G N Swe

CW01604262

NARCISSUS

A Tate Randall Thriller

Viv

Enjoy.

G Swe[illegible]

First published in paperback by
Michael Terence Publishing in 2023
www.mtp.agency

ISBN 9781800946323

Michael Terence
Publishing

Ness… for believing.
And your continued encouragement and support…
Forever more… x

Michelangelo Merisi was born in Milan in 1571.

From the early 1590s to 1610, he established himself as a prominent painter in Rome, Naples, Malta and Sicily.

Like many of his contemporaries, he took his byname from the village he grew up in. Caravaggio.

The tempter, or the tempted, who sins most?…

Measure for Measure
William Shakespeare

This book includes media links…

Explore artworks, locations and more.

Go to gnsbooks.com (Interactive) or scan the QR code to unlock images, maps and facts as you read.

29th May 1606

Via della Scrofa

Rome, Italy

PROLOGUE

The ball court was shrouded in darkness due to the late hour. Two figures, both dressed in black, stood at its centre. A gathering of onlookers mingled in the shadows to either side. Gesturing erratically with the blade in his hand, the shorter of the two figures harangued the other in an aggressive yet slurred manner. A waning crescent moon offered little light to the altercation. However, the occasional glint of its reflective glow danced across the burnished steel surface of each advancing blade.

The second figure also wielded a sword. Its blade, like its holder's demeanour, was at this very moment in a defensive disposition. The blade deflected the periodic advancement of the other sword as the figure defended his honour and physical being.

The other figures clustered within the shadowed fringes on either side of the court were supporters to one of the two duellists. Here to not only offer support, but to ensure fair play, prevent stab in the back tactics and to literally pick up the pieces should their challenger be the less fortunate of the two. Individuals within the defenders group frequently raised their own voices, offered a bombardment of opinions and made advances towards the fighting pair. If they made an attempt to intervene, they were hauled back and hushed by others within their throng. The supporters accompanying the other duellist were more subdued. Offering little support and backing to their swordsman, they showed more interest in the bottle of grog being handed amongst them and to whom in their gathering currently had the shared tobacco pouch.

As the altercation continued, both men gesticulated, voiced accusations and frequently thrust their sword in their adversary's direction. The taller man continued to defend his honour from a constant volley of allegations and a parry of sword feints. The shorter bearded man, although unsteady on his feet, probably due to whiling away numerous hours in a nearby taverna, held his ground and hollered further objections in his rivals direction.

'You deserve no woman, Signor Tomassoni,' he brandished the tip of his sword towards the face of the other.

'Why do you worry yourself so much Merisi?' replied Ranuccio Tomassoni as he too waved his blade in his opponent's direction, 'And over a common whore indeed.'

Defending the strike, Michelangelo Merisi continued.

'Courtesan Melandroni may not be a lady of the gentry but no woman, no matter her class, skin or faith, deserves the back of a man's hand as frequently as you like to offer yours.'

'You treat her like she is yours and yours only. She is no more a whore to you, than I,' taunted Ranuccio. He could see and feel the anger building within his opponent.

'And that is where you and I differ so, Ranuccio. I always see Fillide is paid sufficiently, whether her services to me are as a model or of a sexual nature.' Michelangelo raised his voice further as his anger took control. 'You, my friend, take it upon yourself to frequently forget payment in silver and settle for a pounding of the flesh.'

'And may I remind you,' proclaimed Ranuccio as he wielded the tip of his sword towards his rivals face in a series of jabs, accentuating each word as he spoke, 'in case the matter may have slipped your mind once again, we meet here today due to your inability to repay your outstanding gambling debts. Monies you fail to pay and most probably wasted on that insipid whore.'

With that Michelangelo could contain himself no longer and lunged forward, catching his opponent unaware and momentarily off balance. Ranuccio fell to the floor. His back pounded into the sandy covering, his feet flew into the air and his sword clattered away from his grip. Michelangelo stood astride his fallen opponent. The tip of his blade hovering over the fallen man's genitals. The sudden fracas had caused Michelangelo's band of merry men to divert their attention away from tobacco and wine and back to the matter in hand. Ranuccio's supporters were all desperately trying to restrain his brother from entering the quarrel. Michelangelo pushed the blades tip further into Ranuccio's groin.

'I shall make you pay for your heavy-handed ways. A pound of flesh for a pound of flesh,' he declared as his opponent cowered back on his haunches. 'I shall see to it, so you will never again need the services of a lady.' He stood his ground and pinned one of Ranuccio's legs under his boot. He exhaled and announced his next intention with bravado.

'I will take payment on behalf of Signora Melandroni by relieving you of your manhood.'

With that, he whipped back his sword and in one single momentum swiped it down in an arc towards Ranuccio's genitals. Just as the blade cut through the cloth of his trousers, Ranuccio twisted his lower body to shield his groin and the approaching blade entered his inner thigh. Realising he had missed his target; Michelangelo withdrew the blade. Instantaneously, a jet of arterial blood gushed from the open wound. Michelangelo staggered back and dropped the sword from his hand.

Ranuccio screamed.

His brother wrestled free and rushed to his side. Michelangelo took two more steps backwards in disbelief and was joined by his supporters. Ranuccio was surrounded by his group as his brother tried to stem the flow. But the blood kept coming.

Then Ranuccio was no longer screaming.

The skin of his face was draining to grey and his lips turning a pale shade of blue.

One of the onlookers inconspicuously tugged at Michelangelo's shirt sleeve in a gesture to retreat from the scene as the rest of his supporters stumbled away into the darkness. Michelangelo bent forward, picked up his sword and with his head bowed down, he too followed the others into the depths of the night.

Lazio District

Rome, Italy

Present Day

1

The Narcissus plugged a micro-USB cable into the mobile phone. Unlike a standard cable, the other end was spliced into two single cables, each with a crocodile clip wired at its end. These clips were attached, blue first, then red, to specific electronic terminals inside the circuitry panel. An eerie hue from micro-LEDs emanated in a blue fluorescent glow. The digital screen in the Narcissus's hand began scrolling through number sequences. Within a few seconds, the first digit stopped at the number three. Moments later, digit two froze, closely followed by digit three. When the final digit dropped into place, the Narcissus sighed,

'Really, that obvious!' The Narcissus spoke in a whispered hushed tone, '3.9.0.6.' The two-digit international dialling code for Italy followed by the double figure area dialling code for Rome. The Narcissus touched a red circular icon on the hand-held screen and the fluorescent glow from the circuit board's LEDs turned from blue to red.

Having overridden the property's outdated alarm system with relative ease; using state of the art digital technology, the Narcissus now traversed the perimeter of the building, staying in the shadows, so as to avoid any active surveillance cameras.

The country residence had been created in a gothic revival style by the current owner's ancestors in the mid-19th Century. It was romantic and picturesque, but macabre, barbaric and crude in its architecture and structure. A grand central frontage with flying buttresses, loomed over a pair of twin towers with pinnacle spires, each forming the East and West wings. Pointed arches, a large central rose window, ribbed vaults and ornate façades formed the tracery of the building's exterior.

The Narcissus approached a large stone corbelled bay window looking out to the rear of the property. The original cast iron windows set into the stone façade would make the next stage of entry relatively easy. The leaded light casement frames had simple drop latch handles. With the magnetic contact switches de-activated along with the alarm system, they offered little resistance to any attempted forced entry.

The Narcissus was dressed head to foot in black special services tactical apparel with a ski mask obscuring the face. An oversized archers quiver was worn across the shoulders. Reaching into an external pocket, the Narcissus removed an oversized multi-tool and selected a medium length blade. Sliding this between the sash and the frame, just below the ornate scrolled handle, enabled the Narcissus to quickly ease the window. With a clear view through the glass pane, the Narcissus observed the trajectory of a sweeping 180-degree security camera. The next stage of the operation would have to sync with the cameras movements. With the grace of a gymnast, the Narcissus hopped up onto the stone sill and slid through the open sash.

Once inside, the Narcissus waited for the security camera to complete its current orientation. Then as it swept past for a second time, the Narcissus hopped down from behind the windows drapes and crouched behind a high-backed Queen Anne chair. Whilst the surveillance system completed a third sweep of the room, the Narcissus prepared the next stage of the operation. Removing a small aerosol can from one of the many pockets in the leg of the combat trousers, the Narcissus attached an extension tube to the can's valve. The aerosol contained a highly viscous paint, which would instantaneously harden on contact with any surface. As the camera's arc passed the chair one final time, the Narcissus moved swiftly across the room, remaining low beneath the recordings field of vision, before backing into the corner directly beneath the camera. Extending the aerosol, the Narcissus carefully depressed the cans actuator, spraying a small amount of black paint onto the lens above. This would sufficiently obstruct any further recordings in this room. From this point on, any viewed footage would be in 'video frame black out'. The procedure would be repeated in the next room and once again in the study.

Minutes later, the Narcissus stood undetected in the book lined room and a self-gratifying smile spread across the face hidden behind the mask. The prize that was sought tonight was hanging on the wall to the left. The Narcissus took a moment to admire the work within the frame. The painting was exquisite. At a little over one metre high, the oil on canvas depicted a female seated before a black background. Thought to have been painted by Caravaggio whilst living in exile on the Colonna estates during the summer of 1606, 'The *St Mary Magdalene in Ecstasy*' shows the saint seated in a slouching position with her hands clasped to one side. Her head is tilted backwards allowing the hair to flow loosely and her eyes and mouth are gently closed in a blissful moment of divine contemplation. A white chemise falls from her bare shoulders exposing the flesh of the upper chest. Caravaggio's interpretation elucidates a woman lost in the solitude of a spiritual encounter. The figure's lower torso is covered with the painter's signature ruby red drape. With numerous copies of the work appearing throughout the following centuries, it was not until the 1970s that a confirmation of authenticity was granted.

Having been transfixed in the moment, the Narcissus suddenly remembered the situation and approached the painting. Running a hand delicately across its surface with the care of a consoling friend, the Narcissus removed a third instrument from an inside pocket. The endoscope camera was blue toothed to the phone in the Narcissus's jacket which in turn was blue toothed to the micro screen in the upper corner of the digital glasses the Narcissus now wore. Sliding the endoscope behind the frame gave a close-up view of the gap between the picture hangings and the wall. The image uploaded to the glasses showed two wires, one yellow, one blue. Each linking magnetic terminals from the wall to the picture. With meticulous precision, the Narcissus manoeuvred the tips of the surgical scissors to sit across the yellow wire. A sense of nervous anticipation caused the briefest of hesitations. Even though the Narcissus knew that the yellow circuit was the correct one to cut in order to deactivate the pressure switch, the heat of the moment was unsettling and a single bead of sweat trickled from brow to temple. Taking hold of the situation once more, the Narcissus cut through the yellow wire.

No alarm sounded.

After replacing the endoscope in the pocket from where it had originally come, the Narcissus removed the frame from its wall hanging.

Still no alarm sounded.

Holding the frame close to the chest, like the warming hug from a long-lost relative, the Narcissus walked over to the study's oversized desk and placed the framed picture side down.

Time was now of the essence.

Removing the picture quiver from its shoulder strap and engaging a blade once again in the multi tool, the Narcissus set about removing the backing from the picture. Working quickly yet methodically, so to prevent any damage to the frames contents, the Narcissus one by one removed the wooden backing slats that held the canvas in place. Within a few minutes, with careful pressure applied at the appropriate point, the picture had been removed from the frame.

Unscrewing the end cap from the picture quiver, the Narcissus removed a ruby red cloth from within. A long handled staple gun was wrapped at its centre. The Narcissus put the tube's contents to one side and started to gently roll the Caravaggio canvas, so that it would comfortably fit where the red cloth had been before. This was probably the most time-consuming part of the entire operation, as care was needed to prevent any unnecessary cracks or creases to the thick oil on canvas.

Finally, with the painting safely secured within the picture quiver, the Narcissus's attention returned to the gilded 17th Century frame. The Narcissus ran both hands around the length of the wooden assembly.

Once.

Twice.

Then on the third rotation stopping at a slightly raised wooden knot. Pushing the newly discovered knot with a thumb, whilst twisting it between two fingers, caused a minute mechanism within the frame to engage. With the softest of clicks, a small tube, no wider than a stick of chalk protruded from its surface. The Narcissus gripped the end of the emerging cylinder with a thumb and forefinger and with a slight twisting motion the small wooden cylinder, no more than two inches in length, came away from the surface. The Narcissus examined the tube from all angles, eventually noticing a small wooden plug had been inserted into one end. Removing the plug allowed the Narcissus to see the cylinder's contents. Within its centre and easily removable, the tube held an aged paper scroll. Unrolling and unfolding the parchment from the cylindrical coils from which it had been furled for several hundred years, revealed a square picture approximately six inches across. As the paper uncoiled, a beautiful woman's face began to appear. The Narcissus placed the unfurled paper on the desk and gently patted it flat. The drawing was clearly that of the same female who graced the painting of which the frame had enclosed. In the lower left corner, the sketch had been signed,

'Michelangelo'.

After running a gloved finger tenderly over the signature a couple of times, the Narcissus re-rolled the paper, enclosed it in its wooden casement and slid it into a zippered pocket on the chest of the combat jacket.

Returning to the frame, the Narcissus rolled the red cloth out over its perimeter and using the stapler, fixed the cloth where the painting had once been. Then, turning the frame and its new contents over, the

Narcissus rehung it in its original position, before standing back and admiring the work. The golden embellished frame was now simply adorned with a ruby red drape.

Taking no more than a few seconds to savour the moment, the Narcissus gathered up the instruments and strapped on the picture quiver. With one last glance around the room, the Narcissus turned and left.

Retracing the route back through the house would be relatively quick and easy as the camera lenses were still obscured with the black-out paint. Exiting through the same window sash, the Narcissus rounded the building, reset the buildings alarm system and retraced the shadowed route back across the garden so as to avoid the external security cameras once again. A few minutes later, the Narcissus had scaled the perimeter wall, dropped to the road below and was now quietly vanishing without trace.

Hyde Park
London, England

2

The two swimmers were cutting through the water at quite some pace as they front crawled, heads down, across the lake. It was never a race to the finish line, but always about pushing the limits to challenge each other. With the ever-present waterfowl still roosting and no other swimmers braving the early hour, the rest of the Serpentine's surface was undisturbed and presently shimmered like a mirror as the morning's low rising sun shone across its length.

The lake was created in 1730 at the request of Queen Caroline, the wife of King George II. The Queen had asked the Royal Gardener Charles Bridgeman to redesign both Hyde Park and Kensington Gardens and to create a recreational lake at the heart of the parks. The damming of the river Westbourne created a long sweeping 40-acre water. A distinctive curve at its Eastern end, gave it the appearance of a snake and hence its name. A rectangular swimming area segregated by a line of buoys from the rest of the lake was opened as the Lansbury Lido in 1930 and the Serpentine Swimming Club was formed. Open during the summer months to the general public, the Lido area is strictly members only between 6 and 9.30am each morning, to accommodate enthusiastic club swimmers on their dawn patrol rituals.

The swimmers kicked hard and stretched their stroke length, taking large amounts of oxygen on each third stroke as their heads emerged from the water to take a breath behind their bow wave. One of the swimmers was Tate Randall, head of the Metropolitan Arts & Antiquities Investigation Department. A relatively new operation set up to investigate, locate, retrieve and return stolen art and historical artefacts. The other swimmer was Jonathan Harvey, Tate's best friend and colleague. They had first met at the Cambridge University Swimming Team trials while both were first year art students. After graduating they had gone their separate ways. Tate had joined the Met and eventually risen through the ranks to Detective Chief Inspector. Jonathan had taken a job North of the border with an art restoration business. But they had remained in touch through their shared passion for all things water based. Without fail they would meet every September for a week on Cornwall's Southwest Peninsular to surf the early Autumn swells.

The two swimmers emerged from the lake at the Lido platform, Jonathan moments before Tate. Both with their bodies still in the water, they laid their arms up and across the deck whilst resting their heads to one side. They did not talk to start, each taking deep breaths as they re-oxygenated their blood supplies. Tate was first to speak.

'You were certainly pushing it in there this morning. Where did you find that extra half stroke?' Jonathan took a deep breath in through his nose, filling his lungs before replying.

'Might have been the Filet Mignon with Mama Rous's béarnaise sauce I devoured at La Gavroche last night.' Tate let out a short chuckle.

'And which page of your little black book did one lucky lady appear from?' He paused, fist on chin, mimicking the thinker. 'No, don't tell me, let me guess. A certain Miss Jocelyn Roberts,' joked Tate at his friend's expense. 'The Librarian. You take her out any more frequently and you'll have to start calling it a relationship.'

'She just really respects the finesse of fine cuisine, as do I,' Jonathan retorted, continuing the witticism.

'Yeah, and it's got nothing to do with what you both share for dessert?' Tate held his nose between his thumb and index finger, blowing out to clear his sinuses. Jonathan continued his justification.

'Anyway, it can't be classified as a relationship, as she never stays over.'

'That's because you kick her out before she starts to get cosy.' Tate gave his friend a playful shove at the shoulder.

'No… a man just needs to sleep after a hearty dessert.' Jonathan placed his hands on the Lido platform and propelled his body from the water before turning to sit at its edge. He waited for the ensuing frivolous wisecrack.

'That's ironic, coming from the Tin Man.' Tate had referred to Jonathan as the Tin Man since University because of his early onset of silver hair or more significantly his lack of a heart.

'Ok, enough. Let's stop there before you go into your usual details of how dessert was served. I believe you touched first, so it's your choice.'

As always, their early morning ritual finished with the swimmer home first, choosing where they ate breakfast. Jonathan being a devoted foodie sometimes took a while to ponder his options.

'While you digress, I'm off to take a shower,' and with that Tate thrust upwards out of the water and on to the platform next to Jonathan. Patting his friend on the shoulders, Jonathan replied.

'No need, decision made.' He broke into a mimicking well-spoken accent, 'this morning's breakfast will be taken at The Black Penny.'

'Covent Garden… very bohemian' replied Tate as the pair headed up the jetty.

Surrey Quays
London, England

3

The Narcissus watched the video feed on the laptop screen. The laptop was sitting on a coffee table alongside an array of reference books, a glass of red wine and an auction catalogue spread open at its centre. Beyond the table, a snapshot of the Canary Wharf skyline could be seen through the apartment's balcony doors. The afternoon sun penetrated deep into the room, casting shadows of the furnishings across its carpeted floor. The video feed currently showed the seating area of an auction room steadily filling with potential buyers, whilst early bird bidders were already sitting and shuffling through the pages of today's itemised catalogue. Earlier, the Narcissus had bypassed the auction rooms security system and tapped into the companies four live camera feeds. One recording the auctioneer, another capturing the lot display area and the final two filming the sales floor. As the cameras swept across the ever-increasing crowd, the Narcissus scanned the images looking for familiar faces and sizing up potential competition.

From the comfort of an apartment in a recently regenerated part of the capital, the Narcissus relaxed back into the chair as the first lots of the day came and went. As the auctioneer continued numerically through the catalogue, his gavel falling to signal further items changing hands, the Narcissus quietly sat assessing the floor of buyers. Watching the preceding lots would give an indication of the financial calibre within the room. With the majority of the lots meeting their reserve but then selling relatively quickly, the Narcissus surmised that the item of interest later in today's catalogue would probably do the same. Watching lot eleven sell for four hundred pounds above its reserve price, the Narcissus sipped at the Merlot before plugging a prepaid phone into a digital voice manipulation unit.

Over the next couple of hours more lots made their reserve, before being whisked away by auction assistants to be rehomed in a new owner's collection. The occasional lot would fail to meet its reserve and would wait in storage or return to its current owner before making an appearance in another catalogue somewhere in the foreseeable future. The sun was beginning its slow descent towards the horizon and the mid-afternoon shadows elongated further into the room before the lot in which the Narcissus was interested approached the gavel. Very soon now, it would be time for the Narcissus to acquire a new acquisition.

The prepaid mobile started to ring and vibrate across the surface towards the tables edge. The Narcissus took a long slow mouthful of the wine, letting it invade every corner of the mouth whilst savouring its body and depth of flavour. As the aroma of the wine escaped the glass, the Narcissus glanced across at the small pencil sketch of the woman's face. It had been encased in a simple glass frame and currently sat at the end of the table. The Narcissus allowed a satisfying smile to materialise in a sign of respect to the figure in the sketch.

This was the moment. Within reaching distance of a hand on the prize.

The Narcissus swallowed the wine, took a deep breath, gained composure and reached for the phone. The voice on the other end of the line spoke first.

'Dr Coster?' questioned the caller to check they had dialled the correct number.

'It is,' answered the Narcissus, the tonation of the voice altered by the DVMU.

'Ah good, its Geoffrey Legg here, from the Thames Art & Antiques Auction House.'

'I've been waiting on your call,' interrupted the Narcissus, cutting the caller off to keep conversation to a minimum.

'Oh good. Can I first check you are still interested in bidding on Lot thirty-eight in today's catalogue. The "Rendezvous a la mer" by Emile Moreau,' conferred Mr Legg with a slight trepidation in his voice. The Narcissus simply and purposely replied,

'I am.'

'Excellent news.' Mr Legg expelling a deep relieving sigh. 'Then I shall be your eyes and ears during the process, if that's OK with you Dr Coster?'

'It is.'

Both parties experienced a moment of exasperated silence on the line before Mr Legg continued.

'There are a couple more lots before the Moreau, so if you don't mind, we could utilise that time to clarify a few incidentals. It will help things run smoothly when the bidding gets underway.' Again the Narcissus replied instantaneously allowing Mr Legg no leeway with his words.

'Begin.'

Feeling slightly hesitant now due to the Narcissus's phlegmatic tone, Mr Legg began.

'Yes, yes, good, um, firstly, have you considered the maximum you wish to bid for the item in question?' The reply was just as curt as before.

'There is no limit.'

Taken back by the response, Mr Legg paused before staggering into his next sentence.

'S, s, s, so, am I correct in understanding that your wish is for me to continue bidding on your behalf no matter what value the picture reaches?'

'Correct,' came the reply with an assertive authority. Feeling slightly uneasy, Mr Legg continued trepidatiously.

'There… are… some eager… bidders… in the room… including a gentleman who is a keen collector of 19th century French impressionism.' Mr Legg waited for a response, but it didn't come. 'It may be quite a battle.' The Narcissus gave a simple arbitrary retort.

'As long as we get the picture, Mr Legg.'

'Very good, I will do my best Dr Coster, but sometimes the competition can be unsubmissive.' The Narcissus remained dogmatic, refusing to listen to reason.

'Just ensure the battle is victorious, Mr Legg.'

The Narcissus's cantankerous demeanour was beginning to gripe with Geoffrey Legg,

'Yes, yes, very good, things seem to be moving along in the room a little quicker than I expected. One final question before we commence. Could you please confirm how you wish to pay should the outcome of today's purchase be successful?'

'Electronic transfer!'

30th May 1606

Rome, Italy

4

The unlit street was dark and soulless. The only light to penetrate its blackness, was the occasional glow from a fire's dying embers or the naked flame of a sooty candle escaping through the ageing cracks of shrunken window shutter boards. The street smelt of defecation, rot, decay and was aptly home, to maggots, rats, lice and plague. It was paved with cobbled brick, sloping gently from the walls of buildings to a central culvert. The culvert ran along the street's centre before disappearing down an iron clad drainage hole at the end of the road. The remnants of the previous days slop buckets were trapped in its crumbling joints. Faeces, blood, entrails, fat deposits and vegetable peelings, all adding to the street's despair.

The figure was dressed in midnight blue galligaskins, a close-fitting doublet and a black hip length cape. Not the regal attire of a gentleman of nobility, nor the thread of the lower classes, but tailoring of bourgeois and distinction. As the figure lurched forward, it grasped at the darkness, hands fumbling ahead in search of further support. The alleyway being so narrow, only an arms width between its flanking walls, helped the gents onward progression. He palmed off the walls on either side, only to stumble when the walls gave way to door or window recesses. The occasional falter into a doorway allowed for a momentary recovery of the senses before again pitching onward into the blackness.

Late into the night, the man had lost the final hours of the day drowning himself in the bottom of a bottle in the stale recesses of an unsavoury taverna. The bar in which he had sat was in a notoriously desolate quarter of Rome. The vicinity was home to the poorest of the poor, the destitute, vagrants and pilgrims from distant shores who came in search of lands of milk and honey, only to have their dreams shattered upon arrival by a false utopian nightmare. A territory where the primary vocation was a life of crime. Here within its streets, the penniless rob the penniless, the destitute steal from merchants who barely scrape a living and cutthroats slaughter the nameless for the cost of their next meal.

The bar itself was in stark contrast to the impoverished world outside its door. It was a reasonably small establishment, well-kept and shipshape, with a modest footfall of thieves, prostitutes, gamblers and those lucky enough to have rubbed together enough for a glass of cheap grog. In its simplicity, it was just two adjoining rooms, each with a single window looking out onto the street beyond. In the far room a simple iron fire grate held a single half charred log. The logs smouldering embers producing a small amount of light rather than adding a little warmth to the atmosphere. The fires chimney breast crept across the gable wall. The remainder of the two rooms were a mismatch of old wooden chairs, tables and stools. All showing the rigors of time and constant repair. Each table had a single candle at its middle. However, each table was also adorned with all manner of paraphernalia depending on its occupants. Discarded hats, the end of a pair of booted legs, the odd sword or two and various glasses, bottles, jugs and carafes. Wine and ale were served from a small back room by its proprietor, an ex-navy cook who had spent more time at sea in the brig for brawling than time in the kitchens cooking.

The man had taken a seat in the shadows away from any natural light that may still have been penetrating the windows. He had chosen a table in a quiet corner and sat in semi darkness, having refused the serving girls' request to light the candle upon entering the establishment. He sat there alone, ignoring prying eyes and doing his best to hide the evident blood staining to the front of his tunic. Sometimes he rested his elbows on the table with head in hand, sobbing. Other times letting his inner rage escape in a pounding of his fist. But all the while drowning the pain and numbing his conscious through carafe after carafe of wine.

It was those previous hours that now hindered his perception and ability to negotiate the blackness engulfing him. A sudden scurrying at his feet caught him off balance and sent him careering towards the gutter. Unable to prevent the inevitable, he managed to get one hand down towards the rapidly advancing floor. That hand however met with faecal matter and grime. His feet skated on the sloping brick and he ended up sitting on his backside half in and half out of the culvert. He remained sitting in the gutter as he regained his composure and grumbled at his surroundings. After a while, he sluggishly wiggled his rump to one side of the street and by shifting his back against one wall, he managed to slowly edge his way up to standing again. He wiped the remnants of his soiled hand across his shirt front, where it joined stains of blood and wine from the evenings previous exploits. Brushing himself down, he adjusted his belt and realigned his cape. Regaining his poise, he refocused on his surroundings to find the quarry he had sought was only yards ahead. He let out a little chuckle to himself.

'Una caduta all'ultimo ostacolo.' *A fall at the last hurdle.*

Woolwich District
London, England

5

Geoffrey Legg stood behind a wooden lectern to one side of the sales hall. He touched the side of the headset he wore to momentarily pause any further communication between himself and his client. He took a few seconds to compose himself, taking a series of deep breaths and exhaling slowly. He'd had a run of demanding customers of late and this current one was no exception. In fact, no. This one took the biscuit. Cold, abrupt and downright rude.

Geoffrey had spent his entire life working in the auction trade. Starting as a young boy in the back rooms, he worked his way through the rank and file and for the last 8 years had been an Absentee Representative Manager. Acting on behalf of individuals unable to attend an auction in person. In the real world, the heady heights of a telephone bidder's bidder.

Movement in the corner of his eye brought Mr Legg's focus back into the room and the task at hand. Two auction assistants dressed in customary brown work coats had just appeared on the small staging area next to the auction block where the auctioneer was fussing through papers in his hand. The two assistants were holding a picture in a simple Victorian frame, one also held a card with a number on it.

'Lot 38,' announced the auctioneer, now holding and referring to a single sheet of paper. 'An outstanding example of 19th century French impressionism. "Rendezvous a la mer" by Emile Moreau. The work comes to us today from a private collection in Italy, where it has been since it was acquired from the artists commissioner in the early 1920s.'

Geoffrey Legg touched the headset on his right ear and reconnected the call with his client. 'Sorry for the short delay, Dr Coster. Lot 38, the "Rendezvous a la mer" is now on the stand and we are about to start. Are you still happy for me to continue on your behalf as we have discussed previously?' As he was now accustomed the reply was short and decisive.

'Yes.'

'I am delighted to say there is a keen interest in the room today for this lot and we have two postal bids and also three telephone bidders represented by our client managers to the left of the room,' declared the auctioneer as he gestured towards Geoffrey and his two fellow associates. The auctioneer then gestured to the room in front.

'Shall we start the bidding at say two thousand pounds?' Immediately a gentleman in the bidding hall raised his number to confirm a starting bid.

Geoffrey Legg touched his headset to remove the mute setting.

'Dr Coster, I can confirm, the opening bid has been placed at two thousand pounds. Do you wish to counter bid at this stage? My advice would be to wait at present.' The reply came.

'Wait.' There was no please. There was no thank you.

Another bidder in the room waved their number agreeing to raise the bid to three thousand. Geoffrey confirmed the bid with his client. Several more bids came from the room and a couple more from one of the telephone bidders, raising the cost of the lot to ten thousand pounds. Geoffrey continued to keep his client up to date with the current selling price. Having reached the ten thousand mark with a series of bids in quick succession, the auctioneer judged the anticipation in the air.

'Who will offer me another two thousand pounds to make twelve?' The gentleman in the room, who Geoffrey knew as a keen collector of French impressionism, tipped his number towards the auctioneers block. A first bid from another telephone bidder, followed by another raise of two thousand from the floor, took the total to sixteen thousand. Geoffrey conveyed the situation as it played out to his client, unaware that Dr Coster was in fact watching the rooms every move after hacking into the auction house's security camera feed earlier in the day. The silence from Geoffrey's client did not shock him. He was becoming used to the doctors stand-off attitude. He was however shocked at the ensuing words.

'Twenty thousand!' echoed through his earpiece. He immediately came to his senses and declared the bid to the room. The auctioneer repeated the number.

'Twenty thousand pounds I am bid on the phone to my left. Is there anyone interested in offering me twenty-four thousand?' The collector went to offer his number towards the block, but the other telephone bidder beat him to it.

'Twenty-four thousand on the second phone on my left. Will you offer me twenty-eight thousand?' gestured the auctioneer towards the collector sat in the third row on the floor.

'Thirty thousand!' came the reply, with a silent gasp from the crowd. Again the auctioneer repeated the bid.

'At thirty thousand pounds with the gentleman on the floor,' he declared. Geoffrey talked briefly with his client before offering a bid of thirty-five thousand pounds. The auctioneer looked to the collector in the third row and to his colleague managing the other telephone customer. The room went still and silent for what seemed like an age until the auctioneer began again.

'Thirty-five thousand pounds with Mr Legg's client on the phone. The postal bids have been surpassed. Is there anymore?' The other associate on the phone shook his head to end their line of bids. The collector looked to the ceiling thoughtfully, before tipping his number card and announcing an increased bid.

'Thirty-seven five hundred,' he declared. The auctioneer repeated the offer and looked across to Mr Legg. Whilst Geoffrey talked with his client, he again repeated the new highest bid for the painting.

'The bid is with the gentleman in the third row on the floor at thirty-seven thousand and five hundred pounds. Have I anymore, or any new bidders?' The hall remained still.

'Thirty-eight thousand five hundred,' came the shout from Geoffrey Legg. Again the crowd murmured and some turned to look at the collector who this time looked down. The auctioneer with his gavel in hand scoured the room for any final offerings.

'Thirty-eight and a half thousand pounds I am offered.' He extended his gavel in the collectors direction. 'Fair warning. I am selling at thirty-eight thousand and five hundred pounds?' Once again, he extended his gavel. This time letting it sweep out across the entire room in front of him. The collectors head remained lowered and shook slowly from side to side. The auctioneer got the message.

'One final time, the "Rendezvous a la mer" by Emile Moreau selling at thirty-eight thousand and five hundred pounds,' he paused, more for effect than inviting another bid.

'Sold!' he pronounced.

'Mr Legg, you may inform your client they are the new owner.' Geoffrey let out a smile of self-gratification as he reached to unmute his headset. But before he could do so a voice on the other end of the line came through.

'Thank you.'

Taken aback by the surprising polite response, Geoffrey's hand hovered above the mute button. His mind raced for an answer. How did the doctor know they had placed the decisive bid? He had yet to tell his client of their success.

Thorney Street
London, England

6

'Black, Columbian, four sugars,' the voice announced. Tate span his chair through 180 degrees to face the source of the voice.

'Nice tan' he declared. The focus of his compliment was leaning against his office door jamb with one foot back against the frame exposing a bare knee below the hem line of a short tight fitting black dress. She held two large take-out style coffee cups and purposely over played the 'look at my tan' pose.

Lena Johnson was five feet eight but was frequently just shy of six foot due to her obsessive passion for heels. Her slender frame led to legs most women would die for and were further accentuated with the four-inch Christian Louboutin stilettos presently adorning her feet. She always dressed with panache and invariably in black. But always with a splash of colour to highlight feminine elegance. Today's splash came by the way of the signature red leather soles and heels of her Louboutin shoes and the deep ruby red varnish embellishing her nails. Lena was a woman who took pride in her appearance and would always allow time to ensure she looked good. The icing on the cake was her hazel eyes and jet-black hair with a natural wave. Like Tate and Jonathan, she too was an art graduate. She had graduated in Fine Art from Oxford and gained a master's in art history at University College London. During her relatively short career she had become an authoritative figure in the world of renaissance painting. Her expertise and knowledge lay mainly in the late Italian renaissance and baroque periods. She had been top of Tate's list when he had first started to recruit for the divisions new investigational team.

Lena crossed the room and took the seat opposite Tate, handing him a coffee as she sat down. Tate's office was one of four rooms his unit had been allocated on the fifth floor of the MI5 building at Thames House since its conception a little over five years ago. On this floor they also had an open plan outer room where the remainder of the team had desk space, multimedia stations, filing and research areas and a small interview room.

They had also been allotted a room in the sub-basement. A bare concrete cavern filled with steel tables, chairs, filing cabinets and open backed steel shelving. Every available surface within the basement room was piled high with reference books and catalogues. A systematic chaos where only its creator would know exactly where to lay his hands on a particular resource. The room looked like a cross between a mad scientists laboratory and a collector-maniacs library. It was here that recovered artefacts came to be identified, restored and hopefully returned to their rightful owners. It was also where Tate's long-term friend, Jonathan, now spent the majority of his working days.

In stark contrast, Tate's office was spartan and meticulous. It was modestly furnished with a classical two drawer oak desk, leather back swivel chair, a five-drawer filing cabinet and a plain wooden six tier bookcase, vigorously maintained in chronological order. The only items on the desk were a telephone console, a monitor, mouse and keyboard. Two large Georgian windows at the far end of the room offered some light and a view across the Thames to the South. The walls of the office were simply embellished with three works of art. Not your run of the mill style paintings but works relating to Tate's fondness of nineteen seventies progressive rock music.

The first was a print of the cover of the 1971 release of an album called 'Nursery Cryme' by Genesis. The cover painting by Paul Whitehead, depicted a Victorian garden scene with a game of croquet in progress. However, decapitated heads instead of balls were being struck through hoops by mallet wielding Victorian ladies. The picture framed opposite to this was a print of Mark Rogers artwork for the album cover of 'Beyond the Waves' by Neptune's Finger. A barnacle encrusted hand with a single finger pointing skywards is seen emerging from choppy seas. The final picture, mounted in the prime location at the centre of the offices main wall, was Tate's pride and joy. It was a numbered edition artwork for Pink Floyds 1977 release of the conceptual album 'Animals'. The cover image created by the Hipgnosis pairing of Storm Thorgerson and Aubrey Powell was of Battersea Power Station with a giant 40-foot inflatable pink pig tethered between its famous chimneys. Tate had obtained the work at a memorabilia charity event a few years back. He had paid more than he had initially anticipated. However, he knew all too well, that if one day finances required, there were plenty more like-minded fans who would kindly reimburse the cost. The picture was not only an early edition, but it was also signed by Thorgerson, Powell and members of the band.

The only other fixture in the office was an ornate photo frame on the top shelf of the bookcase. It contained a picture of Tate's parents, Joseph and Olivia Randall. It had been taken in Tate's teenage years during his first trip to Florence. Joseph and Olivia had met when both were in first year scholarships at the Tate Gallery in London. They had married within 2 years and Tate was born a few years later. Both continued to work at the gallery until they took early retirement in their late fifties to travel and have more time to indulge in their own artistic works rather than that of others. To this day, Joseph still maintained that his son's birth name reflected the location of his conception. Joke or no joke, a fact neither Tate nor Olivia appreciated Joseph divulging.

Tate blew lightly across his coffee to cool it before sipping from the cup.

'So how was Corsica?' Tate asked, placing the coffee on the desk in front of him and stretching his arms above his head. Lena relaxed too and crossed her legs.

'Challenging but enlightening and eye opening.' Lena had just returned from a two-week break. The first week she had spent on the French Mediterranean island of Corsica at a painting retreat, participating in a program run by a renowned landscape artist. Not only did Lena have an unparalleled knowledge in her particular field, but she was also a very accomplished portrait artist. She had exhibited many times since graduating and sold several paintings at respectable prices.

'Challenging?' questioned Tate, as he tried to sip his coffee once more, only to withdraw as the scalding liquid seared his lips.

'You know landscapes are not my forte,' Lena replied taking another mouthful from her cup before placing it on the table in front of her. 'However, I really enjoyed painting in a different medium. I wanted to broaden my artistic horizons and I think the course proved successful.' Tate's computer bleeped to inform him of an email arrival. He ignored it and continued.

'I can see the Sardinian sun delivered just as you wished.' Lena had spent the second week of her break on the neighbouring island of Sardinia, where she had rented a villa in the mountainous central region. Lena stretched her arms forward exposing her bare forearms. She turned them palms down, then palms up as she admired her deep tan.

'Yep. Sunbathed, read a couple of novels, sunbathed some more and even managed to try out my newly acquired watercolour techniques and painted a couple of landscapes from the veranda of the villa,' said Lena as she uncrossed and crossed her legs once more. Tate tried his coffee a third time as his computer sounded another incoming email.

'What did you put in this coffee, molten lava?'

'You should cut down on the sugar and add a little milk,' Lena suggested as she habitually picked at the quicks of her fingernails.

'I don't want to ruin it, I just want to be able to drink it,' quipped Tate as he pushed the cup to one side. 'So I take it you're recharged, invigorated and ready to get stuck straight back into a little A&A after a little R&R?'

Lena let out a breathless sigh, 'first day back after a holiday is always a pleasure.' Tate reached to his left and opened the top drawer of his desk and retrieved a folder.

'Well, let's bring you up to speed with what's been happening around here while you've been away sunning yourself.' He opened the folder. 'The Corrigan case is closed. The court hearing was last Thursday as you know.' Tate reached for the coffee cup once more. 'Guilty on three counts, theft, possession and intent to sell. Sentencing is Monday week.' He finally sipped from his coffee and savoured not only the taste but also the aroma as the first mouthful teased past his lips.

'New evidence has come to light on the Montagues missing 18th Century porcelain. The Goya that turned up in a private collection on Anglesey, has proven to be fake after extensive forensic analysis by Jonathan.' Lena nodded as she listened intently to Tate's briefing update. She stared into her cup as she swirled the final dregs of her coffee, thoughtfully contemplating and processing the information Tate was disclosing. She sat back and continued to listen. 'I assume your mountain retreat wasn't too remote and you have heard about the stolen Caravaggio in Italy.' Lena sighed heavily once again before replying.

'Yes it even had running water and an outside loo.' She paused to change tack. 'Yes it was all over the news as I'm sure it was across the globe.'

'The Guardia di Finanza Art Recovery Team would want us to keep our ears to the ground and our noses in the wind in case the said painting raises its head above the waves on this side of the channel.' Lena continued to pick at the quicks of her fingers as she talked.

'It was probably the mafia. It wouldn't be the first time they've been suspected of acquiring a Caravaggio by some ill-gotten gains.'

Caravaggio's 'Nativity with St Francis and St Lawrence' was stolen by two thieves from the Oratory of San Lorenzo in Palermo, the capital city of Sicily. To this day it has never been recovered and rumours still persist that it was the work of the Sicilian Mafia. It remains on the FBI's top ten list of stolen art with an estimated value of $20 million.

'Let's hope it's not another masterpiece lost in the bowels of history.' Tate's computer pinged once more with an email alert.

'You're popular this morning' declared Lena as she continued to pick at a stubborn callus of skin on her little finger.

'Only if I want to buy something I don't need or provide all my private details for the chance to win a £500 supermarket voucher,' mocked Tate as his hand hovered over the wireless mouse. 'They will still be in the unread queue later.'

Tate pushed his chair back and got to his feet. Running a hand through his hair, he smiled at Lena. 'Good to have you back, the place was beginning to look a little scruffy without you around.' Lena stood too and smoothed down any creases gained in her skirt from sitting. She picked up her empty take out cup.

'I do hope my credibility is still a little more than the team cheerleader,' Lena jousted as she leant over to clear Tate's cup too. Tate beat her to it and drained the last of the coffee before handing the empty cup to Lena.

'Far from it, you were and always will be my first choice.' She grabbed the cup from him and pretended to bat him with it. Both Tate and Lena had a lot of respect for each other and enjoyed their two-way banter.

'I've looked over the Harry Booth forgery case files whilst you've been away and if you agree I think you should continue with the lines of enquiry you were already following.' He leaned on the back of his chair. 'Files are back on your desk,' he added as Lena moved towards the door. The sun broke through the heavily clouded London skyline as Lena turned to Tate before departing.

'Good to be back too,' she smiled before turning again and exiting the office. Tate stood behind the chair, shaking his head and laughing quietly to himself as he watched Lena overplay her swagger as she headed back in the direction of her workstation.

Tate pushed the chair to one side and leant forward on his desk. Reaching for the wireless mouse, he clicked on the mailbox icon on his home screen. The icon had a number 3 over it. Opening the inbox, the first two mails were exactly as he had fore mentioned. Junk mail. The third mail however perplexed him even before he opened it. Apparently, it had been sent to his mailbox from his mailbox. His hand again hovered over the mouse's left button. Momentarily he thought it might be a malicious malware. But shaking his head and tutting to himself he hit the button. A simple message appeared on the screen.

Tate Randall
Tate Randall

17th July, 09:48

Why can you not see?

Who the enemy can really be.

Narcissus

Surrey Quays
London, England

7

The Narcissus released the wire muselet cage. Holding the cork and turning the bottle, the Narcissus gently teased the cork from the Veuve Clicquot estate La Grande Dame 2006 Champagne. The bottle sighed contently as it finally gave up its cork and after years of patiently resting, it released its distinctive aromatic notes of apricots, quince and sweet almond. Holding the bottle by the punt, the Narcissus delicately poured a small amount of the pale golden liquid into the champagne flute. The bubbles plumed before collating into a shimmering mousse at the sides of the glass. The Narcissus smiled as an overwhelming feeling of serenity, pride and fulfilment permeated every muscle and bone with a tingling warmth.

Thoughts and recollections flashed through numerous memory cycles as the Narcissus recalled all that had happened to arrive at this very moment. The bidding competition at the auction had not been expected to be quite as keen as it had turned out to be. The Narcissus had hoped not to raise any unwanted suspicions with someone paying well above the reserve for a painting by a relatively unknown French impressionist. However, the interest expressed by numerous others to add the 'Rendezvous a la mer' to their collection had in hindsight only alleviated the Narcissus's need to remain inconspicuous. With the auctioneer dropping the gavel at thirty-eight and a half thousand pounds, Thames Art and Antiques would be jubilant with their seller's percentage fee. Little did they know, that not only had they just sold an Emile Moreau for a very respectable amount of money, but they had also aided and abetted the transportation of a multi-million-pound Caravaggio into the country.

The very same night that the 'St Mary Magdalene in Ecstasy' had been removed from the private residence in Rome, the Narcissus had travelled across the city to the Casa D'Aste del Barberini. Having previously researched the Italian Auction house, the Narcissus had discovered their connections with Thames Arts and Antiques in London. The two houses frequently transferred works for auction between the two cities. Further scrutiny of their current catalogue of works proved fruitful, as a painting of the appropriate proportions was due to be transferred to London within the following few days.

Upon arriving at the premises of the Italian Auction house, the Narcissus had bypassed the buildings security system in a similar way to the private residence hours earlier. Once inside, the Moreau was reasonably easy to locate and the Narcissus made quick work of removing the backing board from the picture. It took less than twenty minutes to remove the Caravaggio from the picture quiver, temporarily fix it behind the concealing painting and replace the backing boards. Again, retracing the entry route, the Narcissus had reactivated the security system and nobody was any the wiser. The transfer would go ahead as planned and the picture and its travelling companion would be under the gavel in London the following week. All the Narcissus had to do was sit back, wait and place the highest bid on the day of the auction.

Refilling the glass flute, the Narcissus remained transfixed in thought and once again the sound of the escaping carbon dioxide bubbles in the sparkling mousse led a journey back into the subconscious.

Once the electronic transfer of monies had been deposited in the Thames Art and Antiques account and the relevant paperwork completed, the auction house had arranged for the painting to be couriered to the address supplied by the Narcissus in the guise of 'Dr Coster'. Arriving at the given address twenty minutes before the estimated courier delivery time, the Narcissus had used a duplicated door entry security swipe card to access the entrance lobby of the apartment block. Using an android plug-in override programme, the Narcissus had bypassed the buildings access intercom system and diverted the incoming signal for the couriers drop off address to a mobile handset. The Narcissus had then remained out of sight in the internal fire escape stairwell. Within a few minutes of the scheduled delivery time, the courier had arrived and using the lobby's entry intercom informed the occupant of his presence. Unbeknown to the courier, from that point onwards he had been talking to the Narcissus on a mobile phone rather than the occupant of 4B. To avoid having to make visual contact, the Narcissus had spun a yarn to the courier about presently being in the shower after returning from a run and would buzz the door so the courier could leave the package in the lobby. However, the courier had insisted that a signature was needed or he could not leave the package. An exchange had then begun between the Narcissus and the courier. The Narcissus attempted to beguile the courier with "I'll be at least ten minutes if you can wait." But the courier declared he could not wait that long as he was on the clock. The conversation then continued backwards and forwards with references to the courier's busy schedule tomorrow and whether he really needed to fit in a rescheduled delivery. Finally, the Narcissus convinced the courier to sign the electronic signature pad with the surname 'Coster' as nobody could write effectively enough on the touch screen for someone at the other end to verify authenticity. Having won the verbal battle over the intercom, the Narcissus had remotely released the lobby doors locking mechanism and allowed the courier access to complete his delivery. Moments after the courier's van had driven away, the Narcissus had appeared from the stair well, retrieved the package, exited the building and had made the short drive home.

The glass in the Narcissus's hand was again almost empty, due to the unconscious sipping of champagne whilst running through the memories of recent events. The choice of the celebratory Champagne had been indicative. The Veuve Clicquot La Grande Dame 2006 was befitting of the occasion. For Madame Clicquot had been the first woman to control a Champagne house and in the early 19th century she was referred to by her male peers as the 'Amazing Dame of Champagne' in acknowledgment of her audacity and determination. Her reputation in the pursuit for distinction and unrivalled quality remains to this day.

The picture laid out across the glass table before the Narcissus bequeathed a comparable legacy. For the creator of the 'St Mary Magdalene in Ecstasy' was also a visionary and profoundly influencing figure during his turbulently short lifetime.

30th May 1606

Rome, Italy

8

Oblivious to the time of night, he pounded his fist against the door with no care or consideration for the occupant or those of neighbouring properties.

'La mia padrona, la mia padrona, aiutare il mio cuore sanguinante;' *my mistress, my mistress, help my bleeding heart,* he bellowed as he continued to strike out at the wooden threshold. 'Salvami dai miei peccati;' *Save me from my sins.* He halted his pounding and instead lent forward at full stretch, resting the palms of his grubby hands and his forehead against the door. 'Amante, non ti senti il mio dolore;' *Mistress, do you not hear my pain,* he now pleaded as his lean became a slouch and he started to slide down the door, his cheek now caressing the wood.

Inside, the woman who had only moments before been awoken by the fracas at her door, let out a long-winded sigh as she slid her arms into an over gown and tied its frayed band at her waist. Due to the nature of her business, it was not unusual for her to be woken in the early hours of the morning by inebriated men, drunken soldiers, truant husbands or bruised and battered ladies of the night who had fallen foul to the back of a bad tricks hand. She slid a finger into the single brass ring of the candle holder and padded bare foot to the top of the stairs. Living in a three-storey house had its benefits when it came to sleeping. It being further from the constant noise emanating from the street outside and benefitting from being further from the stench of the ever-present effluent gulley was a godsend. However, the stairs between the floors were always a chore. The three-storey property was in a relatively poor district of Rome and like most of the other buildings in the vicinity, its foundation footprint was minimal. Smaller footings allowed landowners more room to cram in further buildings until residents were literally living on top of each other. The building the woman occupied was basically a room upon a room, upon a room. The third floor was her private space and where she also slept. Floor two was used to entertain her clients and the ground floor was for washing, eating and other domestic chores. She started to descend the stairs hoping that at this early hour it was a regular client who needed a quick fix, rather than an alcohol induced, '*my wife doesn't understand me anymore and I don't know what to do*,' or the repentant father who wished to declare his undying love for her.

The drumming at the door had momentarily ceased but she could still hear the pathetic needy whine of the person on the other side but could not put a face to the drunken slur. As she descended the stairs on the second floor, her mind dredged its past for a name. To no avail it fought itself for an answer as she descended the final flight of stairs. She broke the darkness of the ground floor with the luminescence radiating from her solitary candle. The pounding at the door started once more as the uninvited guest asked if she could hear his pain. She stopped, uneasy with the situation, and gathered her thoughts. 'H*ow can I not hear your pain and suffering as you pound on my door*'.

She crossed the cold flag stones of the ground floor as she hurried to relieve the neighbourhood of any further disturbance. She stopped briefly to adjust the plunging neckline of her gown, retightened the waistband and in doing so enhanced her sagging cleavage. She reached the door and started to disengage the lock. As she did so, she was finally able to put a face to the now familiar voice on the other side. It had been the slurring of the words and broken sentences which in turn had caused her the difficulty in matching the two. She quickly continued unlocking the door, only to be knocked aside as the weight of the leaning body caused it to swing sharply inwards as soon as the lock was released. The gent fell through the opening, grasping at the void where the door had once been and ended upon his knees where he continued his whining confession.

'Signor Merisi, What on earth… Look at your… How on earth…,' she spluttered as she tried to string a sentence together in her astonishment of the scene that now played out in front of her. He looked up at her from his position of repentance. His small goatee beard and moustache were matted with the remains of the earlier liquid encounters.

'Signora Antognetti, forgive me,' he begged as he reached out his arms to her.

'Michelangelo. I have no problem with you appearing at my door in the small hours of the morning, as you have done on numerous occasions before. But did you have to announce your arrival in such a fashion that may even have woken the dead?'

'Forgive me, I do not recall how I possibly got into such a state and I could think of no other place to go. So I…' The sound of footsteps in the street outside broke his sentence. She noticed the look of concern spread across his face and with that she turned a heel and kicked the door shut. With the world outside banished, she offered him her hands and pulled him to a standing position.

'Come, let's get you seated,' she said as she gestured towards a table and chairs on the far side of the room. He staggered forwards in the direction she had indicated, each step alien to the last. She had gotten used to him visiting in a similar state. However, she had lost count of the number of times he had visited her in a drunken stupor but could still count the number of occasions she had seen him sober on the fingers of one hand. Nonetheless, tonight was exceptional. She could not recall seeing him this bad in a long while. She eased a chair from beneath the table and helped him to a sitting position, all the while maintaining a sturdy grip on the back of the chair. No sooner had his backside made contact with the seat before he slurred a demand.

'Some wine if you please.' She was about to question the necessity when he cut her short, 'Just bring the bottle.'

She had learnt over the years that it was easier to relent to a man's demands, whatever they maybe, than to argue until your cheeks are the shade of deep red roses. She crossed the room to the area used for preparing and cooking, a kitchen of sorts and removed a bottle from a sideboard. She collected a glass from a bowl filled with water and other soiled cups, plates and cutlery and used the hem of her gown to wipe it clean. Grabbing the bottle on the way, she crossed the room and re-joined him at the table, whereby this time Michelangelo's head was laid cheek down with his arms stretched out across the surface. She poured a glass of wine and placed it forward of his head. Immediately he sat up and drank the whole glass in one, like a rabid dog in desperate need to quench it's thirst. He slammed the glass back down on the table, wiped the excess wine from his beard with the back of his hand and grabbed the bottle.

'Really?' she questioned as he raised the bottle to his lips. She made a move to take it from him, but even in his intoxicated state he was too quick for her.

'Mistress,' he declared, 'if you could begin to understand the kind of day I have had then you would realise my need.' With that he took another large swig from the bottle, before placing it within comfortable reach at the side of the table. As he did so, she stood from where she had been sitting opposite him and moved around the table to stand behind his chair. Gently she placed her hands on his shoulders and started to apply a small amount of pressure as she manipulated the tightness of his muscles. She spoke softly.

'Unleash your burden, a problem shared is a problem halved.' She leaned forward a little so he could feel her breath on his neck and whispered in his ear.

'Tell me.'

Thorney Street
London, England

9

Tate left his office on the 5th floor, walked straight through the anterior office and into the corridor beyond. Turning right he headed to the twin elevators at the far end. The temperature outside was steadily increasing as the stifling heat of the inner city set in. The inner sanctum of the air-conditioned corridor provided a much appreciated, yet momentary escape. Reaching the end of the corridor, Tate stopped at the sliding doors and pushed the button to call the elevator. As he waited, he hummed a tune in his head and drummed a rhythm on his thigh with his fingers. The ping of arrival broke his thought process and he stepped through the opening doors. Turning to face the entrance he pushed the button for B -2. As the doors slid together and the descent to sub level two began, Tate slouched back against the rear wall and continued where he had left off with his humming and drumming. He was in an exceptionally good mood today and was hoping nothing would dampen this feeling. Lena returning from her break meant the team was back to full strength and for some unseen reason, Lena always seemed to lift his spirits. As he continued to hum the melody from 'Owner of a Lonely Heart' he began to question the reason for his current ear worm. Was he slowly growing closer to Lena? Maybe too close? Were his feelings for her becoming irrational? Lena was an incredibly good-looking woman and under the cool, calm façade, he was just your everyday hot bloodied male. A second ping announced his arrival at Sub basement two and snapped him back into reality. The doors opened and Tate stepped out into a fluorescently lit concrete corridor. This one also being invitingly cool, although not air conditioned, as the warmth of summer did not penetrate this far down. As he walked down the corridor, his thoughts moved to the strange email he had received the previous day.

'How had the email been sent from his own account? Had he been hacked? Was someone trying to suggest he was not doing his job effectively? What was the significance of the strange signature?'

Reaching a door on his right marked 2C broke his thought process once more. He tapped his knuckles twice on the door before easing its handle and entering slowly. His double knocking was not out of politeness, but to alert the rooms occupant to a visitor, rather than suddenly startling them whilst they focused on a delicate work process. The knocking of the door had however been in vain, as the rooms occupant was unaware of Tate's entry. He was absorbed in the work before him, whilst he too hummed along to a tune. His tune came from the over-ear headphones that at present covered both his ears. Noticing Jonathan was using a scalpel to gently scrape paint from the surface of a painting on the easel before him, Tate quickly thought of a way as to not make his friend jump out of his skin and damage the work. He caught sight of the light switch to the left of the door and leant across, clicking the switch on and off in quick concession so as to flicker the lights quickly. This had the immediate effect he had wished for and Jonathan looked up from the job at hand.

'Tate!' he bellowed over the music before he placed the scalpel to one side and slid the headphones down around his neck.

'What are you listening to?' enquired Tate as he moved further into the room.

'Marillion, debut album, side one, track three?' Another of their friendship bonds was their shared taste and passion for the same genre of music and this was one of the private little games they enjoyed sharing together. Using the traditional format of two-sided vinyl, one would need to guess a songs title from the information given, relating to the tracks position on the album.

'Script for a Jesters Tear. The Web?' replied Tate with a huge smile on his face. 'I believe I may have walked in just at the right time.'

'Yeah, pretty much,' smirked Jonathan, 'Bit of an easy one really.'

'Never an easy one unless you know the answer.' Tate walked over to Jonathan's workstation and rested a hand on his friends shoulder. 'One day my friend, one day.' Jonathan stood and nodded his head in agreement.

'Yes. One day soon, I shall topple the mastermind of rock trivia!' as he threw a pretend punch at Tate's chin. 'But for now what brings the great one to the bowels of the earth?' Tate rounded the table to their left and picked up one of two porcelain figurines.

'How's it going, any luck in finding the owner of these two little darlings?' said Tate as he turned the work over and over in his hand, admiring its intricate beauty.

'I think we may have a lead. A description from a house break in Surrey eighteen months ago pretty much matches the data we have accumulated at this end. I checked them both for authenticity and they match the provenance exactly. They have not been swapped for fakes. They are the genuine article.' It was sometimes known for criminals to swap originals for top quality fakes before returning them to the open market. The figurines had been found amongst an antiques horde when the police raided a recognised 'steal to order' thief after a tip off about other stolen artefacts. Jonathan picked up the other figurine and he too turned it over in his hands. We have the registered owners coming in next Tuesday to verify the pieces and provide evidence of ownership.'

'Good work buddy. How's the oil painting coming along?' questioned Tate as he placed the figurine carefully back on the table and walked over to the easel where Jonathan had been working on his arrival. Jonathan joined Tate and picked up the scalpel he had previously been working with. He moved the scalpel through the fingers of his hand and used it to motion towards the painting.

'The work has had numerous repairs and over paints, its proving difficult to get back to the original.' Jonathan motioned towards the bottom corner where he had previously been uncovering the layers of over painting. The area was about the size of a passport photograph.

'Just started to reveal part of what could be a signature.' He handed Tate an eye glass. 'Here, take a look!' Tate took the optical cylinder and leant forward towards the bottom of the painting before raising it to his right eye.

'What's the Tin Man's best guess?' Tate moved the eye piece articulately across the area in question.

'The brush stroke tailing to the left, may well be the tail of a "G", but I'll need to do some more exploratory work to confirm my suspicions.' Jonathan picked up a pencil and as Tate stood, he traced the next letter with the pencils tip.

'This second figure is almost definitely a letter "A",' he pointed out whilst once again tracing its outline with the pencil. Tate began to nod in agreement.

'So, all the signs so far are pointing towards it being a genuine Chagall.' The Tin Man pursed his lips and he too nodded in agreement.

'The spectrograph, x rays of the overpainting and the paint analysis certainly all lead to the same conclusion. It could well be a Chagall.' As they both returned their gaze to the picture, the telephone on the desk behind them began to ring. Jonathan reached across and picked up its receiver.

'Restoration, Jon speaking.' Tate continued to study the possible Chagall as his friend took the call, nodding and responding to the caller with a series of yeses. He hung up the telephone.

'That was Joanne from the call centre,' began Jonathan, 'there is a call waiting in your office. She said it was a Ricardo Moretti from the Carabinieri T.P.C.' Tate looked at his friend, gestured with his palms up, bottom lip curling and his eyebrows raised.

'I wasn't expecting a call. I'd better get back surface side, it could well be important. There is the small issue of a missing Caravaggio if I had to second guess a reason for the call.' He tapped his hand on the easel. 'Let me know what you find as soon as you have something solid.' With that, Tate turned and headed across the room.

'No Problemo, Mr Boss man,' quipped Jonathan as Tate slipped out through the now open door.

Bruton Place, Mayfair

London, England

10

Grayson Art Gallery had a modest yet affable façade. A large picture window adjacent to a full-length glass entrance door occupied the best part of the building's street side exterior. The frames of both the door and the window had been taken back to their original wood patina, giving the gallery's frontage a sense of venerability. The glass in both the main window and the door had been replaced with 11.5mm laminated anti-bandit glass. Secure enough to withstand the full-blown swing of a 20lb demolition sledgehammer. Signage above the lower aspect, was again unembellished and endearing. The lettering was written in a simple grey on black period font. The sign itself was framed in a wooden surround with a patina finish similar to the casements below.

The large picture window framed a single portrait of a noble looking gentleman. Painted in oil on a fruit wood board, the picture sat on a barebones easel and took centre stage of the galleries kerb appeal. Even though the shops frontage on Bruton Place was minimal, the space within was considerably different. Three open-plan spaces extended back from the smaller anterior room and the galleries front window. The reception room had a single antique leather topped, twin pedestal desk with a matching Gainsborough captain's chair to one side. A single brass Bankers lamp, a cordless telephone with charging port, a flat screen monitor, keyboard and mouse and an array of auction catalogues covered the desks surface. The three inter-linked rooms extended back towards the rear of the property through an arched opening on the back wall of the room. The walls of all three rooms were painted a mandatory gallery off white and lit by soft up-lighting. More precise accent lighting captured various works hung in specific locations along the walls. Occasionally paintings were displayed on free standing easels to utilise some of the rooms empty floor space. An incredible deal of thought and effort had been put into the location of each work. The orientation of every painting had been chosen to highlight the works uniqueness and draw viewers to its focal heart. The gallery was far from over-crowded with pieces, but certainly not spartan. Enough works to entice the appetite of passing trade and generous enough to encourage potential buyers to consider further purchases.

The gallery, although meticulously laid out, was only a front for a shadier more lucrative side of the business. Paintings within would frequently sell for reasonable sums of money, but the true value of the proprietor's business lay in the darker world of black-market transactions fulfilled when the shops doors were closed.

Thorney Street
London, England

11

Tate re-entered his office. It still smelt of polish and window cleaner. Still fresh from the previous night's cleaning. Briefly glancing at Pink Floyd's 'Animals' artwork on the wall, he crossed the floor space to where the telephone console on his desk was currently flashing to alert the user of a waiting call. He parked his backside on the edge of the desk and retrieved the handset from the opposite side. Then, casually crossing his legs, he hit the hold release button.

'Tate speaking.' The voice on the other end of the line sounded slightly startled when he spoke. Probably due to having waited for almost five minutes on the open line whilst Tate had made his way back through the building to his office on the 5th floor.

'Inspector Randall, its Joanne in the call centre, Sir.' Tate tossed the name around in his head trying to put a face to the name. Joanne had patched calls through to him on numerous occasions before and they both worked in the same building. But he could not picture her. Tate wondered if in fact they had ever met. They may have passed each other in a corridor or shared a lift without knowing. Each a nameless face to the other.

'Sorry to have taken so long. I was probably as far away from my desk as physically possible whilst still actually being in the building,' Tate declared. He made a mental note to pay the call centre a visit and introduce himself. He liked to be able to visualise a colleague's face when talking with them.

'Not a problem, Sir. I have a call holding for you from the Carabinieri T.P.C in Rome. An Inspector Ricardo Moretti. I explained the situation and asked if he would like me to take a message and get you to call him back, but he was keen to hold.'

Tate pursed his lips and mused over the credentials Joanne had just given him. He had a very good mental picture of the holding caller. Ricardo Moretti had a strong Roman nose and a full head of suave silvering hair. He was Italian through and through, with strong features you would not forget too quickly. Tate had worked alongside his Italian counterpart on several occasions in recent years and they had become good friends.

'Shall I patch him through, Sir?'

'Yes, Joanne, please do,' said Tate as he fingered the phones traditional spiralled cord to allow him to move around the desk to his chair on the opposite side.

'Probably best not to keep him waiting a minute longer.' The line clicked and Joanne disappeared once more into the corridors of nameless faces.

Tate leaned back in his chair as far as the phones cord would allow.

'Ispettorre Moretti. My friend. How are you?'

'I'm very well thank you. And yourself?' came the reply in explicable English with a distinctive syllabic Italian accent.

'Yes, I'm very well too, thank you,' replied Tate. 'Sorry for the wait. I was in the bowels of the building in the Conservation and Restoration Workshop with Jonathan. Seven floors and several corridors between there and here. But, anyhow, it's good to hear your voice?'

'Likewise,' replied Inspector Moretti, 'anything has got to be better than that awful on-hold music you English believe comforts waiting callers.'

'I couldn't agree more. Apologies again for the wait. I thought it would be best to take your call in the privacy of my own office, therefore affording you my full attention.'

It had been just under eighteen months since Tate and Inspector Moretti had last met face to face. Tate had travelled to Florence to attend a meeting at the world-renowned Uffizi gallery. Senior figures from art investigation units across Europe had gathered for a two-day seminar hosted by Inspector Moretti and the Carabinieri T.P.C. The rapid movement of stolen art and antiques throughout Europe had increased ten-fold in the last decade and along with the French and the Dutch, the Italians and the British had forged a strong alliance in the cross-continental investigation and recovery of missing artefacts.

The Carabinieri Command for the Protection of Cultural Heritage had been the world's first specialist task force formed to investigate art crimes. Located in the heart of Rome at the Palazzo Sant'Ignazio it was held in high regard by its European counterparts as being the leading authority in combatting antiquarian crime. Formed in the late 1960s to aid in the recovery of paintings and artefacts looted by Nazi soldiers during the second world war, it is now involved in far more than just the theft and the illicit trading of art. The agency engages in the monitoring and control of sites of archaeological interest and is charged with the safeguarding and protection of artworks in disaster zones and war-torn countries. Other divisions under Moretti's command are tasked with forensic analysis, forgeries and fake identifications. Their investigators are also responsible for the management of the LEONARDO database. Containing the details of over six million artworks, including some one and a half million listed as missing, stolen or illegally excavated, LEONARDO is the world's biggest art database. The coalition with their European partners has led to a yearly recovery of approximately 150,000 artefacts, worth an estimated value of half a billion euros. Inspector Ricardo Moretti was a leading figure in the T.P.C. He had a distinguished recovery record and an astonishing depth of knowledge and expertise built over 25 years of service. Tate had an enormous amount of respect for his senior Italian counterpart.

'I'll come straight to the point of my telephone call,' declared Moretti, suddenly sounding very official on the other end of the line. Tate adjusted his buttock position and sat up straight in the chair like a pupil ready to engage in a favourite topic.

'I am currently leading the investigation into the stolen Caravaggio, here in Rome.' Roberto Moretti knew he need offer no further headline information to Tate regarding the disappearance of the missing artwork. An incident of this degree was splashed across the globe by the worlds media within hours of its initial reporting and he knew Tate well enough to know he would have acquired himself as much information as he felt necessary.

'We have attained vital evidence and CCTV footage which strongly suggests that the work has been trafficked to British shores,' Roberto declared, reeling Tate's attention even further onto the line.

'We are led to believe the Caravaggio was hidden inside another work and freighted along with other paintings to an auction in Woolwich.' Tate removed several sheets of paper from a ream in the desks bottom drawer and started to jot a few notes as Roberto continued.

'I was wondering how you would feel if I were to suggest we joint task force from our respective positions during all further investigations, just as we have done on several other occasions in recent years. You to follow the trail of our current leads from when the suspected host painting arrived in Woolwich. We will continue investigations from our end and I will manage, oversee and piece together operations from here in Italy.' Tate had said little, preferring to let his senior counterpart explain his thoughts and ideas. Only occasionally did he offer a couple of words to confirm an understanding. He had always been a good listener. He allowed others to talk, express their opinions and was patient when others wished to explain their reasoning. Tate's preference to listen, allowed him time to gain some clarity on a situation, process the information and to consider his options. He liked to step into a situation, rather than jump in with both feet first. Tate listened intently to Inspector Moretti's suggestion of a combined task force. He was always open to opportunities to develop further relations with his European allies. Coupled with the sense of veneration felt from the offer to work once more under the wing of a man recognised by his peers to be the leading authority in his field, left no doubt in Tate's mind that this was a concurrence of circumstances too good to be missed.

'My team and I are always welcome to any collaboration beneficial to an investigation. It would be a pleasure to work alongside you once again, old friend.' He relaxed back into the chair once more and repeatedly clicked the push button at the top of his ball point pen.

'I was hoping that would be the case,' replied Roberto. 'This could well turn out to be the most significant art crime on Italian soil since the Monza enquiry a few years back.' Tate continued to listen and whilst doing so speculated over the Monza case in his mind.

After multiple meetings and telephone conversations to discuss the possibility of purchasing some major art works, two potential buyers had met with a dealer in a neutral location to view the prospective works. During the viewing, the two buyers had asked for a moment in private to further discuss aspects of the purchase, only for the dealer to find on his return that the buyers had vanished along with a Rembrandt and a Renoir. To Tate's knowledge there had been no success in locating either of the paintings to this day.

He double clicked the pens push button. Realising how potentially annoying the clicking of the pen may have been to the caller on the other end of the line, he put the pen down and sat forward to the desk just as his email alert sounded.

'I have just forwarded to you all the relevant case files and the CCTV footage we have obtained from the night the Caravaggio was concealed inside another painting. The perpetrator had bypassed the security system but luckily for us, was unaware of the companies secondary surveillance measures.'

'A Secondary surveillance system?' probed Tate, who had picked up the pen again and added to the notes he had already taken.

'It seems the company had been having some internal affair issues. It was only by chance that whilst reviewing surveillance taken on some extra hidden cameras, they happened to stumble across the footage of the concealment.'

'An unfortunate occurrence or a fortunate occurrence, depending on which way you view it,' declared Tate.

'Yes, a stroke of luck in our eyes. It opened a direction we may never have taken without it. Have a look for yourself when the footage arrives. Once you've had time to look over the files, perhaps you could return the call and we could discuss things further.'

'I will give it my immediate attention. Unless anything untoward happens, I'll do my best to get back to you later today.'

With that, the conversation ended. At this stage, there was no more to be said. So, no further words were exchanged and the pair said their goodbyes. Tate put the phone back on the cradle and reaching for his mouse, he clicked on the email icon.

Regents Park
London, England

12

The Narcissus put the prepaid SIM into the phone and went through the process of registering the credit. Sitting in a quiet corner of Regent's Park, the Narcissus looked like every other city worker taking their lunch on a bench in the sunshine. With the credit accepted, the Narcissus rang the pre-memorised number. The phone rang five times before connecting. A man's voice answered.

'Grayson Gallery, Jeremy Grayson speaking.' The Narcissus waited momentarily before replying.

'Mr Grayson, my name is Dr Valentine.' The Narcissus paused again to induce an effect of authority. 'I believe I have acquired an item which may be of interest to you.' Again the Narcissus waited, but this time scanning the immediate vicinity for prying eyes and ears.

'May I ask what the item you believe I would be interested in purchasing would be?' retorted the voice from the other end of the line.

'Oh I do not want you to buy it,' stated the Narcissus, 'I want you to sell it!' Feeling suddenly cautious and slightly nudged from his throne, Jeremy was hesitant in his reply.

'Ah. I see. And what is it you believe I could be of help in selling?' The question had been in vain as he was rudely ignored.

'Let me start by saying, I know how you go about your business and that you are not averse to, shall we say, getting a bit of dirty paint under one's fingernails from time to time.' The statement took Jeremy by surprise and he was slightly aghast at its impertinence. He tried to interrupt but to no avail, as he was ignored for a second time.

'Come, come Mr Grayson, we both know your gallery is a ruse. You don't get to drive an Aston Martin from selling mediocre Flemish realism at two thousand pounds a pop.' Jeremy tried to interject once more and once again the Narcissus paid no attention and continued to control the conversation.

'The real money is made in a much darker place than that, Mr

Grayson. Wouldn't you agree?' Jeremy responded but the Narcissus did not hear the reply. A passing mother with a pram and a teenager on roller blades had drawn the Narcissus's attention. Whatever the response had been, it made little or no difference.

'If I tell you the painting will attract a seven-figure price tag and your five percent sellers commission would be a tidy little sum.' Jeremy Grayson interrupted circumspectly.

'Sorry, I am afraid my fee is fifteen percent of the gross value, with a two percent estimated value transaction fee, payable in advance!' The Narcissus waded back in without any consideration for Grayson's previous remarks.

'Five percent of seven figures is far greater than five percent of nothing, Mr Grayson.' There was a silence from the other end of the phone. Eventually Jeremy spoke.

'If I were to consider acting on your behalf, I would need to see the work, so as to ascertain its authenticity, condition and estimated market value.' Again he was allowed no time to hesitate.

'That is why you will meet me at your gallery tomorrow evening after you have closed for the day.'

'I'm afraid tomorrow evening is inconvenient, I already…'

'You will close,' the Narcissus curtly demanded, 'the shop as per usual and remain within the premises. I will arrive there shortly after.' Jeremy was about to respond before there was a click and the line went dead.

The Narcissus lent back into the park bench as an elderly lady took a seat at the far end. She smiled across towards the Narcissus as she removed a plastic bag of bread crusts from the top of her shopping trolley come walking aid. Throwing the first of the scraps to a squadron of pigeons landing at her feet, she smiled once more and advocated,

'if you feed them the right thing, they will come back for more!' The Narcissus returned the smile and nodded in agreement.

Thorney Street
London, England

13

Lena sat at her workstation, her fingers dancing frantically across the keyboard as corresponding words appeared on the screen in front of her. Movement in the corner of her eye caused her to slow her word count and whilst still typing at a generous pace it allowed her to focus on the source of the distraction. Recognising it was Tate approaching, she minimised the current screen on her monitor and ran a hand through her hair, sweeping it back from her temples.

'Tate!' she said trying to sound surprised, 'to what do I owe the pleasure? I do hope you have come to offer to take this hard-working gal to lunch?'

'We could in fact discuss what I have to talk about over a bite to eat,' Tate replied as he lent forward and rested on Lena's monitor. He leaned in closer and peered around so to get a better view of the monitor's screen.

'What's your current work situation like?' Lena tapped a couple of keys and the monitor screen jumped back to life.

'Just following up on a couple of leads relating to unclaimed items included in the "Aladdin's Cave" feature that aired on the BBCs Crime Watch whilst I was away.'

Occasionally, the Arts and Antiquities Investigation Department would use media like the weekly television programme to reach a wider audience of witnesses. The increased public awareness would lead to a greater percentage of stolen items being reunited with their rightful owners. They would occasionally produce reconstructions of crimes to gain information from the public audience or feature 'Wanted Faces' caught on CCTV during news bulletins and other daytime programmes. The wider audience had proved useful in creating further lines of enquiry and had frequently led to successful arrests and convictions.

Lena tapped a finger on the screen to indicate each item.

'Had much response?' Tate asked, looking at the list of items Lena was referring to.

'Seventy-eight enquiries since the screening. Once you sort out the chaff and the fraudulent claims, there will probably be 10 to 15 legitimate leads to follow through.'

'Is this something you could hand over to Tom?' Looking slightly puzzled, Lena replied tentatively,

'Uh, yeah. I don't see why not.' Tom was the new blood on the team. Still wet behind the ears, but not drowning, Tom was straight out of recruitment training. Brought in by Tate to increase his head count and more importantly with the increase in organised crime of late, to spread the workload and increase his man hours on the relatively low budget afforded to him by the MET. Tom had shown promise at the interview stage having grown up alongside his father's antiques business in Suffolk.

Still being cynically quizzical, Lena was keen to question Tate's intent.

'Why, what's come up that's so important?'

'Something a little more up your street, shall we say.' Tate pushed back from the monitor and straighten his spine to regain his posture. 'I'll tell you over that lunch you suggested.' With that, Lena promptly shut down her computer and put her monitor to sleep, before grabbing the Coach handbag hung on the back of her chair. She did not need asking a second time.

'Where are we eating then?' she buoyantly inquired over her shoulder as she headed for the door without the slightest hint of hesitation.

30th May 1606

Rome, Italy

14

Michelangelo bent an arm backwards and placed a hand upon her hand as she continued to massage his shoulders. He gently patted her hand, briefly exposing a repressed affectionate side very rarely unmasked. He clasped her hand once more and lifted her arm to his side.

'Come, sit with me and I will tell you,' he conceded as he steered her hand to rest on the back of the chair to his left. He took another quaff from the bottle, took a deep breath, exhaled with a sorrowful sigh and began.

'I am at a loss; I fear this time there may be no salvation.' He stuttered and lost his composure. This time she reached across and took his hands in hers. Many times in the past she had consoled him after he had turned up at her door looking for redemption after scrapes with the law or fellow drunks and rogues who had wrongly crossed his path.

'What have you gotten yourself mixed up in, that now troubles you so?' she said as her thumbs gently caressed the backs of his hands. He cleared his throat and gave himself a moment to contain his thoughts.

'You are acquainted with Signor Tomassoni, are you not? I believe he has used your services on a number of occasions.'

'Signor Tomassoni's coin is as good as any man's,' she retorted in an unnecessarily defensive tone. She withdrew her hands from his and feeling a little uncomfortable, she placed them in her lap beneath the table.

'We had a little misunderstanding, a small altercation you could say. Apparently, you were not the only courtesan he frequented.' Still feeling slightly out of sorts she replied,

'Using one or more mistress is not a crime, is it not?'

'No. but,' his speech was slow, he was finding it difficult to find the words due to his continued intake of wine. However, he was doing better than one would expect, considering his alcohol intake during the previous few hours. 'No lady deserves to be paid for her services with the blackening of an eye and a bruising of the ribs.'

'Don't tell me, you took the law into your own hands and taught him a lesson,' pressed Signora Antognetti.

'Of a sort. I owed him money from an unpaid gambling debt, but I thought it only right he paid for his ill gained ways first.' The chair made a bone penetrating screech as Michelangelo pushed away from the table and its wooden legs resisted against the stone floor. 'So, like on many occasions in my past, my temper got the better of me and I challenged him to a duel.' He tilted the bottle towards the candles luminescence to see how much if any wine remained. 'What happened next, I neither planned nor wanted to happen.' He rolled the corner of his moustache between his thumb and fore finger as he contemplated how best to continue his tale.

'We met last evening at the court on Via della Scrofa,' He paused and mused for a moment. 'We exchanged words and during the engagement of blades, he fell to the ground and I saw right to take my chance.' He paused long enough to swig from the bottle and swallow. The wine dribbling into his matted beard. 'I only meant to maim his manhood so he would no longer have need of a woman's services, but the stupid fool turned away to protect himself at the last minute and the tip of my blade ripped open his thigh.'

Michelangelo covered his face with his hands.

'He dropped to the floor immediately, wailing like a banshee,' he shook his head, doing his best to hold himself together. 'The blood flowed from his leg like a spring tide river. When his brother and friends gathered to his side to stem the bleeding, I thought it would be best to disappear before they turned their attentions on me.' Michelangelo once again reached for the bottle. However, this time Signora Antognetti forestalled his advance and removed the bottle from within his reach. Michelangelo followed his arm and his head slumped down across the table.

'I think enough is enough,' Signora Antognetti asserted as she cleared the table of its wares. She crossed the room, putting the bottle and glass to one side, before heading to the door where she slid its heavy deadbolt back into place. She looked back. Michelangelo was still pitched across the table, his mouth garbling drunken slurs. It was not long before his mumblings metamorphosed into a series of snorting snores. Knowing she had not the slightest chance of shifting his drunken bulk up the stairs to where he could comfortably sleep off his wretched state, she climbed the stairs herself to the first floor. She pulled a heavy woollen blanket from the bed and turned tail down the stairs once more. With the blanket spread across her outstretched arms, she returned to the table. The candle at its centre flickered repeatedly as it burnt its final offerings of animal fat. Signora Antognetti folded the blanket in two and laid it across Michelangelo's shoulders. She leant forward, placed a hand across his forehead and gently kissed Michelangelo on the crown of his head. She whispered tenderly, 'lasciate che il sonno abbassa la tua mente;' *Let sleep unburden your mind.*

With that, Signora Antognetti retrieved the candle from the table and padded across the stone floor in the direction of the stairs one final time. As she began to climb the first flight, the candles fuel supply finally diminished, the flame snuffed out and the room was once again shrouded in darkness.

Southbank

London, England

15

Tate and Lena sat in the window of the OXO Brasserie on the eighth floor of the iconic South Bank landmark. Originally built at the end of the 19th Century as a power station to supply electricity to the Royal Mail post office, it was subsequently purchased as a cold store by the Liebig Meat Company, the manufacturers of Oxo beef stock. Skyline advertising at that time was banned along the Southbank, so when the building was rebuilt to its current Art Deco design by Albert Moore in 1928, the tower was cleverly constructed with three vertically aligned windows on each of its four sides. Coincidentally, the windows happened to be in the shape of a circle, a cross and a second circle.

The window in which they were now sitting, offered a panoramic view across the river Thames to Saint Pauls Cathedral and the London skyline beyond. Having each ordered a glass of Isabel Estate Sauvignon Blanc, they both mused over the lunchtime menu offerings. Lena was still wondering what Tate held so secretly to his chest having been mysteriously nonverbal during their short tube hop from North of the Thames. The brasserie not only boasted stunning views of the city but had a mouth-watering menu to accompany it. All set-in period surroundings emphasised with modern detailed furnishings.

Putting the menu to one side, Tate sipped his wine before easing back into his chair. Casually he began to speak about the matter in hand.

'Rome called this morning,' he said all blasé, 'they believe it's here!' Tate need say no more. Lena knew exactly what he was referring to. The disappearance of the Caravaggio was the biggest story to break within the art world for some years.

'There is significant evidence that the painting has been shifted out of Europe and onto UK soil. It looks to have been hidden inside another work being transported here for auction.' Lena, who was sipping her wine lowered the glass from her lips,

'Nice, old-school skulk,' she replied before Tate continued.

'They have CCTV footage of a suspect stowing the painting.' Tate stopped mid-sentence as he noticed a shadow cast from behind spread across the table between them. The waiter had returned to take their orders. Tate gestured to Lena to go ahead and she ordered Scallops, chorizo sausage with sweetcorn puree and samphire. Tate followed suit and ordered Falafel, red pepper and feta salad with a spiced pomegranate dressing. When the waiter was no longer within earshot, Tate continued, 'It is understood the painting was then couriered along with several other works to an auction that took place at Thames Art and Antiques on the 25th of July.' Having been fiddling with her cutlery setting whilst Tate was talking, Lena used her fork to gesture as she replied,

'so unbeknown to them, Thames Art may have sold a masterpiece hidden within a lesser-known work? What was the name of the piece within which it was smuggled?'

'Rendezvous a la mer' by Emile Moreau,' replied Tate as he took another sip from his glass and tilted it to the windows light to reveal the wine's true colour.

'So, some lucky so and so may have a Caravaggio in their possession and be none the wiser.'

'Maybe,' exclaimed Tate, placing the glass on the table. 'A more likely train of thought is that it was purchased at the auction by someone who knew what truly lay within.' Lena started to put the pieces together within her head.

'They stole it, hid it within a work to move it and picked it up again in their desired location.' She pondered for a moment. 'So all it would take was a bit of prior planning to find a similar size painting that is scheduled to be transported and sold in the desired destination.' She chewed the facts over in her head before continuing once more.

'Why go to the effort of breaking and entering to stow the Caravaggio and then wait to purchase the concealing picture at the desired auction?' she mused as she now tapped the fork on her front teeth as she thought. 'Why not just break in again at the selling auction house and remove the work as before.'

'Quite possibly not a one-man job,' replied Tate, 'More likely to be an organised job with people on the inside at both ends.'

'Or maybe someone wanted the thrill of buying the concealing painting, knowing all too well what lay beneath. Affording them the pleasure of wallowing in the glory and the over whelming sense of achievement of pulling the wool over the institutions eyes!' enthused Lena. A waiter serving an adjacent table caused Tate to again pause momentarily.

Both he and Lena took sips of their wine. Lena let the wine circulate in her mouth to appreciate its true depth of flavour. Fresh green mango followed by passionfruit and guava. Tate continued as the waiter departed back towards the kitchen.

'So, the Italians would like to collaborate with us hand in hand. They would like us to investigate the trail on British soil, from when the painting arrived, was processed through customs and prepped for auction at Thames Art. Then to follow the trail from the selling of the concealing work, its purchase, collection and through to who and where the painting and its current owner are now.' Tate paused once more as diners filed behind Lena.

'The Italian Bureau, for the moment, will continue to investigate both the break in to remove the Caravaggio and the break in to conceal it within the Moreau.' Lena put an empty glass down on the table.

'You keep referring to "we" and "us." Do you mean the department or "us",' she gestured with a finger to and fro across the table before them? Again, Tate let the wine wet his lips before commenting.

'The nature and gravity of this investigation and more importantly the media attention it will bring, means we must give the Italian Bureau the strongest support we can offer and that means putting our most experience team on the case.' Tate paused. 'So, yes, that means you and I.' Lena let slip the slightest of smiles. 'I thought we might tag team this one together.'

A passing waiter noticed Lena and she tipped her empty glass in his direction. Knowing exactly what she meant by the gesture, he acknowledged her and headed in the direction of the bar. Tate and Lena continued to discuss the information they had already gained. Tate providing Lena with a summary of the emails and files he had received from Moretti. Occasionally Lena would ask for clarification or probe for more detail on specific facts. Finally, the waiter returned with two plates of food.

'Pan-fried scallops, for Madam,' attentively moving the recently delivered glass of wine to one side, so as to place the plate in front of Lena.

'And the Falafel, red pepper and feta salad for Sir,' placing the other plate at Tate's serving. 'Another drink for Sir?' enquired the waiter before leaving.

'No, I'm fine with just water thank you, we have a busy afternoon ahead,' replied Tate, raising his eyes and gesturing towards Lena's second half empty glass.

Bruton Place, Mayfair
London, England

16

Jeremy Grayson paced about the room. As he did so, he nervously checked his watch every two minutes or so. '*Why had yesterday's phone call from Dr Valentine made him feel so apprehensive and uneasy?*' He had dealt in stolen art for the biggest part of his life.

Jeremy Grayson was the sole proprietor of the Grayson Gallery. The gallery had been at its current location for a little over ten years, having derived from different guises and locations over the previous twenty- five years. Its owner, now in his mid-fifties was a tall well-presented man and every inch of six feet six. He was broad at the shoulder and lean at the waist. Clean shaven with a strong chin, square jaw and a good crop of thick brown hair. He was meticulous about his appearance. Jeremy was always well groomed and dressed to the nines. More often than not in three-piece Canali suits, made to measure on the Via Borgognona during one of his frequent visits to Rome. However, Jeremy had not always been of such a suave nature. Born Jimmy Presley, he had been a gangly teenager, reaching the six-foot mark just shy of his thirteenth birthday. The loftiness married with a geeky awkwardness and the unfortunate surname had led to an adolescence of taunts, exclusions and bullying. It was during this period of his life that the then, Jimmy Presley, first discovered a passion for art. He withdrew from the real world he loathed and despised and immersed himself in the alternative universes offered by the Marvel and D.C publications. Over the coming years he became somewhat of an expert on all things comic related. During his final school years, he began trading Batman, Superman, Captain America et al with other likeminded introverts. Often, obtaining copies of hard to come by editions from unknowing fledgling readers and selling them with a substantial profit to 'Got to Have' ardent collectors. He sold his first stolen piece when he was Fourteen. A Spiderman Edition left in an unattended satchel in the school playground.

Leaving school at sixteen, he continued to trade comics, other related paraphernalia and found a niche in the adult market for vintage collectable trading cards. By the age of eighteen he had made enough money to comfortably rent a small shop, where he sold reproduction posters of classic Marvel & D.C comic front pages and dealt in the black-market trading of first editions and rare covers. During this period, after years of relentless schoolboy taunting and verbal bullying from phrases such as "Oi Elvis, where's your Blue Suede Shoes?" or "Elvis, is it lonely at Heartbreak Hotel?" and the tedious referral to "Presley, what as in Elvis?" He decided to change his name. Like his comic book heroes, he too would have an alter ego. That day, Jeremy Grayson emerged from the shadows.

As his confidence grew with his new-found persona, so did his acumen for back hand dickering and illicit deals behind closed doors. He soon discovered he had a talent for unearthing and coercing potential buyers to pay 'over the odds' for an item they could not live without.

During his twenties, Jeremy discovered an interest in Pop Art and the works of artists such as Paolozzi, Hamilton, Rauschenburg and in particular Roy Lichtenstein. As he continued to explore, expand and diversify his comprehension of a larger cross section of art, he found his own tastes metamorphosing and a new-found love for the early twentieth century Surrealist movement. Like his favoured comic book artists, Surrealists had the ability to mould the worlds of dream and reality into alternative avant-garde worlds.

Jeremy's recognition and prestige in numerous art circles promptly escalated as he began dealing in works by artists such as Breton, Magritte, Ernst and Dali. So too did his bank balance. Commissions from works such as these were far in advance of the few pounds made in the transactions of comics and posters. Jeremy's business began to flourish, better premises came and went, profits grew, dealings in different genres multiplied and soon Jeremy became a name to be reckoned with on the London art scene.

He adjusted his bowtie in the reflection of the front door and continued pacing the room.

'*What was it in the tonation of the doctor's voice that put him so on edge?*'

He had dealt with a multitude of rogues and rapscallions over the years. However, there was something about the doctor he could not quite put his finger on.

At five o'clock on the nose, Jeremy Grayson locked the front door of the gallery and flipped the traditional hanging 'Open/Closed' door sign to Closed. Returning to the desk on the far side, he sat back in the chair and was just about to commence shutting down the computer, when the phone rang. Jeremy picked up the phone on the second ring and held it to his ear. No sooner had he done so and before he could speak, a voice at the other end announced,

'I do like a man who is a punctual timekeeper!'

Jeremy had anticipated the call, but possibly not quite as promptly. It was just like he was being watched. With the cordless phone still pressed to his ear, Jeremy shuffled across the room and hesitantly looked up and down the street outside. The caller continued.

'A courier will arrive in five minutes. They will deliver the painting to you. From then on, you will have forty minutes to view the work before the courier will return for its collection.' The caller continued with further instructions, giving Jeremy no opportunity whatsoever to respond.

'During this time, you will take no photographs!'

Jeremy opened his mouth to remark and the caller hung up.

Bruton Street, Mayfair
London, England

17

The Narcissus was dressed in full black motorcycle leathers, armoured shin protection boots, a full-face helmet with a dark smoke shield visor and was sitting astride a Honda CBF 500. Again, finished in black. Leaning the bike slightly to the right, the Narcissus pushed a button in the side wall panel and the rear doors of the Mercedes Sprinter van began to open on small hydraulic piston hinges. At the same time, a galvanised ramp emerged from below the tailgate and lowered itself to the road surface below. A soft electronic bleep signalled the completion of the ramp lowering and the Narcissus carefully negotiated the bike forward and down onto the road.

The Honda CBF 500 is the preferred bike of many inner-city courier services. The CBF 500 is a user-friendly solid but lightweight ride. The bike has a low seating position, good for stop/starting in traffic and pinpoint steering makes u-turning easy in tight streets. Some may say it is a little under-powered, but as the average speed in London traffic mirrors that of the horse and carriage limit at the turn of the last Century, this causes no problems.

The Narcissus had stood towards the end of Bruton Place and watched as Jeremy Grayson had closed the gallery. Happy that Mr Grayson was adhering to yesterday's instruction, the Narcissus had exited the street and simply rounded the corner into neighbouring Bruton Street. Waiting there was the black Mercedes Sprinter which the Narcissus had paid and parked earlier that day. The van had been specifically parked in a 'blind spot' to avoid detection from any on-street cameras. The Narcissus had used the van and motorcycle combination to avoid any chance of the motorcycle being tracked on ANPR surveillance. The motorcycle could therefore be captured entering and leaving the area of Bruton Place but be tracked no further.

Whilst returning to the van, the Narcissus had once again phoned Jeremy Grayson with further instruction on the arrival of the courier and picture.

A gentle push of the electronic ignition and the CBF 500 quietly rumbled to life. With the picture safely secured in the vertical pillion carrier, the Narcissus looked in the off-side mirror, let an approaching car pass and pulled out onto the one-way street. All the Narcissus need do now was to turn left onto Bruton Place and follow the one-way system back around the block and pull up outside the Grayson Gallery.

Bruton Place, Mayfair
London, England

18

On cue, five minutes later, a courier pulled up outside the gallery on a black motorcycle. Jeremy instantly noticed the unusual shrink-wrapped wooden casement in the bikes rear carrier as he walked towards the gallery's front window and once again looked up and down the street. Apart from the customary hand full of 'On the dot-five o'clock' workers scurrying to Happy Hour at the Coach and Horses around the corner, the street was relatively deserted.

As the courier dismounted the bike and started to remove the wrapped wooden casement, Jeremy paranoidly checked the street for activity once more before moving to the door and re-opening its locks. No sooner had he done so, when he had needed to instantly step to one side, as the courier was already pushing the sash open with a buttock, whilst carefully manoeuvring the encased picture with both hands. The courier continued into the room and without even acknowledging Jeremy, promptly put the wrapped frame down on top of the brochure covered desk.

Just as Jeremy was thinking, '*I know who you must work for*', the courier turned and exited the building as expeditiously as they had entered. Then within a blink of an eye, the courier re-mounted the bike and was gone.

Feeling slightly shaken and stunned by the swiftness of the delivery, Jeremy turned towards the picture, before remembering the need to return to the door and secure the gallery once again. After one final check for prying eyes on the street, Jeremy collected the packaged casement and carried it through the gallery to a small private viewing room at the very rear of the property.

Placing the picture down on a small table in the corner, Jeremy glanced at his watch.

'*Forty minutes.*'

He began removing the shrink-wrapped plastic to find the whole package was in fact inside an over-sized polyethene zip-lock bag. Removal of the bag revealed a large wooden casement, not unlike a generously sized flower press. Two sheets of laminated wood, slightly larger than the contents inside were secured at each corner by bolt and wingnut clamps.

'Better not waste any time,' he thought.

Jeremy released the wingnuts on all four corners and lifted the upper laminated sheet from the bolt threads to reveal a bright red velvet cloth. This had obviously been placed between the wooden laminates to protect the painted surface of the canvas within.

'Don't rush. This needs to be done professionally and correctly.'

Before proceeding any further, Jeremy opened a drawer that ran the entire length of the tables underside and withdrew a pair of cotton gloves. Pulling a glove onto each hand, he then gently lifted the velvet cloth away from the painting it concealed.

Time froze.

Minutes passed. Jeremy was transfixed by the image before his eyes. The realism and beauty of both the physical and emotional state of the subject held his gaze. The artist had captured the figure in a single shaft of light within a deeply shadowed background. It created a contrast between the light and shaded skin tones to draw the viewer into the intensity of the subject's face. Jeremy found himself becoming lost in the intimacy and vulnerability of the subject.

He snapped back into the real world and lifted the cuff of his jacket so to check the time.

'Only 25 minutes remaining. If I call and ask for more time, I already know what the response will be.'

He looked at the picture once more. Sometimes you just know. It was a matter of instinct and this time his gut reaction was telling him this was the real deal. But Jeremy had also done his homework. To verify the authenticity of this painting he needed to get a look at the rear of the canvas. Carefully, he replaced the velvet cloth over the painted surface and relocated the wooden covering before steadily turning the entire frame over. He removed the bolt heads from the four corners, so that this time he could remove the other board and reveal the back of the canvas.

The marks were quite clearly there. As he had discovered whilst researching the painting over the previous twenty-four hours, there were at least eight indistinguishable copies thought to exist across the world today. However, only the original had the two distinctive markings clearly visible at this very moment to Jeremy. The first was a wax stamp only used by Vatican customs during the seventeenth century and secondly a hand-written note declaring the 'Reclining Magdalene' had been commissioned by Cardinal Scipione Borghese. Jeremy was now reasonably sure that the

'St Mary Magdalene in Ecstasy' currently in his possession was the bona fide Caravaggio.

Glancing at his watch once more and anticipating a phone call at any minute, Jeremy hastily removed a small digital camera from the drawer beneath the desk and took a close-up shot of each of the painting's rear markings. Like a naughty schoolboy, he then hid the evidence back in the drawer. Jeremy then re-assembled the wooden casing and re-sealed it within the polythene bag. He was removing the cotton gloves when the phone rang on cue just as he had prognosticated. This time however, it was Jeremy who was first to speak.

'The provenances are correct and I am satisfied that the painting is an authentic Caravaggio!'

'I know,' came the reply, 'I stole it myself.' Before Jeremy could comment further, the Narcissus continued.

'The courier will return in fifteen minutes. Have the painting ready for collection. I will contact you shortly with further instruction.' Jeremy was expecting the caller to hang up, but before they did the voice spoke once more.

'And I thought I told you "No photographs" Mr Grayson!'

30th May 1606

Rome, Italy

19

Signora Antognetti woke from her sleep to the sound of Rome's ever-present pigeons scratching and cooing on the tiled roof above. She let her eyes remain shut as the sun's rays spread across her face and gently warmed her skin. A Mediterranean rejuvenation of sorts. Signora Antognetti was an extraordinarily beautiful woman. She had been blessed with an ethereal appearance and skin as delicately white as new porcelain. It was as if she had emerged sculptured from the purest white marble in a Bernini masterpiece. Her flawless skin was offset by thick raven black hair that flowed across her shoulders before cascading down her back like a stallion's mane. She came from a family with a long lineage of courtesans. Like her sister and her mother before, she was a 'Daughter of the Night' and made a respectable living by providing upper class gentry and members of the aristocracy with pleasures of a carnal nature. Her exquisite elegance also allowed her to attain numerous sittings as a model during a period when Rome's artists frequently used live subjects to add a new desire for realism to their works.

Sat in a chair in the corner was the man she had left covered with a blanket before she had come to bed in the very early hours of the morning. He was smoking a pipe. His eyes were glazed and looked like marbled steak. As he drew on the clay pipe with one hand, his other held a pencil which he now used to continue the sketch currently sitting across his lap. His unkempt hair clung to the side of his face. With the hand holding the pipe, he swept the dishevelled hair from his temple before lodging the pipe once again into the corner of his mouth. He continued to move the pencil over the paper, only occasionally drawing his gaze from her face to glimpse at the progression of the sketch. His clothes were feculent from last evenings encounters and he was fetid and malodorous as his body sweated stale alcohol from every pore. As he continued sketching Signora Antognetti, he did not notice as the pipe upturned in the corner of his mouth and the ash fell away onto his tunic. The ash adding further to his filthy attire.

A short time later, Signora Antognetti stirred in her bed once again. The warmth of the sun had caused her to nod off and she awoke unsure of her surroundings. She rubbed her eyes with the backs of her knuckles and stretched her arms and legs simultaneously. She opened her eyes and as her vision adjusted to the light in the room, she glimpsed the ungodly sight staring at her from the corner. Realising that this was reality and she was not on the edge of a dream, she let out a short cry. As she processed the scene before her, she pulled the outer most bedsheet to her chin as a protective wall. She cowered behind her linen battlements and started to recall the events of the earlier hours. Then as the pieces started to fit into place, she realised who the uninvited guest must be.

'Michelangelo,' she murmured. 'What are you doing in my room?'

'You were still sleeping when I awoke. I came to check on you. You looked so beautiful whilst you slept, I thought I would capture the delicacy of your repose in a sketch,' responded Michelangelo, thinking nothing of the occasion.

'But this is my space. You know I do not allow others above the second floor.'

'Forgive me, my angel. It was only with my best intentions…' A noise in the alley, probably a cat seeking a feathered feast, broke Michelangelo's train of thought and he returned to his drawing. Still weary of emerging from her slumber, Signora Antognetti pushed aside her annoyance of Michelangelo's presence and instead occupied her mind with thoughts of pity for the man who sat before her.

'Look at him, the poor soul. Why does he continue to get himself into such a state? A genius trapped inside a tortured mind,' she thought to herself as she adjusted the pillows behind her head and continued to scrutinise the artist sat in the corner.

'Why you? What is it about you that pulls at my heart strings so? Why you Michelangelo Merisi?' With the thoughts trapped in her sub conscious and the question stranded in her mind, she pulled the bed sheet across her shoulder and turned her back on the intrusion once more.

When she woke again, later in the day, the intruder was gone. Composing herself, she re-plumped the pillows and sat up. As she did so, she noticed the two small squares of paper at the foot of the bed. Reaching forward she retrieved the papers, patting their edges to unfurl the encroaching corners. Each square contained a pencil drawn portrait. Each portrait delicately illustrating her own face as she slept. Each face a flawless moment in time captured by the artist's hand. Each drawing was signed in the corner…

Michelangelo.

Bring the pages alive…

Explore artworks, locations and more.

Go to gnsbooks.com (Interactive) or scan the QR code to unlock images, maps and facts as you read.

Southbank

London, England

20

Tate pulled the Land Rover Defender out onto Thorney Street and into the flow of traffic on Millbank, as Lena continued to fight with the traditional style lap belt still fitted to Tate's cherished motor. Tate still had vivid memories of the first time he had driven his grandfather's 1954 short wheel-based Land Rover around the family farm in Dorset at the age of six. It had kick started his love of all things Land Rover. He had started with the collecting of die-cast models, followed closely by technical specification posters on his bedroom walls and finally to the gift of his then late Grandfathers Landy on his fourteenth birthday. He passed his driving test in the very same vehicle, twelve days after turning seventeen. The model Tate drove today was a 1963 SWB Land Rover Series IIA, considered by numerous enthusiasts to be the most robust model to ever leave the production line.

Tate followed the traffic flow and turned onto the Lambeth Bridge. Situated between Westminster and Vauxhall bridges on the site of the old Westminster horse ferry, the bridge is one of the main traffic arteries for crossing the Thames to the South Bank. It was first constructed in the mid Nineteenth Century before being replaced in 1932 by the current five-span steel arch structure. Its striking red paint scheme duplicates the red leather benches of the House of Lords situated on its northern banks in the Palace of Westminster. Tate had frequently crossed the bridge during his childhood. Each afternoon upon finishing school on the South Bank, he would use the bridge to cross the river and meet his parents from work at the Tate gallery on Millbank. His father had consistently quizzed him as to why he thought the twin obelisks at each end of the bridge were topped with pineapples. To this day, Tate was still unsure if they were indeed pineapples or just simply pinecones. Urban legend led to popular belief that they were in fact pineapples, as a tribute to 17th Century Lambeth botanist, John Tradescant the Younger who is attributed to have grown the first pineapple on British soil. As he drove the Land Rover past the obelisks at the exit to the bridge, Tate smiled to himself as he recalled the different stories his father had given him for the pineapple obelisk tops. He also thought how ironic it was that after so many years he had also ended up working within spitting distance of the bridge itself.

'Do you think they look like Pineapples or Pinecones,' Tate mused. Lena looked up momentarily.

'What?'

'The obelisks! Do you think they resemble Pineapples or just plain and simple Pinecones?'

'They look like Artichokes to me,' said Lena as she returned her attention to shuffling papers laid in her lap.

'Artichokes,' pondered Tate, 'Dad never once suggested Artichokes.'

As the traffic crawled onto the South Bank, Tate concentrated on the congested traffic and Lena shuffled her way through a selection of files they had put together late yesterday afternoon. She occasionally circled a name or a location and linked some with inter joining lines like a spider diagram. Periodically Lena would express her thoughts with a Tut, Hmm or Ahh, whilst sucking on the end of the Bic biro for inspiration.

Upon their return from lunch yesterday, they had thoroughly digested all the files, documents and evidential information that had been emailed across from their Italian counterparts. Tate had again spoken with Moretti to clarify specific details, confirm communication channels and receive a series of further updates.

With the sun now rising to its midday peak and the heat of the inner city steadily climbing the mercury scale, Tate and Lena were heading out across the city to investigate the paintings entry into the country through the doors of Thames Art and Antiques. As they rounded the Elephant and Castle and turned onto the A201, Tate drummed his fingers on the steering wheel to the rhythm of the music coming from the cassette tape player inserted into the metal dashboard. It was just above the spring loading ashtray currently filled with spare change instead of discarded cigarette ends.

Lena looked up briefly from the files scattered across her knees and gestured towards the dashboard with the wand like pen in her hand.

'Do we have to listen to this incessant noise,' moaned Lena. 'Can't you get Capital radio on that thing?'

'That noise happens to be By-Tor and the Snow Dog, a classic early seventies Rush track from the Fly by Night album,' said Tate with a '*really, have you no idea*' tone to his voice.

'By whom and the what dog,' begged Lena. Ignoring Lena's naivety,

Tate continued his witticism.

'And unless they are still transmitting Capital radio on Long Wave, then the answers no!' Lena leant forward, held the files on her knees with one hand and moved the other hand towards the tape players controls. Tate raised and held one finger from the steering wheel. Lena recognised the signal and recoiled into her seat. She had no idea which knob, button or slider would mute the sound anyway.

As they made headway towards Woolwich, they continued to discuss the how's, why's and maybe's of how the painting had entered the country in such an ingenious way and how Thames Art and Antiques had possibly and unknowingly sold a painting within a painting for an incredibly generous price. As the sun continued to roast, the humidity intensified and they edged their way through the sprawl of summer tourist traffic. Whilst they were stuck in the stop/start of the congestion, Tate and Lena averted their thoughts to the possibility of inside moles on both this side and the Italian side of the situation. They also discussed the idea of the Caravaggio being stolen to order and the feasibility of a media enticer. Occasionally a lesser-known work would hit the headlines to spark the media's attention before a more recognisable work would be offered for auction. Or alternatively used to draw the public's attention away from a major acquisition or discovery that was likely to cause a considerable commotion within the art community. The 'St Mary Magdalene in Ecstasy', being a lesser-known Caravaggio may well fit the criteria to be used in either scenario.

The temperature inside the vehicle rose further still as they sat at a traffic junction and watched the lights change from red to amber to green and back again to red without the traffic moving.

'I don't suppose this rusty bucket of bolts happens to have air conditioning of any sort,' mused Lena as she wiped a bead of perspiration from the tip of her nose.

'See the metal cleat to your left. If you pinch that between your thumb and forefinger, you can slide the window back. Then if you put your arm out of the said open window and angle your palm appropriately, you should feel the airflow to your face when we start moving again. If you require a higher rate of flow, just let me know and I'll try to speed up a little when the traffic and speed limits allow.'

Bruton Place, Mayfair

London, England

21

The daily horde of tourists passed by the window heading to New Bond Street or Burlington Arcade to gape through the windows where the other half shopped. They would amass along the pavements hoping for a chance encounter with a footballer or a pop star or at best the glimpse of someone they recognised from a reality show. The occasional couple would stop and admire a painting in the gallery's window. They would stand and chat, sometimes point at a specific aspect of a work, but commonly they would pass on by, ignoring the fact that the gallery had a door with an open sign displayed in plain sight. Jeremy Grayson was accustomed to window shoppers.

He perused through the artwork he was currently displaying at the gallery. As he wandered, he critiqued each paintings position and if its current lighting emphasised the best aspects of the work. He tried his best to focus on the job at hand, but his thoughts were elsewhere. It had been two days since the viewing of the Caravaggio. He had expected to receive further contact from Dr Valentine by now. Although the doctors voice put him on tenterhooks every time they talked, Jeremy was still keen to be part of what may turn out to be one of the most lucrative deals of his entire career. Over the past few years, Jeremy had built a considerable reputation and become somewhat of a name to be reckoned with. Even if it was within the darker shady side of the business. He had acquisitioned paintings for multi-million-pound business owners, film and tv stars, a super model and he had even procured a pair of Monets for a well-known billionaire. Paintings would frequently change hands and nobody would be any the wiser to changes of ownership. Most involved large money transactions from one offshore account to another. With Jeremys increasing exposure to the iniquitous side of the business, he had already considered several clients who would possibly show an interest and be potential buyers for a stolen Caravaggio.

His attention was drawn back into the room by a tapping on the gallery window. Three middle aged women were conversing over the window's current display. One of the trio was generously leaving her greasy fingerprints across the glass as she traced the detail of the painting whilst probably explaining her interpretation to her jovial companions. Jeremy instinctively knew they would be 'walk-bys' and focused on his collection. He scrutinised a picture from a couple of different angles, before adjusting a mini spotlight which had been positioned to throw more light diagonally across the canvas and draw a viewer's focus to the left side. After a couple of minor tweaks, he was satisfied with the way the light now shone across the picture and he returned to the desk at the front of the gallery. His instinct had been correct and the silhouettes of the three women had vanished but welcomely being replaced by the refection and warmth of the sun. Jeremy clicked on his mailbox icon to view six new messages awaiting his attention. The first was a discount code from a leading restaurant chain. The second and third were offers from websites he had visited in the past. The fourth however was not an automated circular, it was from a private email address. It's subject line was:

'Valentine message.'

Jeremy had waited all day for further contact and now his finger hovered over the mouse button. Even without hearing the doctors voice he felt uneasy and lacked self-confidence for the first time in many years.

'Pull yourself together man. Get a grip. This could be the deal of a lifetime.'

He moved the cursor over the address line and clicked the button. The email was short and to the point. Just as he would have expected. He read through it twice. On reading it a third time, the corners of his mouth turned upwards and a slight smile started to spread across his face. Dr Valentine had confirmed Jeremy's participation in the selling of the Caravaggio and the two percent advancement would be transferred to his account. However, the doctor had asked him to compile a list of prospective buyers. Was the doctor looking to entice a bidding war? Jeremy's smile intensified. If that was in fact the case, there would be a greater chance of a more lucrative deal.

Woolwich District

London, England

22

Tate coerced the Land Rover into the only vacant parking space. The space between two previously parked cars being so narrow, both he and Lena struggled to exit the vehicle. A sign on the wall in front declared, 'Thames Art & Antiques. All vehicles and contents are left at the owners own risk. The management will not accept responsibility for any damage, accidents or losses.' Tate chuckled to himself as he edged between the Land Rover and the neighbouring vehicle. *'I hope the same doesn't apply to items they are holding in their possession on the other side of the wall.'*

Tate and Lena headed across the parking lot to the entrance of the Thames Art and Antiques warehouse. The property was built in traditional London brick with wrought iron framed casements running around the entirety of its perimeter just below the roof soffit. Large expanses of the roof were also glazed, allowing an abundance of natural light to penetrate the building's interior. Located in the historical maritime district of Woolwich, the warehouse was acquired by the company when the Navy finally sold off its remaining portfolio of properties during the 1930s.

Tate held the door and let Lena enter first. They had purposely not phoned ahead to announce their arrival. Broadcasting their visit may forewarn a possible mole to pre-empt an alibi, discard vital evidence, alert outsiders or instigate a cover up. Tate and Lena had discussed how they would approach their inquiries during the remainder of the journey through Greenwich and on through to the Woolwich basin. It had been decided that Lena would lead the inquiries and questioning, leaving Tate the opportunity to observe and analyse any information they obtained. Their course of action would start with acquainting the Company's Director with the reason for their visit, followed by their initial inquiries. This would involve interviewing anyone who had had contact with the concealing Moreau painting or had been involved with its transportation or sale in the first instance. They would also be collating fingerprints of all members of staff who may possibly have had any contact with the picture.

Customs handling documents would also need to be collected and scrutinised.

As they approached the reception desk, Lena removed her police identification card from inside her jacket. The reception area was an antique in itself. The room was of oval shape with walls clad in art deco walnut cladding. The far side of the curve was dominated by an oversized art deco bow fronted office desk. Made in a dark walnut finish, it had a double pedestal with two lines of four drawers on the seated side and cupboards to the front. The receptionist sat in a stylish leather and chrome art deco chair to match. The curving walls to either side displayed a matching pair of art deco leather cigar club sofas. The room was a statement piece to all who entered.

The woman behind the desk greeted them with the obligatory, 'Good morning, how can I help you today.' Lena raised her ID.

'DI Lena Johnson and this is DCI Tate Randall from the Metropolitan Arts and Antiquities Investigation Department. We understand a Mr Rupert Hawkins is the Managing Director of the business. Would he be available to spare us a few moments of his time?'

The receptionist responded with a silent nod and keyed an extension number into the small switchboard on the desk.

Woolwich District

London, England

23

Mr Hawkins welcomed them into the room and gestured that they take a seat in the two chairs on the opposite side of the desk.

Rupert Hawkins had followed in his father's footsteps and recently taken the helm as Managing Director of the family business. Started in the late nineteen hundreds by his now late Grandfather, what had begun as a small house clearance business had grown to become a very reputable European auction house. From the humble beginnings of dealing in small bric-a-brac and household furniture to a company now importing and exporting exquisite antique furnishings and fine arts.

Rupert was in his late fifties. A large man of portly stature, an inch or two shy of six feet and the wrong side of sixteen stone. His rounded face and thread veined cheeks were accentuated by a large dark brown handlebar moustache. His appetite for all things antiquated was bolstered in his archaic attire of dapper tweed suits, whose waistcoats strained at the buttons across his ample paunch due to his additional appetite for hearty food and real ale.

The air of his office, where Tate and Lena were now seated in a pair of Victorian walnut wing back chairs, hung with the smell of his third passion.

Cigars.

Rupert sat behind his late Grandfathers Druce & Company kidney shaped mahogany desk, whilst the Vasco da Gama corona he had been smoking before their arrival continued to smoulder in the 1920s German cigar-rest to his right. Rupert leaned back in his chair, clasped his hands together behind his head and stretched his legs forward beneath his desk in a conspicuous show of pompous authority.

'So, my secretary informs me you are with the Art & Antiquities Investigations Department. Is that correct?' he enquired as he flexed his elbows back behind his head. Lena sat forward on the edge of her chair.

'I am Detective Inspector Lena Johnson and this is Detective Chief

Inspector Tate Randall,' she said gesturing towards her partner. 'Yes, we are both with the A.I.D branch of the Metropolitan Police Department.'

'I think you will find everything is in order here, I run a very tight ship and have a family reputation to uphold,' said Rupert defensively, as he released his grasp from behind his head and re-interlocked his fingers in front of his chest.

'We are fully aware of the credibility and prestige your company holds within antiquarian circles. It is held in high regard by many within the business,' replied Lena. She could tell the ostentatiousness was for show and a different man lay behind the bravado. However, they needed to keep his demeanour neutral. Their enquiries would be more difficult if Rupert put up his defences and was not open and honest about operations within his company. So, Lena continued to subtly gratify his cause.

'You've had some high-profile pieces pass through your doors recently. That must afford a wonderful sense of achievement having only taken the reins of Managing Director a little less than a year ago?' Rupert reached for the corona, drew hard on its butt and exhaled a long vaporous trail of smoke above the heads of Lena and Tate.

'The business is,' he paused for effect, drawing once more on the cigar, 'going from strength to strength, auction by auction.' He exhaled once more. 'Technological advances are progressing exponentially. However, it appears people are now keener than ever to hold onto the past and furnish their homes with features that nod to the bygone days.' He took another long draw on the cigar and placed it back on its wooden rest. Again, showing no concern for his guests, he slowly exhaled a ribbon of smoke in their direction. As the smoke dissipated around them, Tate could no longer contain himself and a cough spluttered from his mouth.

'I am sorry,' exclaimed Rupert. 'With a blanket ban on no smoking in any public spaces, I find solace in the sanctuary of my own office, but I do forget how others do not share my desires.' He reached for the cigar one final time and tapped the ash from its tip into the ashtray and gently snuffed the butts dying embers.

'So enough of the pleasantries, what's the real reason behind your visit today?' Tate coughed once more and spoke for the first time.

'We are currently investigating the whereabouts of a particular painting. We have reason to believe the work passed through your company and was sold at an auction you held here earlier this month.'

'What was the title of the painting?' asked Rupert as he brought his hands together in a prayer pose and placed his thumbs on his chin.

'Rendezvous a la mer by Emile…'

'Moreau,' Rupert cut him off mid-sentence. 'I remember it well. It gave up quite a fight. Unexpectantly, it made over three times its reserve.' Rupert's manner appeared to change direction slightly and his pretentiousness began to diminish. He seemed strangely excited by the enquiry into the painting.

'Made us a tidy percentage too,' he beamed. 'Of course, we have all the relative paperwork, authenticity certificates and import duty statements, should you need to see them.'

'If we could start by seeing those, that would be wonderful,' Lena intervened as she stood and crossed the office to an internal window that overlooked the auction room. As she surveyed the floor below, she scratched at the cuticle of her thumb nail with the tip of her index finger. It was one of those things she did subconsciously whilst thinking or contemplating.

'Yes, no problem. I'll get my secretary to look them out right away,' said Rupert as he reached for the phone station on his desk. As his finger hovered over the intercom button, Lena turned back from the window.

'We do not wish to raise any unnecessary suspicions at this stage. We would appreciate it if we could keep this as low key as possible for the time being. The fewer people aware of our enquiries, the better. I think you would agree that only those in authority need know,' declared Lena, knowingly aware that she was further feeding his grandiosity and he was still more than happy to take the bait.

Woolwich District

London, England

24

Rupert responded to Lena's request and had collected the file for the sale of the Moreau painting himself. He had however, asked his secretary to make some tea as he passed by her desk on his way back to the office.

The secretary finished pouring tea for Rupert and Tate and turned to Lena as she headed towards the door. '

And a cup of coffee,' she grumbled as she presented Lena with a bone china cup and left the room.

'May I apologise,' said Rupert, 'Karen believes tea making is below her job description. She has been known to respond to such requests with, "I'm not a bloody vending machine."' Rupert smirked at his little anecdote, 'I think, however, we may have gotten off lightly today.' Ignoring the niceties of the situation and the newly found charm in Rupert's persona, Lena returned to the situation in hand.

'May I take a look at the file, please.' Rupert stood. This enabled him to pass the file over the desk to the waiting extended hands.

'Like I have already said, I think you will find all the paperwork is as it should be.' Lena placed the file on the desk in front of herself and Tate and opened the cover.

'As you can see,' proclaimed Rupert, 'firstly there is the Certificate of Authenticity, followed by the customs paperwork to receive the work into this country. Customs clearance declarations and import duty tax receipts are all documented on subsequent pages.'

Lena flicked through the pages as Rupert chronicled the paper trail. Pointing at the paperwork, Rupert who by now had rounded the desk and was currently stood behind the pair forged ahead with his explanations. As Lena turned a new page, Rupert would rattle off a summary of its details. His clarifications confirming the documentation of procedural paperwork. All of which Lena and Tate were fully aware of and would rightly assume to have been there. Tate gave Lena a knowing glance and the pair let Rupert continue. He seemed to relish his newly found openness.

However, Tate felt slightly uneasy with Rupert now perched at his shoulder and this new position no longer afforded him the opportunity to read Rupert's body language.

'Why the sudden change of heart? The man had gone from a closed book to an open catalogue in a matter of minutes.' Tate had noticed the change in Rupert's composure from the moment he had discovered their enquiries where focused on the Moreau painting. It could well be possible that Rupert had no inclination to the concealment of the Caravaggio. Tate recognised that sometimes people with something to hide, pasts to conceal, previous misdemeanours or simply a guilty conscience, try their absolute best to cover their guilt by being over the top with their helpfulness. Once Rupert had discovered the true nature of the investigators visit, he had visibly let his guard down.

'Was he now assisting their enquiries having been relieved to know they were not investigating some other misdemeanour? Had he been concerned over a tax evasion cover up or the occasional back of the hand cash sale?' Right from their initial introduction, Tate had had a gut feeling that Rupert Hawkins had plenty to hide.

'Whose responsibility would it have been for the paintings collection and customs clearance?' asked Tate.

'That will be Tony Wilkinson. He deals with all works imported from the Continent. He would have personally seen all paintings through customs that day.'

'And who else would have had access to the painting on its arrival?'

Rupert swallowed a mouthful of tea and returned the cup to his desk. He reached for his cigar, but quickly thought better of it.

'I cannot say for sure, but the Customs officer at Dover would have cross checked all the relevant documentation and that each painting matched its paperwork. His signature will be on the paperwork in the file.' Lena handed Tate a document with a HM Customs and Excise logo in the top corner and Tate made a note of the attending officer's details.

'We shall need to talk with Mr Wilkinson in due course,' affirmed Tate, as Lena continued to leaf through the papers.

'That is the Declaration of Ownership from the previous owner, followed by statements authorising the sale and paperwork confirming the paintings market value appraisal, reserve price and the third-party agreements of sellers' fees.' Although he had happily let Lena handle the documents, Tate had been studying each page for any inconsistencies and taking note of any particulars and questions worthy of further investigation. He made a note of the previous owners' details.

'Could the previous owners have arranged the export of the painting, knowing its size would be ideal to enclose the Caravaggio?' Lena rifled through several more pages detailing the paintings background and the details included in the auction catalogue. All the paperwork they had thumbed through so far would be relevant to their investigation, but the ensuing pages would be far more significant to their primary enquiries. It recorded the paper trail of those who had shown an interest in purchasing the painting, those who had actively participated in the bidding during its sale and most importantly, who had placed the winning bid and purchased the painting. Rupert continued to convey the detail of each page.

'You will no doubt recognise those listings,' he offered as he pointed to the pages Lena was currently perusing.

'A list of the telephone and postal bidders and their allocated auction representative and a complete list of those who registered to bid.' Rupert's helpfulness was now becoming tedious and Lena needed some breathing space.

'We shall of course need copies of these pages. Mr Hawkins would you be so kind,' motioned Lena as she handed Rupert a handful of documents.

'Yes, of course. I'll do it immediately. It won't take a moment; I'll be straight back.'

'There's no need to hurry Mr Hawkins,' exclaimed Tate as he knowingly glanced at Lena once more. 'Take your time.' Lena thumbed through the list of registered bidders and handed the sheet to Tate who did the same. Neither recognised nor recalled any of the names on the register.

The final pages of the file documented the purchase of the painting. The first sheet was a record from the Auction Block of the series of bids culminating in the sale of the painting. It registered the value of the bid and tied it to a registered bidder. The concluding pages were the sales invoice and a copy of an electronic transfer of funds receipt. A transfer of thirty-eight and a half thousand pounds from the account of a Dr Adam Coster.

The highest bidder and the new owner of both 'Rendezvous a la Mer and St Mary Magdalene in Ecstasy.'

Woolwich District

London, England

25

Tate sat back in the chair and thumbed through the notes he had taken. Lena stood and strolled about the office. They used the small amount of time and space to contain their thoughts. They had interviewed Tony Wilkinson regarding the transition of the painting through UK customs. From the statement they had taken, it was safe to say, Mr Wilkinson had followed the procedure to the book, as he had done numerous times before. He had seen the painting, along with several others, through the customs procedure, completed all the necessary paperwork and was most probably totally oblivious to the Caravaggio laying within.

Lena continued to pace the room. They had a few minutes before Mr Legg would arrive to give his statement.

'Let's run through possible scenarios,' said Tate as Lena crossed behind the back of the chair in which he sat. 'The Caravaggio was removed from the Moreau before it left mainland Europe.'

'The least likely scenario,' Lena stated, perching her bottom on the corner of the desk so as to face Tate. 'Two,' she continued, raising her index and middle finger together in Tate's direction. 'The painting was removed from its carrier between arriving in the UK and the Moreau being sold at auction.'

'Three,' She raised her ring finger to join the previous two. 'The buyer bought the 'Rendezvous a la mer' knowing that the Caravaggio was concealed within.' Lena paused for a moment's thought and Tate continued for her.

'Four, the buyer of the Moreau has no idea of what lies within the painting.' Lena nodded in agreement. 'They bought it legitimately and at some point, in the future it may be stolen, so the Caravaggio can be retrieved.'

'Five, the buyer bought the painting for a client and is also oblivious to the concealed Caravaggio.' A knock at the door interrupted their speculative theories. The door opened and Rupert Hawkins re-entered the room followed by a short spectacled gentleman.

'Officers, this is Geoffrey Legg. One of our most loyal employees. He's been with us since my father's time.' Tate offered his hand to Geoffrey.

'This is DCI Randall and DI Johnson from the Art and Antiquities Investigation Department. As I explained on the way up Geoffrey, they would like to ask you a few questions about the selling of the Rendezvous a la mer,' declared Rupert as he ushered his associate around the desk to the chair on the far side. Geoffrey stood nervously looking at the chair, then to his employer and back to the chair again.

'Yes, yes, Geoffrey sit, sit, you may use my chair.' Tate noticed his discomfort.

'Mr Hawkins, we'd appreciate some time with Mr Legg, if you don't mind.' Rupert took that as an indication to busy himself elsewhere and excused himself from the room.

Having read through the auction houses paperwork trail for the selling of the painting, it was clear that Geoffrey Legg's involvement in the entire process was little more than acting on behalf of a client in the auction hall. The key factor of interest to Tate and Lena was that Geoffrey Legg was the only employee to have had contact with the so-called Dr Adam Coster. Lena broke the silence.

'Mr Legg, thank you for taking the time to help us with our enquiries.' Geoffrey nodded in agreement.

'Please, call me Geoffrey.' He seemed unsettled sat in the boss's chair and looked awkward and lost in its vastness.

'We would like to ask you a few questions about your interactions with Dr Coster during his acquisition of the Moreau painting. Can you remember when you first had contact with him?'

'I never met him face to face. Our communications were entirely over the telephone. He had initially shown his interest in purchasing the work through our online enquiry page. As an Absentee Representative Manager, I picked up the enquiry and followed it up with an indication of interest phone call.' Tate and Lena had learnt from the client file, that the contact number was a mobile. Probably, prepaid and untraceable.

'We only talked twice more after that. Once to confirm details and to clarify my representation on his behalf. The only other time was during the auction I'm afraid.' As Lena continued her questions, Tate made further notes with his notebook and pen. Tate still liked to do things in a traditional way. Or 'Old School' as Lena often reminded him.

'How would you describe Dr Coster from the way he sounded to you over the phone. Old? Young? Did he have any accent? Foreign sounding or a regional one perhaps?'

'He didn't sound old or particularly young. Middle-aged I would say. Well spoken. He did have a strange tone to his voice. Raspy, almost sort of robotic.' Lena gave Tate a short puzzling glance.

'Was there any hint of an accent?' Geoffrey paused to think for a second and adjusted his glasses across the bridge of his nose.

'No, I'm afraid not. Middle of the road English. To be fair, he did not say a great deal. Answered my questions with the fewest of words. If I can be brutally honest, I did not like the man. He was incredibly rude and abrupt. Frequently cut me off when I was speaking. I have never taken to people of that nature. They seem to have no time for anyone but themselves.' Tate retracted his pen and looked up from his note taking.

'Did you have any contact with Dr Coster after the auction?'

'Only by email, at the address in the file. Confirmation of the purchase, the verification of the electronic transfer and confirmation of the address for the paintings delivery.'

'Is there anything else during your conversations with Dr Coster that stands out? Maybe something he said that was unusual or seemed peculiar in that instance.' The answer came instantaneously this time, Geoffrey did not need time to think as the words came tumbling from his mouth.

'Oh yes, most definitely. I remember thinking it was most unusual at the time.' Geoffrey shuffled his backside so as to perch himself on the edge of the chair and lent forward, not unlike a reader on Children's Storytime. 'After the gavel had dropped to indicate the acceptance of our winning bid, Dr Coster thanked me, before I had even had chance to confirm our final bid had been successful. It was like he had been there all along watching the proceedings.'

Geoffrey Legg was your stereotypical law-abiding citizen who never stood out of line. He paid his bills on time, offered his seat on the train to others and never departed church without leaving an offering in the donation box. Tate knew there was nothing more Geoffrey Legg could give them. He looked to Lena in a muted agreement that their questioning had come to an end. Lena pursed her lips and nodded silently.

'Well, that's all the questions we have for now Mr Legg. If you remember anything else relating to Dr Coster that you think maybe of interest to us, please give me a call.' Tate handed him his card. Geoffrey took this as a cue and raised himself from the chair.

'May I just ask, is the painting safe?' Tate looked at Mr Legg and perceived his concern.

'All I can tell you at present, is the location of the painting is unknown.'

Euston Road

London, England

26

Two children scrambled around the plinth of the sculpture. They clambered and crawled their way up to the base of the bronze structure.

'Look at me, Mum,' shouted the smaller of the two, as both children proceeded to play 'Peekaboo' between the arms and legs of the leaning human form. Their imprudent mother sat below. She paid little attention. Heedless to her children's misdoings, she occasionally looked up to shout, 'be careful you two' and now and then diverted her attention from her phone long enough to take a photograph of the mischievous siblings.

The sculpture of Sir Isaac Newton overlooks the piazza at the entrance to the British Library. Eduardo Paolozzi based his large bronze casting on William Blake's 1795 print, 'Personification of Man Limited by Reason'. The sculpture portrays a seated Newton leaning forward seemingly taking measurements with a pair of dividers. The joints of Newtons body are joined at the shoulders, elbows, knees and ankles with mechanical bolts to emphasise an association between nature and science.

The tranquillity and open space of the enclosed courtyard at the British Library offered a haven from the bustle of the city surrounding it. People could often be found reading, drawing, studying or simply taking time for contemplation within its reposeful atmosphere.

The Narcissus had done just that. For the previous thirty minutes, the Narcissus had sat in the solitude of an empty bench and allowed life to quietly float by. Finding solace in the ability to escape from the world for the briefest of moments. That moment had however been stolen by the arrival of the two unruly children. As the Narcissus continued to watch the rug rats using Newton's torso as a climbing frame an amusing thought materialised.

'If Newton's laws of motion and gravity are indeed correct, then there would be a high probability that one of the children may very soon take a tumble and ironically come back to Earth with a bump'.

The Narcissus smirked at the anecdote, whilst a recently inserted prepaid SIM activated within the phone. After a few minutes of registering the card and linking it to a false email account, the Narcissus once again tapped in the digits of the memorised number and waited for the call to connect.

'Grayson Gallery, Jeremy Grayson speaking.' The Narcissus said nothing, letting the line remain silent for the briefest of moments. Just long enough to generate a feeling of apprehension.

'I hope you have taken the opportunity to compile the list I have asked for?' There was no reply. This time however it was not for effect, it was a pause to gain composure. Finally the response materialised.

'Just as you had instructed. I have chosen noteworthy collectors, all of whom I have represented in the past and all of whom are affluent enough to consider a purchase such as the one you are offering.' Upon receiving the email from Dr Valentine, Jeremy had created a list of potential buyers. Each meeting the particular criteria outlined so insistently by the doctor.

'If I may say so,' floundered Jeremy, unsure whether he should continue, 'I do not understand the need for such a list. I could choose any one name from those I am providing and be certain of a successful outcome in the first instance.'

'That will be for me to decide, Mr Grayson,' instructed the Narcissus.

'I was just trying to save you the inconvenience of…'

'The names, Mr Grayson. Who do you advocate as a worthy buyer of the Caravaggio?' Jeremy writhed silently, biting his lip to subdue his exasperation.

'Sir Christopher Roebuck would be my first choice. We have secured many…' Once again, the Narcissus cut Jeremy short.

'Just the names for now, Mr Grayson.' At the other end of the line, Jeremy composed himself and calmed his agitations before continuing.

'Sir Christopher Roebuck.'

'Anatoli Nikolaev.'

'Tristan Campbell.'

'I have no need to deal with Tristan Campbell,' the Narcissus implied in the usual curt and terse manner. The remark took Jeremy unaware and derailed his train of thought. Once again, he fought to remain calm and maintain his serenity.

'Ashley Denning.'

'And Hendrik Pietersen.'

'And there will be no offer of an opportunity to view the Caravaggio that concerns Hendrik Pietersen,' insisted the Narcissus with an air of authority that suggested there was no room for negotiation. Jeremy held his tongue but began to wonder why the doctor had requested his services in the first place.

'However, I have two further names I require you to make contact with,' stipulated the Narcissus, 'I shall email them to you, along with how we shall proceed from here.' Jeremy was poised to raise a concern but remained silent. He had already learnt that any opinion would be in vain and futile where the doctor was concerned. He was offered no opportunity to do so as Dr Valentine continued.

'I will also confirm which prospective buyer shall be the first to be invited to view the Caravaggio. I must insist you have no contact with any of the other potential buyers until you have my authorisation,' declared the Narcissus. 'If the Caravaggio is purchased at the first offer, there will be no further need to contact the remaining four.' Jeremy remained bewildered at Dr Valentines insistence. However, with his role seemingly minimal, he may as well sit back, remain tight lipped and simply collect his handlers fee.

'Do I make myself clear, Mr Grayson?' Feeling like a schoolboy chastised by the Headmaster, Jeremy responded.

'As clear as day.'

There was the slightest indication of disdain in his reply. Nonetheless, it was swept under the carpet and quickly ignored as the Narcissus continued.

'One final thing. If you are satisfied, as you should be with the authenticity of the painting.'

There was a noticeable pause.

'Delete the photographs, Mr Grayson!'

The call ended.

The Narcissus eased back on the stone bench and began to remove the back from the phone. A shriek from the direction of the Newton statue reverted the Narcissus's attention back to the vexatious children. The shriek had however, not been a cry of alarm, but a cry of joy. The mischievous pair were shinnying down the walls of the plinth, enticed by their mother, who was currently unwrapping cake and biscuits. The Narcissus found contentment in the moment as a quote from Shakespeare sprang to mind.

'The tempter or the tempted, who sins most?'

30th May 1606

Rome, Italy

27

They spent the remainder of the day deliberating Michelangelo's next move. They talked for short periods of time. Michelangelo drank. They ate bread and cheese. Michelangelo drank some more. Between times Signora Antognetti carried out day to day chores and Michelangelo slept in a chair at the table with his torso spread out across its wooden surface. When they talked, Michelangelo spoke of remorse. He cried. He pleaded with his conscience. He had never intended to inflict such an injury on Ranuccio. She had to believe him. She said she did. But was it just words? It had been a terrible accident. He ran the altercation back, over and over in his head. He had only wanted to teach his biggest adversary a lesson he would never forget. Images of that moment kept repeating in his mind.

'If the stupid fool had not still been thinking about his bloody cock, even at the very end. Things would be different if he had not turned to protect his dignity.'

His head hurt. His body ached. *How could events be undone? How could he stop the pain?* So many questions repeated in his head.

'Were they already looking for him? Should he run? Who could he seek for forgiveness? Most importantly, who could he now trust?'

Signora Antognetti tried to reassure him. She continued to comfort him although it became increasingly more difficult as Michelangelo drank excessively to dull the pain and drown his misery. But no amount of drink would alter the fact that he had caused the serious wounding of another man. There could be no turning back of the clock. They would have his head for a crime of this nature.

Late in the afternoon, Michelangelo awoke from another alcohol induced sleep to find Signora Antognetti had bathed and was presently tying an outdoor cape at her chest.

'Are you leaving?' enquired Michelangelo as his eyes fought to open from their drunken slumber.

'I have a previous engagement I cannot afford to miss,' Signora Antognetti replied as she continued to ready herself to leave.

'I should be back before dark. I have left some food on the side for you. You are safe here. Nobody knows of your presence. I think it would be wise to stay hidden for now. Please Michelangelo, do not leave. There is more wine if you must. When my work is done, I will find out all I can.'

'Where and who do you go to?' Michelangelo asked hesitantly. He knew better than to ask. However, his insecurities were heightened and a darkness gnawed from deep within causing him to even question the trust of those closest to him.

'My affairs are not your business, Michelangelo. You know better than to pry into things that do not concern you.'

'Please don't tell me you are modelling for that damn Carracci again,' Michelangelo demanded, slamming his fist into the table.

'That's precisely why I didn't tell you. I knew exactly what your response would be, and you have justified my silence. Annibale's money is as good as any man's.'

Annibale Carracci was another influential painter held in the same high regard as Michelangelo. Both artists frequently failed to see eye to eye. Each was as outspoken as the other and both were frequently forthright with derogatory remarks about the others accomplishments. Their rivalry came to a head when both were chosen to paint works to stand side by side in the new Cerasi Chapel of the Santa Maria del Popolo. Annibale had won the prize commission to paint the alter-piece, whilst Michelangelo had to bite a bitter pill, swallow his pride and settle with the commission to paint the two side panels. However, some feel Michelangelo may have had the last laugh. With Annibale's 'Assumption of the Virgin' taking pride of place at the head of the alter, was it by coincidence that Michelangelo's 'Conversion on the way to Damascus' was hung on the alters right side with a large horses' backside pointing directly at Annibale's work.

Signora Antognetti stood at the door poised to leave. She looked back across the room in the direction from which bitterness and anger had once again been thrown.

'*Why did she have such feelings for such a spiteful man. Was it part of the internal mothering instinct in-built into women?*'

Occasions where he had shown her heart-felt consideration, love and affection, were few and far between these grievous episodes. She held those lesser moments in such high regard, that the malicious outbursts paled into insignificance.

Shooting a fleeting glance in Michelangelo's direction, Signora Antognetti surrendered one final smile and without saying a further word, she turned and stepped out onto the street.

Isle of Dogs

London, England

28

Harriet Stone pulled the BMW 320d into a vacant, dedicated residents parking space and looked up through the windscreen at the building rising in front of her. The recently prolonged spell of idyllic English weather looked likely to end as the clear blue heavens were succumbing to a bank of ominous looking clouds across the capitals horizon. As she looked skyward the evening sun bounced prismatic colours across the buildings glass façade. The apartment block was situated on the Isle of Dogs. Nestled on an elbow of land where the river Thames meanders a full 180 degrees to the east of the city, the docks and canals of London's commercial past had in recent years seen a heavy regeneration scheme. With many major corporations and financial institutions now relocating to nearby Canary Wharf, the Isle was fast becoming a thriving destination for luxurious residential property. The building she now sat outside was a seventeen-floor glass and steel constructed residential tower. Nestled at the foot of the Isle, it offered uninterrupted views across the Thames to the Cutty Sark, Greenwich and beyond. It consisted of a ground floor entrance lobby with twin elevator towers servicing fifty-six residential apartments over fourteen floors. Floors fifteen and sixteen housed four further large apartments and the top floor housed a single penthouse.

'Ready?' Harriet enquired to the man in the passenger seat. She opened the car's door and swung her feet out onto the tarmac. As she did so, the cool sanctuary of the car's air conditioning instantly evaporated and she was taken aback by the warmth of the city for this time of the evening. The passenger responded with a slightly hesitant nod of the head and followed her across the parking area in the direction of the buildings entrance.

As Harriet and her fellow investigating officer approached the door, a uniformed police constable stepped forward. Recognising DI Stone, he lifted the crime scene tape currently restricting entry to the building. Harriet and DS Iain Richards walked through, showing their identification cards as a matter of procedure.

'The tech team are already inside Ma'am. Floor Nine,' offered the constable.

'Thank you, Constable,' replied Harriet as the pair continued into the building and crossed to the pair of elevators.

As the lift rose towards the ninth floor, they both removed plastic over shoes from their pockets. Harriet steadied herself with one hand on the elevator's wall and pulled an overshoe on to her boot.

'So, what do we have so far?' she enquired. DS Richards finished fitting his own over shoes before removing his mobile device from his pocket. He held his thumb over the mobiles home button and the fingerprint recognition feature unlocked the device. Iain touched an icon on the home screen and a data file opened instantaneously. Long gone were the days of a policeman's notebook and pencil.

'Single male body, mid-twenties to early thirties, of oriental origin,' he paused briefly.

'Decapitated.'

Harriet looked up as she finished adjusting the over shoes on her boots. 'Your first decapitation?' she enquired.

'Second Ma'am. The first was a tube jumper though,' Iain replied as the lifts automated system announced their arrival at the ninth floor. Harriet studied the interior of the elevator car.

'No cameras,' she declared as the doors parted, and Iain followed her out into a small corridor.

The corridor offered four doors, each to separate apartments and a single door to the stair well. The one they sought was at the far end and was distinguishable by the crime scene tape and again a constable outside. This time Harriet did not recognise the constable and announced their ID's.

'DI Harriet Stone and DS Iain Richards.' The constable responded silently with a nod of the head and a purse of the lips before detaching the tape and opening the apartments door. He then recorded the time of their entry in the logbook he held in his hand. Harriet and Iain stepped over the threshold and waited. In a connecting room, a female dressed in full length white forensic overalls, turned and noticed their presence.

'Ok to proceed, Ma'am. Primary evidence has been completed,' she stated, before turning back to the procedure she was currently completing. Both Harriet and Iain took that as their cue to proceed and each donned a pair of latex gloves before moving further into the apartment.

Penelope Carter-Moore placed an 'evidence indicating number' on the floor where she was presently crouching and took a trio of pictures. Each picture frame slightly tighter than the previous. Each showing details of blood pooling patterns on the hardwood floor. She carefully placed a 'length indicating rule' alongside a particular blood pool, re-adjusted the focal length of the digital SLR and took another series of shots. Before standing, she opened the cameras viewer and clicked through the captured shots. Happy with the files, she stood and crossed the room to greet the two new attendees.

'Good to see you Harry, present situation aside,' declared Penelope. They would normally have shaken hands, but protocol would not permit due to possible cross transference of materials.

'Always a pleasure to discover we have your expertise at the scene, Penny,' declared Harriet as she started to survey the scene opening before her. 'It's reassuring to know the department appoints the most knowledgeable on a case of this calibre.'

'No one else was available,' jested Penny as she returned to the macabre scene of the apartment.

Penelope Carter-Moore was a senior forensic investigator with the National Crime Agency. Penny, as everybody knew her, grew up in a leafy suburb of Surrey to very affluent parents. Her father was a surgeon at the Royal London hospital and her mother practiced as a local GP. Following in her parent's footsteps, Penny gained a biological sciences degree at the Imperial College London with full intentions of following it with a master's degree in medical sciences at Oxford. However, a chance encounter with a lecturer of Investigative Sciences opened a door to a whole new world, where she found an un-paralleled passion and un-discovered ability to diversify into a career as a forensic scientist.

Under the hood of the ever-present white overalls and thick rimmed owl-like spectacles, Penny Carter-Moore was a 'Plain Jane'. Swap the overalls for an evening dress, remove the spectacles, let down the shoulder length blonde hair and the duckling emerges as an elegant swan. However, the overalls were more on than off and Penny had recently turned thirty and was still on the available list.

'Sewn into those white overalls is Penny Carter-Moore, Senior Forensic Investigator for the N.C.A and one of the best the country has to offer,' Harriet advocated, as she introduced Penny to her colleague.

'And this is the newly appointed D.S. Iain Richards. Joining us from North of the border.' Both Penny and Iain smiled and gave an acknowledged nod.

'So Penny, what have you got for us?'

Isle of Dogs

London, England

29

Harriet surveyed the scene playing out in front of her. No two crime scenes were ever the same. Even crime scenes originating from the same perpetrator differed in many ways. It was all in the detail. Each miniscule factor or infinitesimal particular was as important as another. Nothing could be overlooked, no matter how trivial it may seem. Something that may not appear relevant at the time could be significantly compelling to the bigger picture at a later date. Harriet approached every new crime scene in the same way. She called it the ABC of detection. Assume nothing. Believe nobody. Check everything. Harriet had always inculcated her fellow officers to gather evidence not only with your eyes, but with all your senses. Not only, what am I seeing? But what am I hearing, smelling, feeling? Is there a strange or familiar smell? What is creating a particular sound? Where is the draft coming from? Why is the surface sticky? Leave no stone unturned, no question unanswered. Perceive and retrieve, anything and everything.

Harriet was like a hawk. Eagle eyed you could say. As her eyes moved around the room, photoreceptors in her retinas gathered the individual details of each visual observation. The gathered information then travelled along a series of optic nerves to be processed in the visual cortex of her brain. The entire pathway taking milliseconds to travel. Finally, each impulse was processed and stored in her visual memory. As she appraised the situation the process repeated thousands of times within the initial minutes of Harriet being at the crime scene.

The apartments main space was open planned. Kitchen, dining and living spaces all integrated into one large room. Running its entire length, the south facing aspect was a heat retentive wall of glass, with floor to ceiling drapes currently opened to one side. The floor throughout was laid with solid birch hardwood flooring, with an occasional deep piled rug between furnishings. To the left of the entrance hall was an extravagant ultra-modern kitchen. Its cupboards, surfaces and islands, finished in brilliant white and silver. Two sinks, numerous built-in appliances and an abundance of chef friendly culinary gadgets, all as fulgent as the day they came out of the box. A cinema sized TV screen covered the entire wall at the other end of the room. Four deep snug leather chairs were arranged in an arch at the optimum viewing distance from the screen.

The centre of the open planned area accommodated another lounge with sofas arranged across a sunken floor and a large dining area with a ten-place glass table and chairs at its centre. It was here that Penny currently stood.

'Single victim, male, of oriental origin. Decapitated,' declared Penny.

'Estimated time of death, between 8 and 10pm yesterday. Body temperature has reached ambient temperature and rigor is in full Rigid State.'

Body temperature and rigor effect are commonly used to primarily assess time of death at a crime scene. A deceased body will decrease in temperature by one and a half degrees centigrade per hour until it reaches the temperature of the environment around it. The stiffening of the body, commonly known as Rigor Mortis, normally appears within the body around two hours after death. Adenosine Triphosphate, the substance that allows energy to flow to the muscles, dissipates and without it the muscles become stiff and inflexible. Although Rigor begins throughout the body at the same time, the smaller muscles, like those of the face and neck are affected first. A complete stiffening of the body, technically referred to as Rigid State can take up to 12 hours.

The headless torso was sat at the head of the table. '*Ironically befitting of a victim of beheading,*' thought Harriet as she joined Penny. Iain remained a short distance back. The body was still fully clothed and sat upright in the glass backed chair. A small amount of blood splatter could be seen. However, a red blanket wrapped around the torso's shoulders like an oversize shawl covered the majority of the blood patterning. The victims neck protruded from the folds of cloth. The skin of the neck, severed tendons and ruptured capillaries spewed from the gaping cavity in a volcanic eruption of bloody sinew. Ripped, torn and lacerated flesh hung from dissevered bone. The wounds were ragged and scraggy from the dismembering of the head. The chalky white of the severed spinal column could be seen at its centre. One arm of the torso was extended across the table. The hand at its wrist was grasping the decapitated head by its hair, holding it upright over a golden serving platter. A small amount of blood had coagulated in a puddle on the plates surface. A single over-sized gold ring dressed a finger of the extended hand. The face of the severed head had drained to an ashen colour and the eyes had fallen to stare at the blood pooled platter.

Penny continued, 'blood patterning would suggest that the head was removed over there.' She pointed to the area where she had been working when Harriet and Iain had first arrived. 'Primary blood analysis and the relatively small amount of pooled blood would suggest the heart had stopped before decapitation. The blood pattern would have been far more dramatic if it had still been beating.'

'Am I right in thinking a saw was used to remove the head, rather than a bladed implement?' interrupted Harriet.

'At this stage, I would suggest a fine-toothed saw, possibly surgical. We will know more when the cutting striations are observed under a microscope.' Whilst she had been breaking down the crime scene, Penny had noticed that Iain had continued to stand on the fringe of the room. Only having just met him, she could not decide if he was being cautious and limiting the footfall around the crime scene or whether the beheaded torso was having an unfavourable effect on his stomach contents. She re-focused her attention on Harriet.

'The lack of blood trail from the decapitation site to the table would advocate towards the head having been placed on the tray before it was removed to the table. The red blanket around the upper torso was probably used to drag the remaining body to its current position.' Harriet looked along the travel line and back to the head on the platter. Iain remained at his safe distance. He continually tapped at his mobile device, recording every detail of Penny's observations.

'Has anything else been moved?' enquired Harriet.

'Not as far as we are aware. Apart from the curtains. The cleaner had apparently come by to clean the apartment after a rental departure. She informed the first on scene that she had activated the electronic curtain and the lights from the control panel in the entrance hall. As she entered the room and the curtains parted, she saw the head on the table. She said she got no closer than the end of the kitchen island before she high tailed it back out the door. The neighbour heard her screams and found her hyperventilating in the corridor.'

Iain removed a handkerchief from a trouser pocket and dabbed the perspiration from his brow before continuing with his notes.

'And the neighbour?' asked Harriet.

'He says he came in, no further than the hallway to check for himself before dialling 999. They're both still next door with a female officer. One of the forensic team will bag their clothes for cross fibre analysis.'

Harriet looked across at Iain as Penny finished speaking. His skin tone had now faded to a bloodless taupe and his brow was again glistening with sweat. Recognising the signs, Harriet thought it best to excuse her colleague.

'Probably best if you follow up with the cleaner and the neighbour, Iain.' Mopping his brow once more, he nodded and turned to leave. As he did so, Iain got his first look at the head's face. He swallowed deeply, forcing the rising bile back down his throat.

'I know,' he gulped, 'who this,' he held his hand to his mouth and swallowed again. Taking several long deep breaths allowed him to finish his sentence.

'He's been all over the news lately. It's Hidetaka Yamamoto!'

Isle of Dogs

London, England

30

The voice in the earpiece announced they would be live-on-air in 20 seconds. With a final glance at the notes on her tablet, she dropped a shoulder, rotated her neck and flung her perfectly coiffured mane of GHD straightened blonde hair back from her face.

Rebecca Crawford struck a pose.

A pose she had held numerous times before. Confidently, with a hint of a welcoming smile, she clasped the microphone to her chest, stared straight into the barrel of the camera's eye and on through to the eyes of the viewing public beyond.

She stood on the fringe of the yellow crime scene tape. Beyond the exclusion zone, an apartment block with a further florescent barrier at its entrance dominated the skyline. Apart from the usual police presence and the arrival or departure of the occasional white coveralled forensic officer, Rebecca and her camera man held an exclusive media presence at the tape line. A handful of inquisitive onlookers had started to gather on the other side of the restricted area. Mainly locals with a nose for gossip and the ever-familiar faces of fanatical ambulance chasers. Usually there would be a throng of media personnel from numerous news channels jostling for prime positions to broadcast their reports. But today was different. Rebecca had received a heads up. A source had given her the whisper. Information was easy to obtain if you had the right contacts. A radio ham with a passion for scanning the emergency services radio frequencies was always happy to give Rebecca a nod in exchange for a bottle of single malt.

For now, she had an exclusive breaking headline. But it would not last long. As soon as she went live, the pandemonium would begin. Every man, dog and reporter would crawl out of the media woodwork and be racing to join her at the tape. But she had a head start on the rest of the pack. This was her breaking story. Moments like this were few and far between. She was going to savour every single moment and do her utmost to stay one step ahead of the stampede.

'And 3,2,1, yours,' came the direction from the studio via her earpiece. She stood strong and spoke with confidence as the light on the camera confirmed they were now live to the nation.

'This is Rebecca Crawford bringing you an exclusive breaking story from Universal News. We are live from the Isle of Dogs in London, where we are led to believe that celebrity playboy Hidetaka Yamamoto has been found deceased under suspicious circumstances.'

Lee Valley Park
London, England

31

The wheel hit the kerb and with a slight adjustment of weight, the rider bunny hopped the bike onto the tarmac. The high traction compound tyres found little resistance as the bike crossed the pavement and dropped down once again onto the gravel path of the park. Harriet double clicked the speed trigger shifter and the gears accommodated the new terrain. Easing up from the saddle to stand on the peddles, she increased her pedal rate and manoeuvred the bike across the increasingly uneven ground. Standing on the pedals also allowed her to absorb more of the shock from the larger ruts in the path through her legs. After about five hundred metres, she abruptly deviated the bike from the path onto a series of narrower tracks which traversed a treelined area of inclines and declines. With the change of terrain and an increase in the angle of the slope, Harriet once again shifted the gears. This time decreasing the ratio to allow for a greater crank rotation. She pushed harder as the bike climbed the hill. Feeling the lactic acid starting to build in her thighs, she pushed through the pain, shifted the gears once more and increased her crank rotation rate. The tyres slipped as they fought for traction on the gravelled terrain as she made steady progress up the incline. Reaching the backbone of the ridge, she negotiated the bike through a series of deep hollowed switchbacks before shifting her weight forward over the handlebars as the tabletop of the ridge gave way to the decline on the other side. Tucking her backside low and to the rear of the saddle to counterbalance the weight of her upper torso over the handlebars, Harriet sat on the pedals and freewheeled the bike down a set of wooden steps, through another sequence of gullied switchbacks and through a shallow stream at the foot of the slope. The water flicked off the tyre treads and mixed with the thick dusty layer that already coated Harriet's calves. Together they formed tiny rivulets of mud that trickled down the backs of her legs, to stop, only when they met the tops of her ankle socks.

Following the flow of the stream, she picked up her pedal rate once more as the ground began to level out. Sections of the path to the side of the stream were graded with pebbles to form a rough terrain known to mountain bikers as Rock Gardens. Harriet rode the bike standing on the pedals and used her knees once again as shock absorbers to counteract the uneven surface. Adrenaline burst through her veins as she pumped harder to traverse the obstacle. As her adrenal glands converted amino acids into dopamine, Harriet's heart rate increased and her respiration system started to work overtime. But this was the rush she sought by pushing her body to the extreme. The buzz she longed for. The fix that she got. Her early morning burn also allowed Harriet to clear her mind and contain her thoughts before being swallowed by the pandemonium of the job.

She inhaled large amounts of air to re-oxygenate her blood as she pushed herself to the limit knowing her early morning session was nearing its conclusion. Maintaining her accelerated momentum, she dropped off the end of the Rock Garden and followed a short, gravelled track around a series of banked curves before turning back onto one of the park's main arterial paths. From here it was only a short distance back to the bike locker and an invigorating shower.

The Lee Valley velodrome mountain bike park was built as part of the London 2012 Olympic offer. Its legacy afforded off-road cycling to the capital's residents without travelling outside the M25. An opportunity that Harriet took advantage of whenever time and the shackles of the job allowed.

Having returned the bike to the rental area, Harriet had showered and was now changing her compression fit, transferable moisture cycling lycra for something a lot more street savvy. Black jeans, a white open neck blouse, cropped tan leather jacket and brown ankle boots had become her trademark attire since becoming Detective Inspector. Sometimes to the amusement of her team, who jested that she probably had a wardrobe at home comprising five or more identical outfits.

Harriet stared at the reflection staring back at her from the mirror as she applied a fine dark pencil line to her upper and lower lids. The eyeliner accentuated the deep turquoise of her eyes. All her adult life, she had never felt the need or necessity to apply any further make-up to her face. However, she thought the face she saw now told a different story and perhaps now would be a good time to start thinking about it. Amused by the thought, she smiled at the smiling face in the mirror and ran her hands back through her shoulder length brown hair, before grabbing her rucksack from the bench and heading for the door.

A short walk to Stratford tube station and a couple of stops on the Central line train and she would still be at the Bethnal Green MET building for the 9am briefing.

Bruton Place, Mayfair

London, England

32

The weather outside was becoming increasingly inauspicious. The skies had darkened as large Cumulonimbus storm clouds gathered across the Capital. The dense clouds contrasting the skyline by enveloping the city with an alternative atmospheric structure of domes and towers. London had seen its first rain in over a week. Although it had only lasted a mere twenty minutes it was enough to break the oppressive weight bearing humidity of late. The heavy shower had also been enough for people passing the gallery window to couple with their trusty umbrellas once again. Occasionally, some would venture into the gallery to admire his current collection or to shelter for a few minutes whilst a heavy downpour passed.

Today, Jeremy Grayson wasn't paying attention to the faces at the window. His attention was on the news feed currently streaming live on his desktop monitor. The live report held his attention for two reasons. Firstly, he had a thing for Universal News roaming reporter, Rebecca Crawford. Not only was he enchanted by her cover girl allurement but was drawn by her fortitude to prevail in the face of adversity. She also had a cute smile. He often imagined how she would dominate him in the bedroom too. However, today she played second fiddle to the news item she was breaking. Jeremy listened intently as Rebecca disclosed her story on the screen. He did not notice the shimmer in the highlight of her hair. He looked beyond the cerulean blue of her eyes. His fixation today was the subject of her story. The screen showed Rebecca reporting at the perimeter of a crime scene on the Isle of Dogs, whilst a tic-a-tape news feed at the bottom of the screen scrolled the breaking headline. 'Hidetaka Yamamoto found dead under suspicious circumstances.'

As he watched, his mind struggled to comprehend the situation. Surely it was purely coincidental. He had arranged an introduction between Dr Valentine and Hidetaka only a few days ago. Where and when they had arranged a viewing of the Caravaggio, he did not know. Anyway, it was to sell a painting, not murder someone. The stupid playboy had probably gotten himself topped in some sort of revenge killing. He hadn't done himself any favours. He'd agitated more than one person with his social media exploits of late. Perhaps, someone thought a lawsuit wasn't quite enough to shut him up. Jeremy wondered if Hidetaka had even had the chance to view the painting. Maybe they had already met and a deal had been discussed. Either way, you can't complete a deal with a dead man and the doctor would not be happy.

Bethnal Green

London, England

33

Harriet swallowed the last mouthful of the Relentless energy drink, crushed the empty can in her hand and tossed it into the corridor's bin before joining the rest of her team in the incident room. She brushed through the doors with an air of authority and purpose. As she entered the incident room, all those present turned to acknowledge her arrival. Some looked up from telephone calls and in response to Harriet's entrance, proceeded to bring their conversations to a close as soon as conveniently possible. Others looked up from hypnotically glaring at computer monitors, saved their currently opened files and diverted their attention to the front of the room. Those who had been chatting with colleagues, broke their conversations and gathered as a team around the incident boards where Harriet now stood. Some casually leaned against the nearest wall, others parked their backsides on the corner of a desk, and some of the sitters scooted their swivel chairs to more opportune positions. No matter where they settled, they gave Harriet their full attention. An air of silence and respect swept across the room.

'Morning crew,' declared Harriet, addressing the room in her routine way of breaking the silence. She had used the opening since hearing a quote at a managerial workshop when she had first become a Detective Inspector. It had referred to having a crew with a common goal to keep your ship afloat. It had struck a chord and stuck.

'OK, looks like we've got ourselves a media frenzy coming our way.' She nodded at DS Richards, who stepped forward. He cleared his throat with a raspy cough, glanced briefly at his notes and continued.

'Single deceased male.' He pointed to the Facebook profile headshot pinned to the profile board. 'Some, if not all of you will recognize the victim. Hidetaka Yamamoto. Playboy. Son and heir of the Japanese industrial tycoon Akihiro Yamamoto. He's been stealing the headlines of late. Seems to have been getting his kicks from posting online videos of his nocturnal activities with more than one or two fellow celebs.'

He paused as a couple of sarcastic remarks were thrown around the room. 'A couple of injunctions have been imposed to have the videos taken down.' Harriet interjected.

'This is fresh. Next of kin have yet to be informed. Family is in Japan. We don't want them finding out via the media. Get onto it, Andy. Contact the embassy. The usual diplomacy for a foreign national please.' DC Stevens was sat on a desk corner and raised a thumb in acknowledgement.

Iain shuffled the top page of his notes to the back and looked across to Harriet for reassurance. None came. This was only the second time he had addressed the whole department since relocating South of the border and joining the team. He continued.

'The body was discovered yesterday at approximately 4pm when the cleaner entered the property off the Ferry Road on the Isle of Dogs. The apartment had been rented for 3 days via the Sleepezy B&B website. The owner is a Mr. Alex Reynolds. According to the cleaner, he frequently works away in Zurich. Rents the property when he's out of town.' Harriet cut in once more.

'Chase this one will you, DC Evans. Look into the B&B booking. Who, when, how etc. Locate Mr. Reynolds. Tell him there's no need to rush home. Probably won't be too pleased to hear he won't be using his apartment for a while.'

'No probs, Ma'am,' replied DC Jake Evans. He was the baby of the team. Still a little wet behind the ears, but all things internet, cyberspace or cloud based were his forte.

Removing a trio of A4 sized photos from the paperwork bundle in his hands, DS Richards moved forward of Harriet and map-pinned the photographs individually to the incident board.

'The victims head had been removed, probably postmortem and along with the torso moved to the dining area and seemingly posed at the table.' He attached a further two pictures to the board and continued. 'Initial indications suggest the decapitation probably took place in the lounge area and the dismembered parts were moved using the red drape you can see wrapped across the torso's shoulders. We shall know more when forensics have completed.' He added one final picture to the board. It showed a close-up of the neck stump.

A deathly stillness swept through the room. Fidgeters stopped fidgeting, pencil twirlers stopped twirling and the pen suckers stopped sucking. Individually, one by one, they all took in the macabre detail of the picture. As if on cue, a lone siren cried out from the street below and broke the rooms eerie silence allowing DS Richards to continue.

'Minimal arterial blood patterning, and the uniformity of the cutting striations, again support the theory that the heart had stopped beating before the head was removed. The cleanliness and precision of the cuts to both flesh and bone, point towards the use of a surgical grade tool.' Harriet stepped forward, indicating to Iain that she wished to interject once more. She stretched an arm out across the photographic line up and using two fingers tapped the three photos detailing the body posed at the table.

'Crawford and the rest of the muckrakers are going to be swarming all over this like flies on shit.' As she continued, she crossed back and forth in front of the incident board.

'As soon as they snare the cleaner, they will know the head was decapitated,' she declared, pointing to the close-up shot. 'I don't want the fact that the body was posed leaving this room. That's a card we are going to hold awfully close to our chests. It's the one thing the press and the public aren't getting. It will help to sort the chaff when the phones start ringing.' She let her gaze wander the room, until she found the body she sought.

'Sar. Run a profile through HOLMES. Input search parameters for "decapitation" and "posed victim", please.' A woman with extremely long hair, wearing a dark blue sari, lowered a 'Keep Calm and Push Delete' mug from her lips, swallowed the mouthful of its contents and acknowledged Harriet's request.

'On it as soon as we're finished.'

Pivotal to any major investigation was a team of office-based profilers and indexers, responsible for the input, retrieval, collation, and interpretation of information crosschecked through a Home Office database known as HOLMES 2. Sarika Rajamani was the team's senior indexer, Harriet's go-to and ranked highly on the department's biscuit thief suspect list. Sarika had worked her way through numerous administration jobs within the force, before transferring to an indexers role when the crime support database system had started to become more widely used in major investigations. The HOLMES 2 system finds common traits in a wide variety and volume of information. The analysed data is then prioritised for relevance to any on-going investigation.

'While you're on it, can you run up a personal profile of the victim too,' Harriet asked, directing the question once more in Sarika's direction. A silent nod confirmed her acknowledgement.

Like a tag team act, DS Richards took his silent cue and continued with the crime scene summary.

'Primary forensics have collected the usual suspects from the scene. With the apartment on a regular rental turn-over, hairs and fibers are abundant. There is no CCTV within the building, although there are several street cameras in close proximity.'

'George. The cameras are yours. Run the last 72 hours. Look for repeats, ins and outs, and anything capturing the victim in the vicinity,' said Harriet as she walked across the front of the room and parked her bum on the nearest available desktop. 'Door to door as soon as possible too, please George. Take a handful of uniforms and DC Thompson along for company.' A stout bearded officer sat to the rear of the room, momentarily paused tapping a biro between his front teeth. 'Be my pleasure,' he replied in a strong East London accent, before continuing his metronomic clicking. DS George Quinn was a stalwart police sergeant. A pedigreed beat pounder for much of his career, before two replacement hips forced him into his current investigative role. George was the backbone of Harriet's team. Happy with the drudgery of the daily slog. He kept his nose to the grindstone and was more than happy being handed the donkey work. Harriet had a lot of time and respect for DS George Quinn. A fact she was unashamed to endorse.

'Anything more at this stage Iain,' asked Harriet.

'You and I have the postmortem later this morning and there will no doubt be a press conference at some point,' he replied before stepping back as if offering the floor to Harriet. She remained seated.

'Any questions?' She extended a momentary glance around the room and in return received a series of pursed lips and shaking heads.

'Good. We'll reconvene back here, same time tomorrow.' As members of her team returned to workstations, left the room, or resumed conversations, Harriet stood and crossed to where Iain was still standing.

'Good job,' she said, tapping him twice across the shoulders in unison with the words. She continued to talk as she walked away.

'Forty minutes, OK? We'll leave for the PM. I've got a few things to take care of first,' she declared before entering the SIO office and shutting the door behind her.

Croydon Police Station

London, England

34

Scott Edmunds sat in the interview room nervously biting his nails and picking at an annoying nostril hair. If only he'd held his ground and done his job by the book, then he wouldn't be sitting here now. If he lost his job over this, his mother would give him what for. He had only started 3 months ago and had lost his previous two jobs within 6 months due to continual lateness. He looked around the room, but his gaze was continually drawn to the mirrored screen on the side wall. He tried his best not to look there.

'Were they watching him from the other side like they did in the movies? Were they analysing his behaviours, so they would know how to break him.'

He told himself not to be so stupid. He'd only left a delivery in the entrance hall as the customer had insisted. It was their fault if the damn thing had gone missing. The customer had been the one who had suggested he forge the item delivered signature. If Global Deliveries gave their drivers a more realistic time allowance per delivery, then he would have thought twice about leaving the parcel like he did.

Just as Scott's brain began to over exaggerate the situation further, the door to the room opened and in walked a man closely followed by a woman. Both were carrying Starbucks take out cups.

'Cup of coffee?' said the man, extending a cup in Scott's direction.

'Uh, yeah, thanks,' replied Scott reluctantly, wondering if they had laced it with some sort of truth inducing serum. The man sat opposite Scott and the woman who was carrying two cups, gave one to her partner and sat in the chair to the side.

'DCI Tate Randall,' said the man, offering his hand across the table.

'Hi,' replied Scott as he hesitantly took the handshake, but whilst thinking he had seen this scenario many times before on his favourite police dramas. The old good cop, bad cop routine.

'This is DI Lena Johnson and we are from the Art and Antiquities Investigation Department. Thank you for coming into your local station voluntarily today.'

'I ain't come in voluntarily,' thought Scott. *'My supervisor heavily suggested it might be the right thing to do, and I'm missing a day's pay for it.'*

'We were hoping you could help us with our enquiries in association with a case we are currently investigating,' continued Tate, 'We have a few questions we'd like to ask you about a delivery you made to an address in West Brompton on Friday last week. The delivery in question was for a Dr Coster at Apartment 4, Willowbrook House.' Scott fiddled with the lid of his coffee cup, DI Johnson re-crossed her legs and turned the cup she held in her hands. Tate took a sip from his coffee and continued.

'Could you recount your movements for us, from the time you arrived to make your delivery?' Scott moved uncomfortably in his chair, put his cup to one side and started to pick at a hard piece of skin on the thumb of his left hand. He did not look up.

'We are not here to accuse you of anything Scott, we just need you to provide us with a few details of the delivery you made.' Scott's imagination began to run away once more.

'What's the maximum sentence for forgery? Delivery driver sent down for impersonating a customer.'

'Perhaps you could start with when you arrived at the building,' said Tate, reaching across and handing Scott's coffee back to him. Scott took the cup from the good cop and tentatively glanced over his shoulder at the bad cop sat to the side. He took a sip of the coffee.

'When I got to the street there was nowhere to park, so I did a quick once around the block. When I got back, there were still no bloody spaces. I was just about to say sod it and double park, when a van pulled out on the other side of the street.' Tate put down his own coffee and interrupted.

'Do you remember the make of the van?' Scott sipped his drink once more.

'It was a Doorstep Organic Larder van. I remember cause that stupid cartoon carrot was on the rear doors.' A movement to his left caused Scott to hesitate. He glanced over his shoulder once more and noticed the bad cop was writing something down.

'Probably profiling me, to help break me later.' Tate noticed Scott's unease.

'DI Johnson is just noting down anything that might be of interest and may later help us with our enquiries.' Tate was keen to continue. He wanted to keep the kid talking. 'So, you parked the van, then what happened?'

'What I always do!' replied Scott quite insistently. 'I grabbed my tablet from the dashboard and then went around to the back of the van, found the parcel in the back and went into the entrance foyer across the street.' Tate noticed a slight assertiveness in Scott's tone.

'That's fine, can you tell me what you did next?'

'I used the buildings intercom system to phone up to the apartment to let them know I had a delivery for them.'

'So, did they answer straight away?' enquired Tate as he noticed it was becoming harder for Scott to supress his agitations.

'Yeah, she answered almost immediately, like she was sitting next to the intercom waiting.' Tate was slightly taken aback by the answer.

'You said, "She", it was a female who answered?'

'Yeah, when I asked for Dr Coster like on the address label, she said it was Dr Coster speaking.'

'Are you absolutely sure it was a woman's voice.' Tate glanced over at Lena, who returned the glance with raised eyebrows.

'Course I'm sure, I know the difference between a man and a woman, mister. I ain't no faggot!' Tate ignored the frivolous reply and enquired further.

'Did the customer come straight down to collect and sign for the parcel?' Scott again shifted his position uncomfortably in the chair and swallowed hard.

'Yeah, she said she'd be down in just a jiffy and came straight down.' Scott fingered the neckline of his hoody. He was starting to feel uncomfortable. He was getting too hot and he could feel his heart starting to beat a little faster. If he'd had a top button, he would have loosened it.

'Was it getting hot in here due to the weather outside?' He listened for the hum of the air conditioning unit. It had gone silent. *'Turn off the air conditioning and sweat it out of him.'* Just like the hostage situation in a Desert Storm movie he had seen recently. *'Had the good cop given him a hot drink, knowing it would increase his core temperature?'*

'So, you waited in the foyer and the doctor came straight down.'

'Yeah, came down in the lift, signed for the delivery, took the parcel and went straight back up!' Scott picked at the edge of the raised lettering of the Adidas logo embellishing the chest of his hoodie.

'Can you describe the doctor for me? What did she look like? The colour of her hair. What was she wearing?' Scott had found a loose thread on one of the letter's corners and began to twist at it between his thumb and forefinger.

'I didn't pay much attention. I was on the clock and needed to get going. I don't know.' But his tongue began to run away with him.

'Maybe blonde, good looking, tall. Yeah, good figure. I remember, cause I thought she looked like that Jennifer Lawrence from the Hunger Games movies. But not like she is in the films. When she's got the blonde hair in real life.' Scott looked back across at Lena. She was still making notes. They were buying his description.

'Can you remember what Dr Coster was wearing when she came down?'

'She had on a short red skirt. That I remember, cause I noticed she had a crackin' set of pins.' Scott's confidence was growing. He was on a roll now. 'Stiletto heels and a black blouse, unbuttoned at the top.'

Tate watched Scott carefully as he replied to his question. Scott's eyes looked up and right. A sign that he was looking to his imagination for an answer rather than his memories. Classic body language signs that he probably was not telling the whole truth.

'For someone who didn't pay much attention, you seemed to have remembered a great deal, Scott,' said Tate changing his tone slightly.

'You see, Scott. There is a small problem with the information you're feeding us.' Scott pulled at the neckline of his hoody once again.

'There is no Dr Coster registered at that particular delivery address. In fact, there is no Dr Coster residing anywhere in that building!' Tate clasped his hands, put his elbows on the table and lent forward.

'And what is most unusual, Scott. The customer misspelt their surname whilst signing for the delivery. I don't believe that's a common occurrence for anyone. There is no 'A' in Coster, Scott. Its ER, not AR.' Scott's confidence diminished, there and then.

Tate remained silent.

Waited.

Finally, Scott caved in.

'OK. OK. I signed the bloody delivery accepted signature. It was her idea though. She said she was in the shower and I'd have to wait. I didn't have time to wait! We have a deliveries per hour schedule. If I fall behind the clock, I get my pay penalised. She suggested I sign as nobody can read the digital signatures anyway and told me to leave the package in the foyer. It's her own bloody fault if someone stole it, not mine.' Tate sat back in the chair and crossed his arms.

'So, you didn't see Dr Coster, but you did talk to her through the buildings entry intercom system.'

'Yeah,' receded Scott. 'I just did what the customer said, so I could get outta there pronto and onto my next drop.' Tate pushed the chair back and stood up. He crossed to the corner of the room and opened the door.

'Thank you for taking the time to come in, Scott. Your statement has been a great help.' He gestured towards the exit.

'Am I free to go? You won't be pressing any charges?' declared Scott hesitantly as he stood to leave.

'No, Scott. You're free to leave and can be rest assured this won't be going on your criminal record.' With the weight relieved from his shoulders, Scott stood and looked for a bin to discard his empty cup.

'Just leave it on the table,' sighed Tate and with that Scott headed for the door.

'What about my job? Do they know about the signature? I can't afford to lose this one. Me mum will have me out on me ear.'

'They are most probably none the wiser, Scott. Who checks those signature squiggles anyhow?' said Tate as Scott passed him in the doorway with the air conditioning unit still quietly humming away above him.

Bethnal Green
London, England

35

She removed the wrapper from the Jackmans original and placed it in her mouth. The soothing menthol vapour of aniseed and eucalyptus slowly drifted from the taste buds on her tongue and on through her nasal passages like an early morning river mist creeping ever further upstream. The menthol hit, not only cleared her nasal and sinus cavities, but helped to clear her head and direct her focus.

Harriet sat in the SIO room, a small glass partitioned area at the far end of the incident room. The space was used by the Senior Investigating Officer and higher-ranking officers to direct live operations. In her own mind, Harriet compared the room to a fish tank with her inside. Swimming round and round, forever searching for the answers and more often than not, looking for the questions to the answers she already knew. The room also afforded her some solitude and a private space when needed.

It was this private space she now used to her advantage as she took her mobile phone from the top drawer of the desk and dialled a number from her contacts list. As the call connected and started to ring, she laid her head back, closed her eyes and welcomed the calming effect of the menthol sweet. The call connected and she was about to speak when the contacts answer message cut in.

'Hi, you've reached Rebecca Crawford, reporter with Universal News. I am sorry I cannot take your call at the moment. Your call is important to me, so please leave your name and number and a short message and I will get back to you as soon as possible.' With her head still lying back and her eyes closed, Harriet massaged her temples as she continued to hold the phone to her ear. After a short pause, the answer phone beeped and she left a message.

'Hi, Becks. It's me. Give me a call as soon as you pick this up.' She disconnected the call and opened her eyes. As she did so, DCS Leslie Gibbs appeared outside the fishbowl. Harriet sat forward in her chair, placed the mobile on the desk and scrunched her hair. The door opened and a tall well chiselled black man dressed in full police regalia entered the room.

Detective Chief Superintendent Gibbs removed his cap and placed it under his left arm. A full head of thick silver hair and a matching moustache stood out in contrast to his dark obsidian skin. His face was accentuated with an angular chin which had taken a punch or two over the years, a very pronounced nose and deep-set hazel eyes. There was no denying it, he was a good looking and well-respected man.

'Harriet.' He extended a hand across the table. A heavy gold watch hung from his wrist. She greeted him with a strong shake of the hand.

'Chief Superintendent.'

'Let's cut the formal crap, Leslie, from now on, please.' The DCS took the seat opposite Harriet and ironically placed his cap on top of the paperwork in her 'in tray'.

'So, the beheading of a Z list celeb,' exclaimed Leslie as he brushed his chevron style moustache down from the philtrum to the corners of his mouth with his thumb and index finger. 'They're normally only seen losing their heads in an argument with fellow contestants on one of those "stuck in the jungle" reality shows.' A small chuckle to his own pun escaped from his mouth. 'Haven't got the time of day for it myself. But the wife seems glued to them 24 hours a day.'

'Can't say I have a lot of time for them either,' replied Harriet. 'Not that I'll have a lot of time for anything once the media frenzy hits this one.' Harriet's phone bleeped, buzzed and started to vibrate across the desk. She picked it up and glanced at the caller ID. Pushing the call divert button, the phone froze and she placed it back on the desk. Moments later it buzzed once more, the screen illuminated and a missed call message icon appeared.

'Shall we say 3pm for the press conference?' Leslie enquired rhetorically. The sentence was definitely weighted more towards a statement than a question.

'DS Richards and I should be back from the postmortem by then. Do you want me to,'

'That's fine. I'll take care of the arrangements myself. I've got an hour or so before my lunch date with the Commissioner. Hence the attire!' He retrieved his cap, stood and pushed back the chair with the backs of his legs. 'I take it, we won't be needing to inform Miss Crawford," as he threw a cautionary glance across the desk at Harriet's mobile.

'I'll make sure she's aware. Nothing more than that. I'll do as I usually do, Sir. Stick to my guns. Talking shop is strictly off limits and she knows it.'

'Just err on the side of caution,' he said, as he half turned to the door. 'We wouldn't want the rest of the wolf pack sniffing at our loins.'

Brixton Area

London, England

36

Tate and Lena had left Croydon police station and were heading back towards the city. Traffic was slow due to major road works around the Streatham Hill area. They were currently ensnarled in a bottleneck of traffic due to temporary four-way lights at the junction up ahead. The heat outside was oppressive and stifling. Tate's Land Rover offered little to no respite. The longer they sat, the warmer they became. Eventually Tate turned off the engine in fear of it over heating. Having the windows open or shut made little difference.

Lena raised her eyebrows in a disapproving manner, inhaled over excessively and let out an exasperating sigh. Tate knew all too well it was targeted in his direction. Both the heat and the congestion would be his fault. He sensed Lena's agitation further as she began to fidget. After a few minutes of rubbing and picking at the edges of her nail polish, she turned her attention to the collection of cassette tapes in the Land Rover's open access glove compartment. She removed half a dozen or so and placed them in her lap. She then proceeded to pick them up one at a time and ponder their titles.

'Brain Salad Surgery,' she frowned.

'A Farewell to Kings, The Lamb lies down on Broadway,' she dropped them back into her lap as she was drawn to the cover of a fourth.

'In the Court of the Crimson King,' she curled her lip in a fake sneer.

'I'm glad you didn't choose this picture for your office wall,' thrusting the tape case in Tate's direction. Tate just raised his eyebrows. He crawled the Land Rover forward a few feet to the bumper of the car in front.

'Close to the Edge and the Point of Know Return,' continued Lena reading the spines of two more cases.

'Yes, I think we probably are,' Tate murmured sarcastically, keen to change the conversation. 'So, what are your thoughts on two-person involvement?' said Tate, leaning forward and looking across to gain eye contact with Lena.

'It does seem that both a male and a female have been involved on different occasions,' replied Lena as she fumbled the cassette cases back into the glove compartment. Tate fretted but held his tongue. The tapes were no longer in chronological order. He edged the Land Rover forward a full two car lengths this time.

'It is not unknown for a couple to instigate and perpetrate a crime together. We have separate witnesses both of whom seem to have communicated with individuals of opposite sexes.'

'I agree,' Lena declared. 'However, with the advances in audio technology, it is now entirely possible to digitally enhance a voice to sound like that of the opposite sex.'

'It's unfortunate that Thames Art and Antiques have no audio record of their telephone communications. It could have been beneficial to the investigation if we had been able to analyse the conversation,' added Tate as he began to move the Land Rover forward at a more constant pace. The lights ahead must have changed and the traffic flowing in their direction was crawling forward.

'Voice changing software can also de-scramble a voice to its original form,' added Lena as she reverted back to polishing her nails with the pad of her thumb as she continued, 'If a recording of Dr Coster's voice had been available, it may have been possible to reverse the pitch variation and find the voices primary tone. It would also have allowed us the opportunity for the delivery driver to compare that voice to the one he had talked with.' She paused for a moment to think.

'Maybe both of the voices were digitally enhanced. Although we have no evidence to prove so. We can speculate and that may well point to a single perpetrator.'

'Or if the crime is that of an organised group,' interposed Tate as he stopped just short of the lights as they turned red once more, 'we may have two separate individuals tasked with different parts of the operation. Or simply, the use of voice enhancement to deny any involvement at a later date. It's a bit of a brick wall really.'

'Mr Legg at Thames Art and Antiques did say the voice sounded, how did he put it?'

'Robotic,' interjected Tate once more. 'It may not have been a good choice of words at the time though. I think it might be a good idea to have another chat with Mr Legg and explore that avenue a little further.'

The lights changed once again and Tate fought with the Land Rover's gear stick, crunching it into gear before slowly pulling away. Lena looked down at the area of the offending sound, frowned and shook her head.

'He also said that his questions were answered with the minimal of words. Again, this could point towards somebody trying to hide their identity.'

'So, where does that leave us?' pondered Tate whilst focusing on the now moving traffic.

'If the voice was digitally enhanced it could well point heavily in the direction of someone working alone. Well, at least on this side of the channel. Has Inspector Moretti's team uncovered anything indicating possible involvement numbers?'

'Nothing from the property where the Caravaggio was taken. Scene was pretty much undisturbed. The CCTV footage of the painting being concealed, clearly shows a single individual. But they could easily be one of a larger team.' Lena gestured towards the windscreen with her hands for Tate to keep going as the lights were changing back to amber.

'We can assume the unsub had tapped into the entry system intercom when intercepting the Moreau paintings delivery. The alarm system in Rome was overridden the night the Caravaggio was stolen and the individual who purchased the concealing painting could possibly have used voice enhancing software. Whether it's an individual or not, they are definitely technologically minded.' Lena tapped the dashboard of the Land Rover.

'That probably rules you out then, Tate.' He was used to Lena's constant ribbing about him being stuck in the past. However, in contrast, Lena always had the newest phone and the latest gadgets.

The traffic began to ease after they had passed through the roadworks. At times Tate was able to gain enough speed to generate a small amount of air flow through the vehicle and offer a brief respite from the intensifying heat.

'I have a telephone meeting arranged with Inspector Moretti tomorrow,' said Tate, finally managing to get the Land Rover into fourth gear for a period of more than a couple of hundred metres, 'to update each other on our progress so far, review all current lines of enquiry and discuss the direction of the case and any areas of interest which may warrant further investigation. You know the protocol, the usual sort of things. Perhaps you could arrange another meeting with Mr Legg?' Lena shuffled in her seat to allow the wind flow to waft across her face.

'No problem. I'll make a call as soon as we get back. I've already arranged a meeting with customs in Dover tomorrow to examine the Moreau's import procedure and inspect their paperwork. Dotting the I's and crossing the T's really, but you never know, something might come up. I'll find out if Mr Legg is available for the following day.'

'That would be great. I will also arranged to interview a Mr Fredric Breakwell at his home in Chelsea. He counter offered the penultimate bids during the Moreau's auction. Again, most probably legit, but you never know.' Lena nodded in agreement, but her attention had been drawn to another of the cassette cases in the glove compartment. She reached forward and retrieved it.

'Queen. A Night at the Opera. Is that Rhapsody song on this one?' she asked, as she once again thrust a case in Tate's direction. Tate plucked the tape from her grasp.

'It is actually.'

'Could you put it on?' she said enthusiastically, 'I can't believe you actually have a song I know!' Tate removed the tape from the case and studied its mechanism.

'I could put it on for you. However, we are now only a few minutes from the office and the song is at the end of side two. I'll have to fast forward and rewind the tape to find the right place.'

Lena never heard the song.

Southwark

London, England

37

They drove across town to attend the Postmortem, zigzagging their way through reasonably quiet back streets, trying to avoid transecting as few of the city's main arterial transport routes as possible. The capital's streets were overflowing and seemed to be bursting at the seams at every round-about and junction. It would have been a lot quicker to take the underground, but that would be packed to the gunnels too. However, the time in the car would afford them the opportunity to discuss the initial details of the case. It would also be a pleasant respite from the ever-increasing mercury scale of mid-summer. The BMW's air conditioning once again provided not only a cool sanctuary, but a freedom away from prying ears as they continued to deliberate aspects of the crime scene and the statement DS Richards had taken from the cleaner.

As they arrived at the building on Southwark Street the pavements were bustling with the first wave of office lunchers. Coffee shops, sandwich bars and restaurants were already brimming with a flurry of sitters as city workers fought to satisfy their grumbling bellies in the short time their office break afforded them. Take-away queues snaked down the pavements as many took advantage of the good weather and looked to lunch in one of the many small green spaces dotted along the South Bank. The smell of fried grease, roasted coffee and toasted bread hung in the air. Harriet, anticipated a gap in the oncoming traffic, indicated at the last minute and abruptly swung the car to the right and down a ramp into the bowels of the building's underground carpark. From the outside, the building was a monstrosity of nineteen seventies brutalism architecture. Its block-like form of raw cast concrete muscled its way skywards in a rugged fortress like mass. It's cold, unappealing appearance was contrasted by the revival of much of the local vicinity in a modernist regeneration scheme. But it was built to last and here it would stay. Controversial and contentious as it was, today it was seen as in vogue and had been granted a Grade II listing.

Harriet and Iain exited the lift having travelled up a single floor. It had taken longer for the doors to open, close, and open again at their destination floor, than it did to travel the ten or so feet through one level of horizontal concrete. They arrived in an ultra-modern reception area. In contrast to the rough-hewn 'beton brut' external façade, the inside had a clean, transparent, almost imperceptible nature that fully embodied the new modernist era. The entire building had been given an internal face lift around five years ago. The interior structure now looked like the inside of a giant glass Rubik's cube. The reception room was at the very heart of the building. It was located on the ground floor at the bottom of a central atrium that rose through the building to a glass dome with an oculus at its apex. Walls on each side ascended skywards in a series of inter-connecting glass panels. No two adjacent panes were the same shade or tint. Some were clear, others monochromatic. Some almost black. Others were sepia tinted or dark amber. Side by side they created a mosaic of glass walling.

A shallow square pool with a cascading mirrored waterfall occupied the atriums central floor space. They circumnavigated the pools perimeter to the far side of the atrium, showed their ID's and signed in at the front desk. The receptionist working at the desk acknowledged their credentials. She then placed an access card attached to a lanyard around her neck into a card reader within the control panel of her workstation. She hit several keys on her computers keyboard. Back on the far side of the atrium, the lift doors re-opened. Iain thanked the receptionist and they retraced their path to the awaiting lift. As they did so, Harriet noted a subtle hint of chlorine in the air, further adding to the overall effect of purity. It reminded her of entering the changing rooms each Sunday morning, when she had attended swimming lessons as a child at the local swimming baths. The smell had given the then young Harriet a sense of cleanliness and safety. If she'd have known back then, it was to counterbalance the boys in her class peeing in the pool, she would have quit and joined the ballet class. As they entered the lift, Iain noticed there had been no control panel on either the inside or the outside of the door. Just a solitary internal card reader slot.

'*You're only going where your access card, or the receptionist allows you in this place*,' Iain mused to himself. The lift doors closed behind them and they travelled up two further floors.

They exited the lift onto a glass walkway that seemed to float like a glacial outcrop. The hint of chlorine from the waterfall pool below was suddenly replaced by the musty odour of sterilizing formalin. A formaldehyde and methyl alcohol mix that smells like ammonia. The new scent grew heavier and now reminded Harriet of visiting her elderly Grandmother as she lived out the final years of her life in a nursing home. Once again masking the smell of human urine and funnily enough, here it was again, covering the smell of numerous bodily fluids.

They ventured out across the walkway, which opened on the left side to overlook a large expansive autopsy room. The length of the room below was divided into three separate sections. The first section was encased with a glass ceiling enclosing the four walls. This was the receiving area and was kept refrigerated at 4.5 degrees centigrade. Bodies were transported in and out of the morgue from this area. Stainless steel gurneys lined up across the room. Most held the deceased in white body bags. The occasional gurney supported a black body bag. Those in white bags were thought to have died of natural causes, accidentally or having committed suicide. The black body bags indicated homicides or suspicious deaths. The room also contained a refrigeration unit for body parts and samples, alongside stainless-steel digital flatbed scales used to weigh bodies on arrival. Double glass swing doors connected this area to the next section.

This central room was where the majority of autopsies took place. Four stainless steel counters were spaced equally along its length. Each counter drained into its own individual sink, which in turn drained into a fluid holding tank below.

Two figures dressed in green medic overalls were attentively removing internal organs from polystyrene cool boxes and placing them back inside the flayed torso of the body currently occupying the counter between them. The arrival of the two figures on the balcony caught the eye of one of the pathologists.

'Franklin autopsy concluded. 12.13pm,' he said, tapping his earpiece to stop the recording. 'Could you continue to replace the organs, please David. Then re-sew the Y-Incision and finish.' David raised the lung in his hands as a gesture of confirmation and the other man turned his attention to the visitors above.

'The cadaver you are seeking, DI Stone, is at the far end,' he said, motioning for them to usher themselves along to the third section of the room.

Southwark

London, England

38

The third section of the workspace was the solitary autopsy room. Having changed his green coveralls and passed through another set of interconnecting doors, Happy Jiang stood looking up at the two detectives. The solitary autopsy room was reserved for examining homicides, special circumstance or suspicious deaths and decomposing bodies. Mostly black bag cases. It was sealed from the rest of the facility during the examination of a body, thus reducing the chance of cross contamination and loss of evidence.

'So, how's things Harry? It must have been all of three weeks since I last had the pleasure of your company,' declared Happy, with an ever-present beaming smile across his face. 'Back again, so soon. If I were paranoid, I'd think you were checking up on me.' He looked up at Harriet and Iain and chuckled to himself.

'I just can't keep myself away, its murder out there you know,' Harriet retorted as Happy's smile increased, and the chuckle grew louder.

'Well, this one's a bit different. Delivered in a bag and a box.'

Happy Jiang was happy. Although he spent most of his waking day with corpses, he had a knack of finding things to make himself and others around him smile. If attitudes are contagious, then his was worth catching. He was the first son of second-generation Chinese immigrants. He had come by his given name through a simple misunderstanding. As his father had held him in his arms for the very first time, his wife had simply said 'Happy?' inferring to how her husband was feeling. Looking down at the child in his arms whilst caught in a moment of euphoria, his father simply nodded and replied, 'Yes, Happy,' and the name stuck. Happy continued with what was to become a family tradition, naming his children Joy and Lucky.

Harriet looked down into the room below. Whenever the line of duty dictated her need to attend an autopsy, looking down into Happy's glass tank always sparked memories of looking down into the giant oceanic pools of Sea World whilst holidaying with her parents in Florida. As a child, she had been fixated by the life in the pools. However, every visit to Happy's tank would only mean another rendezvous with death.

Below, Happy stood at the far end of the autopsy table. Directly in front of him at the head of the table was a clear plastic box containing the deceased's head. The rest of the torso was laid out, chest up, neck to feet away from him.

'With the head and the torso arriving in a separate bag and box, we could be foolish to assume the cause of death to be decapitation by the severing of the spinal column, resulting in a loss of blood flow and oxygen supply to the brain,' said Happy as he moved from the table to the space below where the two investigating officers were stood. 'The scenes of crime report,' he continued, motioning with a file in his hand, 'and preliminary observations suggest the removal of the head was probably postmortem.' He tapped the corner of the file on the box containing the head. 'If not postmortem, from the look of the serration marks, it would have bloody hurt,' Happy jested again as he turned his attention to the decapitation area of the torsos neck. He removed a stainless-steel probe from a kidney shaped sterilization tray and gently used it to lift, separate and examine the serrulated flesh around the exposed bones of the upper neck.

'The lack of capillary haemorrhaging around the cut marks would on first appearances suggest the head was removed postmortem.' He returned his focus to the body and used the probe to examine the bones themselves. He ran the probe over several areas where the ends of the bones showed the greatest degree of cutting serrations. After a brief examination of the area, he went to a stainless-steel cabinet at the rear of the room and removed a pair of surgical binocular loupes. He slid them over his own glasses as he returned to the table. Adjusting the magnification to their maximum focal length, Happy leant forward over the opened neck wounds and examined the serration marks once more. As he further studied the decapitation point, he took a series of close-up pictures with a digital macro lensed camera. Within each picture, he carefully laid a 'micro measuring scale' parallel to the direction of the cutting marks. After several minutes, he removed the glasses, crossed to the back of the room once more and removed a small postmortem saw from a drawer.

'It would seem that two cutting implements have been used. Firstly, a long-bladed knife to separate the external tissues and to cut through the capillaries and tendonous materials. The head itself would then have been removed with an implement similar to this,' he said walking in the direction of the viewing gallery and gesturing with the saw in his hand. 'The blade used has 14 teeth per inch. Saws commonly used in the butchery trade would fit the mark. The point where the separation was made, is not surgically precise. But whoever did this was calm and collected. It has not been rushed in any way as the saw marks all follow a similar line.'

Happy looked up at the viewing gallery and in his usual gregarious way, he continued, 'Butcher, Baker, Candlestick maker, they could all be suspects. But that part of the game is yours, hey, Harry.'

'Yeah thanks, Happy! What else can you tell me?' Happy returned his attention back to the table and the body. Starting with the remainder of the lower neck he began a more detailed examination. No sooner had he done so, when he found a small puncture wound surrounded by light purplish bruising on the left side. He activated his voice recorder by tapping the earpiece on the right side of his head. 'Small puncture wound to left side of lower neck, through the area of the Scalenus Medius muscle. Common point with needle entry site.' He tapped the earpiece once more to stop the recording before turning his attention towards Harriet, who he noticed was surreptitiously glancing at her watch.

'Looks like the victim may have been sedated through a hypodermic entry point. The target area would be common with a right-handed offensive from the front or alternatively a left-handed strike from behind.' He picked up a plastic syringe from the sterilization tray and motioned the actions for the two police officers above. 'We will obviously know more when we have toxicology back.'

Having worked with Harriet on numerous cases in the past, Happy was only too aware that during the early stages of an investigation, Harriet's clock was continually ticking. He immediately returned his attention to the task in hand, examining both of the arms in turn. Starting at the shoulder he worked his way around the bicep, the elbow, lower arm, wrist and hand. He examined each area for external trauma, bruising and general markings. He worked in silence for several minutes, thoroughly examining each area for fibres, hairs and other foreign bodies, all of which could possibly have been left behind by a perpetrator. The only sound was the air conditioning unit humming its presence. Happy repeatedly tapped his earpiece and dictated his examination notes. Whilst examining both hands, he clipped and scraped the fingernails for materials trapped beneath which could possibly contain traces of skin or blood transferred during an altercation. Satisfied with his scrutiny of the upper limbs, he turned to address the observation platform once more. As he did so, he happened to catch Harriet checking her watch once again.

'No signs of defensive wounds or any sort of struggle taking place. If toxicology comes back positive for sedative, it would suggest it was administered unsuspectedly, taking effect quickly and rendering the victim immediately helpless.' Harriet nodded in agreement with her friend below and Iain continued to make notes on his phone.

'There is however some lividity evident in both armpits and the teres major muscles, supporting the theory the body was moved postmortem.'

'That fits with Penny's initial findings,' Harriet replied. 'First indications at the scene strongly suggest the body and the severed head were moved and posed at a table.' A look of amusement spread across Happy's face.

'Looks like you may have gotten yourself someone who thinks they're an artist this time Harry,' chuckled Happy. Conscious of his friends clock watching, he returned to the body to begin his external examination of the rest of the torso and the legs. He would also turn the body midway through to examine the back and the buttocks. Harriet continued to observe Happy's examinations but found herself drawn more and more towards the time piece on her wrist. Aware of commitments elsewhere Harriet finally had to interrupt Happy's work.

'I am afraid we shall have to miss the Grand Opening,' said Harriet, referring to the Y incision Happy would perform to open the chest cavity and start his internal examination, along with the removal of the internal organs for analysis.

'Press conference beckons' she continued, 'Gibbs would have my ass if I were late.' The opening of the torso was never Harriet's favourite chapter in any investigation. If she could find an excuse to depart before the main event, she would. Half expecting an imminent departure, Happy threw one last beaming smile in Harriet's direction.

'You must come around for dinner sometime soon, Harry. Mrs Jiang would love to see you again. And you must come too, DS Richards. She keeps onto me about cooking Fuqi Feipian for Harry.' Iain looked perplexed and looked to Harriet for an answer.

'It's one of Happy's little jokes I'm afraid. Fuqi Feipian is a traditional Chinese dish in the Sichuan region from where Happy's family originate. It roughly translates as Husband-and-Wife Lungs!'

30th May 1606

Rome, Italy

39

It was early evening and the sun was waning towards the roof tops of the western horizon before Signora Antognetti returned. Dusk was settling across the city and the pigeons had gone to roost, their earlier presence only evident by the faecal matter upon the roof tiles and the pavement below. The smell of the evenings final discarding's of human waste emanated from the gutter as Signora Antognetti using both hands, hitched her skirt up from the filth and negotiated the final short distance along the street to her front door. The house was still and shrouded in darkness. Its interior emitted no candlelight through the shrinkage cracks of the shuttered windows. She hesitated as her hand reached for the doors handle. She was about to enter when something intrinsically made her stop, turn back in the direction from where she had just come and check the street behind her. It was empty, but for a skeletal black cat lapping at the gutter in an attempt to uncover a vegetable peeling or a fat deposit to alleviate its pining stomach.

After Annibale had dismissed her for the day having decided the diminishing light was creating unwanted shadows and he would paint no longer, she had gone to the Campo Marzio, where Michelangelo resided and had a small studio. She had ventured there to determine how bad the situation had become. Keeping an ear to the ground and her presence as low key as possible by walking and talking in the shadows, she listened to the whispers, spoke with those who could be trusted and gained any snippet of information that may throw further light on Michelangelo's darkening circumstances. However, since turning her back on the area, she had not been able to banish the feeling that she was being followed. Word on the street and the gossip from the gutter suggested that Michelangelo's situation had escalated from bad to worse. Not only were Ranuccio's brothers and cousins hunting Michelangelo in revenge, but the Carabinieri had been instructed to bring him to justice under the direction of his Excellency the Pope. Signora Antognetti had also made contact with several of Michelangelo's closest acquaintances, some of whom had been with him during the altercation. None of whom now had his back. Most of whom denied any fraternisation with him at all. One or two even jumping ship completely and joining the search for him. The malicious hearsay had made her anxious and an unnerving feeling had crept through her body.

She fought with the key in the darkness, fumbling to find the lock, as she longed for the safety of the room on the other side of the door. Away from prying eyes and ears and back in the refuge of her own private space. As it finally married with the tumbler hole, she turned the large iron key and its mechanism released the mortice bolt. Stepping over the threshold into her personal sanctuary, she dropped the hem of her dress from her grasp and patted down it's pleats until it once again hugged her hourglass figure.

She entered the room and her eyes adjusted from the darkness of the street outside to the soft radiance of a single burning candle. The emanating glow was enough to light the table where the candle sat but was insufficient to have much effect on the fringes and corners of the room. The table was strewn with discarded bottles, a plate of food scraps, a chicken carcass and a number of gnawed meat bones. The chair at the end of the table, where hours earlier she had left Michelangelo sitting, was lying discarded on the floor. Its wooden back fractured and splintered from an impact with the stone surface. A small amount of blood had pooled just above the broken pieces. Signora Antognetti suddenly felt uneasy once again, as she scoured the room for further answers.

'Where was Michelangelo? Had one of his pursuers discovered his whereabouts and come to seek justice? How could they have possibly gotten in?'

Even in the darkness of the street outside, she had seen no evidence of forced entry. Perhaps, he had just made his way back to the comfort of a bed to sleep off the excesses in a drunken slumber. The house felt unusually quiet. Nothing stirred. Keen to answer her uncertainties, she headed for the stairs. As she reached for the banister to take the first step, a small, muffled moan from the rooms far corner caused her to stop and turn in the direction from which the sound had come. In the shadows of the corner, furthest from the windows and the outside world, she could just make out the shape of a man cowering in a foetal position.

Michelangelo lay curled on the floor. His shirt front caked with disgorged food matter and spilt wine. The hair on the left of his skull was matted with congealed blood. She crossed the room, grabbed the candlestick from the table and knelt to Michelangelo's side. She cradled his head in her lap and gently examined the bloodied area. As she did so, Michelangelo stirred, mumbling as he tried to string a sentence together. Signora Antognetti bent her head forward, lending her ear towards Michelangelo's hushed tones. As she did so, Michelangelo looked up at her through barely open bloodshot eyes.

'You're back,' he rasped up at her. She continued to gently stroke his head.

'Yes, I'm back,' she replied softly. 'What on earth has happened to you?' Michelangelo tried to move to a sitting position, but reluctantly gave up after very little effort and remained with his head in her lap. He retched and dry heaved. Slowly, he tried to string together a few words to explain the situation.

'I was woken… from sleep… by a commotion… outside… the chair toppled,' he paused to clear his throat once more. He spat onto the stone floor. She noticed the spittle which landed inches from her skirt contained traces of blood. Michelangelo continued, 'A man was shouting… I recognised the voice… that of Giovan Francessco… Ranuccio's brother.' He paused once more and rubbed his eyes as if he were trying to clear not only his vision, but his thoughts too.

'There was a lot of shouting… There were others with him… They pounded the door… He demanded my presence.' Michelangelo slowly pushed himself up from Signora Antognetti's lap and propped himself up against the wall.

'I have to leave… They know I am here,' he said as Signora Antognetti moved to sit next to her desolated friend. He bowed his head into his hands and spoke the words into his palms, 'They will seek revenge… for injury to their friend and brother.' Taking Michelangelo's hands in her own, she slowly lowered them from his face so that she could look him straight in the eye.

'Michelangelo, there is no easy way to tell you this,' she paused to hold his gaze.

'Ranuccio is Dead!'

Bethnal Green

London, England

40

There was a low-pitched jabbering chatter permeating the room. Occasionally it would intensify before snowballing into laughter, but always receding back to murmurings that were once again barely audible. Members of the press and other news correspondents had gathered early within the small auxiliary room used for press conferences at the Bethnal Green station. The usual faces mingled within the kettle of media vultures. Hughes from The Sun, Redman from The Times, Claymore from the BBC, along with reporters and photographers from numerous other TV, Newspaper and online media outlets. Rebecca Crawford who had arrived only moments ago, took a seat to the side of the room.

Individuals took their seats as a volley of camera flashes announced the arrival of the CID press team. Led by Claire Wilson the station's Press Officer, Detective Chief Superintendent Gibbs and DI Stone took their seats at the front of the room. As the final few reporters scrambled to find chairs, Claire stood to address the room.

'Thank you for your patience. Chief Superintendent Leslie Gibbs will make a brief statement. DI Stone will then consider any further questions you may have.' She chose her words diligently before sitting. The Chief Superintendent stood, adjusted the button across the midriff of his uniform and shuffled the pages in front of him. All part of the act. The room was silent aside from the clacking of camera apertures.

'I can confirm that a body found at a residential property on the Isle of Dogs is thought to be that of Hidetaka Yamamoto, the son of Japanese industrial tycoon Akihiro Yamamoto. The body has yet to be formally identified as his immediate family are foreign nationals,' he paused for a moment, took a sip of water and checked his notes. 'Due to an unexpected reporting of these details by a member of the press, we feel it is in the best interest of the family, that we are left with no alternative than to release these details earlier than we would have liked.'

To the side of the room Rebecca Crawford supressed an impulsive grin. A little investigative work of her own had resulted in more than she had bargained for. Neighbours had confirmed the number of the apartment and the owner's name. Twenty pounds had bought his telephone number and his hysterical cleaner had blabbed the victim's name to him during a telephone conversation shortly after discovering the body and contacting the authorities. Luckily, the cleaner had recognised Yamamoto from a reality gameshow.

Chief Superintendent Gibbs continued.

'Due to the nature of the investigation, we can offer no further information at this stage. Further press releases will be issued as and when the situation allows.' He habitually brushed down his moustache and sat down as a second fusillade of camera flashes ignited the room. Claire Wilson stood momentarily.

'DI Stone will now be happy to take any questions.'

Hands began to raise and recording devices and microphones were held forward. Claire indicated in the direction of one of the journalists.

'Dan Burrows, CBS News. Is there any indications that Mr Yamamoto's death is linked in any way to his recent online activities?'

Harriet remained seated; her hands cupped on the table in front of her.

'We are presently investigating,' sporadic cameras flashed once again, 'all angles and avenues, and it is too early to offer any further details at this moment.'

No sooner had she finished her sentence, when a young woman in the centre of the room stood with her arm raised and began speaking,

'Trish Mason, London Evening Post. Can you confirm if any arrests are imminent or if indeed you have any suspects at this stage?' She remained standing, holding a dictating device in Harriet's direction.

'Again, we are only in the preliminary stages of the investigation. My team and I will be interviewing any individuals in connection with the crime as and when the situation dictates.'

Miss Mason nodded and sat down. The room remained silent for a moment. Those present knew all too well that information would not be forthcoming at this time and they would receive little more than textbook statements. Remaining seated, Rebecca Crawford nonchalantly raised her hand.

'Is there any truth,' she did not formally announce herself like others had done, 'in the supposition that Mr Yamamoto was in fact decapitated?' Heads in the room turned in Rebecca's direction before swiftly returning in anticipation of Harriet's answer. Before she could reply, Claire lent forward and interjected.

'I'm afraid that is pure speculation and without firm evidence, postulations do not benefit public interest. Your sources are for once confounded, Miss Crawford.' She looked across at her two colleagues before continuing. 'When new information comes to light, we shall be only too happy to make it readily available. Once again thank you for your continued patience, there will be no further questions.'

In complete ignorance to her final statement, a bombardment of interrogation ensued as she stood to leave the room alongside Chief Superintendent Gibbs and DI Stone. As they shuffled along towards the door, one voice raised above the cacophony.

'DI Stone. Is there anything else Rebecca Crawford knows that we should be aware of?'

Bring the pages alive…

Explore artworks, locations and more.

Go to gnsbooks.com (Interactive) or scan the QR code to unlock images, maps and facts as you read.

River Thames
London, England

41

The Narcissus left the South Bank, passing Shakespeare's Globe theatre before crossing onto the Millennium Bridge. The late evenings departing sun spread a new fire across the capitals heart and threw its last spears of sunset across the dome of St Pauls. The Narcissus punched the numbers into the keypad and lent into the wires of the bridge, looking down into the ebbing waters of the Thames, as the phone tried to connect. The call was picked up on the third ring.

'Good evening. Sir Christopher Roebuck speaking.'

The Narcissus remained silent. A huddle of tipsy giggling female twenty-somethings armed with florescent blue WKD bottles crossed the bridge behind as they headed in the direction of the West End for a night of drunken debauchery. The Narcissus let the raucousness pass before speaking.

'This is Dr Valentine. I believe I have something which may be of interest to you.'

'Ah, yes. Jeremy Grayson said you would be in touch. Would you mind holding a second. I'd like to go into the other room.' The Narcissus could hear Sir Christopher excuse himself, followed by footsteps across a hard floor and finally a door closing.

'Sorry about that. A few too many bodies in the other room. Can't be too careful who's bending an ear these days. If the something I may be interested in is female with an Italian heritage, then you are quite correct.' The Narcissus watched a large Herring Gull swoop across the water below the bridge before landing on the muddy shore and begin to scavenge along the strandline.

'A viewing will be possible on Saturday at 7pm.'

'Saturday will be fine. I have nothing in my diary this coming weekend. I should be able to slip away without too many questions. I take it the viewing will be in the city?'

'I will message you the location in due course.' The Narcissus continued to watch the gull tear at anything it could find just to fill its belly and feed its craving.

'Not unlike some human beings', thought the Narcissus.

'Will Jeremy be joining us? He's such a jolly fellow. He's done awfully well in the past, acquiring me some wonderful works. Above and beyond one's usual playing field.'

'It will be just you and I. Jeremys role is to provide the contact. And only that.'

'Shame. We've enjoyed a glass or two of the old spumante together in the past to celebrate when an offer has been accepted.' The Narcissus could hear the slight disappointment in Sir Christopher's voice at Jeremys absence but ignored the misgiving.

'I must insist you don't use your chauffeur. Leave the driver at home, Mr Roebuck. We won't be needing witnesses.'

'Of course. That will be no problem at all. I very often give the old fellow the weekend off these days. Do me good to drive the private car. Keep my hand in and all.' The Narcissus was starting to get impatient of the jollity in Sir Christopher's tone.

'You talk to no-one. I find out differently. The meetings off.'

'You have my word. I have no reason to talk or share this opportunity outside of Jeremy, you and I. If…' The Narcissus interrupted and cut Sir Christopher off.

'Jeremy is no longer part of the equation now contact has been made. You should have no further need to talk to Jeremy before the viewing. If you wish to discuss the Magdalene's authenticity, provenance or valuation further after the viewing that is your choice. I must insist at this stage of the proceedings, we focus solely between you and I.' Sir Christopher started to object.

'I have never in all my…'

'These are the conditions of the viewing. If you do not find them to your satisfaction, I will find someone who does,' stated the Narcissus, knowing full well that Sir Christopher would not let this opportunity of a lifetime slip through his fingers.

'So be it,' resigned Sir Christopher, 'I understand the sensitivity of the situation and the need for clandestinity.'

'Now I have your understanding, I will send you the location details.'

'Thank you,' said Sir Christopher, 'I appreciate…'

The line went dead.

On the bridge, the Narcissus tapped an address into the phone and hit the send button. The sun was squinting a last peak above the horizon and casting an iridescent orange net, eastwards across the Thames. The footfall across the bridge had become sporadic as the night drew in. The phone bleeped to confirm the message had been delivered. The Narcissus removed the SIM card from the phone and dropped each separately into the receding waters below.

Bethnal Green

London, England

42

Harriet sat in the chair. Not her usual chair. Sometimes when in her office she liked to sit in the chair on the other side of the desk. Sitting there gave her the opportunity to turn her back on everything and everyone. Giving a cold shoulder to the world, but only for a moment. She swirled the vodka, held the glass up to the light and watched its vortex rotate in on itself before savouring another mouthful.

'After dinner drink?' She did not have to turn around to know the source of the voice.

'Only if you class half a KitKat as dinner.' Harriet remained seated. 'This is a first, Happy. What brings you North of the river?'

'Apparently Grey Goose! You don't by chance have a second glass?' Harriet spun the chair to face her colleague.

'No, Sorry. You'll have to make do with a mug!' No sooner had she made the remark when she noticed the sorry state of the coffee mug on the other side of the desk. Streaked and tarnished from neglect and several weeks without seeing hot soapy water. She downed the remnants of her glass, refilled it with a good measure and handed it to Happy before grabbing the empty coffee mug from the desk. She took a quick look at its inside surface, shrugged her shoulders and poured herself a sizeable measure too.

'Hard Day?'

'Long Day,' replied Harriet. She sat back in the chair. Happy rounded the desk and sat in Harriet's usual chair. As he sat, he made himself comfortable, looked around the office and took in his new surroundings. He noticed a framed photograph on one of the filing cabinets.

'Is that you on your graduation day?' he asked pointing at the picture. The photograph captured Harriet in a military uniform alongside a similar aged male again dressed in military regalia.

'Yeah, that's me. Younger, slimmer and still fresh behind the ears.' She took a sip from the mug. Vodka with a taint of coffee.

'Is that your brother?' Happy enquired, wetting his lips with vodka from his own glass.

'Yes, but how did…'

'He looks like you. You have the same nose and chin.'

'He was so proud that day. His little sisters passing out parade. Her joining him, in the rank and file.' She paused and took a sip. 'He died a few months after that photograph was taken. A roadside bombing in Afghanistan.' She downed the last of the vodka in the mug and unscrewed the cap on the bottle once more.

'I'm sorry Harriet. I didn't realise.'

'It's fine Happy. It's been twelve years now. Scars heal, but good memories remain.' Harriet leaned across and offered the neck of the bottle to Happy's glass. He placed a hand across the top.

'Not for me, thanks Harriet. I wouldn't want Mrs Jiang catching it on my breath. She might think the pressures of the job are getting to me.' He smiled. Harriet poured a good measure into the coffee mug once more.

'So, what's the real reason behind me being the lucky girl and having you grace this office with your presence?' Happy coughed twice as he swallowed the last of his vodka. He was definitely not a drinker.

'Firstly, I wanted to let you know the bloods have gone off to toxicology and I have asked the boys in the lab to give them top priority. More importantly, I've got something that may be of interest to you.' He put the glass down on the table, running his middle finger around its rim as he continued. 'After you left earlier, we found something whilst David joined me to closer examine the head. I thought it probably shouldn't wait until tomorrow.' Happy got up from the chair and retrieved a briefcase he had left by the door on his arrival. From inside, he removed a clear plastic evidence envelope and handed it to Harriet.

'We found this rolled up inside the oesophagus, just above the sever point.' Harriet examined the contents of the envelope, turning it over in her hands a couple of times, so to see its contents from all sides. Inside the plastic envelope was a circle of what looked like skin. It was about four inches in diameter. On one side, words could clearly be read.

'I would hazard a guess at this stage that it's pigskin,' said Happy. 'It looks like the words have been tattooed on to it.' Harriet turned on a small desk light to enable her to see the words more clearly. She read the words over silently in her head, once then twice, then finally she read them out loud.

'It's time to listen as the banshee cries
You never can tell where evil will rise
Now you've heard the harpies scream
A nightmare emerges within the dream'

Thorney Street
London, England

43

Tate sat at his desk reading through the statements from the interviews they had taken over the past few days. They had gathered little evidence that proved substantial. The only information they had obtained that seemed to be of any value indicated the involvement of more than one suspect. Possibly a man and a woman. From both the statements of Mr. Legg at the auctioneers and Scott Edmunds the courier driver, it pointed towards the possibility that one, if not both perpetrators, had some depth of knowledge in digital technology. Mr. Legg had suggested that Dr Coster's voice had sounded 'robotic', implying a voice enhancement program could have filtered the phone call. In his witness statement Scott Edmunds declared he had used the buildings intercom system to communicate with someone he believed to be Dr Coster. Had the suspect linked into the intercom remotely, possibly from a vehicle parked on the street outside? Mr. Legg had also mentioned in his statement that the doctor had seemed to know the outcome of the auction before he had a chance to inform him. Had he remotely tapped into the auction houses surveillance cameras too? It did appear that a level of technological expertise was evident.

Tate stood, crossed to the windows at the back of the office and looked out across the river. A single seated rowing boat was being sculled in the direction of Vauxhall bridge. Tate watched as the rower propelled the boat through the water. On each stroke they drove the blades through the surface, raising the face of the oars at the finish of the stroke before recovering them to the starting position and catching the blades back into the water to repeat the entire process time after time. Tate marveled at the efficiency and effectiveness of each stroke and the distance the rower was covering in a relatively short time. As the sculler began to disappear from Tate's field of vision, he mulled at his observation.

'In contrast to the distance the sculler had travelled, his investigation seemed to have covered very little ground so far.'

A notification alarm sounded, drawing Tate's attention away from the window.

Back at his desk, his mail inbox icon was overwritten with a number two. Tate open the first mail. It was a reply from the owner of the apartment where the concealing painting had been misdelivered. It confirmed their consent to arranging a time to give a statement. Tate did not read any further detail as the subject of the other mail had already grabbed his attention. It was another message sent from his own mailbox. Just like the one he had received the previous week. His finger once again hovered over the mouse's button.

'Had someone hacked into his online account and was now having a bit of fun to make him aware of his vulnerability? Or was there more to this than had previously caught his eye?' The last email had made little sense. He had closed it as quickly as he had opened it. However, for some unknown reason he had archived it as a miscellaneous file. He clicked the mouse and the new mail opened on the screen.

Tate Randall
Tate Randall

21 July, 14:17

Raise the anchor on a turbulent tide

To distant shores where treasures hide

Narcissus

Tate read the message. He then read it a second time. This time with an underlying rhythmic tune. He knew the words or rather the lyrics. Tate minimised the page, navigated to his archive mailbox, and retrieved the previous message. No sooner had he opened it and read the words, he realised they too were song lyrics. Standing alone, the second couplet had been more obvious than the first. But now he realised both were lyrics from the album 'Beyond the Waves' by Neptune's Finger. He looked across the room where the cover picture hung on the wall. The pair of lines in the first email were from the albums opening track. A song called 'The Banishing of the Angel'. The second email contained lyrics from a track entitled 'The Last Crossing of Charon'. Tate started to ponder why someone would hack his account and send such messages. His eyes were curiously drawn to the signature on both messages.

'Narcissus'.

He 'Google' searched the name and opened the first related link.

'A character of notable beauty from Greek mythology. Narcissus was a hunter who rejected the love of the nymph Echo. He was punished for his behaviour by falling in love with his own reflection whilst quenching his thirst in a pool of water. However, each time he leaned to kiss the reflection, it would disappear. Unable to leave and with fear of disturbing the water's surface, Narcissus eventually died of thirst and the flower that bears his name emerged from his resting place. The terms narcissism and narcissist are derived from the story. The fascination with oneself and having excessive self-love are identifiable characteristics of a narcissist.'

Tate thought about the signature once more and suddenly a train of thought ran through his mind and exploded out of the tunnel on the other side of his head. He thought out loud and ejected the words.

'You bastard Jonathan!'

The only person he knew who loved himself beyond belief. A man who took vanity to another level. The penny dropped. The content of the mysterious emails were lyrics from prog rock songs. He and Jonathan had spent their entire friendship testing, teasing and challenging one another's musical knowledge. Tate cursed himself. He should have seen it before. It was clear as day now. He reached for the phone console and hit the quick dial button for the Conservation and Restoration room.

Down in the cavernous featureless concrete sub levels, Jonathan slid the magnifying goggles up onto his forehead, making him look like a character from a steam punk movie. He negotiated his path through various benches, racks and tables from where he had been working towards his desk in the corner. The phone was ringing and one of the LEDs flashed, indicating it was an internal call. Jonathan hit the hands-free button.

'Mines of Moria, Balin at your service.'

'One day, wise guy, it will be someone important and your humour will be wasted,' came the reply.

'I save it up just for you, I wouldn't waste it on just anyone, Mi Amigo!' Jonathan wiped his hands on a towel thrown across the back of the chair.

'I was wondering if you had a few minutes to spare. I've got something I would like to run by you.'

'Yeah, no problema,' replied Jonathan, rolling his shirt sleeves down towards his now clean hands. 'You want me to come up there?'

'Yeah, that would be great.'

'Ok. Give me a few minutes. Need to apply my factor fifty if I'm going to come above the subterranean levels.' Jonathan chuckled to himself and Tate hung up.

Tate was in the anterior office photocopying some papers when Jonathan arrived. He picked the copies up from the print tray, placed them on top of the originals already in his hand and used them to gesture towards his open office door. Both men walked into the office and were drawn by the shafts of sunlight to the windows at the far end.

'Weather's looking good again for the morning,' said Jonathan, feeling the suns warmth emanating through the glass. 'If this spell continues the Serpentine is going to feel like swimming in the Med.' He turned to Tate and immediately perceived an unease in his friend.

'Firstly, let me say, I have no problem with your latest lyrical conundrum. And I will admit, I didn't get the answer until I received the second email. What puzzles me most, is how you got into my computer. Did you somehow hack it remotely?' As Tate looked up at Jonathan, he was aware his friend had a vacuous expression contorting his face and sensed he had no idea what he was talking about.

'If it wasn't you then who the hell was it?' Tate walked back to his desk and wiggled the mouse to awaken the screen. Jonathan followed and lent on the desk next to his friend. Tate opened both emails side by side on the screen. He took a few seconds to let Jonathan read the contents.

'I don't understand it,' Tate finally declared.

'Well, they're both lyrics from songs on "Beyond the Waves" by Neptune's Finger. And no. I had nothing to do with it.'

'Yeah, yeah! Like I said I got that part. What I don't understand is who sent them and why?' Both men continued to study the enigmatic emails.

'The address line suggests they originated from your computer,' said Jonathan, tapping on the screen.

'So, who ever created them either tapped in remotely or sat right here and wrote them.'

'The MET's firewall would surely prevent any remote access and its password protected. What's more, if they got into my mailbox, who's to say what else they could have gotten their hands on.' Tate clicked both emails closed and leaned on the desk mirroring his friend. 'I'll get straight onto the Techie boys. They may be able to provide me with some further answers. But that still doesn't answer why. If you didn't send me four lines of Neptune's lyrics, there must be some logical reason why someone else would do so.'

'Beats me too,' said Jonathan. 'Anyhow, just for the record. If it had been me, I would have just sat here and used your on-screen password.'

'How do you know my password?'

'Foxtrot2112.'

Tate's jaw dropped in utter astonishment.

'Come on. It doesn't take a bloody genius to work it out. A mix of words and numbers. You have three prog album cover pictures on your wall. So that's a good place to start. Probably an album title by your favourite band. I already know that's Genesis. You're not so keen on the album "Trespass" and "Nursery Cryme" is hung on the wall. "Selling England by the Pound" and "The Lamb lies down on Broadway" contain way too many letters. So, the logical album is "Foxtrot". You're particularly articulate, so it would start with a capital letter. As for the numbers. Well that's the easy part. There is only one noteworthy prog album with a numbers only title and all of us prog nerds use it without fail for card pin numbers and hotel safe codes. "2112" by Rush. I'd be changing that password if I were you.'

Bethnal Green

London, England

44

Harriet stepped over the threshold of her office door and joined her investigation team in the incident room at nine o'clock precisely. She was feeling unwound, composed and focused having put herself and her body through a forty-five-minute extreme spinning class at Body Fit earlier that morning.

'Ok, Crew. Let's gather round,' she announced, as she strode through the centre of the room towards the incident boards. On cue, the team congregated from various points around the room. 'Ok Iain, fire away.' DS Richards was sat at the desk where Harriet had just perched herself.

'The postmortem pretty much confirms what SOC outlined yesterday. The victim was deceased before the decapitation took place. A puncture wound was found on the lower left of the neck. Probably a needle entry point. No defensive marks or anything that suggests a struggle took place.'

'Apart from he lost his head!'

'Yes, thank you Stevens,' demanded Harriet. The laughter in the room subsided as quickly as it had erupted. Iain continued.

'Cut marks suggest the head was removed with a saw similar to that used in butchery. No such tool was found at the scene. We are now waiting on toxicology results for a possible cause of death.'

'The Lab boys have been asked to give it top priority,' added Harriet. She shifted her position on the edge of the desk slightly, affording her more focus as she questioned the rest of the team. 'Andy, where are we with the family?'

'The fathers private jet touched down at London City airport in the early hours. Border Force confirm the arrivals of the father and brother, but no mother. The father is to formally ID the body,' he hesitated, 'the head.' A small chuckle broke out around the room once more. 'The victim.' He said correcting himself, 'later this afternoon.'

'Support the FLO at the morgue, please Andy and find out from the father and the brother if they have seen or heard anything that may be of interest.' DS Stevens nodded his agreement. 'George, anything so far on the cameras or the door to door.' George pushed the remainder of the Danish pastry he had been eating back into its paper bag and dragged the back of his hand across his bearded mouth.

'Usual procession of delivery drivers, take away deliveries and waste collection.'

'What day was the waste collection?' enquired Harriet.

'Monday.'

'Probably wise to chase the council for the landfill site. We might still be looking for a murder weapon.'

'Thought you might suggest that. Got Thompson on it already.' Greg Thompson raised his hand. The look on his face said it all. He knew exactly who would end up to his knees in landfill should the need arise. 'Door to door have been collecting the licence plate numbers of local residents to cross match with those going in and out of the buildings underground carpark. There is no direct camera, however, there are cameras at either end of the street. So, we are referencing any vehicle that appears not to have travelled straight through. Going to take some time though Ma'am. And no luck so far with the victim's arrival.'

'Thanks George, keep at it.' Harriet glanced around the room and raised her eyes in DC Evans direction.

'You're up next Jake. What have you got for us?' Jake reached for the top page of a paper pile to his right.

'Alex Reynolds, the owner of the crime scene property is cutting his business trip short and returning today. He is coming in straight from the airport. I've spoken to him twice. Once to inform him of the incident. Although, he had already heard from the cleaner. Secondly, to arrange a time for him to come in for informal questioning about the rental. He will be here later this morning.'

'What have we learnt about the booking itself?' Jake picked up a second page from the pile.

'Pretty much as you'd expect I'm afraid. The booking was made seven days ago from a fake Hotmail account with a dynamic IP address and end to end encryption. Probably all done on a burner.' He paused to clarify himself. 'Burner being a pre-pay mobile device. So basically untraceable. Payment was made using a pre-paid virtual credit card. Card was bought using Bitcoin. So once again we hit a dead end. The only threads we have to follow are the Hotmail address, "mstom@hotmail.com" and the booking name of Mr M. Stom.'

Harriet crossed to the incident boards and wrote 'Alex Reynolds' and 'M. Stom'.

'Keep at it Jake, let me know as soon as you get anything.' She turned and leant against the wall. 'How did HOLMES do. Sarika?'

'There have been 27 incidents of decapitation in the Greater London area over the past five years. Eight tube jumpers. Eleven resulting from RTA's. Three construction site related. One boating accident. Two suicides from hanging. Just two which led to murder investigations. The first was 2015. Led to the conviction of the victims brother. Affair with the sister-in-law. Head was removed with a spade in the back garden of a semi in Walthamstow. Open and shut case. Second is an ongoing case from two years ago. Female head was found on waste ground in the Croydon district. The body is still to be recovered. The only relevant case in the rest of the UK in the same time period is a headless male body found in a feeder reservoir near Birmingham last summer.'

'Iain, can you liaise with Sarika and follow up on the two active cases, please.' Iain nodded in the direction of both women. Sarika continued.

'The only hit referencing "posed bodies" was again from 2015. Elderly female in North Tyneside. Cause of death, suffocation. The husband apparently smothered her with a pillow. Then bathed and redressed her, before placing her in her favourite chair. She had early onset dementia. He later jumped off the King Edward VII rail bridge.'

'I think we can rule that one out,' said Harriet as Sarika lent forward and handed her some A5 photographs. Harriet pinned them on the incident board and Sarika continued.

'The victim, Hidetaka Yamamoto. Forty-two years old. Father is Akihiro Yamamoto. Billionaire and owner of Kyoto Oil. Hidetaka is CEO of some of the family's smaller offshoot businesses. Although, he has spent most of his life on the celebrity fringes due to his father's extreme wealth. He has been resident in the UK, on and off for the past 15 years through a sole representative business visa. Joined the celebrity Z-List after appearing on Celebrity Big Brother six years ago. Numerous short-term relationships with other minor celebrities. The most notable being X factor runner up Jodie Fox with whom he has an eight-year-old son." Jodie's photo was one of five Harriet had pinned to the board.

'As Iain said yesterday, Hidetaka has been in the headlines recently for publishing sexually explicit videos of himself and two female celebrities on various social media sites. Both women have taken out court injunctions to have these videos removed. The first is MMA cage fighter Suzie Garcia. The other is the actress Donna Singleton. Her husband is the British

Lions full back Ryan Nicholls, who has been caught on camera stating, I quote, "I'm going to fucking kill him."'

'We are going to need to talk to all three. Jake, fancy the spotlight. Get onto their agents. I want them all questioned in the next 48 hours. No excuses.'

'No probs, Ma'am,' replied DC Evans, smiling from ear to ear, whilst looking around the room for acknowledgement from his male colleagues.

'If that's all Sarika?' Sarika nodded. 'I've got an important development you all need to be aware of. This was found rolled up inside the oesophagus during further explorations of the head during the PM.' Harriet held up the evidence envelope before pinning half a dozen close up photos of the item on the board.

'Happy believes it to be pigskin. He will hopefully confirm this later today. The words appear to be tattooed. Google first page results affirm they are lyrics from a song by a band called Neptune's Finger." She pinned a final page containing the lyrics onto the board.

'Have a delve into this as well Andy. See if you can relate it to anything, anywhere else. If not, find out what the bloody hell it means. Even if you need to dig up the guy who originally wrote it.'

Trafalgar Square
London, England

45

Tate and Jonathan sat in the bowels of the church. 18th Century brick vaulted ceilings were held aloft by stone chiselled pillars to create a labyrinth of arches cascading away on all four points of the compass. The room was lit by numerous uplighters casting an atmospheric glow from the tops of the pillars out across the curves of the ceiling. They had found a nook away from inquisitive ears and they were both currently leaning inwards across their plates to catch any melting butter or sauce escaping from the bottom of a sausage sandwich.

The Café in the Crypt below the church of St Martins-in-the-Fields lay at the North-East corner of Trafalgar Square. It had become a popular food destination with tourists and locals alike due to its ambient atmosphere and its tombstone covered floor. It can be said, there are not too many places where you can take afternoon tea whilst looking down at the headstone of Anne Bradbury 1771.

Tate had chosen todays breakfast location after finishing first on their early morning swim at the Serpentine. He caught an absconding drip of HP with the tip of his finger and re-united it with the remaining sandwich.

'Those emails have been bugging me all night. I have no idea what they are about or who and why they were sent.'

'I'm sure it's just someone with a grudge to bear. Someone you had sentenced after a guilty verdict and now has too much time on their hands.' Tate had to agree. There were many people who had crossed his path who probably still held him in great animosity.

'I've run the words over and over in my head. The more and more I read it, the more it feels like an accusation. It's like someone is accusing me of failing them or failing in my position as Chief Inspector.' Tate took a mouthful of his coffee before adding another sugar to it. 'And each message is signed with the anonym, "Narcissus". At first, I was convinced it was you. What with the Narcissus being someone who fell in love with himself. And you being the only person I know who spends more time in front of a mirror than a drag queen.'

'Got a reputation with the ladies that's hard to live up to,' Jonathan replied, saluting his coffee mug in Tate's direction.

'The thing that puzzles me most, is the fact that they took the time to hack into my mailbox and not just mail it from a false, untraceable email address.'

'Beats me too. Listen. I wouldn't go worrying about it too much. It's probably just some nut job with nothing better to do, who thinks it would be funny to waste your time with a couple of disparaging emails.'

'Yeah, you may be right,' said Tate noticing the café had significantly filled with customers whilst they had been talking. He casually glanced at his watch. 'Good God, it's almost 10 o'clock! I'm going to have to shoot,' declared Tate, as he stood, downed his last mouthful of coffee and grabbed his jacket from the back of the chair.

'You go mate, I'll get the bill.' Tate took his wallet out of his trouser pocket and put a twenty-pound note on the table.

'No, no. My choice of breakfast. My job to pay. Them's the rules. And make sure the church gets the change.'

'As if?' Jonathon jested as he relaxed back into his chair.

'I'll see you back at Thorney Street later. I've got a short stop to make on the way.' Jonathan simply smiled in return. For he knew exactly where his friend was heading.

Trafalgar Square
London, England

46

At this time of the morning there were only a handful of tourists passing through room 32. The occasional one would stop when something caught their eye and maybe take a closer look. Sometimes they would stand back to get a different perspective, but more than often they would move swiftly on, as if they had a train to catch. Which they probably had, or more realistically a cruise ship. Tate sat alone on the Queen Anne bench as the day-trippers flittered by. He liked to come here early before the crowds and tour parties began to gather. It was a good place. Although not always peaceful, but an environment in which Tate found he was able to think best.

Tate had simply crossed over Charing Cross road from St Martins-in-the-Fields and directly into the National Gallery via the Eastern entrance.

The National Gallery first opened to the general public in 1824. It spent its formative years in properties on Pall Mall before quickly out growing its walls. Construction of the current site at the North side of Trafalgar Square on what was then the Kings Mews was started in 1832. Over the next 100 years its collection grew to become what is today one of the World's greatest collections of art alongside the Louvre in Paris and the MET in New York. Its collection includes works by Da Vinci, Titian, Raphael, Van Gogh and is home to many of the best works by British artists such as Turner, Gainsborough, Constable and Reynolds.

Tate liked to choose his thinking space depending on the task at hand. Sometimes he would sit with the works of the impressionists. At other times he preferred the company of van Ruysdael, Berchem and other Dutch landscape artists. Today he found himself enclaved by the baroque paintings of 17th Century Italy. Works by Cortona, Guercino and Gentileschi adorned the walls. Tate had taken up position in front of probably the most influential, yet most controversial of them all. One of the galleries most popular crowd-pulling artists. An artist whom 'Cruise Ship Tourists' made a beeline for. Although most would end up taking a snapshot of the wrong picture before dashing off to do the same in the Da Vinci room.

The 'Supper at Emmaus' by Michelangelo Merisi da Caravaggio filled the space directly in front of where Tate had chosen to sit. Said to be one of the artists most powerful works, it depicts the moment of the blessing of the bread when Christ reveals his identity to the disciples after his resurrection. Painted at the very start of the Seventeenth Century after a long period dominated by paintings in a mannerism style, Caravaggio was one of a group of influential artists who started to bring a sense of realism to their paintings. His use of chiaroscuro, the strong contrast between light and dark, coupled with his ability to place figures in the shadows of darkened rooms, whilst transfixing the principal characters actions and reactions with the use of a solitary shaft of light, executed a heightened sense of drama which enticed the viewer into the scene. Caravaggio had used these techniques to great effect in the 'Supper at Emmaus'. By pushing the figures to the foreground, with little space between them and the darkened wall behind, Caravaggio projects the characters through the barriers of the painting and into the physical space beyond. The extended hand of the apostle on the right and the torn elbow of the arm on the left appear to tear their way out through the canvas. The detailed still life on the table in the foreground looks as if it might tumble over the front of the picture at any moment and again break the barrier between the painting and the real world.

Tate welcomed this invitation to get lost in both the picture and his own thoughts. It had been a couple of weeks now since the 'St Mary Magdalene in Ecstasy' had been smuggled into the country and they were still no closer to retrieving it. Tate played out the scene in his head. *'Where was the Caravaggio now?'* The trail of circumstances pointed towards the Moreau having been purchased by persons knowing what truly lay within. Somebody in the know would surely never have allowed themselves to be out bid in the tens of thousands for something which they knew hid a masterpiece worth several million. The painting would be long gone from its carrier. '*Why a Caravaggio'?* A work of this stature and importance would not have been stolen for its value at re-sale on the open market. Paintings of this calibre were more than often stolen to order. '*Was AKA Dr Coster the beneficiary of the order or the perpetrator of the theft?'*

Tate's thought process was momentarily broken by the bustle of an enthusiastic group of young school children nudging each other forward through the doors at the far end. He watched as they looked, pointed, prodded and giggled at the towering frames on the walls. Tate hoped their energy to explore and discover would be captivated by the gallery. But he knew too well for most it would eventually wane. He had seen the other side. School teachers trying their damnedest to keep the attention of a handful of pupils who were more interested in each other or their mobile phones. Still, now and then, the odd one would slip through the hoop of the mainstream and be swept along into a life within the world of art.

As Tate was swallowed by the painting once more, his eye was drawn to a reflection in the glass jar on the table. The reflection started a new train of thought. One that whisked him back in time to a trip he had taken to Rome when he himself had been in his budding teens. With both his parents being art academics, holidays in those early years were more than often planned around galleries and exhibitions. Unlike his school pals who spent their summers on beaches or at adventure parks.

One of the galleries they had visited held a collection of Caravaggios. It was in this room Tate now found himself. As he continued to focus on the reflection in the jar, his memory moved around the room on that day in the early nineteen eighties. He recounted the colour of the walls surrounding him. The ornate white stucco ceilings and the gilded frames. The thick carpet beneath his feet. And then there it was. On the wall in the corner opposite the picture of 'St Francis in Meditation'. The adolescent boy leaning on both hands as he gazes into a pool of water. Locked in time by his reflection staring back at him.

The Narcissus.

St Katherine Docks

London, England

47

Sir Christopher Roebuck waited in line as the passengers disembarked the ferry. Upon receiving the address details from Dr Valentine, he had decided driving was probably not the best option due to the proximity of the location he had been given. He had boarded the river tours ferry at Westminster pier and taken the short downstream journey under some of London's most iconic bridges to St Katherine pier.

As he shuffled down the gangplank in unison with the other disembarking passengers, his eyes were drawn to the quayside and David Wynne's 'Girl with a Dolphin' sculpture. The artist was noted for his depiction of movement. Sir Christopher admired how Wynne had created the illusion of the figures flying unsupported above the water. He hoped the work he would view in a short while would be as captivating. He stepped onto the pier and walked along the jetty to the quayside. He rounded the sculpture pool to appreciate its beauty once more before heading into the basin of St Katherine Docks.

Now redeveloped as a residential and leisure complex, St Katherine Docks was part of the Port of London right up until 1968. Named after the 12th Century hospital that once stood on the site, the docks finally became an operational Marina in the 1990s.

Sir Christopher was heading for an annual mooring on the East dock. He crossed the road bridge over the main entrance lock. He walked with a strong stride, eager to make his destination without drawing any unwanted attention. Having retired from public view eight years ago, he was still a recognisable face after forty long years in Parliament. Reaching the Southwest corner of the East dock, he rounded the corner by the Dickins Inn and stepped out onto the jetty. The yacht he was looking for was apparently in berth C14. The movement of the walkway on the water made him feel uneasy and he slowed his step. Sir Christopher was in surprisingly good health for a man of his age. Although the stress of his career had aged his features quite dramatically.

Sir Christopher Roebuck had joined the Labour party as a junior member, actively supporting campaigns before becoming an MP in the late 1960s. He gained the position of Home Secretary within Labours 1970s Government and continued in prominent front seat positions for the opposition during the Thatcher years. It was during this time; he was investigated for a pay to enter immigration scandal dating back to his time as the Home Secretary. He was found guilty of fraudulent behaviour and sentenced to four years imprisonment. He served two years in Category D prisons. It was during this time that he wrote his best-selling autobiography 'Home from Home'. He also wrote the first two books in a series of political scandal novels. He then sat in the House of Lords for a period of time, before becoming a non-attending peer. As an antiquary of the late renaissance and Baroque periods, he had often used the services of Jeremy Grayson to acquire works to further his collection. The painting which he was now only minutes from viewing was far beyond anything Jeremy had previously afforded him the opportunity to purchase.

As he headed out across jetty C, he rotated his head from side to side enumerating the berth numbers. He passed all manner of boats. Express Cruisers, Flybridges, a Gulet, Cutters. He knew nothing about boats, despite having lived within a riggings length of the Thames his entire life. To him, the boats registered names were of more interest. The Daphne-Jane, Lagoon Princess, Eternal Sunset, Star Chaser, Pacific Bliss.

He stopped.

Having momentarily been awe-struck by the vessels names, he had walked straight pass berth C14. He retraced his steps and immediately on his right he saw 'Distant Horizons.'

St Katherine Docks

London, England

48

Moored at berth C14 was an Ocean Breeze 120. A six-berth tri-deck motor cruiser. Powered by twin diesel engines, which with a combined output of 1,200 hp, allowed for a top speed of 30 knots. It was a boat enthusiasts dream. Its upper deck supported a central helm, sun deck seating area and a small galley bar. The main deck below featured fore and aft sun decks and the main galley leading through to a generous saloon. The lower deck comprised of a spacious ensuite master cabin and two further guest cabins. An ideal yacht for those craving added luxury during longer durations at sea.

Sir Christopher stepped onto the aft deck of the yacht. As he did so, the Narcissus appeared through the smoked glass doors of the saloon and crossed the deck to greet him. The Narcissus offered a welcoming hand. Sir Christopher hesitantly accepted the handshake.

'Sorry, I was expecting…'

'I'm Dr Valentine, very pleased to meet you.'

'It's just, that on the phone, you sounded…'

'Shall we,' suggested the Narcissus, gesturing towards the open saloon doors. Sir Christopher continued across the teak-laid boarding into the interior of the middle deck. The saloon was finished in multi lacquered American cherry panelling with cream leather upholstery. There was a C-shaped seating and dining area, the main galley and stairs to the lower deck. Integrated ceiling spots provided the only source of light as black venetian blinds were drawn across all the windows of the cabin. The Narcissus noticed Sir Christopher's uneasiness as he sat nervously on the edge of the leather couch. His eyes repeatedly retracing themselves around the louvered windows.

'The circumstance calls for complete privacy,' declared the Narcissus.

'Oh yes. Absolutely. Certainly, no need for any Tom, Dick or Harry to be nosing in.'

'You seem nervous. Maybe apprehensive?'

'Just a little anxious. One cannot be too sure these days. Once bitten, twice shy as they say. Your insistence on Jeremys absence had made one uneasy to start.'

'I am not one to over complicate things. Jeremy has played his part. From here on, it only requires you and I,' exclaimed the Narcissus, sitting at the far end of the C-shaped couch. 'I assume you took my advice and relieved your driver of his duties this evening?'

'Yes. The old chap was over the moon. He mentioned he may even take his wife out to dinner.'

'I take it you drove yourself?'

'As it happens, one decided to take the scenic route on such a lovely evening. Caught a ferry on the Thames from Westminster. Tried to blend in with the sightseers.'

'*Or be seen by the masses,*' thought the Narcissus. Not that it really mattered. 'Then, nobody is aware of your whereabouts tonight, correct?'

'Absolutely. Lady Roebuck believes one is playing Cribbage at the club on Pall Mall. She has always known not to ask too many questions.'

The sound of halyards could be heard gently jangling as a light breeze whistled through the rigging of neighbouring yachts. An occasional chatter of voices or a crescendo of laughter drifted from the many nearby hostelries. All else was still and quiet.

'In which case, we shall continue,' declared the Narcissus. 'The cost of the painting is ten million pounds and the price is not negotiable.'

Sir Christopher nodded reluctantly.

'The money is to be transferred to an online bank account within 24 hours. Once the transfer is confirmed, the painting will be couriered to a location of your choice.'

'I believe one has, very little choice.' The Narcissus stood ignoring the remark.

'Good. Then shall we proceed? The Caravaggio is in the master suite on the lower deck. After you,' proffered the Narcissus motioning towards the descending steps at the end of the saloon. Sir Christopher rose ardently to his feet, forgetting his earlier anxieties. As he moved towards the bow, he mused as a thought flickered into his mind. Scholars believed that Caravaggio had last seen his painting of Mary Magdalene, when he himself had been on a boat, just days before he died. What a strange coincidence that he was on a boat and about to see the very same painting himself. The Narcissus stood to one side as Sir Christopher steadied himself with the stair rail, ducked his head slightly and stepped below deck. As he stepped down into the cabin, he felt a sharp pinpoint of pain in the side of his neck. He spontaneously threw a hand up to where the pain had emanated. No words escaped his mouth and blackness soon followed.

St Katherine Docks
London, England

49

The Narcissus removed the hypodermic syringe and Sir Christopher slumped to the floor. The opioid had induced unconsciousness instantaneously. The Narcissus had injected Sir Christopher with Etorphine, a synthetic opioid with an analgesic potency three thousand times that of morphine. It is used in veterinary practise to immobilise elephants and other large mammals.

Stepping around the body, the Narcissus crossed the room in the direction of the adjoining bathroom. A wheelie suitcase occupied most of the floor space in the tiny en-suite. After unlocking the case, the Narcissus removed a set of all-in-one coveralls before stepping into the shower cubicle, stripping to just underwear and re-dressing in the coveralls. The confined space of the cubicle made the task more difficult than anticipated. But the Narcissus was in no hurry. Disposable over boots, a surgical mask and Nitrile gloves were carefully put on before the hoodie of the coveralls was finally pulled up. Stepping from the shower, the Narcissus returned to the wheelie case and removed a large red drape, a hypodermic syringe, a plastic sampling tube, a pair of stainless-steel tweezers and a large sixteen-inch boning knife.

The Narcissus re-entered the master suite. The king size bed was the focal point of the room and took the majority of the cabins floorspace. All of the other bedroom furniture was built into the hull of the boat, giving a plush sweeping curve to either side of the room.

Taking the red drape in hand, the Narcissus spread the cloth out over the bed to cover the existing bedding. Then the white under sheet was folded down a quarter of the way at the head end and two white pillows were placed upright against the headboard. The Narcissus then manoeuvred the body of Sir Christopher onto the bed. Although the body was limp, it was not too difficult to lift due to the leanness of the aging man.

With the body lying on its back, the Narcissus retrieved the second hypodermic syringe and once more injected the contents into Sir Christopher's neck. The second syringe was much larger than the first. It contained a mixture of two drugs. The first, pancuronium bromide would cause sustained paralysis of the respiratory muscles, eventually leading to asphyxiation. The second was potassium chloride, which would induce an abnormal heartbeat, thus causing death by cardiac arrest. It was the same mixture commonly used during lethal injection executions in the United States. The dose delivered to Sir Christopher's body would take approximately fifteen minutes until the heart finally stopped beating.

Whilst the drugs were taking affect, the Narcissus manipulated the body into what would be its final resting position. The body was turned onto its side with its head looking to the left. The Narcissus then took one of the pillows and placed it under the left arm pit and the upper chest of the now leaning body. Finally, the Narcissus bent the body's right arm at the elbow to ninety degrees. The fingers of the right hand were splayed and the arm propped up so it would look as if it were holding its own weight. The left arm was laid across the bed and the hand made to grasp a handful of the white under sheet. Happy with the pose, the Narcissus checked the body for a pulse. The heart had stopped beating. The Narcissus took a moment to savour the mise-en-scene.

The light was wrong.

The Narcissus turned on a flexible gooseneck bedside wall light and manoeuvred it so that the light was projected across the body's face and right shoulder. The rest of the upper torso was now cast in shadow. The effect transformed the bodies appearance.

Happy that sufficient time had elapsed for the drugs to have had maximum effect, the Narcissus retrieved the boning knife and stood to the right of the bed, behind the back of the now posed body. The Narcissus grasped a handful of hair at the back of the head. Then pulling the head back to stretch the neck, the Narcissus drew the entire length of the sixteen-inch blade across the taught skin of the throat. The blade cut clean and deep into the tendons, capillaries and flesh, through the cartilage of the trachea, only stopping at the bone of the neck vertebra. Even though the heart was no longer beating, there was still a generous amount of arterial blood spatter, due to the pressure remaining in the capillaries. An arc of ejected blood had sprayed across the pillow and covered the hand grasping the sheet. The white sheet slowly started to change colour as it absorbed the dark red liquid.

With the oesophagus and trachea now exposed, the Narcissus retrieved the plastic sampling tube and the stainless-steel tweezers from the bedside dresser. Unscrewing the top from the tube, the Narcissus used the tweezers to carefully manoeuvre the tattooed pigskin from within. The roll of pigskin was similar in size to a Rigatoni pasta tube. Whilst maintaining a firm grip on the tweezered pigskin, the Narcissus cautiously lent over the body and with the tip of the knife separated any remaining soft tissues obstructing the severed opening of the oesophagus. Then with a steady hand, the Narcissus gently pushed the furled pigskin, deep within the wound of the neck. Happy that the foreign body could not easily be seen, the Narcissus carefully pushed the knife back into the wound, leaving the blade perfectly balanced in the gaping cavity of the neck.

Stepping back so as to gain a wider view of the posed body, the Narcissus scrutinised the most minuscule of details. Altering the angle of the head, slightly adjusting the position of the hand and lastly manipulating the light once more to ensure the shadows were thrown so to elevate the contrast between the light and the dark. Only then was the Narcissus satisfied that the image was complete.

The next few hours were spent methodically cleaning all areas of the boat to eliminate any traces of another person having been on board. This was followed by a reversal of the dressing procedure. Stepping into the cubicle once more, the Narcissus removed the coveralls, mask, boots and gloves, turning them inside out, before sealing them inside a plastic bag. This alongside a bag containing the empty syringes, cleaning products and the clothes the Narcissus had worn earlier were returned to the suitcase. The Narcissus then redressed in a different set of clothing, reset the boats security system and promptly disembarked carrying the suitcase.

As the Narcissus stepped down onto the jetty, the babble of chattering and laughter continued to emanate from the numerous eateries that lined the wharf. On the water, the only sound was the chorus of lanyards still tinkling and chiming on the wind.

31st May 1606

Rome, Italy

50

When Michelangelo awoke, Signora Antognetti was still sleeping, her arms across him and her head tucked up tight against his torso. They had made love late into the night the previous evening. Not as courtesan and client, but as two people who had locked away their true desires for far too long. Since arriving in Rome, Michelangelo had frequented the services of numerous Ladies of the Night, in between his many volatile relationships with vulnerable young boys. But his relationship with Signora Antognetti was like no other. There had been a connection from their very first encounter. Although he had always paid for her services, very often they had talked long into the night and no sexual activity had taken place.

Before they had made their way upstairs the previous evening, they had sat at the table and Signora Antognetti had recounted to Michelangelo all she had learnt during her time in Campo Marzio. The situation appeared to be a lot worse than Michelangelo had imagined. He had broken down into a monstrous wailing sob when she had told him that Ranuccio had in fact died. They sat at the table a long while and whilst discussing the situation they contemplated the few options Michelangelo now had. Whichever course of action they played out, it always ended at the same conclusion. Michelangelo had to leave Rome. And quickly.

Signora Antognetti had prepared some pasta, whilst Michelangelo antagonised his situation. They ate. He drank. They talked some more. But the more they talked, the more it became clear, that Michelangelo's only realistic option was to get out of Rome.

When Signora Antognetti finally woke, Michelangelo was sitting on the far side of the room smoking his pipe. As she watched him, he exhaled a long plume of smoke from his nostrils out through the open window. The smoke caught the wind and dissipated as he took another deep toke and looked blankly into the distance. She sat up in the bed and adjusted the pillows behind her back to make her sitting position more comfortable. As she did so, she continued to look across at a man who not in her wildest dreams would she have believed she would care for so much. A man who was now lost and broken. As she continued to watch him, she thought about the times they had shared together as friends and companions since they had first crossed paths. The disgusting drunk who had acquired her services in a taverna behind the Piazza Coppelle, had over the following few years become very dear to her heart.

When she finally spoke, she did so softly. 'I cannot come with you, Michelangelo!'

'I know. I have played it over and over, time after time in my head. It would not be safe for you,' he replied, exhaling a final plume of smoke from his nostrils before tipping the remnants of the pipe into the gutter below. 'I must leave today. It is now too dangerous for you to have me stay here a moment longer.'

Bring the pages alive…

Explore artworks, locations and more.

Go to gnsbooks.com (Interactive) or scan the QR code to unlock images, maps and facts as you read.

Woodford Green
London, England

51

She slid the back of her hand down the muscle of the upper arm, letting her fingernails gently caress the soft skin. A low almost silent moan came from the body lying next to her. Harriet leant forward and gathered the hair on Rebecca's neckline into a ponytail and placed it to one side on her partners shoulder. She continued to lean in closer and softly planted a series of kisses along the back of the exposed neck. Rebecca turned her head and smiled at her muse.

'Morning,' she said, her eyes still closed as she savoured the moment. The kisses continued and traced a line across Rebecca's shoulder and down the bicep of her upper arm. Here they lingered as Harriet gently slid a hand between her lovers arm and chest, cupping an exposed breast. Rebecca took this as a signal and turned over to face her morning calling. Whilst continuing to massage the breast that filled her palm, Harriet leant forward and teased the now erect nipple between her front teeth. The sensation and rude awakening caused Rebecca to arch her back and a second delicate moan escaped her mouth. Taking this as a positive response, Harriet rolled her hips across her partners pubic arch and sat straddling the perfect curves of the body below her. She caught a glimpse of their naked entangled bodies reflected in the mirrored floor-to-ceiling wardrobe doors. The image further accentuated her libido and heightened her sexual desire. Rebecca opened her eyes as Harriet found the nipple of her other breast and softly traced a circle around its areola with her index finger. No longer able to hold back, Rebecca slid her hands down the outsides of her exposed thighs and up onto the hips of her straddling partner, whilst each started slow rhythmical movements. Harriet closed her eyes as she felt a hand slide between the soft velvety skin of her inner thighs. She swallowed and took a sharp intake of breath.

The vibrating snapped her from the moment, seconds before the ringing started. The phone lit up and began to dance to the edge of the bedside table. With the lightning responses of a praying mantis, Harriet lunged to the bedside and caught the phone mid dive. Swinging her naked legs to the edge of the bed, she turned her head over one shoulder and quietly whispered,

'Sorry,' before hitting the call accept button. She had a fairly good idea what the call would mean as soon as she saw the caller ID on the home screen. Harriet lowered the phones volume and sat with her back to Rebecca on the edge of the bed.

'This had better be seriously bad,' she demanded whilst stretching out a leg and hooking a pair of discarded knickers with her big toe.

'Sorry Ma'am, but another body has turned up with a similar MO as the Isle of Dogs decap.' Harriet turned to see if Rebecca had overheard or was attempting to listen. To her surprise Rebecca had turned away and was now facing the wall on the other side of the room. Her pert buttocks and slender thighs captured Harriet's thoughts for a split second before the voice at the other end of the call broke her lustful temptation.

'Shall I pick you up Ma'am?' With the phone now gripped between her neck and shoulder, Harriet began wrestling and wiggling the captured panties up her legs.

'Yes, that will be fine. And Iain! Stop at a Nero's. Triple shot Americano and a chocolate croissant!'

'No problem, Ma'am. Should be about thirty minutes with the coffee stop.'

'Make it twenty,' replied Harriet as she pushed the call end button and released her neck grip on the phone, allowing it to drop to the bed. Snapping the elastic of the knickers around her waist, she turned and leant towards her naked friend.

Feeling the pressure of the mattress sink behind her, Rebecca spoke without turning.

'Yes, I know the score. You're sorry, you can't say anything. I'll have to wait until you know more and an announcement can be made. It's the deal I signed into. Now go find the bad guys!'

St Katherine Docks

London, England

52

A large herring gull was stabbing at a discarded sandwich wrapper as Harriet stepped from the pontoon onto the aft deck of Distant Horizons. The gull clutched the carton and took flight, moving to a new breakfast location at the far end of the jetty. Stopping momentarily, Harriet followed by DS Richards, put their hands into latex gloves to match their already covered shoes. They crossed the rear of the boat into the mid deck saloon where the aft doors to the lower section were already open. Harriet ducked her head inside and immediately caught sight of the forensic investigator in the cramped space below decks.

'What have you got for us, this time Penny?' she said as she continued down the steps.

'Oh, Hi Harry,' replied Penny, looking up from her position, crouched to one side of the bed. Before proceeding into the lower deck, Harriet turned back to DS Richards.

'Looks like there's not so much room down there, best to keep footfall to a minimum to preserve the scene.' Iain nodded in agreement whilst straining to peak over Harriet's shoulder. 'See if you can locate the port authorities and see what camera surveillance they have. I noticed quite a few cameras on the way in. I'd imagine it to be pretty heavy. Some of these boats must be worth well into six figures.'

'Be my pleasure Ma'am, I'm not the best on water, more of a dry land kind of guy,' replied Iain, turning towards the rear of the boat.

'All cameras for the last 72 hours and get a hard copy,' shouted Harriet over her shoulder before finally ducking below deck.

The first thing that hit Harriet as she stepped down onto the floor of the lower deck was the sweet coppery metallic smell of blood. Once you have smelt blood, you never forget it. In some people it stimulates a defence mechanism and withdrawal behaviour, whereas in others it can have the opposite affect promoting predatory behaviours. Harriet fell into the latter group. The smell heightened her senses, aroused her curiosity and ignited the hunting instinct in her. Not a compulsion to pursue further bloodshed, but an instinct to hunt those responsible for the blood that had already been spilt. There was no mistaking where the blood of the victim that lay before her now had been spilt. The bed was saturated in it.

'I'd hazard a guess that the final moments of this poor fellows life ended right here,' Harriet declared as she took in the scene of the lower deck.

'Most probably,' replied Penny as she looked up briefly whilst putting a blood smeared cotton swab into a sampling tube and sealing it.

Harriet assessed the scene before her, as always taking in every detail. Not only the extensive amounts of blood, but the position of the body relative to the close quarters of the scene. As at every crime scene she would scrutinise all aspects of a room, its layout, furnishings, lighting and décor. Did anything look out of place or seem peculiar? She would pay particular detail to the everlasting expression on the victim's face and any clothing, jewellery or tattoos which adorned the victims torso. She noted the position of the arms, hands, legs and feet relative to the other parts of the body. She noticed the smallest detail like a loose cuff button from perhaps a pre mortem struggle or a twisted spectacle arm from a glancing blow to the head. But, right here, right now, her gaze was constantly drawn to the way the head had been drawn back so as to over stretch the neck and emphasize the gaping wound where an oversized large bladed knife was now lodged firmly in its vertebrae.

'There seems little doubt that the body has been posed, much like the previous one. Look at how the pillows have been placed, along with the positioning of the arms and hands. Consistent MO with our previous victim,' observed Harriet as she lent in to get a closer look at the torso and limbs.

'We might be led to misperceive that this time they didn't finish the job. The heads still attached and we have a possible murder weapon,' Penny interjected as she moved her attention to cable tying plastic bags over the victims hands to preserve any cross-transference evidence. 'But I'm with you on this one. The scenes too clean. The whole thing seems blatantly posed for some sort of perverse reasoning. It's like they are purposely leaving real-life sculptures as some sort of symbolism.' Harriet moved to the opposite side of the bed and watched as Penny placed the second hand into an evidence bag. 'As with the previous victim there appears to be no defensive wounds and no sign of a struggle.' Penny pulled the cable tie to tighten the bag on the second wrist. 'Which would point towards the victims in both cases being incapacitated pre mortem.'

'We're still waiting final toxicology reports,' declared Harriet as she leaned in to closer observe the neck wound. 'But preliminaries seem to suggest a possible heavy sedative followed by a drug induced death, which seems to strongly equate with both crime scenes. Neither of these victims could have succumbed to these injuries whilst conscious without showing any indications of a struggle.' As Penny continued to secure possible vital evidence, Harriet turned her attentions to the large blade protruding from the vertebrae of the victims' neck.

'Looks likely to be a single directional cut,' stated Penny, noticing Harriet's focus on the position of the embedded knife. 'From left to right,' she continued, 'with the blade being reasserted from the right after the initial cutting.' Harriet leaned ever closer, as if transfixed by the wound.

'Any evidence of anything inserted into the neck wound apart from the knife?' Harriet asked as she peered further into the open cavity.

'I'm still on my primaries. Why? What are you thinking?'

'Just a hunch, that's all,' stated Harriet. 'Happy found a tattooed pigskin in the oesophagus of the first victim.' The statement seemed to ignite a fire in Penny and she reached for the camera she had left to one side on a bedroom dresser.

'I need to shoot a few more shots of the body in situ and some close ups of the neck wound first, but then we can take a look. I'll need another ten minutes or so.' Having always had an enormous respect for her colleagues expertise, Harriet withdrew from the scene into the lower decks en-suite bathroom as flashes from Penny's camera signalled a series of images being captured.

After what was only three or four minutes, Harriet reappeared from the closet sized room.

'The shower, sink and toilet appear to be dry and unused. I'm not sure your boys will find much in the waste tank either. Clean, clean and more than clean.' Penny looked up from behind the camera lens just as Harriet re-entered the room.

'I think we might have something. I noticed an anomaly whilst taking close-up shots of the neck. Could you pass me the long thin tweezers from my kit bag,' she requested, motioning to the open bag on the floor near to where Harriet now stood. Harriet found the tweezers immediately in the top section of the bag and held them up for Penny to acknowledge.

'Yes, perfect. They're the ones.' Harriet leaned across and handed the tweezers to her colleague. Using the gloved index finger of her left hand, Penny manipulated the open flesh of the wound, moving the sliced muscles of the neck to expose the severed opening of the oesophagus and trachea. She then carefully inserted the tips of the tweezers into the opening and carefully manoeuvred the prongs to either side of the small foreign object she had seen. She gently squeezed the arms of the tweezers together and slowly teased the foreign object from its hiding place.

'Could you lay one of those empty evidence bags out on top of the dresser please,' she said as she carefully moved away from the bed, whilst ensuring she had a secure grip on the tweezers at all times. Harriet did as instructed and Penny placed what now could be seen as a cylindrical roll of skin onto the bags surface. Using the tips of the tweezers once more, she unfurled the cylindrical roll until it lay flat against the bag. Penny turned to ask for another evidence bag, but Harriet was one step ahead and held the bag open. Penny carefully eased the skin into the bag and Harriet sealed it shut. Holding the bag up to the light, the two women could easily read the tattooing on the skin.

'The eighth bell tolls as another soul is taken
Fear amongst men as the Kraken awaken
Greed and gluttony feed each man's desire
As their ship starts to sink to the depths of the mire.'

St Katherine Docks

London, England

53

'As you can see behind me, earlier today London Metropolitan police sealed off an area here at St Katherine Docks. The Docks join the river Thames through a series of lock gates providing visiting boat owners central London moorings adjacent to the Tower of London and Tower Bridge. The area is popular with city workers and tourists alike as a destination to eat and drink in its many bars and restaurants.' As the camera man widened his camera angle and panned the camera through a 180-degree panoramic view of the waterside establishments, Rebecca changed her position to one side and whilst off camera for a few moments she gave her hair a quick flick and patted down her jacket. The camera finished its sweep at Rebecca's new position.

'Personnel from crime investigation units have been seen working in and around a yacht named Distant Horizons moored on the east dock.' Rebecca paused once again. This time whilst the cameraman tightened his angle and zoomed in on a pair dressed in forensic coveralls working on the aft deck of the yacht, Rebecca smoothed down the skin on the bridge of her nose and readjusted her microphone against her chest. Once again, the cameraman returned the lens's focus to Rebecca.

'There is speculation amongst employees here at the dockside that a body was discovered in the early hours and there is a high probability it could be connected to a body found earlier this week at a block of flats on the Isle of Dogs.' Rebecca turned slightly to open her bodies frame to the scene unfolding behind her and the cameraman followed her lead by widening his angle once again.

'We will bring you further updates live from the scene here at St Katherine Docks as soon as further information becomes available. Rebecca Crawford, Universal News.' She held her pose for a moment until her cameraman lowered the lens. As he did so, she gave herself a self-approving smile. She was the only reporter at this stage who could postulate that a body had in fact been found and that there may be a link to the Isle of Dogs investigation. Why else would Harriet have been summoned to a crime scene in the early hours. There was no way in hell that she would be called to a new crime scene without the possibility of it being linked to the high-profile case she was already working. It wasn't all about being fed inside information. Sometimes you just needed to use your intuition.

Thorney Street
London, England

54

Tate was on the phone when Lena entered. He motioned for her to take a seat. As she waited Lena could hear one side of the conversation. Enough for her to make sense of the call. Tate was notifying Capitano Moretti of their progress. As Tate continued to provide Moretti with details of their investigations on this side of the channel, he looked across to Lena, held up a pair of fingers and mouthed 'two minutes'. Lena acknowledged her understanding with a silent 'ok'. As she waited with one ear still on Tate's side of the conversation, her gaze wandered to the trio of pictures on the wall. She wondered why Tate chose to embellish his surroundings with 1970s rock artwork. Still, one man's Picasso is another man's Warhol.

'Yes, I see no problems with that. I'll contact you when we have anything further. Good to talk to you too. Arrivederci.' Tate replaced the handset.

'Sorry about that. As you could probably hear, I was just bringing Capitano Moretti up to speed with things at our end. In fact, I've just been telling him about a couple of concerning emails I have received recently. I'd welcome your opinion too.'

Tate woke up his monitor screen with a nudge of the mouse and gestured for Lena to join him on his side of the desk. With Lena leaning in from the end, Tate explained how and when the emails had arrived, just as he had done previously with Jonathan and Moretti. He leant back in his chair, giving Lena time and space to read the pair of emails, side by side on the screen.

'Well, the signature could be a possible link to our case with the name's association to Caravaggio, but I have absolutely no idea what the message is referring to,' Lena replied as she withdrew from the screen to stand at the end of the table.

'The words resonated with me straight away. The lines are lyrics from songs on the Neptune's Finger album "Beyond the Waves"'. He pointed to the picture across the room, 'which leads towards someone who knows me well. I thought it had to be Jonathan playing one of his little games at first. When I confronted him, he insisted it wasn't and that I believe.' Tate walked towards the picture of the hand rising from rough seas. 'If it's not someone having a giggle and we take it as a possible threat, then it would point to someone having been in this office at some point and noticing the picture hanging there.' Lena crossed the room to join him by the picture. Tate continued. 'It wasn't until I was at the National Gallery yesterday before it struck me that the signature could very well be significant and in some way connected to our missing painting. I knew you would recognise the link straight away. The "Narcissus" being a notable Caravaggio painting and you having mastered in Italian art history. With your extensive knowledge and passion for the early baroque period, I instinctively knew you'd see it. What are your initial thoughts on the using of "Narcissus" as a signature?'

Tate returned to his desk and Lena followed. Once more, she sat in the chair on the opposite side. Crossing her legs, she let the shoe of her raised leg playfully slip from her heel, only to catch it again by extending her toes before it slipped entirely from her foot. She did this repeatedly as she pondered the question.

'Caravaggio's "Narcissus" is not an A list crowd puller like his works in the chapels of Rome, but neither is the "St Mary Magdalene in Ecstasy". Those with a general interest in art would most probably include it on a list of Caravaggio works they'd like to see. As a signature, it would be enough to grab your attention, if indeed it has been used to draw a link to the missing painting. A Narcissist is someone who admires their own being more than that of others but needs the admiration of others to feed upon. So, yes. The messages may well have been sent by someone linked to the theft of the painting. Their feelings of self-worth and grandiosity could point to over confidence, even a state of cockiness. Certainly, enough to taunt an investigation by sending obscure emails.' Tate beamed at his colleagues knowledge.

'What else is locked in that encyclopaedic brain of yours about the painting itself,' he asked whilst typing 'Narcissus' into his screens Google search bar.

'Caravaggio painted the "Narcissus" in Rome at the tail end of the sixteenth century. It was during this period that he gained a greater notability for his works, which in turn led to a series of large religious commissions across the capital. The picture itself portrays the moment when the mythical adolescent known as Narcissus falls in love with his own reflection. The painting is recognised as an early example of his extreme use of light and shadows.' As Lena continued, Tate twisted his monitor in her direction. An image of the painting filled the screen. Lena leant into the desk once more and ran a finger across the screen.

'See how the background is completely obscured in the shadow of blackness, whereas the figure itself is strongly lit across the upper torso, but in contrast, little light is cast into the reflection below. It's an artistic technique known as Tenebrism or dramatic illumination. It's a style of painting that is easily identifiable, especially in his later works.'

'Similar to the "Supper at Emmaus" in the National Gallery,' interrupted Tate.

'Exactly. Some believe the extreme lighting of the face and shoulders empathises the self-centred admiration of a narcissist's own self. However, some scholars and experts are still dubious that the painting is an authentic Caravaggio. It is only recent analysis of the execution of his style carried out during restorations, along with confirmation of an export license dating to 1645 that it is now finally accepted as an autographed work.' Lena pointed at part of the image once again.

'The boy is depicted wearing an elegant, brocaded doublet, similar in material to the under dress in his painting of the "Penitent Magdalene" of the same period. Being a poor artist at the time, meant Caravaggio like many other artists reused costumes and props in many of his paintings to save money. He also painted using live models to achieve a realism in his characters features. He repeatedly used the same friends and prostitutes to again save money. The boy in the "Narcissus" bears an uncanny resemblance to the face of the angel in his "Rest on the Flight to Egypt" painting. These similarities along with stylistic comparisons, again affirm its authenticity as a true Caravaggio.'

'I think we can safely say you know your Italian art. Your elucidation of the painting is even weightier than the one Capitano Moretti gave me a few moments ago.'

'I based the thesis for my masters on the investigations into the theft of Caravaggio's "Nativity" painting stolen in Palermo, Sicily in 1969. I spent an entire summer submerged in everything and anything Caravaggio. It laid the foundations and paved the way for why I'm sitting here today.'

'I'd be interested to read it one day if you'd allow me.'

'God knows where it is. I'd have to find it,' said Lena, before quickly changing the subject. 'Caravaggio's "Narcissus" is at the Galleria Nationale D'Arte Antica in Rome.' Lena paused. A look of deep concern came over her face. 'You don't think it's the next target, do you?'

'I've just discussed that possibility with Moretti. From the context of the emails, we are both suspicious but sceptical. However, he is taking no chances and is going to double security around the picture.' Tate moved and clicked his mouse a couple of times and the thought provoking emails re-appeared on the screen as before.

'I've had the tech boys analyse the source. They say it appears someone broke through the Mets firewall and hacked into my email account from a remote IP address. Untraceable. Each time, they sent the emails from my account to my account. They are as baffled as I am. Why not just send them from the remote source?' Lena raised her palms skyward and shrugged. Tate continued.

'It's the content which baffles me. I understand the connection to Neptune's Finger. But why those particular lines? The first pair,' he pointed to the email open on the left of the screen, 'could it be implying a failure to resolve a situation. Maybe the Narcissus is someone who has been a victim of art theft in the past and is now turning the tables.'

'Or it could just be this Narcissus fellow, vying for attention, taunting us to take his actions seriously,' suggested Lena.

'And the second pair, what do you think,' enquired Tate?

'Tide may signify movement. "Turbulent tide" maybe referring to the movement of stolen works. And "raise the anchor" could be metaphoric for the removal of the painting.' Tate raised a finger and continued the construct.

'Tides are related to seas. Along with "Distant shores" it could be taken to imply the transportation of stolen art overseas. The phrase "where treasures hide" may well be referring to the concealment of the Caravaggio within the other painting.'

'Perhaps this Narcissus is cocky enough to believe they can taunt the investigation with cryptic emails which in turn maybe satisfying their need to attract attention. It might well be their way of seeking admiration by implying that the "Mary Magdalene" is in fact now on British soil.'

Bethnal Green

London, England

55

Harriet was sat in her office, slouched forward in her chair, elbows on her desk and holding her phone in the landscape position. A live feed from Universal News was streaming on the screen. She watched as Rebecca, looking radiant as ever, stood on the waterside at St Katherine Docks for a second day and addressed her viewers in her usual confident manner. A breaking news banner scrolled across the bottom of the screen. Harriet continued to watch as Rebecca reported further details relating to the unconfirmed discovery of a body found aboard a yacht moored behind her. A secured police investigation area could easily be seen over her shoulder. Rebecca continued to hypothesise the possibility of a link to the body found on the Isle of Dogs several days ago. Luckily for Harriet, no further details had been leaked so far, but an inevitable press conference would soon follow.

Harriet was so absorbed in the news feed that she failed to hear the person entering the room. A tactful tap on the glass partition broke her concentration.

'Sorry to disturb you Ma'am. I have a couple of interesting discoveries on the security footage from the dockside and surrounding area. I thought you might like to take a look.' Harriet impulsively tapped the home button on her phone as she looked up.

'Excellent Iain! Ok, I'm all yours. Let's go take a look.'

Bethnal Green
London, England

56

Iain sat in the chair at his desk, whilst Harriet stood with one hand on the backrest and the other leaning inward on the edge of the table. Iain clicked a few file icons and a new pane with a video feed appeared on the screen.

'To start, I ran through the security footage back as far as yesterday afternoon. This first loop shows the victim arriving on the scene and you can clearly see Sir Christopher heading in the direction of the pontoon where the yacht is moored. The time feed on the camera records this at 6.37pm yesterday evening.' Iain tapped his computers mouse a couple of times and the video feed repeated itself.

'Unfortunately, there is no other camera in close proximity to that particular pontoon or any other capturing footage from a location further afield. However, I did pull some footage from a street camera positioned by St Katherine's pier and again he can be clearly seen disembarking the Crown River Cruiser which docked at 6.30pm.' Iain clicked another icon and a further pane slid in. This time a still shot showed Sir Christopher in the boats exiting queue.

'Maybe see if you can find an image of where and when he got on. You never know, it might be of some help later,' Harriet stated as she tapped her fingers lightly on the table. Iain nodded in agreement before continuing.

'So, with the victim arriving at that point, it gives us our first fixed point on the timeline of the crime. From there I viewed the footage from earlier that day. Not only from that camera, but all others positioned at possible entry points to the East docks, looking for arrival footage of any possible suspects. At 4:13pm, you can see from the next clip,' once again he opened a segment of video footage, 'an individual dressed in the uniform of the Royal Mail, wheeling a travel case, enters the area of interest. I have run through footage from cameras at all exit points around this area of the Docklands and the suspect cannot be seen in any further footage or be seen leaving the area in question before the first response team arrives.'

'You don't think someone would have the balls to hang around, hiding out somewhere until after things die down. If so, they could still bloody be there on another yacht,' declared Harriet. 'Get one of the auxiliary lads to give you a hand. Check all camera footage for the rest of the day. Look for anything out of the ordinary.' A small smile appeared on Iain's face.

'One step ahead of you, if you don't mind Ma'am' he mused as he started a feed from a different camera. 'You will see as the images from this camera run through, later that evening at 9.22pm we have an individual of similar build to our earlier Postal worker but this time dressed in the uniform of the London Underground staff. They can be seen pulling a similar travel case and leaving the Docks by the Northwest exit.' He froze the footage with the suspect clearly visible on the screen and looked up to address Harriet directly.

'However, when I ran through earlier footage there is no sign of this second individual entering the area before or after Sir Christopher's arrival. There is a good chance they are the same individual in different guises. Street cameras then picked up the Underground worker outside the Northwest exit and we can follow them on these cameras until they enter the Tower Hill tube station. Once there, they have the Circle line or District line East or West.'

'Or the new walkway to Tower Gateway and the DLR,' offered Harriet as she stood to straighten her back for a minute. 'Obtain the days footage from TFL and check for any further sightings of either suspect.'

'Already put in a request Ma'am.' This time Harriet gave Iain a smile.

'That amount of footage is going to take some man hours. I'll put it to the Chief Super and see if we can bring in some civvies to help sort through it.' Iain nodded in agreement as Harriet leant forward once more and pointed to one of the video panes still on the screen.

'Run this one again for me will you,' she asked. Iain manipulated the mouse once more and the video began scrolling.

'There! Freeze it there! Can you enlarge it and zoom in on the figure?' It took very little time before an enlarged but grainy image of the postal worker suspect filled the screen.

'Good work,' said Harriet, 'Now can you do the same with the suspect dressed in the underground uniform and put them side by side.' Once again, Iain showed his computing prowess and moments later the two stills of the suspects sat together on the screen.

'There. What do you see?' Iain took a moment to observe both images.

'They are both wearing the same cap. With what looks like some sort of triangular logo on it.'

'Exactly. And both suspects are wearing oversized overcoats. The temperature in the city was in the low thirties yesterday. Virtually everyone else who passed by those cameras was wearing as little as possible. Good work Iain. You've possibly found us the break we need. We're out of the starting blocks.' Harriet gave a generous nodding of the head in Iain's direction. 'Can you upload that little lot onto a USB and have it ready with the rest of the team for a briefing at 6pm sharp.'

'No problem Ma'am. Already on it!'

Thames South Bank

London, England

57

It had been only 24hrs since Tate had shared the peculiar emails he had received with Moretti and Lena. During that time, he and Lena had both worked late into the night exploring different avenues of enquiry whilst keeping each other informed of their continuing progress. Lena had been investigating the name of the carrier paintings purchaser. She had found the name to be more predominant than she had first anticipated. The NHS database had listed eighty-six staff currently registered in the name of 'Coster' with the honorific of doctor. The General Register Office of the UK had records for another thirty-one thousand individuals with the surname of Coster in their Births, Deaths and Marriages record. Lena had discovered the surname 'Coster' had become increasingly more common in the Central and Southern regions of England amongst the farm labourers of the 19th Century. Understandably the larger percentage of these would not be listed with the title of Doctor. When Lena had narrowed the search to the Greater London area as a starting point, the number including the professional title presented at fifty-seven. This included eight general practitioners, three surgeons, five dentists, two plastic surgeons, four veterinarians, three dispensing chemists, two archaeologists and numerous others from academical and scientific fields. She had begun to cross reference the Dr Costers currently in the Greater London area with any significant art and antiquities purchases, losses, taxable submissions and import or export duties over the past twenty-five years. So far, she had not had a single hit from hours of data crunching.

Tate had been meticulously examining the surveillance footage from the day the carrier painting had been auctioned. He had thought it important to watch the footage of the auctions entire catalogue that day, rather than just the segment showing the acquisition of the painting at which they were focusing their enquiries. This footage revealed nothing out of the ordinary. With the wonders of modern technology, Tate could move between camera angles as the auction played out and had the ability to zoom in on key individuals at precise moments. He played particular attention to the gentleman in the third row, the final bidder to lose out on the sale of the painting. He showed no signs of heightened anxiousness, no excessive frustrations when over bid and never nervously glanced towards a camera during the entire footage. Tate had learnt from their earlier visit to the auction house that the gentleman in question was a Mr Fredric Breakwell. Earlier that morning, he had visited him at his home in Chelsea. Mr Breakwell was a draper, who had run a prosperous business in the West End of London until his retirement ten years ago. It was obvious from the moment Tate stepped into the riverside property that Mr Breakwell was desirous for a particular period of French Impressionism. The walls of the town house were adorned in nothing but that one style. During his short stay, Tate also came to realise that if Fredric Breakwell had been aware of the masterpiece hidden within the painting, his wealth could have easily afforded him to have continued his bidding.

On his return, Tate and Lena had met in his office, but it wasn't long before Tate suggested they took advantage of the continuing good weather and pop out for a bite to eat. They had crossed the Thames, via the Vauxhall bridge and they were now sat on the upper deck of the Tamesis Dock. A quirky floating pub on a converted Dutch barge permanently moored on the South bank. Tate was sipping a ginger beer, whilst Lena was cradling a long island iced tea. She played with the straw between sips as she mused over the vista the river afforded her. Beyond the curve in the river, she had a rooftop view of the South bank and the tops of the Battersea Power station chimneys.

'What is it about that picture? Why are you so fascinated by it?' she asked as she continued to look in the direction of the distinctive white towers. Tate had followed his partners gaze and immediately perceived the picture in question as it hung on his office wall.

'It's not just the picture. Well, it is. I admire the artwork. But I adore the music, the band, the musical genre and the whole concept of the album.' Tate took a long sip of his drink. "I don't want to bore you as I know it's not your thing, but you did ask. The album follows the ideas of George Orwell and his book "Animal Farm". It depicts a capitalist society where the different classes are portrayed as various animals. A world where "Dogs" prey and "Pigs" rule over a herd of mindless "Sheep"'. Tate stopped himself. 'Sorry, too much information.'

'No, not at all,' replied Lena. 'It sounds very much like the world we live in today. The rich and the powerful feeding off the poor. The rich getting richer, the fat getting fatter and without a thought for the majority falling deeper into the void.' At that point, the waiter brought their food. They had each ordered pizza. Tate a stilton and rocket, Lena a meat calzone.

'Perhaps I'll stick to the Spice Girls as they know what they want,' jested Lena as the smallest of smirks escaped her mouth. Tate took that as a signal to change the subject.

'What's your gut feeling about this one? What's your instinct telling you about the nature of the crime?' Lena plucked at a single strand of cheese resistantly stretching itself between her mouth and the rest of the calzone. She wrapped it around her fork before guiding it safely to her lips. She then lightly tapped the fork against her teeth, as if using it as a thought provoker.

'I think we can definitely rule out an opportunist break and enter or even a general theft by an individual perpetrator. They would both have taken more than one painting or artifact. This is more specific. Whoever stole the painting had done their research, knew it was there and took it for a reason.' Tate was keen to keep the train of thought moving and conducted Lena with another question and a prompting of his knife.

'So, that leads us towards a private commissioned art theft, or an organised crime syndicate.' Lena thought for a second whilst she finished a mouthful of her calzone.

'Organised crime syndicates predominately steal for profit, insurance fraud or to hold an object as a bargaining chip. A work such as Caravaggio's "St Mary Magdalene in Ecstasy" would hold a heavy monetary value but would be difficult to move on the open market due to the publicity of the crime. However, as we know from experience, works of this significance can and do change hands on the black market. However, an Italian crime syndicate would almost certainly want to keep a painting of this calibre within its own borders.' Lena had been cutting her calzone as she spoke and paused to take another mouthful. Tate took this as an opportunity to interject.

'So, we're both swaying towards the same possible scenario. A wealthy collector is the patron of the crime. They have a desire to possess the said painting and the capital to obtain it illegitimately. They pay somebody else to take the risks, plan, instigate the crime and transport the Caravaggio. The patron of the crime then simply sits back and waits for the painting to become part of their collection.' Lena fought another strand of cheese to her mouth and continued.

'Knowing the potential value of the painting, the perpetrator of the crime can charge a considerable amount for their role in the acquisition of the stolen item. The patron of the crime is paying for a service rather than the item itself.' Tate patted the corners of his mouth with a serviette and placed it down on his plate.

'With the painting having been transported into the UK, there is a strong possibility that the patron of the crime is a British resident.'

'Or is a foreign national who resides here,' Lena chipped in before Tate continued.

'So our next avenue of approach is to compile a list of wealthy UK residents who collect and have legitimately purchased similar styles of art in the past. Especially those on our radar who have also been suspected of adding to their collections by other means.' Tate paused for a minute and looked in the direction of the power station. 'The perpetrator of the theft could well be Italian. Moretti has a stronger chance of following that trail with forensic analysis of the crime scenes at his end. Although, it may be worthwhile getting the passport details of individuals known to us checked with border patrol to see if there is any correlation with the dates and times of the crime.' Once again, the trail of thought was bounced into Lena's court.

'The Patron could have used a middleman, an administrator, to plan the details, then select and hire a perpetrator or even an overseas team to complete the job.' Lena gestured to Tate by leaning the top of her glass in his direction, allowing the straw within to prompt like a conductor's baton. 'There are many illegitimate art fences here in London who have been subject to our enquiries in the not too distance past. Messrs Grayson, O'Connor and Dunn to name but a few.' With that, Tate jumped to his feet, retrieved his wallet from his back pocket, took one last sip of the remnants of his ginger beer and placed two twenty-pound notes under the glass as he returned it to the table.

'I think it's time we paid a certain Mr Grayson a visit, don't you? And there is no time quite like the present.'

Bruton Place, Mayfair

London, England

58

After their spontaneous lunch, Tate and Lena had headed back to Thorney Street before taking the tube a short distance to Green Park. They exited the station onto Piccadilly and were jostled forward frantically onto the street within the flow of bodies spuing from the crowded bowels of the underground. London had become considerably busier over the previous few days as a further influx of summer visitors had arrived and engulfed the capital to breaking point. The streets overflowed. Tate and Lena had to fight a path through the constant onslaught of the approaching masses as they made their way along Piccadilly towards Old Bond Street.

Turning North, the perpetual stream of bodies thinned marginally. Tate and Lena were able to walk side by side at times, however they frequently found they had to drop into single file, one behind the other to make steady progress. Old & New Bond Streets link Piccadilly in the South to Oxford Street at its Northern end. Originally developed in the 1720s for the upper classes of neighbouring Mayfair to socialise, it slowly developed over the next century to gain notoriety and a fashionable reputation for prestigious shops and high-end brands. The likes of Aspreys the jewellers and the Fenwick department store established their presence over those early years before being joined by global designer brands such as Tiffanys, Gucci and Cartier in more recent times. The world-renowned auction houses of Sotheby's and Bonhams both hold prominent positions within the street. Tate and Lena were au fait with both properties, having spent many hours within the walls of either establishment whilst investigating previous antiquarian crimes.

The vast majority of the crowds that hugged the pavements were window shoppers, whose wallets were not fat enough and their pockets not deep enough for them to venture over a store's threshold. However, numerous chauffeurs waited kerbside in high-end cars and limousines whilst their clients whiled away the hours, safe within the hands of Prada and Valentino.

'I think the old Land Rover would have looked a little out of place if we had driven,' joked Tate as they passed a Lamborghini parked between a Bentley and a Ferrari. Crossing the road, Tate and Lena continued to bob and weave their way through a maze of mesmerised pavement blockers as they continued their way up the right-hand side of the street.

'There's probably more people here fantasising about how the other half live than the Halcyon Gallery across the road has had through its doors all week,' declared Lena, shouting ahead of herself so Tate could hear. She had just finished her rant as a Chinese tourist turned his hypnotic gaze from a window and shoulder barged straight into her. Lena stopped and stepped to one side. The Chinese man already transfixed on his next shop window was oblivious to the encounter and continued without so much as an apology.

'Unbelievable!' sighed Lena, throwing her hands in the air.

'What did you say?' shouted Tate over his shoulder.

'Nothing,' Lena replied as she quickened her step to catch up with Tate.

Noticing a throng of camera yielding Japanese tourists bearing down in their general direction like a rugby front row rucking for touchdown, Tate made to cross the road once again. Stepping from the curb, he immediately found himself having to sidestep a Deliveroo cyclist he had not seen approaching.

'Woo, that was close,' he said to himself as he skipped the final steps to the opposite pavement. Lena having stopped short of the encounter, looked both ways with intent before hurrying across to join Tate.

They left the bustle of Bond Street behind and turned into the relative quiet of Bruton Place. With the tiny back street being nestled between two transecting streets, the tourist headcount decreased substantially.

'Would you like me to take the lead on this one?' Tate suggested as they rounded the corner at the streets bottom end and headed up the left side to the gallery they sought.

'I think that maybe wise,' replied Lena, 'I don't have a lot of time for the scumbag since our last encounter with him.' Two years previously, Jeremy Grayson had been Tate and Lena's prime suspect whilst investigating the alleged black-market handling of a stolen still life painting by Dutch artist Rachel Ruysch. The painting in question had turned out to be a fake, moreover, the original had not resurfaced to this day. Lena had never held back or hidden her feelings for the man, calling him a snivelling weasel on more than one occasion. Grayson had been on their radar for many years now and he had been subject to their investigations on several other occasions. However, each time, they could never put together sufficient evidence to prove his involvement. Grayson had always carefully covered his tracks and given them very little to go on.

They arrived at the gallery and immediately entered through the door, giving anybody inside truly little time to acknowledge their arrival.

'Won't be a second,' came the call from the rear of the gallery. From the inside of the gallery's main window, Tate and Lena could see through the anterior room to where Jeremy Grayson was running a duster over the gilded frame of a large painting. Moments later, he looked up and upon recognising his new arrivals he hastened to the front of the gallery.

'Well, if it isn't the Dynamic Duo,' he quipped belittling those presently in his company. 'And pray tell,' he continued to mock, 'what good fortune brings two such wonderful characters to cross my path on this glorious summer's afternoon?'

'We were just passing and felt obliged to check nothing unforgiving had become of thee,' Tate retorted, returning the sarcasm. Jeremy stepped forward, strode straight passed his visitors, before taking a seat at his desk. Tate followed suit and took up a position directly opposite him. Lena stayed put, leaning back against the internal windowsill.

'I'll cut straight to the chase. You have obviously heard and seen in the media, reports of the recent disappearance of Caravaggio's "St Mary Magdalene in Ecstasy."' Jeremy showed no sign of being unnerved or perturbed at the mention of the stolen painting. Tate continued. 'We were wondering if you had heard any whispers, murmurs or anything on the grapevine of the said painting arriving on these shores.' Again, Jeremy held strong, secure behind the battlements of his desk.

'And what gives you the slightest inkling that if I had heard anything, I would share it with the two of you,' Grayson declared, pushing his chair away from the desk and back to the wall behind him to be as far from Tate as his current environment would afford him. He crossed his legs.

'I was just chancing my hand, that maybe you had turned over a new leaf and that you might for the first time do your civic duty and help an enquiry rather than hinder one.'

'I'll be sure to give you a call as and when I hear anything. Slight hitch though. I don't appear to have your direct dial number for some peculiar reason.' Tate reached into the rear pocket of his trousers, produced a card and placed it on the desk squarely in front of Grayson.

'Care if we take a look around?' stated Tate as he headed towards the main collection of works without waiting for a reply. Lena eased herself from the window ledge and silently followed Tate. Grayson remained in his chair. Tate was fully aware that the gallery was just a front and that many of Grayson's dealings happened behind closed doors. However, the gallery always held a strong collection of paintings and Grayson's reputation was held in high esteem within many of London's wealthier circles. Tate and Lena wandered amongst the paintings and the occasional sculpture or antique artifact. Occasionally they would stop and view a picture together. Every item was displayed impeccably and each faultlessly lit to captivate a potential buyer's attention.

'I have all the relevant paperwork for every acquisition on display,' came a voice from the antecedent room.

'I wouldn't doubt that for a minute. I'm quite sure you have all the I's dotted and the T's crossed too,' asserted Tate as he stopped alongside Lena at a portrait in oils of a 18th Century man. 'Do you have anything by Emile Moreau?' Tate enquired.

'I don't believe that's an artist I have come across. Which genre is she associated with?'

'He!' exclaimed Tate without turning from the painting and remaining with his back in the general direction of Grayson's reply.

'19th century French impressionism,' added Tate as both he and Lena turned and headed back towards the front of the gallery.'

'Not really my forte.' declared Grayson, still behind his desk. 'That is unless someone is specifically looking for one and they are happy to pay a finder's fee for the expertise needed in locating such a piece.' A smug grin appeared across his face. 'There are more and more buyers these days who, shall we say, know what they want, but are too impatient to wait for the required work to become available. They would rather pay a middleman to find and acquire the work for them.' He smiled once again. 'Legitimately of course.' Both Tate and Lena knew only too well what Grayson meant. 'As you are fully aware, these days the majority of any dealer's transactions generally happen at auction. More and more galleries are going on-line. Traditional galleries are only kept alive by wealthy imbecilic tourists who still seem quite happy to overpay for European art and only then to gain blagging rights amongst friends on their return home.'

Tate was hearing and learning nothing new. He had gotten a sense and a gut feeling from Grayson's reaction and response to his Moreau enquiry. If Grayson was aware of the transportation of the Caravaggio within the Moreau painting, he had shown little reaction when prompted. That did not however eliminate the fact that he might know more than he was letting on about the whereabouts of the Caravaggio. Or even having seen it, or more over, handled it. But no matter how hard they were to knock at the door, from past experience Tate knew Jeremy Grayson would never give up anything further.

'Do yourself and I a favour? If you see or hear anything of the Caravaggio, do the right thing, give me a call,' said Tate pointing at the business card on the desk before turning for the door. As he exited the gallery with Lena close behind, Jeremy Grayson had the final word.

'I'll be sure to call, but obviously it will be subject to my usual 15% handlers fee.'

Bruton Place, Mayfair

London, England

59

Jeremy Grayson watched the two detectives leave. He savoured having the last word. A noticeable smirk beamed from cheek to cheek. The self-congratulatory grin also substantiating his satisfaction that the two investigating officers had absolutely no idea whatsoever about the whereabouts of the Caravaggio or his involvement in its sale. However, Tate's probing of the Emile Moreau fascinated his overly inquisitive mind. He typed the name into Googles search engine. As the web page links filled the screen, the fifth result caught his attention. It was a recent listing from Thames Art and Antiques. He clicked on the link. Grayson skim read the web page in order to get a general overview of the content. The article on the Thames Art and Antiques site was a glossary of items sold at a recent auction. 'Rendezvous a la mer' by Emile Moreau was included in the itinerary.

'So is that how you got the painting into the country?'

Jeremy continued to ponder and speculate the coincidental factors currently presenting themselves. The date line fitted within the period of when the Caravaggio was stolen and to when he had first viewed the painting. He clicked through two more linked pages. As he scrolled through each page on the screen, his eyes scanned the information, ascertaining only the essential key facts. Within minutes he had started to draw his own conclusions. The dimensions recorded in the auction catalogue for the Moreau painting would easily allow for the concealment of the Caravaggio within its frame. The artist was only relatively recognisable for their work. Therefore, the painting would not draw too much attention and would probably not command too high an evaluation at auction. By the time Jeremy returned the computer to its home screen he was reasonably sure he had discovered the Caravaggio's route into the country. He afforded himself another self-approving smile.

Jeremy felt self-assured in knowing he was one step ahead of the game. He'd had an early set back when Hidetaka Yamamoto had been apparently murdered before a deal could be done on the Caravaggio. Still, he had confidence that the second name he had provided would almost definitely acquire the painting. Jeremy had procured several deals for Sir Christopher Roebuck in the past, all with incredibly positive outcomes. Sir Christopher would buy the painting for sure and he could collect his handlers fee without having really lifted a finger. The grin on his face was close to becoming permanently fixed at this rate. Feeling good about himself, Jeremy thought about locking up early. Before he did so, he clicked on the Universal News icon on his computers home page. The top stories appeared in windows on the screen. One news headline in particular caught his attention. He strained forward towards the screen, his eyeballs wide and accentuated. For some strange reason he felt being closer to the screen would make the story more believable and ultimately more tolerable. At first, he found he could not quite take on board what he was reading. He read the article over and over. Each time grasping at the facts as his mind began to fill in the blanks and draw a plausible conclusion. But surely this was just a coincidence.

The breaking headline read, 'Sir Christopher Roebuck found dead onboard St Katherine Docks mooring.'

His smile retracted.

Bethnal Green

London, England

60

The investigation board or as investigators liked to call it, 'Crazy Wall', was beginning to fill with an assemblage of photos, route plans, video stills, micro reports and an assortment of evidential 'Post It' notes. Big Boards had become common practise amongst investigation teams in recent years. These large visual aids are used to collate evidence and profile potential suspects. This enables investigators to analyse and evaluate the current progress and available facts of an investigation. The boards visual presence in an incident room allows for a greater chance of spotting non-obvious connections, the cross referencing of specific details and a greater ability in spotting patterns, trends and hidden links.

Harriet was adjusting and repositioning a number of the current evidential postings so as to collate them around a map of Central London which she had just secured to the middle of the wall. She also made room to systematically place photos and evidence from the second crime scene upon the board. She placed two map pins in the newly positioned map. One in the location of Canary Wharf, the other at St Katherine Docks.

As Harriet turned from the board, she glanced at the clock on the wall. Five to six. She noticed there was a hive of activity throughout the room. Everybody was busying themselves with jobs vital to moving the investigation forward. All would be aware that the smallest detail overlooked or mistakenly dismissed could well have a detrimental effect and return to haunt them during future investigations. As she continued to scan the room it was also evident from the hastened hustle and bustle that her 'Crew' were acutely aware of the approaching deadline. Individuals were collecting and collating any last-minute paperwork and paraphernalia alike for the imminent meeting. In the corner to her right, DS Richards was plugging the last of a series of cables into the back of a large flat screen.

The minute hand swept towards the top of the hour and Harriet's 'Crew' began to nestle into their usual positions, armed and ready with a plethora of writing utensils and drinking receptacles, Harriet took the briefest of moments to take stock of the situation. She allowed herself a few seconds of calm in order to maintain a grip on what was quickly becoming a major investigation. Harriet had always shown a strong ability to act accordingly when under pressure, both throughout her career in the military and on through her early years on the force. It was this capability amongst others, that had carved her expeditious pathway of promotion. Harriet took a deep breath and composed herself. She was ready for round two, her mind and spirit were in equanimity and she stood with a feeling of self-possession ready to address her team.

'Evening, Crew.' She paused briefly. She had used the address to gather everybody's attention and to allow those in the room a moment to settle. A quietude drifted throughout the room. The silence acknowledging the teams respect for their leader. When Harriet spoke again, she spoke with poise and self-confidence.

'The MO employed at the second crime scene is comparable to that of the first with four key markers.' She pointed to evidential posts on the wall to her side. 'The posing of the bodies, the use of a red blanket within each posing, the tattooed pigskin messages and the cocktail of Etorphine, Pancuronium Bromide and Potassium Chloride.' Harriet retrieved a sheet of paper from the file at her side.

'Toxicology reports confirm the presence of all three in the bloods of both victims and in both cases the cause of death was asphyxiation leading to cardiac arrest. A combination of the three chemicals is commonly used as an end-of-life cocktail on death row in the US.' Harriet waved the report in the direction of DC Evans, who was slouched astride the back of a swivel chair.

'Have a look into how easily you can obtain these three in the UK, will you Jake?' requested Harriet as the young Constable lent forward accepting the reports.

'See if HOLMES throws up any comparables with the trio of chemicals too, please Sar?'

'I'll start… a… new… search parameter,' replied Sarika, through a mouthful of ginger biscuit. She looked to her colleagues on either side, swallowed the remains, raised her eyebrows and grinned. Harriet noticed the biscuit packet tucked between the files on the desk. She crossed the room. Sarika shrank into her shoulders, cowering like a naughty schoolgirl who had just been caught doing something she knew she shouldn't have. Harriet simultaneously winked and smiled at her, before reaching past her and retrieving a biscuit from the packet. She took a bite, parked her bum on the edge of the desk and gesticulated with the remaining biscuit in her hand.

'So, as we detailed yesterday,' she took another nibble at the biscuit. 'The second victim, Sir Christopher Roebuck, was murdered and his body posed in a similar manner to our first victim, Hidetaka Yamamoto. Cause of death in both cases, chemical induced cardiac arrest. Wounds were inflicted, post-mortem, on both of the bodies. Happy has also confirmed the knife left at the second scene had an identical blade patterning to that used at the first? However, there is no evidence of the use of a surgical saw on the second victim. If the perp is indeed posing the bodies, there was most probably a significant reason not to fully remove the head in this instance.' Harriet moved back across the room to the investigation board and used the remaining biscuit to point at photographs from both crime scenes.

'Why remove the knife from the first crime scene but leave it at the second? Is the knife significant to the posing of the bodies?'

'Maybe there is some underlying meaning in using a particular knife? If we presume the posing of the bodies is premeditated,' proclaimed DC Evans, 'then we could be led to presume that our Un-Sub had planned subsequent crimes before committing the first. Therefore, knowing that the knife would be consequential to the lasting image of the second posed body, he would feel the need to use it at the first crime scene but would need to take it with him when he departed.'

'And its only used to mutilate the bodies, post-mortem,' added George Quinn before turning to DC Thompson. 'Looks like you've got a reprieve from landfill duties, Kiddo.' DC Greg Thompson acknowledged his senior officer with a nodding of his head alongside a silent smile. Harriet smiled too but was quick to supress George's humorous vein before it accentuated.

'So, the posing of the bodies is our common denominator,' she continued. 'There are no other apparently obvious links between the two victims apart from their celebrity status in the media and public eye.'

'And they are both stinking rich,' quipped George once again.

'Money as we know is more than often the underlying factor, but there just seems to be something more sinister at play here,' stated Harriet, taking control of the room once more. 'There also has to be some fundamental reasoning behind the use of the red blanket at both scenes.' She looked across to DC Andy Stevens. 'Any luck finding anything noteworthy about the cloth?'

'Not really, Ma'am, General fabric. Common place in the textiles industry. Used in the manufacture of curtains. Can be purchased off the roll at your average High Street Haberdashery store.' Harriet turned to the board once more and took a few moments to elucidate the evidence. Whilst trying to build a picture in her mind, she let her thought process wander. She scrutinised the board looking for something to provide that pivotal first connection. She remained with her back to the room but spoke.

'Where are we at present with the booking of the second location, Jake?' DS Evans span the swivel chair through 90 degrees to address Harriet's new position, then sat up and withdrew a file from his lap. He opened the cover.

'Much the same as the first. Booking made through Sleepezy B&B using a Hotmail account. All completed on an untraceable pre-paid phone and payment provided through an online virtual card as before. However, a different Hotmail and booking name this time. A Mr T. Bigot.' Harriet turned back to directly address the 'Crew'.

'The posing of the bodies, the leaving of specific items and now the names, which to me seem awfully particular.' She momentarily paused for thought, 'Why not just use Smith or Jones? DC Thompson. Look into the signatures, would you? M. Stom and T. Bigot. See what you can find. Look for a connection.'

'No probs, Ma'am,' beamed Greg as he looked around the room at his colleagues for recognition. His first investigative lead from the boss had finally come his way.

The bigger picture and possible links were starting to ignite electrical currents within Harriet's brain. She remained staring at the board. Nerve cells began to transmit information to other nerve cells and a transition of information was set into motion as the individual cells started to talk to each other.

'Sarika, feed "Red Cloth", "Stom and Bigot" into HOLMES and see what comes up, will you? Iain, take a look into both Hidetaka and Sir Christopher's interests outside their usual social circles. Jake, check with the owners of each property. See if they noticed anything out of the ordinary. Maybe something in an unusual location. Show them photos of the scenes after the bodies have been removed. The slightest detail might be important. If it makes them uncomfortable, I don't care, press them, I want to know. George, where are we currently with the CCTV at the first scene?'

'A white van captured arriving at the premises on the previous afternoon and not seen again until it leaves on the following morning, has plates which do not match the registered vehicle,' replied George, leaning in his usual position against a filing cabinet. 'There is also no record of any resident within the building registered as the owner of a similar vehicle. Probably stolen with false plates. This could well be our Un-Subs entry and exit.' George lent forward and handed Harriet a series of photographs. 'We have also compiled footage from several street cameras showing an individual of a similar build to Mr Yamamoto, wearing the rudimentary baseball hat over the eyes disguise. We can follow this individuals movements from the platform of the DLR station at Island Gardens to the camera at the East end of the street. The individual is not seen to exit the street at either end. Our best guess would be this is Yamamoto.'

'Thanks George,' Harriet said before turning to her second in command, 'Ok Iain, time to share the footage you walked me through earlier with the rest of the team.' DS Richards ran the footage he had collated from the cameras around St Katherine Docks and emphasised the same key pointers he had accentuated to Harriet prior to the meeting.

'Uniform are currently searching Tower Hill and Tower Gateway stations for any signs of discarded clothing etc. Next step is to liaise with TFL to continue viewing footage for the suspects plausible exit point.'

'Use CIO's if necessary, Iain. I want every possible angle and camera covered,' declared Harriet. CIO's or Civilian Investigation Officers are often used to work alongside sworn officers to gather and document evidence. They are also used to obtain public statements and view the hours of camera footage frequently used in criminal proceedings.

Harriet turned her attention to the board one more time. She swept her hand across the evidential posts, stopping at the pair of photographs showing the messages tattooed onto pigskin. She unpinned the pictures and holding them in her hands, she read out the words.

'Andy, what more did you learn about the lyrics?' DS Stevens shifted through some paperwork on his desk.

'Both sets of words are from the 1976 Neptune's Finger album entitled "Beyond the Waves". The ones found,' he paused to choose his words cautiously, 'with the first victim, are from the fourth verse of a song called "The Pilgrim and the Mariner. The second set are in a later verse from the same song.' DS Stevens handed Harriet a copy of the lyrics which she directly pinned to the wall. 'What it means or refers to, makes absolutely no sense to me. But according to our old friends at Google and WikipediA, it's a concept album. Which apparently means the songs have a common theme based around a central narrative. The lyrics of the individual tracks supposedly tell the story of a fallen black angel who under the guise of a pilgrim travels across barren lands and raging seas in search of the lost souls of sinners, before delivering them to the underworld and in return seeking forgiveness for his own misdoings.' DS Stevens continued to shake his head in disbelief, 'Beats me.'

'Did you get any hits from HOLMES when you fed it Neptune's Finger, Sar?' A few giggles and whispers spread through the room before Sarika could answer.

'Just one link. A suicide in Leicester a couple of years back. A teenager slashed his wrists. The individual in question had a history of self-harming. Left a suicide note containing the lyrics from another Neptune's Finger song called Flight to Nirvana. Apparently, it's on an album called "After the Flood."' Harriet did not respond. She was deep in thought as she played something over in her mind. Eventually she looked up.

'Thanks Sarika. I too, am none the wiser. I am also finding it difficult understanding the significance of why Neptune's Finger lyrics are tattooed on a pigskin. But hopefully I know a man who might just be able to shed some light on the situation.'

'Got an ex-boyfriend who's a butcher, Ma'am?' Harriet did not even contemplate who the jovial question had come from.

'No. Just one who's overly affectionate about music.'

31st May 1606

Rome, Italy

61

Signora Antognetti had twice re-visited Michelangelo's lodgings to collect as many of the items he had insisted he would need to take with him on his departure from Rome. She had gathered items such as clothing, a few personal effects, along with his paints and other art materials. She had also searched high and low throughout his living quarters and the small area he used as a studio to muster as much money as she could find. Earlier, before leaving her home, Michelangelo had revealed the location of several secret squirrelling holes throughout his apartment. He had used them to conceal monies he had been paid for the commissions he had carried out across Rome in previous years. As she hurried herself through the darkening streets of the capital's unsavoury districts, Signora Antognetti once again found herself constantly looking over her shoulder. She tried to shrug off the sense of being followed, the nagging suspicion in her head that she was being watched and the constant feeling that at any moment someone was going to pull her deeper into the darkness. She was more aware and anxious of her vulnerability due to the large amount of money she had hidden about her person. Her mind tormented her with gruesome scenarios where opportunist thieves would leave her barely alive in the gutter, whilst fleeing into the night with much more money than they could have ever of imagined from simply robbing a common whore. She also imagined the outcomes of running into Ranuccio's brothers or an encounter with the strong arm of the law.

After what seemed like an eternity, she finally reached the street where she resided. A sense of euphoria and mission accomplished revived her senses and gave her a sense of security once again. She took the final strides to her front door with determination and a renewed vigour. However, after closing the door on the figments of her imagination, she had to return to reality and check she had in fact turned the key and entered through what was indeed her own front door. The scene she had encountered on the previous two evenings had evaporated. The room before her contained no drunk slumped across the table and no longer smelt of cheap grog and that of a five-day unwashed man. Instead, the room had been returned to its previous fastidious manner. The empty bottles and wine dreged glasses which marred the table had now been replaced with a single vase of dried flowers at its centre.

Movement to her right deflected her attention. Michelangelo stood at the sink in the kitchen area. His appearance and demeanour were in complete contrast to those of the man she had left behind only hours earlier. Gone was the washed-out man, gone was the pungent odour of stale alcohol and gone was the negativity of earlier situations. Instead, she had returned home only to be confronted by a friend she had seldomly encountered before. Michelangelo appeared to have pulled himself from his drunken stupor, neatened his appearance and tidied away the remnants of the past few days. He stood with his back to her. His focus remained on the task at hand. After a few moments he noticed her presence and turned to confront her. As he did so, Signora Antognetti caught sight of something in his hand. He turned towards her brandishing a knife as a devilish smile spread across his face. Taken aback, she stumbled and steadied her backwards momentum by grasping at the rear of a nearby chair. As Michelangelo continued to smile, the hand hidden to the far side of his torso rose to marry the blade. The mischievous smile intensified as his fingers opened to reveal a half-peeled carrot.

'I thought I might prepare something for our last night together.'

Walthamstow
London, England

62

Ashley Denning smiled. She was paid to smile. A smile that was worth millions. Over the years, her smile had earned her Worldwide fame, high regard within the modelling and fashion industries and a fortune way beyond her wildest dreams. And all she had to do was smile.

Today, Ashley was smiling in front of a Norwegian glacial waterfall. The mass of the cobalt blue glacial ice shelf rose behind her from the sea to the skyline. To her left, a waterfall of glacial melt water cascaded from the summit of its leading edge. As its deluge plummeted into the turquoise waters below, sprays thrown back from the sea, refracted with the early morning sunlight to form a multitude of arcing rainbows. Rainbows appearing and disappearing as they danced in and out of the over pouring waters.

Ashley threw one of her broad trademark smiles exposing her perfect dazzling white teeth. Along with the smile, she had recently had them insured for fifty million dollars. Some say her smile had become more famous than that of the Mona Lisa. Her smile beamed and her teeth glistened as the light reflected back from the frozen waters. Ashley raised a small dark blue tube in her left hand. As it became level with her face, she spoke.

'Let Glacial Toothpaste give you the sparkle your teeth deserve.' Ashley tipped her head slightly to one side and held her pose. She knew all too well, that someone in visual effects would later be adding a sparkling glint to that radiant smile.

'Cut!' came the shout from the other side of the room. 'Let's break for ten. Retouch on hair and make-up please.' The glacier behind Ashley disappeared and the screen stage turned green once again.

Ashley stepped down from the small platform and crossed to a high-backed stool. She was hastily followed by two younger women armed with brushes, spray cans and pencils.

'Give me a second, would you girls? I could do with a couple of minutes of my own space.' The girls stopped and looked at each other. Not knowing what to do, they stood still. Ashley decided against the stool and instead headed for a door marked 'EXIT'. She hit the crash bar and stepped out into a small alley. From the back pocket of her jeans she withdrew a vaping pen. She leant against the wall and inhaled on the pen. As she relished the flavour of bubble-gum, she exhaled and gave herself the tiniest of smiles. Glacial Toothpaste and a 50-million-dollar smile. If the eyes of the world were to see her now.

'*The filthy, stinking, toking vape head*'. She smiled, smirked and vaped once more.

She was just thinking about returning inside to re-join the set when her other back pocket began to ring. Retrieving her phone, she retook her position against the wall.

'Jeremy, darling! How are you? It's been a while since we last talked!'

'I'm fine thank you,' came the reply. 'Business has been steady. My client list has grown a bit. All helps to keep the pennies rolling in.' Ashley put one foot up against the wall and hugged her bent knee. Her mobile safely tucked under her chin. She had used Jeremy's services on several occasions. He had secured deals on a number of works to further add to her growing collection of feminine portraits. Amongst those he had procured were an eighteenth-century Dutch portrait of 'The Woman in an Orange Headscarf', a black and white bromide print of Audrey Hepburn by Cecil Beaton and a known reproduction copy of the Mona Lisa used during the filming of a French crime drama. A collection Ashley could now readily afford after a long and successful career fuelled by modelling campaigns for major hair and cosmetic brands.

The door next to Ashley opened and a blonde head appeared, looking left, then right before spotting Ashley. 'They are calling for you back on set and we have still to do your hair and make-up,' declared the peroxide dependent makeup artist.

'Tell them I'll be there in five minutes, would you.' The blonde pursed her lips and nodded, having spotted the vaping pen in Ashley's trailing hand. The door closed and Ashley pushed away from the wall before looking up and down the narrow alley. It was often used as a cut through between several of the sound stages. Ashley wanted to be sure she was not overheard. 'I do hope you are calling with news on the Gentileschi?'

'I fear I am not,' Jeremy reluctantly replied. Jeremy had been working on a lead to acquire a recently re-discovered self-portrait by 17th Century Italian artist Artemisia Gentileschi. Ashley had a passion not only for her work but also for her recognition as a pioneering female artist. She had aspired for some time to own one of the artists paintings.

'Nonetheless, I do believe you may well have an even stronger interest in another painting I have been asked to handle.' Before Jeremy had even finished his sentence, the fifty-million-dollar smile started to reach cheek to cheek across Ashley's face.

'Oh my God, you haven't? How? No, you've got to be jesting me?' Ashley moved along the alley and stood with her back against the door she had exited from. She needed to ensure she was not disturbed again. Ashley had no need to second guess Jeremy. She knew exactly which painting he was referring to. Ashley squatted to her knees and exhaled long and slowly. She needed to calm herself and contain her eagerness before she spoke again.

'Is the Caravaggio in this country?'

'Yes!'

Ashley held her phone away from her ear. She inhaled a long deep breath through her nose and held it briefly, before slowly allowing it to escape her mouth.

'Can you arrange a viewing?'

'I have already set the wheels in motion. As soon as I was offered the chance to handle the Caravaggio, I knew immediately who would desire a once in a lifetime chance to own such a revered piece.' Ashley no longer cared if anyone was watching and silently fist pumped the air. She took a few seconds to contain herself once again.

'I am at this moment at a loss for words. I cannot even start to think about how to thank you for offering me the chance to purchase such a painting ahead of all your other clientele.' The words escaped her mouth in an explosive rambled orgy. There was no self-control. Jeremys response was simple.

'You are always first on my list!'

Bethnal Green
London, England

63

Harriet paced about the SIO office. With her head slightly bowed, she tapped the index finger of each hand gently against her temples. She often did this when she could steal a few precious moments alone. It helped her clear her mind and provide an open pathway to cognition. She continued in this semi-meditative state, only pausing occasionally to look through the glass curtain walling of her office, as her team continued to busy themselves in the room beyond. It had been almost two weeks now since the discovery of the first victim. Although everyone was working a number of strong leads and numerous lines of enquiry, they still had not uncovered that substantial game changing piece of evidence. The one single break needed to prise an investigation wide open. Iain's CCTV footage analysis had momentarily opened that door, although it now hung in the wind whilst they trawled through hour upon hour of TFL footage looking for the suspects exit point. So far, HOLMES had not thrown out anything comparable or even worthy of further investigation. Evidence from the forensic lab strongly suggested the crimes were the work of a single suspect. The line of inquiry into the Sleepezy B&B bookings had hit a stone wall. The Un-sub's knowledge, understanding and ability to hide their identity in a wall of technology, left no trail to follow through the internet or on-line banking systems. They were a ghost haunting the investigation, hiding deep in the shadows of cyberspace. The tattooed pigskin messages were Harriet's best chance of turning over that stone of perpetual hope. However, that meant she would need to contact someone she had not spoken to in an awfully long time.

Harriet removed her mobile phone from her pocket and continued to pace the room. She tapped the phones screen against her puckered lips as she continued to mull over her situation. Her memory flashed back to her early years on the force and her time at the MET training college. She had been fast tracked through training along with others with a military background. It was during this period and the ensuing years as a new recruit, she had met and formed a strong physical and emotional relationship with a fellow trainee. They had shared several years together before the pressures of the force tore them apart.

It was this very person that she knew only too well was her best chance of unlocking the meaning behind the lyrics tattooed on the pigskins. She felt a sense of anxiety balling in the pit of her stomach. Making contact would open the door to emotions and feelings she had locked away many years ago. There were skeletons in the cupboard of which she was anxious not to unleash into her world once again. Although the reasons not to, outweighed the reasons to do, Harriet knew it was a phone call she had to make. She needed to pull herself out of the world of speculation and back into the reality of the presence.

She found herself perched on the corner of her desk, but had no recollection of doing so, or of how long she had been sitting there. She was still tapping her phone thoughtfully against her lips. Without giving it any further thought, Harriet opened her mobiles phone book. She had kept the number. Hell, it was still in her speed dial list. She hoped the calls recipient had kept their number too. She hit the dial button and waited for the call to connect. She nervously drummed her fingers on the surface of the desk. The call rang for what seemed like an age before finally transferring to answerphone. She listened to the pre-recorded announcement. A small sigh of relief escaped her upon the realisation that the contact had kept the same number. She swallowed, composed herself and waited for the beep.

'Hi… This is Harriet Stone. It's been quite a while… Listen, I hope you don't mind me calling after all this time… I'm currently working a high-profile case and we've hit a stumbling block with one particular piece of evidence. You were the first person who came to mind, who may be able to offer some clarity on the situation. Totally understand if you're too busy… or the timing is just wrong. Anyways… would appreciate it… if you feel you can. You can contact me 24/7 on this number. Maybe talk soon. Bye for now.'

She pushed the disconnect button. Leaning back slightly, Harriet ran her fingers through her hair. She exhaled a long slow relieving breath, before easing from her perched position and heading straight to the lower desk drawer and the bottle of Grey Goose.

Southbank
London, England

64

Lena had spent the best part of the morning with a MET surveillance team. Under the guise of a utilities maintenance van they had been monitoring the comings and goings at Grayson's gallery for the past couple of days. Pictures had been captured of anyone entering or leaving the property and in turn scrutinised for possible suspects and known acquaintances. So far the operation had not proven fruitful. There had been nothing suspicious to report. Grayson had arrived around 9am each day, left promptly at 5pm and no further activity had occurred overnight. They hoped their phone surveillance would be far more rewarding.

It had been around Midday when Tate slipped unnoticed into Bruton Place and discreetly joined the team in the van. The majority of his morning had been consumed in another lengthy case review with Moretti. He had then collected take-out lunches for Lena and the two MSO's. As he handed them around and the sandwich cartons were torn open, he had learnt of another morning of inactivity and the justification of further surveillance had been discussed. Tate and Lena had then remained with the surveillance officers for a further two hours before leaving them to continue their reconnaissance alone.

After retreating from the van, they avoided the mob of late-afternoon tourists by taking the lesser frequented and quieter surroundings of Berkeley Street as they headed South towards the parks. They stopped at a coffee house to grab a coffee-to-go. Tate taking his usual sugary caffeine bomb, whilst Lena was much more conservative with a flat white. Whilst they waited for the barista to brew their order, Tate and Lena sat on two bar stools at the counter end. The heat from the afternoon sun radiated through the shops front windows creating a warming comfort alongside the aroma of dark roasted coffee.

'I don't believe he is not in some way involved,' announced Lena, voicing her opinion. 'If the Caravaggio is being moved on the black market, Grayson will be sure to have his dirty little fingers in the pie.'

'We both know the way the man works,' Tate stressed as he swivelled the head of his stool so as to directly address Lena. 'And we are both fully aware that we have missed out by a cat's whisker of linking his involvement to several cases in the past.'

Lena interrupted. 'But we never get anything substantial to convict. He's always got someone, something or someway to cover his ass.'

'We have come close on a couple of occasions. One day Jeremy Grayson will get his comeuppance.'

'Yeah, and I hope to be there to enjoy every minute of it,' interrupted Lena once again as she rubbed her thumb across the nails of her other fingers. Tate noticed her habituation, but he was not surprised. Lena was fanatical about her nails. He diverted his attention from Lena's hands and glanced across the counter in the direction of the barista machines. It looked like their order was next in line to be brewed.

'If someone is indeed looking to move the Caravaggio, then the whispers in the backrooms of the art world would most probably have led the seller in Grayson's direction. He is, as we know, recognised within certain circles to be the go-to for potential buyers.' The steam wand of the coffee station behind them screamed as the barista purged the wand before steaming a pitcher of milk. It drew Tate's attention once more before he continued. 'If the word on the street is someone is seeking to move the Caravaggio then our next port of call is…'

'Tommy. Of course,' imparted Lena, raising her hands in resignation.

'If people are talking, there will be rumours and gossip disseminating within the art community and Tommy's ears will be pricked and flapping in the wind.'

'Triple expresso americano and a flat white,' called the barista from the far end of the counter. Both Tate and Lena hopped down from their bar stools and headed to collect their take-outs. Tate immediately removing his coffees lid to add an unhealthy amount of sugar.

Ten minutes later, coffees in hand, Tate and Lena were casually strolling through Green Park in the direction of Buckingham Palace. Formerly known as Upper St James Park, it was first enclosed by Charles II in 1668. Its lack of formal planting and hence its name is rumoured to have been derived from the Queen's order to remove all flowers after catching her husband picking blooms for another woman. In the 1800s it was a common haunt for highwaymen and a notorious duelling ground.

Tate and Lena casually chatted as they continued to stroll down the Queens Walk on the East side of the park. The North to South path had been laid out in 1730 for Queen Caroline, wife of George II.

'Are you still planning on getting away early this afternoon?' Tate questioned as he stopped to admire the façade of Bridgwater House, one of the many grand houses that lined the parks edge.

'Yes. If that's ok with you,' replied Lena turning to stop alongside Tate.

'This house was once home to one of the greatest private art collections in the world including the majority of the Orleans collection,' mused Tate. 'When I was around eleven or twelve, my father took my mother, brother and I on holiday to Edinburgh. It was there that I first saw part of the Orleans collection on loan to the National Gallery of Scotland.'

'You had some real exciting holidays whilst growing up,' Lena mocked as she nudged Tate with her elbow.

'If I had gone to Butlins, I may have ended up being the host of a dodgy gameshow on regional TV. I'm pretty happy the way things turned out. How about you?' smiled Tate, lifting his coffee towards his lips.

'Mostly winter holidays, skiing in the Dolomites. With my parents running a hotel business, they were always busy during the summer months. There was a girl of the same age who lived across the road in our village. So I did go to Sardinia with her and her parents a couple of times.' Tate pointed with his cup in the direction they had been walking and they continued.

'So what have you got planned for the weekend?'

'Oh nothing special really. Just booked a little bolthole to spend the weekend with a friend.' They stepped over a single chain barrier onto the lawn and began to meander their way through the assemblage of deckchairs and picnic blankets, as Londoners took advantage of the pleasant afternoon weather.

'I'm happy to see if Tommy's around, and if so, find out if he has heard anything which might be of use. So if you want, feel free to scoot off. I'm going to cut through St James's to Birdcage Walk,' said Tate, throwing his now empty cup in a nearby bin, before offering his empty hand to Lena in a gesture to do the same for her.

'I'm not quite finished yet. I'll take mine with me.'

'Is it not cold by now?'

'Waste not, want not,' Lena retorted before turning and heading in the direction of Constitution Hill.

'See you Monday,' she called out as she threw a look over her shoulder and was gone.

Tate cut through St James's Park as he had intended. He crossed Blue

Bridge, stopping halfway to admire the view across St James's Lake to Duck Island at its east end. As he was about to turn to go, a pair of Pelicans flew in overhead. He watched the birds glide elegantly across the water's surface before landing on the shoreline, where more pelicans and waterfowl basked in the sun and hung their wings out to dry. The Pelicans have been resident at St James's Park for 400 years since they were presented as a gift from the Russian Ambassador to King Charles II.

Tate continued to watch the birds. He was in no hurry. He took a moment to allow himself to bask in the glory of the afternoons good weather and hang his own stresses and strains out to dry. He allowed time to stop. The clock kept ticking and the world kept spinning, but for the briefest of moments Tate's reality paused and he enjoyed the simplicity of his present surroundings. Tate believed it important to find time each day to gather his thoughts, along with the freedom and space to free his mind. His early morning swims with Jonathan were a great way to cleanse the mind at the dawning of each new day. Tate also swore by the theory that taking time out where possible for lunch, helps the mind be more creative during the latter hours of the afternoon. His hypothesis was also heavily weighted by his well-known passion for good food.

It was a good ten minutes before he re-joined the procession of bodies crossing the Blue Bridge. From there he continued along one of the main arterial paths that cut through the park towards the Southeast corner. In stark contrast to the borderless lawns of Green Park, the abundant flower beds of St James's were in full bloom. The smell of Geraniums and Marigolds filled the air with a bouquet of summer fragrances. Couples sat on benches and children pulled at their mother's arms as they strained towards the lakeside to feed the ducks. Cyclists and roller skaters bobbed and weaved along the paths and Tate sauntered amongst them, enjoying a few final minutes of contemplation.

When he exited the park at the junction of Birdcage Walk and Horse Guards Road, he felt liberated. He continued along Great George Street, past the Mahatma Gandhi statue, through Parliament Square and onto Westminster Bridge. Tate was nearing the centre of the bridge when his phone began to ring and vibrate in his pocket. As he went to retrieve the phone, he spotted Tommy on the South Bank footpath. Knowing that Tommy was his immediate priority and not recognising the caller's number, he declined the call, re-pocketed the phone and let the call divert to answerphone. Tate continued across the bridge and descended the steps to the riverside pathway below.

Tommy squatted on the edge of a short-legged drummers' stool. To his side were eight aerosol cans in an old metal milk carrier and a wooden box containing an assortment of stencils and carded shapes. He was encircled by a small crowd of onlookers who watched intently as he sprayed an aerosol across the painting on the floor before him. He worked quickly, making definitive sweeps with the aerosol, whilst using the edge of a piece of card or a stencil to shield or mask an area as he worked. Upon removing the card, precise horizontal or vertical marks could clearly be seen, as an image of the buildings across the river began to materialise.

Tommy had two preferred locations from where he liked to work. The view from where he now sat, across the Thames to Westminster Bridge with the Houses of Parliament and Big Ben was his favourite. His other frequented patch was Jubilee Park, painting the view of the London Eye and Big Ben. He had found over the years that he could shift more copies of these views to the tourists than many of London's other familiar sights.

He had graduated from the London School of art, but shortly after, he had gotten caught up in the South Bank's Street art scene. His passion for graffiti had caused him to drift away from mainstream art. There were strong rumours that he was one of Banksy's long-term underground crew.

Tommy continued to work, constantly swapping aerosols and stencils, as the picture revealed itself. The crowd looked on in awe. Some moved around the circle to get a better view of how the artist was working, whilst others were happy just to stand back and look on in amazement. With one last flourish of aerosol, he added his moniker to the corner of the painting and the circle of onlookers responded with a ripple of applause.

Tate had stood back unnoticed and continued to do so as the crowd dispersed. Tommy chatted with a few of the bystanders who had remained and sold a couple of pictures he had completed earlier in the day. As he turned to thank his final customer, he noticed the figure stood by the wall.

'Tate! My man. How you doing?' Tate walked forward offering his hand.

'Good to see you too Tommy. Things are looking prosperous,' declared Tate as they shook hands.

'Can't complain. London seems to be awash with tourists who seem happy to part with their cash.' Tommy busied himself, packing his materials into a small box trolley. 'I was wondering when you might show up.' Tate shrugged his shoulders in response. 'Come on, Man,' quipped Tommy, 'There's a stolen Caravaggio in the country.' He placed a couple of paintings on top of the box and pulled the trolley over to the wall where Tate had been previously standing. Tate joined him. Tommy knew all too well the reasoning behind Tate's impromptu visit. 'I'm guessing you want to know what I've heard?'

'That would be good.'

'Usual agreement?' Tommy quizzed as he looked to his left and right along the walkway. Tate reached into his pocket and handed Tommy a twenty-pound note. Tommy slipped the note into the front pocket of his jeans.

'Apparently, the painting was smuggled into the country inside another painting.' Tate nodded in agreement. 'The word is that the Caravaggio is here to be sold. Grayson has supposedly been asked to provide five potential buyers. Unfortunately two of the stupid idiots,' Tommy stopped and smirked, 'Hidetaka Yamamoto and Sir Christopher Roebuck have gone and gotten themselves murdered before they even got an opportunity to see it.' Tate listened intently. The information Tommy gave him and how he managed to obtain it never ceased to amaze him. 'By all accounts, that cute model Ashley Denning has bragged she is hoping to buy it and Anatoli Nikolaev, you know the one who owns the F1 Racing team, is allegedly up to view it. There is no word at present on who the fifth one is though.'

'And you're pretty confident this is legit,' said Tate, knowing too well that information Tommy had provided in the past had always panned out well.

'Unfortunately, or maybe fortunately for some, people just can't keep their mouths shut. You know the old saying, "if I tell you something, will you promise not to tell a soul." Never happens. People can't help but blab.' Tommy smiled at Tate who again nodded in agreement and smiled in return. 'Last thing I've got is a name. "Dr Valentine". Apparently, it's the geezer who's trying to sell the painting.' Tate's smile broadened. Bingo. He had gotten what he came for. Tommy had provided once again. Tate had found the link he needed. A lead that would inevitably lead back to Jeremy Grayson.

Tommy had provided a name that could well be conceivable. But strangely, not the same name Tate had obtained from his earlier investigations at the auction house.

Markham Square, Chelsea
London, England

65

Ashley Denning exited the Uber cab and watched it drive away. As the car rounded the corner, she removed the sunglasses, wig and coat as she had been instructed and stuffed them into the oversized shopping bag slung across her shoulder. She had carefully chosen each garment of her attire so as to draw as little attention as possible. As a child growing up in a nondescript area of East London, Ashley had drawn little attention at first. Just another run-of-the-mill school kid. A chance encounter with a model agency receptionist whilst hanging out with teenage friends at a local shopping mall, plucked her from obscurity and a long and lucrative career beckoned. Unlike so many teenagers who were scouted for their ample cleavage, Ashley had matured into a beautiful young woman who stood out from the crowd simply for her unparalleled natural beauty and symmetrically proportioned features. Add to this a radiant smile and impeccable teeth, Ashley had it all to give. And give it all was precisely what she did for the next twenty years. The contracts kept coming and Ashley kept working, knowing very well that every model has their moment and someday a new face would come along to take her crown.

The Square in which Ashley now stood was in stark contrast to her childhood pastures. Markham Square, London, SW3 is one of the most sought-after residential garden squares in Chelsea. Built in the 1830s adjacent to the Kings Road, it allowed its residents convenient access to the areas prestigious boutiques, restaurants and cafes. It soon became one of the most desirable addresses in London. Its Georgian period town houses were built to be spacious and comfortable. They were typically built over four floors affording their affluent occupants the ability to accommodate their staff on the upper floor. The lower ground floor was then often used for kitchens and other domestic duties, thus leaving the middle two floors as the main living area. Large sash windows surrounded by ornate iron railings dominate the main facades. In today's housing market, many of the properties ringing its perimeter can frequently be seen to fetch in excess of four to five million pounds.

As the last rays of the evenings fading sun dropped behind the properties on the squares Southwest corner, Ashley crossed the road to the centre of the square. Feeling a slight sense of diffidence, she looked up and down the street. She turned, took a brief moment to survey the empty windows of the properties directly behind her, before disposing of her unwanted attire amongst the shrubbery of its central garden. She leaned one hand on the surrounding railings and a pair of collared doves on the grass caught her attention. One appeared to be bowing its head on every other step, as it walked towards the other bird. It reminded Ashley of a royal subject walking towards a monarch. What she assumed to be the male bird continued to bow as the female bird simply turned her head in a sign of complete disinterest. She smiled to herself.

The power of femininity.

Ashley had spent years and sometimes large sums of money to surround herself with works of art associated with the feminine form. No one particular style. Just beautiful paintings of beautiful women. As she continued to watch the flirtatious dove, she allowed her mind to wander and wonder.

'If all goes to plan tonight,' she thought to herself. *'I could soon be the privileged owner of a Caravaggio.'*

The 'St Mary Magdalene' would take pride of place amongst her private collection at her country house in Kent. She was imagining it hanging between the 'Penitent Magdalene' and the 'Magdalen Weeping' when the collared doves took flight. The beating of their wings snapped her back into the present moment. Ashley looked up from where the birds had once been and realised she had been daydreaming. She hoped it had not been for too long. She often tended to drift off for minutes at a time. She turned and strode back to where the taxi had first dropped her off. The house in front of her was No.16. The property she sought was on the other side of the square. Not only had the doctor told her how and where to discard her disguise, she was also specifically instructed not to loiter on the street. As Ashley hastily made her way around the North end of the square, she thought back to the telephone call she had received from Dr. Valentine. After having been invited to view the Caravaggio, the doctor had been extremely specific about her movements prior to viewing the painting. The doctor had insisted that she was to leave her penthouse apartment on the Pontifex Wharf and take the 344 bus from Southwark Street to Clapham Junction. From there, she was to board the London Overground to West Brompton and then take an Uber cab to Markham

Square. She was to arrive no later than 8.30pm.

Ashley checked the Vacheron Constantin on her wrist. *8.20pm.* Bang on time. She turned the corner and checked the house numbers once more.

'30 and 31. Just up here on the left,' she mused.

Moments later Ashley stood at the steps to No.35. She admired the black front door set in the stucco of the ground floor and the black railings embellishing the brick façade of the upper floors. The white cornicing of the Georgian windows adding to the overall elegance of the property. Once more she contemplated.

'I wonder what field of expertise the doctor specializes in. This isn't your average GP's house?'

Ashley removed her phone from the back pocket of her jeans and used her selfie camera to check her appearance before switching off the phone as instructed. She walked up to the front door and without hesitating she rang the bell. No sooner had she done so when the door opened.

'Hi. I'm Ashley,' she proclaimed. 'I'm here to see Dr. Valentine.'

'I am Dr. Valentine. Miss Denning, please come in.'

Ashley, surprised by the doctor's appearance, felt a comforting smile materialise.

Markham Square, Chelsea

London, England

66

The Narcissus led Ashley through the entrance hall and into a large reception room furnished to accommodate high-end modern-day living. The room had high ceilings and still bore the cornicing, sculpted coving, ceiling roses and ornate lighting of a Georgian period house.

'Please, have a seat,' offered the Narcissus in the guise of Dr Valentine. Ashley chose a deep, low backed Italian style single armchair positioned opposite a matching twin sofa. She sat. The Narcissus remained standing in the centre of the room.

As Ashley took in her new surroundings, her gaze continually reverted to Dr Valentine. She could not help but notice that the doctor was incredibly attractive. However, the Narcissus was acutely aware that Miss Denning was trying to unsuccessfully divert her eyes. The Narcissus spoke to break the unease.

'Jeremy Grayson informs me that you have quite a collection of feminal influenced works. Be it a female subject or the artist themselves being feminine.'

'Yes, you could say I have a penchant for the celebration of womanhood and the female form,' Ashley declared, 'My celebrity status has enabled me to purvey the empowerment of women and my collection is a reminder to myself.'

The Narcissus heard the words but paid little attention.

Now was not the time for small talk.

'According to Jeremy Grayson,' said the Narcissus, eager to move the conversation forward, 'you were the obvious choice for a potential buyer considering the paintings subject matter.' Ashley felt a wave of self-satisfaction flow over her body. Ashley was never smug. But she liked the fulfilment of being recognised.

'Jeremy has been such a darling over the years,' continued Ashley, relishing the small talk. 'He has located works to satisfy my desires and offered me first come, first served privileges when the occasional, shall we say, out of the ordinary work becomes available. Between you and I, I think Jeremy also has a little soft spot for me. He's such a sweetie really.'

The Narcissus was tiring of the chitchat. Looking past Ashley at the clock on the wall, the Narcissus decided to waste no more time.

'So, let's get down to the reason why you are really here! The "St Mary Magdalene."' Ashley stood up from the chair. The Narcissus could sense the delirium building behind Ashley's eyes as she struggled to contain her composure.

'Is she here? In this room?' Her eyes darted from one side of the room to the other.

'Had the Caravaggio been staring her in the face before she had taken the offer of a seat?' Ashley was suddenly aware of her avidity and its accompanying behaviour. She took a deep breath.

'If you would like to follow me into the dining room, I shall bring the Caravaggio through for you to view.' The Narcissus motioned towards a pair of double doors at the far end of the room. Ashley moved forward and joining the Narcissus, they walked together towards the doors. As the Narcissus reached for the handle, Ashley leant forward and stopped the Narcissus's hand.

'Before you open those doors, doctor. I must ask. How much are you asking for "The St Mary Magdalene in Ecstasy?" So far, nobody has mentioned the asking price!' The Narcissus removed the unwanted hand and moved towards the doors' handles once again.

'Do not worry yourself about the value. Not before you have had an opportunity to view the painting for yourself,' said the Narcissus, pushing aside the double doors.

The dining room was furnished in a similar style to the previous room. The furnishings once again had clean, modern lines, whilst the fixtures and fittings continued to nod towards the houses earlier period. A contemporary eight-seater dining table sat at its centre. However, the focal point of the room was the original Georgian fireplace with deep set alcoves to each side. Ashley was immediately drawn to the picture hanging above the mantle on the chimney breast. The reproduction picture hung in an ornate gilded frame and practically covered the full width of the chimney breast. Ashley moved closer to appreciate the pictures finer details.

'The Kiss or *Il Bacio'* by Italian artist Francesco Hayez was painted in the late Eighteen Fifties. The painting is regarded by many as an iconic piece of 19th Century Italian Romanticism. The painting simply depicts a couple embraced in a passionate kiss. The man is dressed in a brown cloak, red tights and wears a feathered hat. The woman wears a light blue full-length dress. Neither face of the lovers is easily seen as the artist wished the focus to be centred around the kiss itself. The intensity of the embrace and the man's foot poised on the lower step suggest that his departure is imminent and the kiss is a final farewell.

'I have always thought this painting is wonderful,' said Ashley, holding up her hands in an accepting gesture as she contemplated the composition in front of her. 'I can clearly remember the first time I saw the original at the Brera in Milan. I was in the city on a photo shoot for Prada. The painting instantly drew me in from where it hung at the end of the room. I must have lost at least a couple of hours in that room that day. I was totally enthralled by the embrace and the lingering of the kiss captivated me.' She continued to evoke her memories. 'I almost managed to purchase one of Hayez later versions when it came up for sale at Christies in New York a few years back. Unfortunately, some wealthy American obviously wanted it more than me, as it ended up selling for some stupidly ridiculous price.' Ashley suddenly realised that once again she had drifted and gone off on somewhat of a tangent. She began to turn back from the fireplace and the painting.

'Listen to me jabbering on like…' She stopped mid-sentence.

Time froze.

The doctor stood in the doorway with a crossbow levelled at the waist. The Narcissus spoke a single sentence.

'You do not deserve the Caravaggio!' and pulled the trigger.

Ashley screamed.

But no words escaped her mouth. The crossbow bolt hit Ashley in the chest and the metal tail was now protruding from her ruffled blouse. Immediately blood started to stain into the whiteness of the material. Ashley looked down, not believing what had just happened. She could not comprehend the situation any more than a reason why. Her hands clasped the tail of the bolt, but the world around her started to evaporate. The room closed in around her like someone folding in an envelope. She made no further sound. Within moments Ashley slipped into unconsciousness.

Markham Square, Chelsea
London, England

67

The room now had a slight clinical smell. Not dissimilar to the aroma that greets you when you first enter a freshly cleaned hotel room. The Narcissus had dressed in coveralls and cleansed the rooms in which the encounter with Ashley had taken place. There had been no need to go further into the property and increase the chances of leaving unavoidable forensic evidence. The property had been meticulously cleaned for the rental booking and the Narcissus had been careful not to touch any unnecessary surfaces. Therefore, satisfied that all traces of another person in the property had been sufficiently eliminated, the Narcissus set about posing the body in a similar fashion as the previous two scenes. Before manipulating the body, the Narcissus spent a few moments contemplating the corpse's final position and imagining how the finished scene would look to those who would eventually discover it.

Ashley's lifeless body had slumped to the floor after she had lost consciousness. The Narcissus lifted the body, repositioning it so that the centre of the back was leaning against the fireplaces mantle. A rope looped under the armpits was then secured to the mantle in each of the two alcoves. This would prevent the body from falling forward or collapsing back to the floor. Ashley had naturally grasped at the crossbow bolt in her dying moments and the Narcissus needed to do very little to position the hands across the torso. The fingers just needed to be interlinked around the tail of the bolt to stop the hands from falling away. Finally, the Narcissus tilted Ashley's head forward to rest on her chest, implying she was looking down at the wounded area during her last moments.

Still dressed in the anti-contamination coveralls, the Narcissus removed the signature red cloth from an oversized divers holdall. Diligently, the Narcissus wrapped the cloth around the body's lower half, paying particular detail to how the folds of the cloth fell to form a V-shape directly below the clasping hands. Another large fold of the red cloth was then draped over Ashley's right forearm and shoulder. It gave an appearance similar to that of a flowing dress. The Narcissus stepped back and critiqued the work. After a few minor adjustments to the folds of the cloth and an alteration to the position of the legs to better support the dead weight of the rest of the body, the Narcissus was satisfied.

After spending several minutes admiring the artistry of the posed corpse, the Narcissus removed a small plastic tube from the chest pocket of the coveralls. The tube was of the sort used by Entomologists to collect and view small insect species. From the same pocket, the Narcissus retrieved a pair of tweezers and used them to carefully remove the contents of the plastic tube. The pigskin contained within was rolled back on itself to form a translucent tube. The Narcissus unfurled the skin with the tips of the tweezers to reveal the words tattooed on its surface.

Lost soul, it's not yours to reason why
Loneliness in the desolation of your eye
Pleas of mercy, no mortals adjudge your call
Retribution circles, to catch you when you fall
Narcissus

The Narcissus read the words through.

Once. Twice. Three times.

Satisfied that the words would be significant to their intended recipient, the Narcissus re-rolled the pigskin and cautiously moved across to the corpse once more. Bending slightly at the knee, the Narcissus knelt below the corpse's bowing head like a votary proclaiming faith and receiving the offering of bread at communion. However, this genuflector would be making the offering. Using a gloved finger, the Narcissus cautiously manipulated the lips and mouth of the bowing head to create a small opening and access to the back of the throat. Forcing the bottom jaw down, the Narcissus manoeuvred the rolled tattooed pigskin to the back of the mouth and with the tips of the tweezers delicately placed the offering to the rear of the throat. The Narcissus reclosed the mouth and checked the head was still in its original position. Once more the Narcissus stood back and took a few moments to admire the creation of another still life.

The Narcissus cleansed the area in close proximity to the body before gathering a dive bag and retracing the previously cleaned route back to the front door. A black leather jacket and trousers hung from a coat hook in the hallway. Standing on the door mat, the Narcissus put on the oversized motorcycle leathers, directly over the coveralls. The Narcissus then pulled on a pair of armoured motorcycle boots, slipped on the dive bag like a rucksack and collected a black motorcycle helmet from the top of an umbrella stand on the other side of the hall. After putting on the crash helmet, the Narcissus exited the building, returned the property's keys to the sentry safe and crossed the road to a black motorbike parked aside the central gardens railings. Within seconds, the Narcissus had started the bike and was accelerating away in the direction of the Kings Road.

1st June 1606

Rome, Italy

68

The room smelt of animal fat. The result of continual candle burning. However, today there was a further smell. Eggs. Signora Antognetti was stood over a large cast iron skillet suspended over an open hearth as Michelangelo descended the final flight of stairs. A small iron cooking pot and a copper kettle hung on chimney hangers in the smoke blackened fireplace.

Upon hearing the creaking of the stair, Signora Antognetti turned to find Michelangelo dressed in his usual black attire. He looked decidedly alert and perky considering the early hour.

'Smells good,' he said as he crossed the short space from the stairs to where Signora Antognetti stood. He kissed her gently on the cheek before making to warm his hands over the fire.

'Eggs and polenta,' proposed Signora Antognetti, 'a man needs more than bread and jam before a long journey.' She wrapped a cloth around her hand before lifting the kettle from its hook. She poured warm goats milk into two mugs and handed one to Michelangelo.

'How long before you will be leaving?'

'I think it would be wise to be outside the city walls before sunrise. My passage through the city will be safer whilst it is still dark,' he replied taking his milk and sitting at the table.

The previous evening, they had talked and reminisced whilst sharing a simple meal of stewed vegetables and gnocchi. Knowing it could well be their last night together, they had kept their spirits high. As they laughed and recollected, they toasted each other's good luck with a carafe of wine. Michelangelo drinking surprisingly little on this occasion. They had retired to Signora Antognetti's bedroom far earlier than usual, before once more making love late into the night.

Signora Antognetti spooned the polenta on to plates and topped it with the eggs, before joining Michelangelo at the table. They sat and ate in silence for a short while, each now lost for words as Michelangelo's departure beckoned. Eventually, Michelangelo wiped his mouth with the back of his hand, took a large swig of his warmed milk, before retrieving a large purse of coins from the bag at his feet. He placed the coinage on the table between himself and Signora Antognetti.

'I wish to leave you this,' he declared, pushing the purse slightly further in Signora Antognetti's direction, 'do not think of it as a payment for services, but a gift from one friend to another.'

'I cannot possibly accept such generosity. You may well be in greater need of it during your travels.' Michelangelo placed his hand firmly on top of the coins.

'I still have sufficient should the need arise,' giving the bag on the floor a sideways shove with his boot. 'Besides, as soon as I have found refuge in the hills of the Colonna territory, I will no doubt take up the brush and find a portrait or two to paint.'

Signora Antognetti placed her hand atop Michelangelo's. She reached across and lifted his other hand, gently kissing the ridge of his knuckles before gazing longingly into his eyes.

'And I, would like you to keep this,' she said reaching into a pocket at the waistline of her skirt and retrieving a small square of paper. She handed it to Michelangelo. He averted his eyes from hers and unfolded the paper. 'It is one of the sketches you drew whilst I slept the other morning.' His curiosity returned to her eyes for an answer. 'I shall keep one, I wish you to keep the other. That way I shall never forget you.'

'And I too shall never forget you, Maddalena.' They stood and embraced. Neither spoke. Neither felt the need of a kiss. They remained in each other's hold. After what seemed like an age, Signora Antognetti pulled away slightly and finally kissed Michelangelo on the forehead.

'You should go.'

Michelangelo realising the picture was still clutched in his hand, refolded the paper and placed it safely inside the pocket of his shirt. He took both of Signora Antognetti's hands in his own.

'Come with me?'

'You know I cannot.' Michelangelo had already known the answer before he had asked. He let her hands drop and retrieved his black cloak from where it lay draped across the back of a chair. He picked up the bag beside the table and retrieved another from the bottom of the stairs. They stood together once again at the door. Signora Antognetti placed a hand on his breast where she had seen him place her picture in the pocket only moments earlier.

'Remember me,' she whispered.
'I shall. For one day, I will return and paint you once again.'

King Road, Chelsea
London, England

69

Nicola Perry skipped along the pavement as she quietly hummed along to the song currently playing in her earbuds. The trees lining the street rustled as a warm summer breeze drifted in and out of the branches. The street smelt of roasted coffee, bagels and freshly baked bread. The coffee houses were beginning to fill with their second wave of customers. The empty seats vacated by early morning commuters were now being filled by a surge of late to rise tourists. It was just another Chelsea Monday. Nicola had herself stopped briefly at her favourite coffee chain. A large coffee-to-go was now perched in one hand whilst her other hand fought the balancing act of maintaining a grip on her phone whilst desperately trying to thumb type replies to an endless barrage of rings, dings and buzzes. Passing a street side floral vendor caused Nicola to momentarily divert her attention from her virtual friends. The fragrance of Jasmine, Freesia, Rose and Lavender now filled the air and registered with Nicola that she was much further along the street than she had realised. Her second cleaning job of the morning was only a few hundred metres further along the street.

Nicola had been a cleaner for the best part of her adult life. Short maternal breaks for each of her four children and a brief spell in a shoe store were her only respite from the labours of the mop and bucket. However, in recent years the laborious task of dusting and polishing had become much more manageable. Gone were the nightshifts cleaning high rise offices and split shifts turning round an unreasonable number of rooms per hour for budget hotel chains. A couple of years ago, Nicola had stumbled into a job with a cleaning agency who provided services for opulent cash rich clients. She now spent her working day inside some of West London's most illustrious properties. Nicola would visit many of her customers on a twice-weekly basis to carry out general domestic cleaning, but the job was slowly evolving as more and more clients required their property readying for the ever-increasing short-term holiday rental market.

It was a three-day rental that Nicola was returning to today.

Still humming along to a song by a female artist whose name she could not place, Nicola turned towards her clients front door. Knowing the property should have been vacated, she would need to retrieve the keys from the lock box. She tapped in the combination to the current rhythm of the music and did a little Cha-cha-cha on the top step.

As soon as she opened the door, the smell hit her. It smelt unusually cleaner than when she had left it the Friday before.

'Perhaps the weekend rental had fallen through. Just my luck,' she thought. *'No cleaning would mean no payment.'* Still, she was not going to let that sour her high spirits this morning. She continued to bop and shimmy further into the house, whilst the music in her earbuds began to build and intensify. She entered the lounge on her right.

She stopped mid shimmy.

The music seemed to evanesce and the coffee dropped from her hand.

Nicola stood in the doorway for what seemed like minutes. She stared through at the body, not believing the macabre scene in front of her own eyes. Not only could she not apprehend the current situation, but she struggled to believe just whose body it was.

'That's not just anybody's dead bloody body,' she fretted, *'it's Ashley bloody Denning's dead bloody body.'*

She started to gyrate, but not to the forgotten music. She was subconsciously moving her arms and legs as the shock began to release adrenaline throughout her body. She reached for the pocket of her jeans and fumbled her phone free. Instinctively, she punched in the 3 digits instilled since childhood to summon help. But before hitting the connect key she stopped. A sudden thought had just entered her mind. She remained still whilst she played through the various scenarios.

'Could she do it, was it ethical, could she possibly be arrested?'

Whilst Nicola weighed up the possibilities and outcomes, she suddenly realised that whilst being lost deep in thought, she was now sucking on the end of her phone. She looked to the body, then back to her phone and back to the body once more.

'Perhaps this was an opportunity too good to be missed?'

She pondered a while longer. The opportunity had presented itself and maybe it was that one chance for Nicola to cash in. She and her husband had never had a great deal of money, but they always got by. The chance of a reasonable sum of money would make things a whole lot easier. She gingerly manoeuvred her phone in front of her face and hit the camera icon. Before she knew it, she had moved in closer to Ashley Denning's body and taken a series of pictures from numerous different angles. Then without any realisation of what she was doing, she hit the 'video record' icon and panned the phone around the room. As the time lapse blinked two minutes, she stopped filming. Once more, she stood silently still and contemplated what she had just done.

'Don't think too much into it… just do it,' she willed herself. But her guilty conscience was fighting its corner. She shook her head as if trying to clear her mind or shake away the negative thoughts. Nicola took a deep breath and steadied her hands. She typed two words into the search bar on her phones home screen… *Universal News.*

Bring the pages alive…

Explore artworks, locations and more.

Go to gnsbooks.com (Interactive) or scan the QR code to unlock images, maps and facts as you read.

Markham Square, Chelsea
London, England

70

Within 15 minutes of receiving the call, Rebecca and her trusty cameraman, Mikey, had decamped from an earlier outside broadcasting position beside the Thames. They had been delivering news of amphetamine packages washed up on the shoreline overnight. They had thrown their equipment into the back of the corporation's staff car and sped across London towards Markham Square. A lighter than normal mid-morning traffic, a series of lucky green lights and Mikes knowledge of fixed speed camera positions allowed him to stretch the speed limits where possible. It all helped them make good time through the capitals busy West End. During the journey, their news editor had forwarded to Rebecca's phone, a short video clip, photos and some accompanying information they had received just minutes earlier. When Rebecca had played the video footage, Mikey had found it hard to divert his inquisitive eyes away from the phone and keep them on the road ahead. If the information they had received from their editor led to be correct, then this would definitely be a headline story. However, it would need to be handled cautiously. Rebecca and her editor had discussed the ramifications and subsequential consequences of running with the story during the short car journey. Between them they had formulated a strategy to minimise any media fallout, additional complications and the further implications of going live with breaking news where the authorities had yet to investigate the crime scene or identify the victim.

It was breaks like this that reporters dreamt of, but Rebecca knew all too well, that if not handled with rectitude it could ultimately send you to the gallows. She had discussed the imputations of negligent behaviours and industrial misconduct when covering such a story with her editors in the past. Rebecca was eager and enthused to run with the idea, but she was definitely not going to hang herself in doing so.

As they drove into the square, Rebecca had still been deep in conversation finalising details, when she had immediately spotted a nervous looking middle-aged woman leaning against the central gardens railing. The woman continually looked up and down the road whilst biting at her nails. Rebecca had motioned frantically at Mikey to pull over to where the woman was standing, whilst she finished her conversation with the editor. She then spent the next twenty minutes or so, clarifying an agreement with Nicola and confirming that she would be paid twenty-five thousand pounds for her exclusivity. They also discussed Nicola's role and the actions she would now need to take to ensure that both parties were acting in accordance with the law. It had been decided that Nicola would firstly inform the authorities as to the discovery of the body. She would then wait alone outside of the property for the first responders. Rebecca and Mikey would set up their equipment and be ready to record those arriving first at the scene. They had also pre-recorded a short interview with Nicola to edit into their footage, knowing she would be questioned as soon as the investigative team arrived. Finally, they would not go 'live to air' until a police perimeter had been installed and the investigation was active. This would still give them a breaking exclusive ahead of their competitors.

Rebecca had 'gone live' with the breaking story a little after 1pm. The studio had edited and interspersed the footage from Nicola's phone with 'Live' updates from Rebecca at the scene. They had also shown for the first time, the initial interview with Nicola, who had played to the camera exceedingly well. A spectacular mix of emotion and shock at only finding the body within the last hour.

So far, nobody had even so much as speculated how Universal News had arrived at the scene so promptly. In fact, with everyone so focused on the task at hand, nobody had even registered Rebecca and Mikey's presence at all.

But that was all about to change.

Bethnal Green

London, England

71

The empty energy drink can dropped into the bin beside the desk. Harriet did not hesitate or look up from the paperwork she was currently studying. She thumbed through page after page, skimming pages to gather the general detail of the case material. Occasionally, when something more substantial caught her eye, she would slow the process and scan the document to retrieve the more relevant and specific facts.

She reached for a half-eaten doughnut, again without diverting her eyes from the task at hand. She instead grasped a three-day old cream cheese bagel. She took a bite, returned the remains in the general direction of the plate and continued head down gathering essential information, all without noticing the soured taste in her mouth. The investigation had been gathering pace in the last few days and Harriet's current case load might be a cause for concern to your run of the mill DI. But Harriet took it all in her stride, burning the candle at both ends, only leaving her office on the odd occasion to clarify with a colleague the understanding of a particular document or statement. She had not been home in seventy-two hours. They had gained further CCTV footage of both the victims and the suspects arriving and departing from the crime scenes. Individuals within Harriet's team were also chasing leads for the Sleepezy B&B bookings, vehicle hire and location traces on the victims phones. Considering the high profile of the case, and the media coverage it was receiving, Harriet felt comfortable with the investigations current momentum and coupled with the fact that the Chief wasn't clawing at her door for constant updates or on her back twenty-four-seven made her workload all the more bearable. She was in the throes of interpreting and deciphering the detail of Happy's autopsy report on the second victim when a knuckle rapped on the door.

'I think you might want to see this,' declared DS Quinn, hanging on the doors jamb with his head poking around from behind.

'Is it something that can wait George?' Harriet replied, 'As you can see, I'm up to my elbows.'

'Very sure Ma'am,' replied George with a more weighted tone. 'This is priority one.' Harriet looked up for the first time, took off her reading glasses, dropped them onto the pile of paperwork in front of her and looked to George for a further explanation. The words 'priority one' had gotten her full attention. George motioned towards the team incident room and Harriet sprang from her chair and swiftly followed George into the adjoining room. The rest of the team currently present were huddled below the small flat screen TV hanging in the far corner. As Harriet crossed the room, the image on the screen and the need of her inclusion clearly became more evident. She stood behind the group in a state of perplexity and disbelief.

'You've got to be kidding!'

Markham Square, Chelsea

London, England

72

Harriet turned off the Kings Road and abandoned the BMW in the first available space, paying no attention whatsoever to the individual parking bay markings. They had blue lighted their swift transit across the city from Bethnal Green. DS Richards had held firm to the grab handle above the passenger door throughout the entire journey. No sooner had the car come to a stop, than Harriet exited the vehicle. She paid little consideration to the fact that the engine was still idling or she had left the hand brake off, the driver's door wide open, the blue lights still flashing and a shell-shocked DS in the passenger seat. Harriet stormed towards the square's central green space with her quarry firmly in her sights. She crashed through the wrought iron gate into the garden with the ferocity and barbarity of a charging savage intent only on maiming its prey.

As Harriet continued to boil, she strode across the square's inner sanctum, already extending an arm towards the intended target of her wrath. Her cage had been rattled and her inner rage had been lit. She was not so far from breathing fire.

'You've really done it this time,' she screamed, unable to control her aggressive tone, as she stabbed a finger in Rebecca's direction and continued to march abruptly towards her.

'There is crossing the line and then there is crossing the bloody line,' she hollered, her nostrils flaring on each word with infuriation. 'I should have you bloody arrested.' Harriet shoved Mikey the cameraman to one side and stood between him and Rebecca to make her presence felt. Mikey raised a hand towards Harriet's shoulder.

'Don't even…' said Harriet, not even having to finish the sentence.

Mikey backed off.

Harriet held her ground.

She stood directly in front of Rebecca, merely inches from her face. Rebecca shrugged and raised her eyebrows before responding in the only way that seemed fit.

'Just doing my job,' she replied, dismissing her actions as something indifferent. The reply did not sit well with Harriet. She once more raised a finger towards Rebecca. The veins on her temples visibly bulging. She opened her mouth, but no more words escaped. As her anger boiled, she was left with nothing further to say. She clasped her temples in her hands and shook her head with infuriation. There were many occasions where Harriet could not comprehend the actions of others. This was one of them. She could not understand how frequently people thought solely about their own gains and not the impact or consequences it may have on others. She looked up at Rebecca one final time. She waited for a response.

Nothing came.

Exasperated, she turned and walked away.

DS Richards was standing at the gates to the gardens as Harriet marched towards him across the lawn.

'Everything OK, Ma'am?' There was no reply. He was about to enquire further when he saw the look in his bosses' eye. He thought better of it. The awkward silence was broken as two more squad cars on blue lights pulled into the square, stopping short of a property where a PC was currently securing an area with scenes of crime tape. Both cars parked across the roadway to create a cordon. Still enraged and on a war path, Harriet focused her frustrations on the young Constable.

'Make that secure area at least twice that size,' she barked before turning her attention to the two officers exiting the squad cars.

'If either of those two,' she hollered, pointing in the direction of Rebecca and her cameraman, 'come within a yard of that crime tape, you have my permission to frogmarch their asses out of this square. Do you hear me?' Both acknowledged their superior officer and nodded in unison.

Harriet headed back to her own car and with both arms outstretched she leant on the roof and lowered her head. She took a series of long deep breaths. Her usual cool, calm, composure had melted. Instead, a fire had been ignited. Ignited by the one true constant in her life. Someone who she now no longer knew if she could trust. She closed her eyes for a second, searching for her lost serenity. She needed to take control of her emotions and stay true to herself.

Footsteps approaching from behind broke her moment of tranquillity.

'Give me a moment, would you Iain?' she asked without turning.

'Bad Morning?' enquired a familiar voice. Harriet turned and smiled wistfully.

'I've had better. I take it you have seen the news?' Harriet stepped forward and leant on the wing of the car.

'Yeah. Saw it at the lab, before I even got the call,' exclaimed Penny, before sitting on the bonnet next to Harriet.

'If you had arrived a moment earlier, you would have borne witness to a public chastisement by yours truly, followed by an impetuous five-minute meltdown.' Penny had no need to question who the recipient of Harriet's vexation had been. Penny was fully aware of Harriet's relationship and the difficulties it presented.

'Maybe she might have cause to think twice next time?'

'I doubt it,' replied Harriet, looking soberly across to where Rebecca still stood. 'One thing, we both know what to expect when we go through that door,' she continued, pointing across the street.

Penny eased herself from the bonnet, retrieved her forensics box she had left by the curb and made to move towards the awaiting scene. Harriet remained leaning on her car.

'Ok if I leave you to carry out your preliminaries to start with? I feel a black coffee maybe beneficial. Clear my head, get focused, you know the score.' Penny paused. Looking back at her colleague she gifted her an affirming smile.

'Absolutely. I prefer to be alone on the prelims. Less chance of secondary transfers.' Penny playfully winked at Harriet and continued across the street.

As Harriet watched Penny depart, she noticed DS Richards was still patiently standing at the garden's gates.

'Hey Pen' one more thing. Could you tell DS Richards it's safe to come over now.'

Markham Square, Chelsea
London, England

73

By the time Harriet and DS Richards returned from their impromptu coffee, with Harriet having de-stressed, there was a mass of activity around the usually tranquil square. A carnival of paparazzi and news crews had arrived and were now colonising every inch of available space. Presenters conversed with the lenses' of cameras and flashes erupted in sporadic bursts the moment any sign of activity spilled from the door of No.35. A cavalcade of media vehicles, brandishing all manner of aerials, transponders and satellites, along with forensic vans, police cruisers and press agency cars were abandoned at all angles in and around the square. The roadside was currently reminiscent of the aftermath at a demolition derby. Residents of the neighbouring properties milled on each other's doorsteps, gawking and speculating as they watched the media circus unveil their undisturbed corner of suburbia to the eyes of the world.

Harriet and DS Richards showed their ID to one of the officers at the outer police cordon. The officer, who Harriet recognised from earlier, lifted the tape and Harriet and Iain ducked under.

'They are still here,' he nodded, whilst motioning in the direction of the central green space. 'But they have kept their distance.'

'Thank you, Constable,' replied Harriet in a far more placated and composed manner than their previous encounter. The pair continued down the street to the inner cordon and repeated the entry process. However, when they ducked under a tape for the second time, their presence was registered by a series of camera flashes and shouts of 'Any comments?' from the media massed at the perimeter. Ignoring the barrage, they continued to the door and the young constable stationed on the front steps logged their entry time.

After slipping into the required protective coverings in a small cubicle tent erected over the steps and the front door, Harriet and Iain entered the building. Members of the forensic team were busying themselves taking fingerprints in the hallway and gathering fibres from the ground floor reception rooms. Iain showed his ID to the SOC officer currently dusting a light switch in the hallway.

'DS Iain Richards, Metropolitan Investigation Team. Could you dust the key safe outside the front door for fingerprints when you've finished there?'

'No problem,' replied the SOCO, looking up only briefly to acknowledge a response.

'Good shout, Iain,' declared Harriet as she moved further into the building. 'The key safe could well point towards a rental property and a Sleepezy B&B link once again.' They turned into the main reception room, carefully manoeuvring around several evidence markers positioned on the floor. Harriet raised her nose and sniffed. The smell of disinfectant hung in the air.

'*No surprises there*,' she thought. '*The unsub has cleaned the scene once again before departing*.' Harriet looked to Iain who nodded in agreement.

'Yeah, I smell it too. Pretty safe to assume all surfaces have been wiped clean.' Penny stepped into view from behind one of the double doors leading into the adjoining room.

'Harry. Iain. I was just beginning to wonder if you had forgotten about us?' she teased, knowingly conscious that Harriet would have cleared her head and be welcome to a little banter.

'We thought about bringing you a luxury hot chocolate take out with whipped cream and sprinkles, but didn't want to chance contaminating your crime scene,' Harriet batted back at her colleague.

'Spoil sport.' They both laughed. Iain smiled.

'She's in here.' Penny stepped back into the room from which she had come. Harriet and Iain followed.

The body of Ashley Denning was slumped against the fireplace on the far side of the room. Blood pooled at her feet, where it had dripped from the arrow she grasped as it protruded from her chest. She appeared to be looking down despairingly at the wound. Harriet stopped as they entered the room so she could first view the body and its surroundings from a distance. It allowed her to create a bigger picture of the situation. Iain stopped beside her, he too processing the scene before them. They had both seen the footage and photographs taken by the cleaning woman before they had departed Bethnal Green. Although nothing can quite prepare a person for seeing a dead body in the flesh, so to speak. Penny broke the silence.

'The body is definitely posed once again. The torso is supported under the armpits with a rope secured to the fire surround.'

'Posed and lit,' Iain interjected. 'Those floor lamps have without doubt been positioned to throw light across the corpse in a particular fashion. When the owner of the property at the Isle of Dogs was shown photographs from the first crime scene, he confirmed the floor lamp in his property was not in its usual position and had been moved to the location seen in the photographs.' Harriet had been moving around the corpse. First one side, then the other, so she could scrutinise the smallest details from various different angles.

'Find out from the constable on the front door where the cleaner who opened this can of worms is now? Will you Iain?' she said as she turned her attention from the body back to her colleague. 'I would imagine she is still out there revelling in the attention she is receiving from the press. Put a stop to it. Get her in the back of a squad car. Have her look at the footage she took and confirm the lamp has been moved. Then I want her escorted back to the station to provide her statement. Call Andy, ask him to handle it. And whilst you're at it, get George and Greg down here pronto to start door to door. The local residents seem curious to know what's happening, let's hope at least one of them was peeking around the curtains yesterday.' She paused for a moment to collect her thoughts. 'Check if a security firm has a close circuit contract in the area. Take a look around the street for individual security camaras. Have the footage pulled from the street cameras on the Kings Road too.'

Iain took that as his cue to leave.

'I'll get straight onto it, Ma'am' and back tracked his way out of the building.

Penny continued to walk Harriet through her findings, although there was once again little physical evidence as there had been at the previous two scenes.

'As you are probably aware, the scene has been thoroughly cleaned once again and the unsub appears to have only entered the bare minimum of rooms.' Harriet nodded in acknowledgment, but Penny could see her colleague was absorbed in thought. Harriet pinched at her chin as she pondered and deliberated for a moment longer.

'Why the change of MO? Knives were used at the first two scenes and the necks were cut. This time the victim appears to have been shot with an arrow.' She continued to speculate. 'If I'm not mistaken, that's a crossbow bolt. That means our suspect must have walked in and out of here with a crossbow. Not an easy thing to hide.'

'I completely agree with you, Harry,' Penny added, pointing towards the wound area with the stainless-steel forceps in her hand.

'Primary observations around the wound would suggest the bolt had entered the body at force rather than a penetration performed by hand. So, you would be correct to assume the bolt had indeed been fired. Happy will be able to confirm this at autopsy.' Penny stepped back slightly, giving Harriet a clearer view of her next evidential pointer.

'The pooling and the large volume of blood indicate the victim was alive and the trauma caused by the entry wound has a high probability in being the cause of death. Again, this differs from our first two crimes, where evidence has shown that the cause of death was chemically induced and both corpses were mutilated post-mortem.'

'So are the MO's?' Harriet stopped for a moment and debated with herself, turning her current thought over in her mind before continuing, 'Are they differentiated enough to suggest a second suspect or a copycat?' She continued to ruminate the idea.

'Had there been sufficient media coverage to sensationalise the previous crime scenes to inspire a copycat killer? Surely the timeline between the crimes had so far been too short to influence a second suspect. She continued to turn the thought process over in her mind. Penny interrupted.

'I believe the posing of the bodies is too particular. The way the bodies have been left holds more weight than the cause of death. Although I do think the weapons themselves may be more significant than we first thought.' Harriet cut in this time.

'So, the killer has created an image in their mind prior to committing the crime. Their intention is to leave a lasting image. It's like they are painting a picture for us.' The last sentence resonated with Harriet. 'Have you had an opportunity to check the body for our Unsubs other recurrent MO?' she enquired, 'although the concealment maybe different from the others due to the lack of a neck wound.' Penny turned to the forensic box behind her and retrieved a sealed evidence bag. The familiar tattooed skin was sandwiched between its plastic sleeving.

'The roll of skin was in fact in the neck. It had been placed in the back of the throat. I believe we can safely assume we have a single perpetrator,' Penny declared, offering the bag in Harriet's direction. Harriet took the bag. 'This evidential marker has not been released or leaked to the media,' continued Penny, 'so that narrows the possibility of a second suspect or copycat.' Harriet nodded in agreement but was already reading the words tattooed across the skin.

Lost soul, it's not yours to reason why
Loneliness in the desolation of your eye
Pleas of mercy, no mortals adjudge your call
Retribution circles, to catch you when you fall
Narcissus

The words read in a familiar taunting pattern to those in previous notes and would doubtlessly relate to the Neptune's Finger album once again. However, it did differ from the others, it appeared to have been signed.

'Correct me if I'm wrong,' proclaimed Harriet, 'but doesn't someone with narcissistic tendencies have an inflated sense of their own importance and said to love themselves more than they love others.'

'Yes, I believe they do. They also have a need to seek attention and recognition,' added Penny.

'Seems our Unsub is becoming overconfident, maybe even cocky. They feel conceited enough to give themselves an alias before the Press do.' Harriet read the words through several more times before handing the bag back to Penny.

'Could you send a picture showing the tattooed text through to my phone as soon as. I have someone who may well be able to offer an insight or some clarity to the notes meaning.'

Harriet really needed to try calling that number once more.

1st June 1606

Alban Hills, South of Rome

74

The wheat cart bumped and clattered along the stony track. Its wooden spoked wheels channelling every judder of the rutted surface to shake the bones of the carts occupants. The driver sat hunched at the shoulder. Occasionally he would flick a long withy cane across the oxen's hind quarters to encourage them up a steeper section of the roadway. He champed on a single stalk of wheat, turning it in the corner of his mouth with the non-stop rolling of his jowl. A large hat, sagging at its brim with age, provided little shelter from the searing heat of the afternoon's sun. The carts second occupant had paid for passage so was slumped in the rear of the cart amongst the loaded wheat.

Michelangelo had approached the driver at a river crossing a few hours earlier. They had exchanged conversation whilst the driver had fed and watered his oxen. Michelangelo had offered payment and the driver had agreed to allow him to ride along as far as the crossroads at the South-Eastern border of the Alban Hills. Although the ride had been uncomfortable and arduous at times, Michelangelo was thankful to have departed Rome with little to no aggravation.

The cart's wheels jostled through a particularly large pothole, causing Michelangelo to grasp at the siderails in fear of being tossed over the side. The undulation caused the stack of wheat to shift, further covering him in a layer of chaff and dust. He sat between his bags, upon his cloak, which he had spread out across the wheat when he had first clambered aboard the cart. His shirt was unbuttoned to the navel to offer some relief from the suffocating heat. At one point, he had looked to retrieve his tobacco, but quickly thought better of it, considering the bed of dried wheat upon which he sat. There was little to do but ponder and reflect. He thought about the moment when he had taken Ranuccio's life and the consequences that had followed. He played through numerous scenarios of how he could possibly undo all that had happened. But wherever his thoughts took him, they always returned to the woman he had left behind only hours earlier. He could not throw the image of Signora Antognetti from his mind. He peeked at his shirt pocket to check that the drawing was still safely within. He resisted the temptation to remove it from the pocket for fear of losing it on the breeze. He placed a hand over the pocket and held the picture close to his heart.

A sudden shuddering and swaying of the cart caused him to brace his posture. He held an arm out to either side, securing his bags as the cart trundled through another section of rugged terrain. As he looked up from steadying himself, he caught sight of a carriage on the verge of the crossroads ahead. The rationale for it being there caused him alarm. He stiffened and tensed once more. Anxiety and fear spread throughout his body as he anticipated something bad or unpleasant was about to happen. He felt a wave of nausea rise as he tried to comprehend the situation confronting him.

'Had the powers that be caught up with him? There would no doubt be a bounty on his head by now. A "capital sentence" would mean anyone within the papal states had the right to take his life, claim the reward and be absolved of any blame. All they needed to do was provide his head.'

The driver reined in the oxen and brought the cart to a stop. Michelangelo ran his hand over the leather of his bag, feeling for the outline of his pistol.

'Had Ranuccio's brothers got wind of his departure and discovered his intentions before racing ahead to seek revenge?'

Michelangelo watched as the man approached the cart. He did not recognise the man. He was dressed in the regalia of a royal house. He also travelled alone. Michelangelo watched as the man spoke briefly with the driver before continuing in the direction of the rear of the cart where he sat. As he approached, he spoke softly to enquire.

'Signor Merisi?'

Michelangelo hesitantly nodded, his hand now within the bag gripping the stock of the pistol.

'Do not be alarmed,' declared the man, noticing Michelangelo's hesitant demeanour. 'I mean you no harm. I represent Duke Marzio Colonna.' The man moved closer, parted his cloak and raised his palms. 'As you can see, I am unarmed.' Michelangelo tentatively eased the grip on his own pistol and edged himself into a more assertive position.

'The duke received word of your plight. The Marchesa Costanza sent word with a rider following your departure from Rome.' The man offered Michelangelo his hand in a gesture to alight the cart. He accepted the offering and no sooner were his feet back on solid ground when he proceeded to dust himself down. The man continued.

'I was dispatched in hope of intercepting your passage. The duke wishes for you to take refuge within the walls of his Palace at Zagarolo.'

Bethnal Green
London, England

75

Harriet stood in the shadow of the investigation board. It was growing exponentially, with new evidence and a progression of lead material being added daily. The discovery of a third victim had created new direction for some leads, a greater focus on the key indicators of others and several fresh lines of enquiry. The investigation was gathering pace and they had seen a rapid growth in the diversity of information they had been collating. She perused the photographs, Post-its and printouts which in time would provide the vital links to what was currently a scattering of evidential pieces. And there were still missing pieces of the jigsaw yet to be discovered.

Members of her investigation team milled around the room behind her. Each focused on their piece of the puzzle. Some shuffled through old case files, others typed at keyboards as they searched the web for information and clarity, one sided phone conversations could be heard, as could the constant whirl of the copy machine as it persistently expelled page after page of statements, reports and profiles.

Harriet channelled out the sound as she tried to create an image in her mind. She ran both her hands back through her hair as if subconsciously removing it from her face would further clear her head space. She held the hair back behind her ears and scanned the board. Her eyes crisscrossing the evidence as she started to construct an imaginary network linking key individual facts. Evidential string theory. Much like the interconnecting strands of a spider's web. They had the evidence. But it was making the connections that had so far eluded them.

She focused in on the photographs of the three victims. All had celebrity status. All were wealthy. All had previous criminal convictions. Hidetaka and Ashley having minor convictions and Sir Christopher his publicised immigration scandal resulting in two years imprisonment. But apparently nothing else in common. All three had allegedly been invited to high-end rental properties, again with seemingly no connection apart from all being booked through Sleepezy B&B. Each rental had however been completed with a different name and email account. Stom, Bigot and Strozzi.

Harriet now turned her attention to a new area of the board where a montage of pictures and documents relating to the three names had been assembled. She had asked DC Thompson to look into the three names used to make the rental bookings. And boy had he come up trumps! Stom, Bigot and Strozzi were all apparently recognised artists. Matthias Stom was Flemish, Trophime Bigot was French and Bernardo Strozzi was Italian. They had however, all worked in and around Rome during the early part of the 17th Century. All three reputedly produced religious compositions in a baroque style.

Harriet re-read the information Greg had provided earlier that morning. Matthias Stom had painted a picture entitled 'Salome receives the Head of John the Baptist'. It depicted a severed head being offered on a golden platter. She thought back to the first crime scene. *'The head had been removed and placed on a large serving plate upon the table.'*

Harriet looked at the printout Greg had provided of the Stom painting. She could see the similarities. She then read the descriptions of the second two paintings. 'Judith cutting off the Head of Holofernes' had been painted by Trophime Bigot in 1640. It showed the moment Judith the Widow draws a sword across the neck of General Holofernes. The final painting by Bernardo Strozzi is an oil on canvas entitled 'The Martyrdom of St Ursula'. It captured the death of St Ursula as she is shot in the chest with an arrow. As she read both descriptions her mind was each time drawn back to the crime scenes and the way the bodies had been so meticulously positioned. Each was almost identical to the original painting. She thought back to the boat at St Katherine Docks. *'Sir Christopher had been left in the same position, lying across the bed with a sword severing his neck.'* Her memory then moved to the most recent murder. *'Ashley Denning's dying moments had been captured as she looked down at the arrow protruding from her chest.'*

Harriet continued to deliberate the newly discovered facts and information. Her mind began to process and prioritise each individual aspect of the crimes. She executed a series of questions through in her head.

'Was the perpetrator copying the works of these artists? If so, what was significant about Stom, Bigot and Strozzi?'

'Did the suspect see themself as an artist? What about the signing of the signature at the last scene? Did the perp now want recognition for their work?'

'Did the signature in some way link to the names of the three painters? What about the pigskins and the lyrics? How did they fit in?'

These questions and more needed answering. And quickly. The time span between each of the murders was relatively short. If the Unsub was becoming more confident with each newly committed crime, then they could possibly kill again in the next few days. Harriet needed to keep the wheels of the investigation turning. It was essential that they get ahead of the game.

She looked across the room, spotted DC Thompson, got his attention and called him over. He joined her at the board.

'Firstly Greg, I'd like to commend you on the quality of the information and the speed in which you collated it.'

'Thank you, Ma'am,' said Greg, with a feeling of fulfilment and acceptance. He sheepishly looked over his shoulder to see if any of his colleagues had overheard the praise the DI had instilled in him. Harriet also took pleasure from the fact that DC Thompson had done such an efficient job. The lad had shown potential. She could therefore rely on the young constable again. Harriet pointed at three pictures in front of them.

'Look for a connection between the three painters and the 'signature name' Narcissus.' Greg nodded inordinately, unable to contain a complacent grin.

'Also see if you can find any links between Neptune's Finger and the three artists. I'm thinking album cover, songs, lyrics?' Greg remained silent, waiting for anything further.

Nothing came.

His boss seemed to have moved on and now looked to be deep in thought.

'I'll get straight on to it Ma'am,' he said moving back towards the desk he shared with George.

'Yes, thank you,' Harriet replied, without diverting her eyes from the board. Harriet deliberated and cogitated, as she pondered her next move. She knew what she had to do and who was best placed to help her.

At that precise moment, her phone began to ring. She retrieved it from her back pocket, almost dropping it when she saw the callers ID appear on the screen. Without hesitating, she headed directly to her office and shut the door behind her.

Thorney Street

London, England

76

A green bird flew past, as Tate leant against the window and looked out across the Thames. He continued to watch as the Ring-neck Parakeet landed in a tree on the river side. He seemed to remember his Father once telling him that the progenitors of London's population of Parakeets had escaped in 1951from Isleworth Studios during the filming of The African Queen starring Humphrey Bogart and Katherine Hepburn. He wondered if there was any truth in the story as he watched the bird pulling at the loose bark of a branch. He placed a call and held the phone to his ear. The bird continued to fight with the bark.

The call connected.

Harriet answered the call. Although she knew the identity of the call from her phones display screen, she still responded in a professional manner.

'Harriet Stone. Metropolitan CID.' There was a moments silence from the other end.

'Harriet. It's Tate Randall. It's been a long while. I hope I'm not interrupting anything important?' Harriet let the words linger. It had been a long time since she had heard that voice, but she could still picture the man behind it.

'So, you did get my call the other day,' she said joyously.

'I'm sorry. I'm not quite sure what you are referring to?' Tate thought for a moment before the realisation hit. The call on the bridge just before he had met with Tommy. He had allowed it to go to answerphone and then had completely forgotten about it. 'Oh God. Sorry. Was that you. I didn't recognise the number.' Harriet felt a little put out. He had obviously removed her from his contacts list. The mishap made Tate feel slightly awkward. He tapped his temple several times against the windowpane and grimaced at himself. Outside, another green Parakeet flew into the tree alongside the first. 'If I had realised it was you, I would have called you straight back.'

'It's absolutely fine. I'm sure you had more important things on your mind.'

'*Oh God. Did that sound a tad pitiful,*' thought Harriet as she nibbled at her bottom lip. They were both walking on eggshells, neither wishing to offend the other after years without contact.

'I was actually calling today as I may have some information that maybe of some interest to you and your current investigation,' declared Tate, hoping his offering might help lighten what was an awkward situation.

'Well, believe it or not, when I called the other day, it was to ask if you would mind looking over some of the evidence we have accumulated from that very investigation,' said Harriet, feeling more at ease with every word she spoke. The ice had begun to break and they no longer had need to tiptoe around the situation. Harriet got up from her chair and leaned against the front of her desk. Tate leant against the window and watched the birds who were now side by side picking at the bark. Harriet continued to explain her dilemma.

'Some of the evidence my team has gathered strongly suggests links to the art world. We have uncovered key pointers relating to three artists and the paintings each of them has produced. Knowing we needed more in-depth information from someone with expertise in that field, I immediately thought of you.' At the other end of the line, Tate allowed himself a self-satisfying smile. It felt good that Harriet had not forgotten him and all the more they were talking again. Even though it was work related, it still felt good.

'I would be more than happy to help in any way I can,' said Tate as his two green distractions, each with a piece of bark, flew off in the direction they had come.

'And the information I have received from a reliable source may well link your three victims to a case we are currently investigating here.' Harriet's ears pricked upon hearing Tate's last sentence. She knew her instincts had been correct and contacting Tate had been the right thing to do.

'Then maybe it would be beneficial to meet in person? Of course, only if you are ok with that?' Tate caught himself smiling once more.

'That's absolutely fine by me. Perhaps you'd like to come here. My office, that is. I'm free tomorrow afternoon if that's any good?'

'That fits with me,' replied Harriet, 'Thorney Street, right?'

'Correct. How does two thirty sound?' It was Harriet's turn to smile this time.

'Sounds like you still enjoy your lunches!'

Bruton Place, Mayfair
London, England

77

Jeremy Grayson paced. He paced from his desk to the shop door. From the shop door to his desk. He paced continually. He did not look up. He could not comprehend what was happening. He had watched the live feed as it was broadcast from Markham Square. He had looked away each time they had shown the footage of Ashley's body. Poor Ashley. She did not deserve this. He'd had a soft spot for Ashley, although she would never have known. Nor would she have had the time or interest for someone as disinteresting as him. '*She was a supermodel for Christ's sake.*' He corrected his thought. '*Had been a supermodel.*'

When Jeremy had heard the news about the murder of Hidetaka, he had simply surmised that the young reprobate had gotten himself mixed up in something much deeper than he had bargained for. Upon seeing the headlines reporting the discovery of Sir Christopher's body he had begun to wonder and postulate if there was any reasonable connection but had quickly passed it off as purely coincidental. However, when the news had broken and images of Ashley's body had been splashed all over the media, it was like a punch to the stomach and Jeremy intuitively knew the deaths of three people on a list of potential buyers had not been a chance occurrence. A list he had compiled and provided. Clandestine buyers willing to illicitly purchase a stolen painting. For many years now he had been involved in black market deals, the movement of stolen paintings, insurance fraud and underhanded transactions, but none had ever involved or culminated in the death of another person. Jeremy could not wash his hands of this. He could very well be charged with third person involvement.

He had felt uncomfortable and sceptical ever since his very first encounter with Dr Valentine. There was something about the doctor he could not quite put his finger on. Something that did not feel quite right or sit comfortably with him. The way the doctor had insisted they carry out their business had seemed unorthodox. Jeremy had also found the doctor idiosyncratic. He had often wondered why they had never met face to face and why the doctor had been so adamant as to when, where and how the painting could be viewed. It now looked to be all part of a plan.

Jeremy continued to pace. His hands held in a prayer pose; he tipped his fingers to his lips as he thought.

'Why invite a potential buyer to view a painting and then murder them? With the painting having been so recently stolen, could the doctor not afford for a prospective buyer to walk away, having not secured a deal? Were they merely seen as collateral?'

Jeremy stopped pacing at his desk. His hand reached for the computer mouse as he sat down. He hovered and clicked the icon on the home screen. 'Universal News Top Stories' opened. He scrolled through the headlines. There were two relating to the murder of Ashley Denning. He opened each and read through the content. He spent the next ten minutes doing the same with other mainstream news channels. It was apparent that the press were 'led to believe' that the murders of Ashley Denning, Sir Christopher Roebuck and Hidetaka Yamamoto were possibly the work of a single killer. At present they were 'inconclusively' reporting that someone was targeting celebrities. There was no reported evidence at present which could in any shape or form be associated with him or the stolen Caravaggio. Jeremy was the only one apart from Dr Valentine who knew about the list of the five potential buyers, He was possibly the only person who could provide a link between the murders. He stood once again, but this time he leant against the back of his chair, whilst his gaze wandered through the shops window to the street outside. Jeremy took a deep breath and focused his mind.

'Was the painting simply being used to beguile the individuals into the doctor's hands for no more reason than to murder them? Doctor Valentine had been adamant to who the five prospective buyers should include. Was it just an avengers hitlist?'

A feeling of unease swept through Jeremys' body. There were still two names on the list. There was no way he could warn them without consequences and incriminating himself in the whole sordid affair. The majority of Jeremy's business was carried out unlawfully and underhanded, but he would never have agreed to his involvement in a deal such as this should he have known. His breathing changed, becoming fast and shallow as a sense of trepidation overwhelmed him. There had been five names on the list. Three of those were now dead.

Would there soon be a sixth name on the list?

And would that name be his?

Thorney Street
London, England

78

Harriet drummed her fingers on the steering wheel, tapping along to the song currently playing on the radio. She recognised the song but did not know its title or who had recorded it. Furthermore, she had absolutely no idea which radio station she was currently listening to. It was the same station that the radio had been tuned to when she had first been designated the department car. Harriet felt buoyant and optimistic regarding her meeting with Tate. Although, after many years without contact, she could sense the tiniest amount of apprehension balling in the pit of her stomach. She had almost run into him last summer. She had been having pre-theatre drinks with Rebecca at a bar in Covent Garden when she had noticed Tate and Jonathan sat at a table in an adjoining room. A quick-thinking remark of 'gosh look at the time' and a hasty departure had avoided her an awkward situation.

She pulled the car into the underground parking area and had her ID credentials cleared at the gate before being permitted entrance. After finding a parking space, she grabbed an attaché case from the passenger seat and headed to the lifts on the far side of the level. As she weaved between the vehicles, she caught sight of the Land Rover parked in the corner. She chuckled to herself. '*You still have that old thing then*'. During their time together, Harriet and Tate had frequently thrown the essentials into the back of the Land Rover and dashed off for a weekends camping in the South-West on the whim of a good forecast.

Harriet rode the lift to the fifth floor. After asking the first person she encountered in the corridor for the whereabouts of the Art and Antiquities department, she rounded the corner and immediately spotted the sign to the left of the door up ahead. The door was open, so she politely knocked and stepped inside. There were three people busily working at computers. All three looked up to acknowledge the visitor.

'DI Harriet Stone. Metropolitan CID. I'm looking for Tate Randall?' The only female amongst the three stood up from her workstation and crossed towards her. Harriet could not help but notice how tall and elegant the woman was. The woman held a hand forward.

'DI Lena Johnson. Nice to meet you.' They shook hands. 'Tate said you would be coming. I'll let him know you are here.' Lena turned back towards Tate's door, but Tate had beaten her to it and was already crossing the floor towards them.

'Welcome to our tiny abode. It's so good to see you. And after so long.' They too shook hands. Harriet felt slightly awkward and the handshake felt a little formal. But what was she expecting? It had been several years since their relationship had ended. It was never going to be a bear hug.

'Good to see you too,' she replied with a warm pleasing smile. They looked at each other, neither quite sure what to do or say next. Noticing the unease, Lena excused herself and returned to her desk.

'Shall we go through to my office,' Tate gestured extending an arm in the direction from which he had just come. Harriet followed Tate through the anterior room. Lena looked up and smiled once more as they passed. Tate closed the partition door behind them and motioned for Harriet to take a seat. She sat and placed her attaché case at her feet. Steam rose from two coffee cups on the desk. Tate rounded to his side.

'Coffee. Black?' He offered, pointing to the cup nearest Harriet.

'Hot, black and bitter. And you? Still having a shot of coffee in your sugar?' They both laughed; And they both relaxed a little.

'So, what's happening in the world of DI Harriet Stone? By the way, congratulations on the promotion.'

'God, that seems like such a long time ago,' replied Harriet picking up the cup and blowing across its surface. 'Running the gauntlet like any other officer in the CID. Work. Sleep. Work, work, eat, sleep, work, repeat.' They both laughed once more.

'I actually almost bumped into you last summer. John and I were drinking in Covent Garden and I noticed you across the bar. When I looked up again, you were gone.'

'Really,' Harriet quipped as she sipped at her coffee, 'Probably had somewhere to be, as always.'

'I assume you are still cycling, kick boxing, finding time for the gym. You look great by the way.' Harriet shied at the comment. It was slightly uncomfortable but it gave her a good feeling. She quickly changed the subject in case she began to blush.

'You still have a penchant for your music, I see,' she said raising her eyes towards the artwork on the wall and coaxing the conversation towards a subject matter she knew was close to Tate's heart.

'It's one of those things that I think will be part of me my entire life.' Tate cringed discreetly, wishing he had chosen his words more wisely considering their past, but Harriet did not seem to notice.

'I spotted the Land Rover downstairs too. Some things never change.' They both chuckled and smiled once again. Harriet noticed the picture of Tate's parents and was about to enquire about their well-being when Tate changed the context of their conversation. He took a large gulp of his coffee and sat upright in his chair. Time to get down to business.

'As you are most probably aware, a painting by the artist Caravaggio was recently stolen in Rome. We are currently investigating the possibility of the painting having been transported to the UK and subsequently being offered for sale on the black market.' Harriet nodded and Tate continued. 'During those investigations we have recently been informed by a reliable source that a potential list of five prospective buyers has been provided by a middleman who is well known to us as a handler of black-market deals. He is a shrewd and cunning man who is reluctant to offer much in the way of information.' He paused momentarily. 'However, I am confident that the information provided by our source is strong. It is on the strength of this information and later discovering a possible significant connection to your case that I felt it was essential to contact you.' Tate again hesitated briefly.

'The first three names on that list… match those of your three victims.' He broke off and reached for his coffee. Harriet sat dumbfounded at what she had just heard. She took a moment to comprehend the information. Eventually she spoke.

'Correct me if my understanding is wrong. You are saying that Hidetaka Yamamoto, Sir Christopher Roebuck and Ashley Denning are on a list of prospective buyers for the stolen Caravaggio.'

'Correct.'

'And you have the names of two individuals who could potentially be our next two victims?' Harriet reached for her coffee and took a larger than normal swig. The caffeine would help silence the alarm bells now sounding in her head.

'Well, not quite.'

Harriet looked perplexed.

'I have a possible fourth name. Our source did not know the fifth name at the time of our meeting. That however may change.' Tate could foresee Harriet yearning for the name. It was written all over her face. He did not hang back.

'Anatoli Nikolaev.'

'The Russian billionaire who owns the F1 team?' she clarified, just to be sure.

'Yes. I believe so.' Tate nudged his mouse and woke up his computer. He double-clicked the mouse a couple of times and a small printer on the shelves behind sprang to life and ejected a single sheet of paper. Tate swivelled in his chair, retrieved the printout and turned back to hand it across to Harriet.

'Mr Jeremy Grayson. Proprietor of Grayson Gallery in Mayfair. He has been subject to our enquiries on many occasions in the past but has always managed to slip through the net. He is a known handler of stolen works and our source points to him as being a possible middleman in the movement of the Caravaggio.' Harriet skimmed through the profile she had been handed as Tate continued.

'We were granted a warrant this morning to obtain his phone records. He made a single call from a mobile registered in his name to each of your victims prior to their murder. I am confident the victim's phone records will confirm this. If he has had dealings with them in the past, as I suspect, his number will most probably be in each of their phone's contact lists.' Tate removed several sheets of call records from a desk drawer and slid them across in Harriet's direction. She shuffled through them, noting several highlighted numbers.

'He has also received calls to the gallery's landline on a number of occasions from several different mobile numbers. We traced those numbers. Each was a pre-paid SIM registered to a fake email address. Records of those numbers show each was used for a single call and never used again. All in all, it points to a burner phone. Used and discarded.' Harriet had found the calls Tate was referring to within the printouts and was scrutinising the detail.

'I will get one of my team to cross reference the calls on the victims phones and also to check for similar in-coming calls from single use numbers.'

'At this stage I do not believe we have enough to make an arrest,' proclaimed Tate, 'however I think there is sufficient cause to invite Mr Grayson to answer a few questions to further our enquiries.' Harriet nodded in agreement before Tate pursued the matter further. 'I believe the Caravaggio is quite possibly being used to entice individuals to locations before they are murdered in cold blood.' The statement was bold and decisive. 'I also suspect that Jeremy Grayson plays no more part than providing the initial contacts, truly believing he is to collect a sizeable handlers fee. If indeed he was involved further, believe me, he has the guile and duplicity to cover his tracks much more methodically.' Tate had laid his cards. He could see Harriet was contemplating her next move.

'I really should make a phone call now. I think there is little time to waste. Anatoli Nikolaev needs to be contacted and offered protection as soon as possible. My team can also start collecting the phone data, there and then.' Harriet swirled the remnants of her coffee and swallowed the final mouthful.

'I'll leave you to make that call,' said Tate, picking up his own cup. 'More coffee?'

Thorney Street
London, England

79

Tate returned with a tray of take-out coffees. He handed them amongst his team before returning to his office with the remaining two. Harriet was currently reading through a file she had retrieved from the attaché case at her feet. Two more files lay on the desk.

'Thanks,' she said accepting the coffee, 'Anatoli Nikolaev is being offered the option of a safe house as we speak. The phone records of the three victims will be processed in the next couple of hours.' She put the coffee down and picked up another file. 'We have so far found no link between our three victims, other than the one you have just provided. However, we have discovered links between the way the victims were murdered and more importantly the positions in which the bodies were found. We believe all three bodies were posed, postmortem.'

'Posed?' The word sparked Tate's curiosity.

'This information has not been given or leaked to the media so far. As I am sure you are aware, what I am about to show you cannot leave this room.' Tate nodded as Harriet removed three photographs from the file and spread them out on the table. The macabre nature of the photographs were beyond anything Tate could have imagined. He needed to look at the pictures more than once, but he was not sure he wanted to.

'One of my team has been trawling the internet for artistic comparisons or similarities. We believe the three victims may have been posed to imitate these three paintings. Harriet removed three more pictures from the file and lay them out in juxtaposition to their counterparts on the table.

'Salome receives the Head of John the Baptist.'

'Judith cutting off the Head of Holofernes.'

'And the Martyrdom of St Ursula.'

She gave Tate a moment to analogise the pictures. 'The three paintings are by Matthias Stom, Trophime Bigot and Bernardo Strozzi,' stated Harriet as she tapped each one in turn. 'Our knowledge ends there and with WikipediA. I was hoping to tap into your expertise and get a second opinion.' Tate continued to assimilate the pairs of pictures. Eventually he drew his gaze away.

'There are definitely a lot of similarities suggesting the corpses have indeed been posed to create a likeness to the pictures.' He pointed to one particular pair of pictures. 'Trophime Bigot was known as the Candlelight Master. To this day, his true identity is still questioned. The other two artists I am not familiar with. Fortunately, Lena who you briefly met earlier, has a far greater knowledge than I do. It may be beneficial at this point if we were to ask her to join us. That's if you don't mind?' Harriet nodded and spoke at the same time.

'I have no problem with that whatsoever. I am always open to the opinion of someone with knowledge in a particular field. An extra pair of eyes can often spot something the rest of us could not see.'

'Give me a minute.' Tate left the room. Harriet watched through the glass partition as Tate talked with Lena at her desk. After several minutes Tate returned with Lena in tow.

'I took the opportunity to bring Lena up to speed and to ensure she was aware of the sensitivity of the situation.' The two women nodded and smiled at each other. Lena leant in from the end of the desk and studied the photographs. One at a time she picked up the prints of the original artworks. As she did so Harriet offered some further clarification.

'The surnames of Stom, Bigot and Strozzi were also used to make bookings through Sleepezy B&B for each of the crime scene locations. Our internet searches revealed all three names were related to painters. It was then we discovered that each had produced a painting comparable to each of the crime scenes.'

'All three painters resided and worked in Rome during the early 17th Century. They frequently painted works of the same subject matter, most often scenes from biblical texts,' imparted Lena whilst the other two listened intently. 'They also, all painted in a similar style using a technique called chiaroscuro. The contrasting effects of light and shadow. Sometimes they would use a single light source to illuminate a particular aspect of the painting.' Harriet cut in.

'There is evidence at all three crime scenes that clearly points towards lighting fixtures having been moved to purposely illuminate the corpses.'

'Perhaps your perpetrator has a passion for 17th Century Italian renaissance,' declared Lena, 'and wishes to emulate them in their own way.' An unexpected tapping on the glass partition interrupted Lena and drew the attention of all three occupants. A head appeared around the doorway.

'I heard there was an attractive lady in the building!'

Thorney Street
London, England

80

Jonathan strode into the room and Harriet extended a hand as she stood to greet him. Jonathan bypassed the hand, instead wrapping his arms around her in a bear hug. He stepped back. Unashamedly and tactless as ever he looked Harriet up and down.

'Looking good,' he declared.

'It's good to see you too, Jonathan,' replied Harriet, 'not looking so bad yourself.'

'Early morning swims in the pond with the boss man. Helps to keep the pounds off.' He tapped his stomach. 'You do know these two were an item a few years back,' Jonathan teased for Lena's benefit, before returning his focus to Harriet.

'And to what do we owe this honour?'

'Harriet has a line of enquiry within the case she is currently working, which relates to works of art,' interjected Tate. 'She thought it may be beneficial to seek our opinion. As you are here, we may as well utilise your knowledge too.' Tate looked to Harriet. She nodded.

They spent the next few minutes bringing Jonathan up to date with all they had previously discussed. He too found the crime scene photographs slightly disturbing. After scrutinising the evidential material for several minutes, Jonathan picked up the photograph of the second crime scene and its companion artist's work.

'This is all wrong. Your crime scene is a mirror image of the original painting and the positioning of the limbs is inconsistent.' He retrieved his phone from his back pocket and tapped an entry into the search engine. After locating the image he sought, he turned the screen for the others to see. 'The way in which the body at your crime scene is posed is more consistent with Caravaggio's depiction of Judith and Holofernes. The positioning is more precise.' He pointed out the comparisons on the screen of his phone. 'I think I am right in saying,' he focused his statement in Lena's direction, 'Caravaggio also produced versions of the other two paintings.'

Lena nodded in agreement before adding, 'amongst many others. There are numerous paintings by Caravaggio that all three of the other artists have also produced.' Jonathan once more thumb typed into his phone. He then turned it once again towards the other three.

'This is Caravaggio's representation of 'The Martyrdom of St Ursula'. Look at the position of the hands. They are grasping at the entry of the arrow. Again its more consistent with the image from the crime scene. In your print-out of Strozzi's painting, you can clearly see a difference.' He pointed down at the picture. 'St Ursula's arms are held to the side.' Tate looked to Lena, who looked to Harriet. All three nodded in agreement.

'I certainly can't argue with that,' Lena inferred, 'Everything John has implied confirms your previous insights and intuitions, but by a different artist. There is definitely more to this than meets the eye.' Tate gaped at his friend in wonderment. Jonathan noticed the bewilderment in Tate's eyes.

'What can I say. I found I had an appreciation for Caravaggio after visiting an exhibition of his works at the Borghese whilst on a romantic weekend away a couple of years back.' Jonathan paused, looking for Tate's recollection. 'You remember. When I took Maria from the Justice Department to Rome.'

'I knew there had to be a girl involved somewhere along the line. You never cease to amaze me, you really do,' chuckled Tate, looking at Harriet and shaking his head.

Tate returned to his friend, becoming aware that he was still pondering something. Jonathan looked up.

'Remind me. What are the two names which have arisen from your enquiries into the stolen Caravaggio?'

'Dr Coster is the name used by the individual who purchased the carrier painting,' said Tate, before turning to explain to Harriet. 'We believe the Caravaggio was smuggled into the country within the frame of another painting.' She indicated her understanding with an expression of surprise. 'And Dr Valentine is possibly a name the Caravaggio seller is using when making contact with Jeremy Grayson,' added Tate, conscious that Jonathan was still chewing something over in his head.

'Got a pen?' asked Jonathan turning over one of the pictures. He began to write out a list of names on the back.

'Stom, Bigot, Strozzi, Coster, Valentine.' He pointed to the fourth name. "Adam De Coster. I believe is a Flemish painter.' He moved the pen to point at the last name. 'Drop the 'E' from Valentine and you get Valentin. Valentin de Boulogne if I am correct is another predominant 17th Century artist.' He added one more word to the list.

Caravaggisti.

'The followers of Caravaggio. All five painters are known to have been influenced by Caravaggio. They all continued to produce works in the style of Caravaggio long after his death.' Lena spoke for the first time in a while.

'Perhaps the unsub sees themself as a Caravaggisti and by posing the bodies they believe they are continuing his legacy to this day.'

'Would have been a damn sight easier to use paints and a canvas,' mocked Jonathan before seeing the steadfast look on Harriet's face and wishing he hadn't done so. She was now focused on the task at hand.

'It still doesn't offer us any further solution towards the reason for the choosing of the three victims,' proclaimed Harriet, trying to redirect the conversation. 'There must be a significant link between all three?' She stopped and thought for a second, searching for a reason, clutching at an answer. 'The link has to be art related. Perhaps they have all crossed the same individual whilst purchasing art on the black market. Maybe they have wronged that individual during a previous transaction. Is it a revenge thing? Someone seeking justice?'

'Perhaps they are being made an example of, maybe as a warning,' remarked Lena. 'Wealth is the common denominator here. Someone in the artworld may be frustrated by the increasingly common use of a wealthy status to illegitimately obtain works beyond normal means. The killings could be their way of making a statement.' Tate waited for the two women to finish speculating before returning to the facts.

'Sir Christopher Roebuck has been unquestionably suspected of illicitly purchasing art in the past and has connections with a certain Mr Grayson. Anatoli Nikolaev has also been subject to our investigations on more than one occasion. It is widely known that both Ashley Denning and Hidetaka Yamamoto have substantial art collections including works bought outside the usual channels. Therefore either of your theories would fit the profile.'

'We will need to obtain the bank records of all three of the deceased,' declared Harriet, 'checking any large money transfers for similarities in the recipient's account numbers.' Jonathan raised a hand before adding a suggestion.

'Maybe you need to look at the paintings in each of the victim's private collections. Singling out those which have not been purchased through an auction catalogue or via gallery transactions. You may well find a common trait, which in turn could lead to someone already on our radar.' The other three agreed and Harriet started to make notes to lines of enquiry they would now need to follow.

'As we don't have a probable suspect and an arrest is not anticipated, perhaps the focus should be on preventing another crime,' claimed Tate digressing the conversation once more. I will re-contact my source with regards to a fifth name.' He then directed a question directly at Lena and Jonathan. 'If the perpetrator were to commit a fourth crime, which of Caravaggio's remaining paintings do you think fits best with the way the bodies are likely to be posed?' They both thought for a minute. Jonathan with a hand cupped to his mouth and Lena scratching the walls of her thumbnails with her index fingers.

'There are several crucifixions. Then there is the Sacrifice of Isaac. Once again, the use of a knife within the scene. There are so many possibilities,' Lena claimed. 'The flagellation of Christ. Crowning with Thorns. The Burial of St Lucy. The list goes on.' Jonathan waited for Lena to finish before adding further titles.

'There appear to be swords in his paintings of the Martyrdom of St Matthew and the Beheading of St John the Baptist,' he continued as he scrolled his phone through a chronological pictorial of Caravaggio's entire catalogue.

'They all sound easily manipulatable in any given location,' proclaimed Harriet as she briefly looked up from writing down all that Lena and Jonathan had been relating. 'I feel we now need to do some additional groundwork and do it fast. The time window between the murders is shortening with each crime. We need to act now. I would like to share the information you have provided with my team as soon as possible. Your insights and knowledge have raised many questions, many of which we cannot answer at present. They have however, given us more direction and provided potential lines of enquiry we can now look to explore further.' She paused, closed the file in front of her and clipped the pen she had been using to its cover. She then looked up to acknowledge the other three people around the desk and express her gratitude and appreciation.

'All of your input this afternoon has been invaluable. I cannot thank you enough. If you think of anything further which may be beneficial to our on-going enquiries, I will always be welcome to your input.' She smiled at Tate in particular.

'You have a great team, Tate. Don't lose them.'

Thorney Street
London, England

81

Lena and Jonathan had said their farewells to Harriet. Lena's having been slightly more formal than her colleagues. Tate and Harriet remained in the office.

'Your team are a credit to you,' she continued to praise as she collated the paperwork spread out across Tate's desk. 'It was really enamouring to see three people spark off each other so. You can feel there is a strong bond between you.' She placed the gathered evidence folders into her attaché case, leaving a single file on the desk.

'Our meeting has certainly opened new directions for both investigations and identified evidence which strongly suggests links between the two cases which will require further exploration from both sides,' proclaimed Tate, as his ever-inquisitive mind could not stop his eyes diverting to the remaining file. Harriet was also all too aware of Tate's unconscious eye movements.

'There is one more piece of evidence I would appreciate you taking a look at before I leave,' declared Harriet reaching for the folder. 'In fact, it is the second reason why I wished to meet with you today.'

'Fire away,' Tate replied, keen to know what was so paramount for Harriet to have waited until now to share with him.

'Our perpetrator has left what we believe to be taunting messages at each of the crime scenes.' She opened the file and handed Tate three enlarged photographs. 'Each message has been tattooed onto the surface of what we now know from analysis to be pigskin.' Tate shuffled through the three photographs taking his time to read the message within each. 'The messages were found hidden within the neck wounds of the first two victims and inserted into the throat of the third.' Harriet could sense an unease in Tate's eyes. 'I presume you will recognise the source of the words that have been used,' she said as Tate took a seat and she continued. 'As soon as we discovered their origin, I instantly knew you would be the best person to offer a possible understanding of their meaning…' She stopped mid-sentence, noticing a sense of disquietude had swept over Tate. He sat, head down in the chair and read through the words several more times. Harriet sat down to be at the same level. She looked across waiting for a response. Eventually it came. But it was not at all what she had been expecting.

'I too have been getting similar messages.' Harriet was momentarily taken aback by the reply and she could not find an immediate response. Neither spoke as the reality of the situation sank in. Whilst both remained briefly lost for words, Tate located the emails containing the messages he had received. He turned his monitor so Harriet could view the content. Eventually he spoke. 'At first I thought it was Jonathan having one of his little jokes. What with the words being from the Neptune's Finger album and our shared fondness of music. But he maintained he knew nothing about it.' He looked across at the picture of the album cover on the wall. Harriet followed his gaze.

'Well, I think we can now fairly safely acknowledge that both of our cases are indeed connected, or at least someone wishes for us to be aware of that fact,' proposed Harriet. 'And like the messages our investigation has uncovered, the ones you have received also appear to be antagonising.'

'I totally agree. I have discussed with my team the possibility of the messages being used in a way to provoke a reaction. However, the signature now makes a lot more sense too.' Harriet quizzically looked at Tate, perplexed by his last statement. Her face wore a look of bewilderment as she waited for an explanation. 'The Narcissus is the title of yet another painting by Caravaggio. It seems our unsub is seeking attention. They have given themselves a "Nom de Guerre" or alias.' Harriet picked up on Tate's train of thought and cut in.

'So they want to be known, or worse, to be remembered. They have a need for an identity. They believe their actions have purpose and wish others to be aware of that fact.'

'The messages are undeniably lyrics taken from songs which appear on the album "Beyond the Waves". At first glance, they could be seen as a means of attracting attention. An almost "catch me if you can" scenario. The perpetrator wanting to be acknowledged for their notoriety.'

'We are currently keeping our cards very close to our chests with this particular line of enquiry,' Harriet divulged, pointing to the photographs which Tate had placed back on the desk. 'The last thing we need now is the press getting hold of this. I do not intend to hand this person the eminence they seek.'

'I completely agree,' asserted Tate, 'we do not need to attract any unwanted attention to either investigation or risk the possibility of the media speculating any sort of link between the two.' He paused for a moment to ponder a thought over in his head. 'On the surface, it appears that the stolen Caravaggio is being used as an enticer. Simply being used to allure specific individuals. If so, I do believe there may still be further underlying reasons for the stealing of the painting. There could well be more to this than presently meets the eye.' Harriet nodded in agreement as she rose from the chair.

'This afternoon has opened many doors. I think it best we update our teams with these new findings as soon as possible.' She collected the remaining file, slid it into her attaché case and held a hand across the table. Tate also eased from his chair, accepting the handshake as he stood.

'May I suggest we keep communication channels between our respective cases open for the meantime?' stated Tate as they held the handshake a little longer than normal.

'Absolutely,' replied Harriet, her eyes locking momentarily with Tate's before diverting down at the desk. Two coffees still sat on its surface.

Both had long gone cold.

Bethnal Green
London, England

82

Harriet headed straight back to the incident room at Bethnal Green, only stopping briefly at Krispy Kreme Doughnuts on the High Street. As she entered the room, she noted that the majority of her team were present. Noticeably absent was DI Richards. The remainder were all absorbed in tasks involving either paperwork, computers or telephones. She dropped the 24-piece selection box on the nearest desk and opened the lid.

'Ok Crew, gather round.'

One by one the team appeared, drawn by the sweet doughy aroma like bees to a honeypot. George was one of the first to delve into the box. He reached for the Double Chocolate Dreamcake at its centre. As he withdrew his goody, his wrist was met with a slap and a finger waggled in his face. He dropped the doughnut back to the centre of the box and settled for a Glazed Raspberry instead. Sarika smiled up at George and retrieved the Dreamcake doughnut. George knew all too well, as did everyone, the Double Chocolate Dreamcake always had Sarika's name on it.

As Harriet's crew began to settle into positions along desk edges, each armed and ready with a doughnut, Harriet found herself a desk corner from where to address the team.

'As some of you are aware, I have just spent an invaluable afternoon with the Arts and Antiquities Investigation team, headed up by DCI Tate Randall. With their extensive knowledge and expertise we were able to establish several potential evidential pointers and uncovered significant links between our crime scenes and a major case they are also currently investigating.'

Harriet spent the next twenty minutes bringing those present up to date with the findings, outcomes and subsequent lines of inquiry arising from her earlier meeting. As she did so, individuals posed questions to clarify or elucidate their understanding. Some took notes, others jotted key points and several retrieved a second doughnut. Satisfied that she had summarised the vital details and that the clock was now ticking, she addressed their current situation.

'Before we continue, would someone update me with the whereabouts of DS Richards?'

'He is currently with Anatoli Nikolaev,' divulged DC Stevens, 'Mr Nikolaev initially turned down the offer of a safe house. He said he was happy with his own security team. DS Richards has gone to explain the severity of the situation with the hope of changing Mr Nikolaev's intentions.'

'Thanks Andy.' DS Stevens acknowledged his superior before taking a second bite of his doughnut. 'Anything further with linking the names of the artists with the name "Narcissus",' asked Harriet, directing her question specifically towards DC Thompson.

'Bit of a dead end I'm afraid Ma'am. Only thing even close was a painting by Strozzi entitled "Woman in a Mirror". It was apparently inspired by the Narcissus fable.'

'Let's change direction a bit, Greg. Can you look into any dealers who are frequently involved in art transactions involving large sums of money. Start with inside the M25 and within the last ten years. Check any suspects you uncover for criminal records.' Greg nodded.

'Andy. Get me a full print-out of the lyrics from the Neptune's Finger album, will you?'

'Already done,' he replied as he crossed to his desk, retrieved a print-out and handed it to Harriet.

'Also nothing so far,' commented Greg Thompson, motioning towards the print-out, 'on links between the lyrics, Neptune's Finger and the paintings.'

'Anything from HOLMES yet, Sarika?'

'Several hits on the parameter "Red Cloth" she replied, wiping the back of her hand across her mouth, 'two hits linked to strangulations and a couple more associated with suffocations.'

'Can you follow them up, please. Look for any connections to art theft, artists, art transactions and art in general.'

'No problem,' nodded Sarika, licking the tips of her fingers. Harriet shook her head and smiled, before looking across the room to DC Evans.

'Where are we with the phone records, Jake?' DC Evans lent forward from the edge of the desk and clasped his hands together.

'The phone companies haven't been too forthcoming due to the celebrity status of the victims. However, we should have them in the next few hours or so.'

'Get back onto them. If they are not here within the next hour, threaten them with subpoenas.'

'No probs, Ma'am. I'll get onto it immediately,' replied Jake, straightening himself back up on the desk.

'And get George to give you a hand when they finally arrive,' Harriet added. Jake and George looked at each other and nodded. George raised the remnants of a second doughnut in recognition. Harriet returned her attentions to Andy Stevens.

'Get onto the banks and credit companies, Andy. We want the account records of the deceased. Look for any large money transactions to the same recipient account.' Andy jotted a note on his pad. Harriet looked around the room.

'Any questions?' None came. Heads shook. 'Good, then let's get to it. And someone let me know as soon as DI Richards returns.' The team began to disperse back to their own work areas. Some collected a second or third doughnut on the way.

Thorney Street
London, England

83

Jeremy Grayson sat alone at the table. He checked his watch. He had been sat there for over twenty minutes, but he knew it was all part of the game. He had reluctantly agreed to a voluntary interview after yet another visit in just a matter of days from the Arts and Antiquities Investigation Department. However, this time it had only been the female DI. She had informed him that he was now a 'Person of Interest' relating to the whereabouts of the missing Caravaggio. At first, he had avoided her questions and offered little in the way of a positive response. After the threat of the possibility of obtaining a warrant to search the premises, he was encouraged to make himself available for questioning. Off the record of course. He had agreed to attend the following day.

So here he sat. Whilst he sat, he pondered what they could possibly have discovered. The longer he sat, the more time he had to strengthen his defences to any accusations that may come. Eventually, the door opened and the DI entered, closely followed by her more senior partner. They both took chairs opposite him. She placed an open folder on the table. He could not make out its detail from where he sat.

'Thank you once again for making yourself available to help us with our on-going enquiries relating to the disappearance of the Caravaggio Magdalene,' said the female detective. Jeremy made no response.

'As I mentioned whilst at your gallery yesterday, some information has recently come to light relating to your possible involvement in the movement of this painting.' Again Jeremy remained blank.

'We have a source, who you will appreciate must remain anonymous, who indicates you have been asked to provide and make contact with potential buyers for the said painting.' Jeremy still felt no reason to reply at present. She continued.

'We were granted a warrant to obtain your phone records.' Jeremy was about to object but thought better. It would be to no avail. 'As you are most probably aware, the first three names we are led to believe you have provided, are all now deceased.' She is choosing her words carefully, thought Jeremy. He began to feel apprehensive.

'The same three individuals have also received calls in the week prior to their murders from a mobile phone registered in your name,' declared the DI, turning the folder in Jeremy's direction. He spoke for the first time.

'Coincidental. They are all existing customers.' He took the opportunity to change his position in the chair. One of his buttocks was becoming numb.

'Can you explain three phone calls from mobile phones which have only been used for a single call to your gallery, each call being received only minutes before you made the calls to each of the victims?'

'I have numerous daily calls from persons unknown, making enquiries,' Jeremy replied, carefully choosing his words too. Two can play at that game. The DI continued whilst her partner started to jot the occasional thing in his notebook.

'Does the name Dr Valentine mean anything to you?'

'It's not a name I am familiar with. Should It?'

'We are led to believe it could possibly be the name of, or being used by, the individual wishing to sell the Caravaggio.' Jeremy did not reply. He just shook his head and pursed his lips. The senior officer tore a page from his notebook and handed it to his colleague. She read it before speaking again.

'If you have indeed gotten yourself mixed up in something much deeper than you may have expected, we may be able to offer you a way out. Maybe you did provide contacts as a middleman in the sale of a stolen work of art. However, at that point you had no indication it would lead to the deaths of three individuals and you are now looking at a charge of aiding and abetting in three murders.' She paused and waited for a reaction. Jeremy remained steadfast. He ran a hand back through his hair and looked at the detective.

'If you were to offer us information relating to the identification or whereabouts of the so-called Dr Valentine, we may well be able to get those charges reduced to aiding and abetting the sale of stolen property.' Jeremy maintained his silence and pondered once more. Eventually he responded.

'I do not know Dr Valentine personally or professionally. I have never met Dr Valentine. However, I have spoken over the phone with someone who alleges to be a Dr Valentine.' Jeremy might have been guilty of attempting to move a painting on the black market, but there was absolutely no way he was being accused of aiding and abetting a murder.

12th August 1606
Zagarolo, Alban Hills, Italy

84

Michelangelo continued to apply the 'grounding' to the canvas which lay on the table before him. He had previously applied a generous layer of animal skin glue, known as 'sizing', to seal the surface of the canvas. The grounding was composed of walnut oil, gypsum dust and pigments of carbon-black, brown-umber and a small amount of white-lead. This would create the dark primary under tones needed to deepen any shadows within the painting, whilst providing a strong base colour for a contrasting dark background.

It had been a couple of months now since Michelangelo had accepted the duke's offer to reside at his Colonna Palace. The remoteness of the location offered a man in fear for his life, a safe haven to continue his work away from his foreboding situation. During that time he had produced two new works. The first was a reproduction of a work he had previously painted five years earlier during his residency in Rome. The 'Supper at St Emmaus' depicted the moment when a resurrected Jesus reveals himself to two of his disciples. Michelangelo was presently a troubled man, whose sombre mood was reflected in the darkness and deep shadows of the composition. The second painting was 'David with the Head of Goliath'. It showed a triumphant David holding the severed head of Goliath the Giant. Again the picture was cast in extreme darkness. The most poignant aspect of the painting was Michelangelo's self-portrait as the disembodied head of Goliath; Strangely symbolic of his own head being offered in a gesture of forgiveness.

Michelangelo continued to apply a second layer of the grounding to ensure the under layer of the canvas was the deep tone he sought. There was a knock at the door.

'Entrare,' declared Michelangelo and a household servant entered the room. The servant bowed. 'Vieni vieni.' The servant approached the table where Michelangelo worked. He carefully put down his palate knife and gave the servant his full attention.

'The rider returned this afternoon. I have been asked to bring this straight to you,' she stated, holding her hand in Michelangelo's direction and offering a folded square of paper.

'Grazie,' he replied, taking the letter and replacing it with a coin. The servant returned her gratitude, bowed once again and exited the room.

A few days earlier a rider and carriage had been dispatched to Rome. On-board the carriage were the two completed paintings. The first, 'Supper at Emmaus' was to be delivered to Ottavio Costa, a previous customer, in hope that his interest remained and he would purchase the picture. The other painting of 'David and Goliath' was to be surrendered as a gift to Scipione Borghese, the head of papal justice. The one man who could offer Michelangelo a full pardon and a return from exile. The offer of a painting with the self portrait of Michelangelo's severed head being a submissive plea to keep his own in real life. Before the carriage had departed, Michelangelo had also entrusted the rider with a letter and instructions for him to personally deliver it to Signora Antognetti.

Michelangelo broke the unmarked wax seal. He read the letter. Tears began to flow from the corners of his eyes. Tears of sadness, that he could no longer be with Signora Antognetti. Tears of joy, for the news she wrote of within the letter. He read one particular sentence, over and over, repeatedly.

'*I am with child and it can only be with you.*'

He comprehended the words and the significance of their context to both himself and Signora Antognetti. He could not return to her at present. Perhaps she may now be persuaded to leave Rome and follow him South. As he contemplated the situation, he came to realise that there was one constant. He must continue painting. Whatever the future held for them, he must be in a situation to provide for Signora Antognetti and the child.

He thought of the woman to whom he had declared his true feelings only days before having to flee Rome. He held his hands to his heart and longed to one day embrace her again. His hands moved to his breast pocket. He had kept the pencil sketch close to his heart since that day. He removed the picture from the pocket and unfolded it within his hands. He studied its intimacy and the emotion it engendered. He gazed at its beauty and allure for a long while.

His next painting would be his repentance.

He would paint a lone female. A solitary woman in a state of desolation and abandonment. He would use Maddalena's image as the face of his new work. He would paint the subject of the painting gently caressing her swollen belly and the child within. He would entitle the painting,

'St Mary Magdalene in Ecstasy'.

Colliers Wood
London, England

85

Jonathan stood at the hob and stirred the rice. He took a sip of the Pinot Grigio he had just poured himself. He welcomed the refreshing aromas of peach and melon and the zesty fruit finish as he teased the wine around his mouth. He held the glass up to the light of the window and the early evenings sun sparkled as it refracted through the translucent pale lemon liquid.

He was in high spirits and a warm cosy feeling enveloped him, hugging his inner self and bestowing a sense of self-assurance. He liked to entertain, but this evening was much more than that. Cooking for Jocelyn for the first time was a big step for Jonathan. Things were changing. He had become more aware of his emotions of late and more importantly of those around him. His relationship with Jocelyn was on the verge of becoming a relationship. At this point, he would ordinarily have become uncomfortable, started to feel trapped and would have looked for ways to escape whilst formulating a relationship exit strategy. But this time it was different. He was at ease with it. He felt with Jocelyn that he could let down the walls a little. Open up and expose the cold heart of the Tin Man to the vulnerability of love and affection. Well, maybe just a little bit.

He took another sip of the wine and returned his attention back to the risotto. He had finely chopped his aromatics; onion, garlic and celery, before slowly sautéing them over a low flame. Or 'Il Soffritto' as the Italians liked to call it. He was currently at the second stage known as 'La Tostatura'. The roasting of the rice. He continued to stir, ensuring all the grains were coated in the oil, watching as he stirred for the rice to become translucent. The next stage was his favourite. 'Lo Sfumato'. He turned up the heat and added a generous glass of white wine to the pan. No need to skimp at this stage. He had a second bottle chilling in the fridge anyway. The cold wine hitting the hot rice grains released an instantaneous aromatic steam. Jonathan lent over the pan and inhaled the intense fragrance of rapidly vaporising wine. It was one of his favourite smells when working in the kitchen. He sipped his own wine once more. After a few minutes, the alcohol had cooked off and he stirred in the first ladle of hot stock. He left the rice to absorb the stock and turned his attention to the remaining ingredients. He was preparing an asparagus and pea risotto as Jocelyn was a vegetarian. He began to chop the asparagus into bite size spears, occasionally turning to stir the rice. He was just about to add another ladle of stock to the pan when his apartment intercom buzzed. He looked up at the clock on the wall, then checked his watch.

'God, she's keen. I wasn't expecting her this early'. He took the pan off the heat and shouted at the intercom.

'Won't be a sec.' Not that anybody could hear him. He tidied the asparagus and the freshly shelled peas to one side, put the chopping board in the dishwasher and washed his hands. The intercom buzzed once again. 'Just coming.' He dashed into the bedroom, kicked off his slippers, wrestled with a pair of socks, before sliding into his leather loafers. He checked his hair in the mirror and untucked his collar. 'Still coming,' he hollered as he bared his teeth at his reflection, checking for stray strands of pea shoots. One more ruffle of the hair and he headed for the intercom and the front door. 'Sorry, I was…'

'Delivery for Mr Harvey,' declared an exasperated voice. Jonathan let out a relieved sigh and lolled his shoulders.

'I'll be right down.' He pushed the lobby entry release button. As he descended the stairs, he could not recall a delivery due today. In fact he could not recall having placed an order. He exited the stairwell just as the delivery van pulled away outside the building. The package had been left in front of the lift doors.

'Must be busy, probably on the clock,' he thought as he picked up the box and headed back up the stairs.

Jonathan placed the box on the kitchen counter, still puzzling at what the delivery could possibly be. The box had no identifiable markings. A thought suddenly hit him and he allowed himself a self-satisfying smirk. Perhaps it was from Jocelyn. He removed a knife from a drawer and carefully cut along the top seal of the box. He placed the knife to one side and slid a hand under the flap of the opening. As his fingers reached into the void below, they were immediately struck by something within the box. He withdrew his hand instantaneously. No sooner had he done so when a searing heat started to permeate up his arm. His hand began to burn and as he grasped at it with his other hand, he noticed two puncture marks just above his thumb. He instinctively realised what had just happened. He knew he had to remain calm, but panic would be the easier option. He grasped for his phone on the work counter and hit the three digits. The pain was beginning to worsen and his hand was starting to swell. Nausea filled his stomach.

The call connected.

'Emergency services. Which service do you require?'

'Ambulance,' he replied in a reasonably calm manner. As soon as the call reconnected, Jonathan immediately explained his situation and gave his address. He listened to the operators advice but the words began to make less sense and slowly they began to dissipate and the voice became more remote as a blackness enshrouded Jonathan.

The flap of the box fell to one side. The head of a small snake appeared over its rim.

Inside the box, a severed head sat transfixed in a soulless stare. An entanglement of snakes meandered within its hair.

St Georges Hospital
London, England

86

Jonathan woke from his dream. A really bad dream. His eyes adjusted and he slowly emerged into the world around him. He did not recognise his surroundings, nor could he comprehend where he might possibly be. Maybe he was still somewhere within his own subconscious. A dream within a dream. A false awakening. Gradually the foggy world began to dissipate and his perception of the situation started to make more sense. He tried to lift his head but it seemed like an invisible force was baring down upon him. It felt like a giant pair of hands were pinning his shoulders to the bed. He tried to lift an arm. It felt unusually larger than it should be. A strange sensation of numbness coupled with a tormenting pain irradiated with the slightest movement. He tried the same with the other arm. This time finding his hand secured to the bed with a series of tubes and wires. A sudden awareness overwhelmed him. His remaining senses came into play. His tongue tasted metallic and his throat felt like coarse sandpaper. He recognised trace aromas of pine fresh and the constant background rhythm of pulsing and beeping. But why would he be there?

A voice funnelled through the dissonance and Jonathan searched for the source of the sound.

'Hey Mate. Welcome back.' Jonathan raised his chin and squinted in the direction of the voice. His best friend stood to the side of the bed. He managed a wan smile. There was also a woman standing with Tate. He recognised her but could not find her name. 'You had us worried there for a moment,' said Tate as he moved over the bed to prevent his friend from stretching to see.

'Wha ha pen?' Jonathan slurred; his face partially paralysed on one side.

'Dr unk ple th.' Tate understood and retrieved a glass of water with a long straw from a bedside stand. He offered it to his friends mouth. Jonathan welcomed the liquid, moistening the desert in his throat. Tate used a wad of tissues to mop the water escaping from the drooling lip.

'Do you have any recollection of last night?' Tate offered the straw once more and Jonathan drank.

'Riss otho' came the reply as Jonathan squirmed and tried to sit himself up a little. Tate perceived the discomfort and electronically raised the head end of the bed. Jonathan adjusted his position and noticed his swollen arm for the first time. He winced slightly as he once again tried to move it.

'So, you were at home last night preparing dinner and it appears you received a delivery,' revealed Tate. 'We know this, because after you were brought here, Harriet and I visited your apartment.' Jonathan smiled at the woman. He now remembered her.

'Tha box,' tried Jonathan, still having difficulties talking, 'E Shn, eek.'

'Yes. You were bitten by a snake from in the box. Luckily, it was a shallow bite and you managed to call for assistance before you lost consciousness.' Harriet moved towards the bed, standing next to Tate. She spoke next.

'The snake was easily identifiable and an antivenin was administered within the first hour. You have received four more vials since then. The partial paralysis of your left side, which is affecting your speech at present, should subside over the next few hours.'

'And your chiselled good looks will not be affected,' added Tate.

All three smiled.

'The doctors say you may have a mild swelling and discomfort in your arm for several days.' Jonathan motioned for more fluids and as Tate accommodated his request, Harriet continued. 'Our primary observations at your apartment, reveal you were sent a severed head in a box. There were also several snakes recovered from your kitchen.' Tate noticed a glint of recognition in his friends eye.

'Yes. The Medusa. The Gorgon from Greek mythology with venomous snakes as hair. Turning all those who gazed into her eyes to stone,' explained Tate. 'Once again, a work by Caravaggio. He painted it on the face of a battle shield. I remember seeing it at the Uffizi whilst I was at a conference in Florence.'

'It appears to be the work of our suspect known as The Narcissus,' declared Harriet. 'The box and the head have been taken for analysis and to check for similarities to the previous crime scenes.' Tate looked across at Jonathan and could tell the pieces were slowly starting to fall into place. A cloud passed across his friend's face. He took his hand as bleakness and desolation emptied his friends eyes.

'There is one more thing,' he said, knowing too well that Jonathan already sensed what was coming.

'The head in the box was Jocelyn's.'

Bethnal Green

London, England

87

Tate had shown his ID, signed in at the front desk and received directions to the incident room.

He was in a sombre mood. His friend had not taken the news of Jocelyn's death at all well. Moreover, there had been no leads to the location of the remainder of the body. The only consolation was the fact that Jonathan had not seen the head in the box. The snake bite had taken care of that. After leaving Jonathan's bedside yesterday, Tate had spent most of the afternoon on a video call with Moretti. He had spent a long while explaining the recently discovered links to the four murder scenes. Both men were now of the firm opinion that the Caravaggio was still somewhere within London. The call had ended with Moretti reassuring Tate that he had every confidence of the painting being recovered.

He was met at the entrance of the incident room by a young Detective Constable named Thompson, who he now followed through a warren of desks towards a glass partitioned office at the rear. Inquisitive heads turned from computer screens as he passed. Harriet noticing his approach, rose from behind her desk and greeted him at the door. They shook hands, both feeling more relaxed and comfortable in each other's presence than on the previous occasion.

'Thank you, Greg,' said Harriet dismissing the Constable. 'DCI Tate Randall allow me to introduce my new DI, Iain Richards.' The man still sitting at the desk stood and they too shook hands. 'Iain has recently joined us, having transferred from the Scottish force.'

"Where were you stationed?" enquired Tate.

'Edinburgh, Sir. Previous to that I pounded my beat in Inverness.' Tate acknowledged the answer and accepting Harriet's hand gesture he sat in the third chair.

'How's Jonathan?' enquired Harriet as she retook her position in the chair on the far side.

'I talked to him this morning. The paralysis has subsided and he's a lot more coherent. Apparently, the bite area is still painful and as he put it, "his arm still looks like an elephant's leg."" Harriet tittered and smiled, before removing an evidence bag from a drawer and handing it across the desk to Tate.

'The pathologist is still examining the head, but early indications suggest the amputation markings have similarities to those found on our first victim. Once again, he discovered our unsub's calling-card within the neck wounds.' Tate examined the item within the bag. It was the first of the actual tattooed pigskins he had handled. He found it somewhat disturbing. He had not expected the ink to be blood red. He studied the chosen lines.

'Pray for forgiveness you dogs of the sea
Last man on ship is the worst place to be
As Plague takes a hold, haunting the madness
Do not misjudge those laid before us
Is this disease a fiend or a friend
Take no prisoners, the downfall of men.'

Narcissus

As Tate digested the words, Harriet offered a suggestion to their meaning.

'The verse could once more be perceived as a threat or a warning. "The dogs of the sea" maybe referring to our victims. The perpetrator may be suggesting the victims are corrupt and they are in fact the offenders. She paused, aware that Tate was pondering something.

'Unless they are a direct warning to me. I don't believe this Narcissus was expecting Jonathan to survive. I think Jocelyn was just collateral damage. I believe Jonathan was the intended target and the threat may well be meant for me. Maybe I'm the next intended target. "The last man on ship." Once again the words point towards misjudgements.' He mused further. There was one thought that troubled him most. He spoke his suppositions aloud for the others to hear. 'Why Jonathan? He had no involvement in this until a few days ago. There was no motive to go after him unless it was to indirectly get at me. Jonathan and I have occasionally referred to ourselves as "dogs of the sea." But only those within our closest circles could possibly know that fact.' Tate felt an overwhelming sense of culpability. Had his friend almost lost his life because of him?

Had others fallen victim for something he had or hadn't done. There was a discomfort inside him but he could not put his finger on its cause. Something sat uneasy with him. He needed to find the answer and extinguish the annoyance. 'Do you have the CCTV footage from the entrance cameras at Jonathan's apartment block?' he asked, frustrated that he currently had more questions than answers. Harriet turned her computer monitor to face the two men and took up a position on the end of the desk.

'Over to you Iain.' He reached over and manipulated the mouse.

'Two cameras. One forwards to the door and the other covering the lifts and stairwell entrance.' The footage began to play out on a split screen so both feeds could be seen simultaneously. 'The time feed is two minutes before the delivery van can be seen arriving outside the property.' They watched the footage through twice, from the arrival of the van to Jonathan exiting the lobby with the package. A total of eight minutes from start to finish. Each time they scrutinised the images, looking for the smallest detail that could eventually lead to the identification of the perpetrator. After the second viewing, Iain, who had been quiet throughout added some further information. 'You will notice that shortly after the van arrives,' he played the footage in slow motion as he explained his presumptive, 'the driver appears from the far side of the van but is not seen to retrieve a package from the back or side doors. However, you can clearly see the box is already in their hands when they round the vehicle.' He re-ran the images once more.

'The driver is then seen walking to the door of the building, before using the entrance intercom. I think you will agree, the driver looks to be female, but the cap deliberately hides the face.' Iain paused the front facing camera on the clearest captured image of the driver. Something struck a chord with Tate. Unsure of his reasoning, he reserved judgement and remained quiet. Iain continued his analysis. 'At this point, the driver must be waiting for Mr Harvey,' he faltered momentarily, briefly looking to Harriet and Tate for consent to address their friend more informally. 'Jonathan,' he corrected, 'to answer the intercom and remotely open the doors before entering. She then leaves the package and exits before Jonathan is seen to enter from the stairwell.' Iain looked once more to Harriet for approval, she nodded, he continued.

'The courier company have confirmed a delivery to a property in the vicinity yesterday evening. The driver on the round is logged as a male. The scheduled delivery was for a Mr Nicholas Wright at an address on the opposite side of the street.' Iain checked his notes from a file on the table.

'I contacted Mr Wright this morning. He confirmed the delivery of a package. However, it appears the item was something he had not ordered. George is currently on his way to retrieve the delivered item and Jake is tracking the source of the delivery's order.'

'Do we know what the item was,' asked Harriet, wondering if it would be consequential to the case. Iain held off for a moment, knowing his reply would certainly put the cat amongst the pigeons.

'Apparently it is a small inflatable pig.' All three knew the significance of the item but Tate was first to speak.

'Yet another link. This time however, to the picture of the Pink Floyd album on my office wall.' Harriet and Iain sat and waited; they could clearly see Tate was once more running something through in his head. Things were starting to add up, but Tate was not sure he wanted them to. Over the past twenty-four hours he'd had his suspicions and his intuitions were now striking chords within his head. However, he could not couple any of his suppositions with conscious reasoning. 'Did the delivery have a pre-designated arrival window?' he finally asked.

'It was scheduled in a two-hour slot between six and eight, which corresponds to the time signature on our CCTV footage,' replied Iain.

'If the perp had been remotely tracking the package's delivery, they could easily have seen when the driver was just a few drops away and parked just before the van arrived. Could you rewind the CCTV to the point before the vans arrival?' Iain re-cued the footage to its start point and no sooner had it resumed when Tate asked for it to be paused. 'Can you zoom in on the car on the far side of the street?' Iain manipulated the footage to tighten the image and eventually an enlarged grainy picture filled the screen.

'That's our delivery driver,' Harriet declared as she moved closer to the screen to get a better look. 'So the van was just a ploy. It was used to cover up a delivery by hand. They waited in the car for the real driver to make the delivery across the street and appeared from the far side of the van giving the impression that they were the driver.' Harriet stopped, having noticed something further within the frozen image. She pointed to a detail. 'You can see the logo on the cap.' Iain played the footage and paused the picture once more at the point where the imposter driver waited outside the entrance to Jonathan's apartment. He enlarged the image as before.

'There,' pointed Harriet. 'You can see the logo much more clearly. It's the same cap that CCTV footage captured our perpetrator wearing at the second crime scene. You can quite clearly see the triangular logo.'

'It's not a triangle,' revealed Tate. He knew exactly what it was. 'It's a prism. It's the cover graphic from Pink Floyds "Dark Side of the Moon" album.' Tate's previous speculations were slowly emerging to be true and a realization materialised that his instinct may have been right all along.

'Is it possible to play the footage of the driver waiting outside the entrance in slow motion?' asked Tate. Once more, Iain worked his magic and moments later the footage ran at quarter speed. As the footage played, Tate attentively watched. 'Can you do the same with the footage of the individual in the car before the van appears?' Again he watched, leaning closer to meticulously observe the finer detail. Iain allowed the footage to continue and they viewed the entrance footage once more. 'In both sections of the footage you can clearly see the individual is rubbing and picking at the nail area of their fingers. It's an anxiety disorder known as Onychotillomania. For many sufferers it's a repetitive behaviour which they do habitually without realising it.' Having made the statement, Tate felt the pit of his stomach fall away. A feeling of disquietude engulfed his body. He was finding it difficult to contemplate what was really happening. He began to question himself. Was it all a great misconception? Was he seeing and believing things that weren't really there? He knew deep down that was not the answer. The evidence was now beginning to outweigh the doubts. The facts slowly substantiating his suspicions. He knew what he was about to share would have an effect on his life for many years to come. He fought for a reason not to do so. But his rationale won over.

'It's Lena.'

Bethnal Green

London, England

88

'Are you sure?'

As reality hit it felt like the world had stopped and time had been abandoned. Seconds passed. A fragile silence froze the room. It's three occupants momentarily unsure how best to proceed. Each remaining quiet, uncomfortably numb with the thought of saying the wrong thing. No one person wanting to offend another. The silence being a sign of mutual respect and understanding. What happened next would have an effect on all three, but in very different ways.

Tate rubbed his eyes and held his hands across his nose in a prayer pose. He was struggling to comprehend what was happening and to where and who the evidence was pointing.

'OK.' The only word he could find as he composed himself. Still not knowing quite where to start. He took a deep breath and sighed. 'There is part of me still hoping I've got this all wrong. But the deeper we dig, the more it seems that my recent suspicions have been right. I am not completely sure at this point of the reasons why. But I do believe in my instincts and what they are telling me.' He paused once more, holding his palm across his eyes and forehead. He grimaced and pulled the hand and his frustrations down the side of his face.

'I believe Lena is the Narcissus.' He had still not wanted to say it, but he had now said it twice and the more he thought about it, the more he realised it was probably true. Harriet broke her silence, curious to understand Tate's reasoning.

'What led you to think it was Lena?'

'There was more and more evidence pointing to someone who knew certain aspects of my personal life and someone who had access to or at least had visited my office. The messages I have received and those left at your crime scenes point to someone who clearly has knowledge of the artworks on my wall.' DS Richards had started to take notes as Tate divulged his thoughts. He had several questions, but at this moment he thought it best to let Tate continue.

'When you met with us,' he gestured to Harriet, who had returned to the chair behind her desk, 'to discuss possible links to the artists you had uncovered, I wondered why Lena was not completely forth coming with information relating to Caravaggio, considering her extensive knowledge of the subject. I felt then, she was holding back. She has as much if not more insight into matters relating to that subject than Jonathan.' The mention of his friend caused Tate to waver. Having come that close to losing him had had much more of an effect on Tate than he could have imagined. That coupled with the fact that his colleague who he trusted and respected could well be responsible for the murder of four people. It did not sit well with him and he was finding it difficult to come to terms with the situation. He rubbed his palms into the corners of his eyes once more.

'Do you believe that is the reason behind the incident at Jonathan's apartment?' asked Harriet. Tate took a moment to respond. When he eventually did so, there was a quiver in his voice.

'Just now, I can't comprehend any reasoning whatsoever. Until we apprehend Lena and question her motives, all I do know is that she would have been one of a few people who knew of Jonathan's relationship with Jocelyn. If she had some form of premeditated list, then maybe Jonathan's murder had been planned all along. Who knows?' There is only one person who can answer that question, thought Tate and at some point, he was going to ask it. He stood for a moment to stretch his legs and leant onto the back of the chair.

'Lena was on holiday on the twin islands of Corsica and Sardinia when the Caravaggio painting was originally stolen in Rome. The islands are situated off the West coast of Italy. Having dual nationality passports would have allowed her to travel from Sardinia to the mainland as an Italian citizen. There would be no record.' Harriet looked perplexed. She had only met Lena the once, but now as she thought about it, she did have strong Mediterranean features. She looked at Tate for an answer.

'I know some of Lena's background but obviously not in great detail. She was born in Italy to parents who owned and ran a respectable hotel business in a small village in the Umbria region. Her parents were both killed during the 1997 earthquake that struck the central area. Their hotel was completely destroyed during the quake and Lena was pulled from the rubble. An English couple who had frequented the hotel for many years and had become good friends with the family had been staying there at the time. They adopted Lena later that year and she came to live with them in England at the age of eleven. Her adoptive father ran a successful chain of family butchers in Suffolk and apparently Lena quickly adapted to her new life, but probably never overcame the tragedy of losing her real parents.'

'The butchery might be important,' said Harriet picking up on Tate's thread, 'it has been suggested that the precision of the cut marks to the wound areas at the first three crime scenes could well point towards someone who is familiar with the tools and techniques of surgery, veterinary or butchery work.'

'Lena has mentioned in passing that she did help out in the shop at weekends as a teenager to earn some pocket money,' Tate added, as his attention was momentarily diverted by his phone pinging in his pocket. He ignored it and went to continue but was beaten to it by a question from DS Richards.

'You mentioned that Lena was on holiday when the painting was stolen. Has she had any other time off since then, Sir?'

'She took a long weekend off last week. She apparently had a property booked for a couple of days to catch up with an old friend.'

'The very same weekend that Ashley Denning was murdered,' stated Harriet, just as the penny dropped and Tate looked wide eyed at the other two officers. He began to rack his brain for Lena's other movements over the last few weeks. He could not remember her booking any other time off. She had however taken a day here and there when their case load had allowed her.

'What was the date of the second murder?'

'The 23rd,' replied DS Richards without the need to check his notes. The dates of the live investigations were firmly planted in his mind. Tate began to wander across the office floor, his head down as he tried to further recall occurrences and run a chronological calendar through in his head.

'I'm fairly sure she was off on both the 23rd and 24th as she had worked the weekend before but I can't be too sure without checking.' Deep down inside Tate realised he had no need to check, he instinctively knew that the dates would coincide. He also knew that if he checked, Lena would have been off when the first murder had taken place too. His phone message alert sounded once more. Again he chose to ignore it.

'How did she seem at work between these dates, Sir?' enquired DS Richards.

'She has been her usual self, busy with the case load we have, being a small team. She has shown frustrations with art collectors of late and has a particular vendetta with Jeremy Grayson, the dealer who is subject to our enquiries into the missing Caravaggio. She has always been rather opinionated about the reasons to own particular art works and believes that it is wrong for people to use it as a status thing.' Even as Tate exposed and uncovered the layers to provide Harriet and Iain with the little he did know about Lena, he was still looking for a stumbling block, the smallest circumstance that would cause them to question Lena's incrimination. It was fast becoming one of those days where he simply wished he had not gotten out of bed. He wanted to bury his head under a pillow and hope and pray that it all would just simply go away or better still to wake up and discover it had all been a nasty dream. But this was not going to go away and they would probably not discover a miraculous lifeline. Tate had felt ill at ease with providing information that may well result in the conviction of a colleague. But he had taken an oath and it was his duty to uphold the law.

'The CCTV footage from Jonathan's lobby corroborated my earlier suspicions. I had become consciously aware of Lena's habitual behaviour during the time we have worked together but thought little of it. Observing a similar behaviour in that footage put the final nail in the coffin so to speak.' Both Harriet and Iain had been listening intently and Iain had continued to take his notes. They were both fully aware how difficult it would be for an officer of the law to incriminate a colleague.

Tate's phone pinged three more times in quick succession. He could ignore it no longer. He looked at the screen. There were five identically copied messages all from the same email address.

All from his own email as before.

Someone desperately wanted his attention. He knew exactly what to expect before opening the first. He read the words as they appeared before turning the phone for Harriet and Iain to see.

Tate Randall
Tate Randall
7th August, 14:23

The hand has risen from beyond the waves

Reaching skywards as all hope fades

Set a bearing to the eye of the storm

Where pillars stand tall and creation was born

Narcissus

Tate read through the words again. Something did not ring true, but he could not put his finger on it. It was not until he read it through a third time, that he noticed the dissimilarity.

'The last line has been changed. The lyrics from the song are, "Where pillars once fell," but this has been changed to, "Where pillars stand tall."' All three looked at each other, each knowing the underlying meaning of the message.

'She's taunting me to confront her,' Tate declared, 'and I know exactly where to find her.'

Battersea Power Station

London, England

89

The Narcissus looked up at Jeremy Grayson as he began to stir. The sedative was wearing off. Jeremy's head hung limp to one side. His limbs twitched as he slowly regained consciousness. The potency of the drug still in his system causing confusion as he battled to understand his situation. He tried to move his hands but only to be confronted with a raging pain as he tried to do so. His mind fighting to grasp at the source of his torment.

Jeremy had been secured to the face of one of Battersea Power Station's iconic chimneys.

He had been crucified.

Earlier that afternoon, Lena had confronted Jeremy at his gallery. She had requested he accompany her to an undisclosed address. A cunning ruse had been contrived implying that the Caravaggio Magdalene had been located and Jeremy's charges of involvement would be reduced if he cooperated and provided them with a confirmation of authenticity. At first he had resisted, but the threat of an impending arrest and an illogical notion that he might just be let off the hook had swayed his decision.

They had journeyed across the city; both being guarded and uncommunicative. Their past feelings and perceptions of each other evident in their silence. Jeremy had become wary of the situation when they had parked at the construction site below the towering building. Lena had reassured him that Tate and the Caravaggio awaited them in an apartment in Phase Two of the recently rejuvenated building.

When they had stepped out of the lift onto a construction site of what was to become roof top gardens and not a residential floor below, Jeremy had immediately known something was amiss. He had tried to insist he was no longer happy to be a part of whatever this was, even if it would mean him facing charges. He was adamant in his decision and had turned to leave. It was a this point that Lena had pulled a gun.

At first Jeremy became argumentative and belligerent. His fury slowly abating as the realisation of the situation started to sink in and it all began to make sense. Then like a shot it hit him. Lena and the Narcissus were one and the same. A panic had swept through him and he had suddenly become fearful for his own life. At gun point, Lena had marched Jeremy across the roof, through the construction works to one of the landmark chimneys. An advertising scaffold shroud hid their presence from public view. She had then forced him to remove his clothing and climb onto the chimney's brick plinth before handcuffing himself to the lightning conductor rod. Jeremy had cried. Cried for his dignity and cried because he was just plain scared of the inevitable. The last thing he would remember was the pin prick as Lena injected the sedative into his ankle. She had then retrieved a rucksack she had stowed the previous evening and set about composing another 'true-to-life' masterpiece.

The posing of the body had taken a relatively short time and Lena, aka the Narcissus, now marvelled at her latest creation. As she took pleasure in admiring its beauty, her mind wandered back to the other works she had previously created. All had been magnificent in their own macabre way. But this she believed was her crowning glory.

Jeremy Grayson's body slumped lifelessly from the cylindrical chimney stack. His hands were pinned to the chimney's walls, a single bolt driven through each palm. He was naked apart from a white cloth dressing his groin. His feet had been crossed at the ankle and bound with rope. His torso was crisscrossed with lacerations and a crown of thorns woven in barbwire had been placed upon his head. Rivulets of blood ran down his face as the barbs of the wreath clawed at his flesh. The way in which Lena had posed the body had been inspired by two similar works that Caravaggio had painted whilst in exile. Christ at the Column and the Flagellation of Christ. Each depicting the flogging of Jesus before his crucifixion.

Jeremy fought to focus his mind and make sense of the falsehoods his eyes were feeding him. His recollection was foggy and a feeling of uncertainty and bewilderment clouded his judgement. Or maybe his eyes were not lying. Pain seemed to scream from every inch of his body. Maybe he had awoken and stepped back into reality and straight into a nightmare.

'Mr Grayson. How good of you to join me.' He heard the voice but could make little sense of who it came from or what was happening. 'The effect of the sedative I gave you is now subsiding and I require your undivided attention.' A crippling pain seared through Jeremy as the thongs of the leather scourge flailed at the already ribboned flesh of his torso. Lena recoiled the Cat 'O' Nine Tails and struck a second time. Jeremy pleaded. His voice almost silent, escaping in nothing more than a whisper as shock overwhelmed his body.

'We are here to bear witness and to pass judgement for the crimes you have committed,' demanded Lena as she unleashed the scourge for a third time. Each strike inflicting further wounds and suffering. 'Are you, or are you not, guilty of selling stolen works of art on the black market?'

'Please. Stop,' Jeremy moaned, the words only just eligible. Lena ignored the plea. She paid little attention to Jeremy's sufferings. His pain and distress were a hardship she chose to ignore.

'Guilty!' she announced, preparing to strike the flagellated body once more. Blood splattered from the whip's tails, tracing the arc of its directional path as it recoiled. Jeremy's body tensed in anticipation of his looming anguish. With each strike he weakened. Unsure of how much more of this affliction his body could bear. As the woman spoke, he heard the words, but struggled to find an understanding. 'Have you actively participated in organised crime to unlawfully obtain works of art?'

'No more. Please,' he pleaded, his strength now failing him and a broken man could be heard in the desperation in his voice.

'Just answer the question.' She showed no concern or sympathy to his pleadings and thrashed the whip forward once more. Jeremy was now beginning to slip in and out of consciousness, his body no longer able to deal with the trauma inflicted upon it.

But Lena had more questions and Jeremy had yet to pay for his misdoings. The flagellation had only just begun. There were more crimes to be answered for.

Until a man's voice interrupted her inquisitions.

Battersea Power Station
London, England

90

As Tate bobbed and weaved his way through the traffic, the Land rover's blue light flashing, endless nagging questions behind Lena's actions swarmed about his head.

'*What had triggered her current state of mind? Had the trauma of her childhood affected her much more than one could have imagined? Why was she so overly concerned with corruption within the art world to feel the need to carry out such unimaginable acts of retribution. And what had he done so wrong, that she felt the need to punish him too?*

Tate had left Bethnal Green without so much as a word to his plan but was relatively self-assured that Harriet being Harriet, she would know all too well where he would be heading. He was also aware that as soon as she arrived, Harriet would set up a perimeter and man all the exits. There would be no escaping. However, Tate had wanted a short time alone with Lena before the place was swarming in blue lights and armed response units.

He pulled the Land Rover to a stop beneath the Turbine Hall of the foreboding building. The sun was still high in the late afternoon sky and scores of vapour trails could be seen transecting the expanse of pale blue between the historic chimneys as planes started their final approach to London Heathrow. Tate looked to the skyline. No pig floated between the towering chimneys today.

The first bricks of what was to become one of the most recognisable buildings within the heart of the capital were laid in 1929. Following the design of distinguished architect Sir Giles Gilbert Scott, Battersea A, a twin towered power station was completed in 1935. Due to the second world war, it was not until 1955 that the identical Battersea B would be completed and the rising of the iconic four chimneys would become a landmark of the London skyline. The station continued to produce one fifth of the capitals electricity until its decommission nearly thirty years later. The building then fell into disrepair and remained empty until the start of a recent restoration and rejuvenation project to bring it back to life as a centre piece of a vibrant new destination on the banks of the Thames.

Tate was still taking the stairs two at a time as he rounded the landing on the fire escapes eighth floor. The lift systems having been out of order, with all the cabins electronically disabled. The stairwell offered a cool haven, but Tate was beginning to feel a rising sweat as he charged up his seventeenth flight of stairs. As he rounded another corner, he glanced up and down the central well and was relieved to find he was further up than he had reckoned. Despite being relatively fit his thighs were now beginning to feel the burn of the non-stop climb to the top.

Although having only been in the stairwell for a very short while, Tate's eyes needed to adjust to the glare as he exited the doors onto the rooftop. As his vision adjusted he scanned the skyline for any sign of movement. At first he saw nothing but the abandoned equipment and building materials of a dormant construction site. The area was lifeless due to regulatory Sunday shutdowns. He briefly looked in the direction of each towering chimney, knowing that if Lena was planning one final statement, her magnum opus, then it would undoubtedly be on one of the towers. He looked to both pairs of chimneys. If she were to choose one, it would not be at the rear of the building, he thought. Lena would want her work to be seen. Tate turned and sprinted in the direction of the two chimneys that towered over the front of the building above the South Bank Plaza and the river Thames.

Movement on the Eastern chimney caught his eye, causing him to stop briefly. He could make out two figures. At first he could not calculate or comprehend the situation, but then the realisation of what may be taking place hit him like a ton of bricks.

She was crucifying someone.

'Lena. Stop this,' he shouted, before accelerating into a sprint towards the scene playing out before him. He covered the ground quickly and as he drew closer to the base of the chimney he was able to identify the subject of Lena's execution. It came as no surprise. When Tate had given thought to the possibility of the next potential victim, Jeremy had been high on the hit list. If he had also considered which of Caravaggio's works the next crime scene might resemble, Battersea's chimneys would only befit a backdrop to his works of Christ at the Pillar.

Tate stopped below Lena, who stood at the base of the chimney. A whip in her hand. Her face and clothes freckled with blood splatter from the recoiling of the thongs. Jeremy hung insensibly from the pillar, his flesh shredded and mutilated. Tate had some idea of what to expect but did not anticipate the extent of Lena's intent. The attack had been far more savage than Tate could ever have imagined.

'This has to stop,' Tate implored, edging closer. Lena turned her shoulder and looked down. Her silhouette imposing and statuesque. A bestial scowl ingrained upon her face.

'Oh… I am only just getting started,' she sneered with a menacing tone to her voice. Lena moved across the plinth to stand directly above Tate. 'He is answering for his crimes and in doing so accepting his punishments.'

'But why do you feel the need to punish these people outside the enforcement of the law?'

'The law has failed us in so many ways and on so many occasions. These people are beyond temptation. They brush the world aside. They believe they are above the law and their wealth can afford them anything they please.' She took one step down towards Tate. 'So they have now paid the ultimate price. All their wealth cannot buy back what I have stolen from them.' Tate could see a pitiless vacancy in her eyes. She showed no remorse. He sensed the wrath and indignation she bore for these people and the sins she adjudged them of committing. He was also aware that Harriet and tactical support would not be far away now and if Jeremy Grayson stood any chance of survival he would require immediate medical attention. But Tate still had questions which he needed answering.

'Why steal the Caravaggio? Does that not infer you are no different from those you have punished?'

'Because it is rightfully mine!' Lena snapped, as she took another step down towards Tate, who looked puzzled and confused by the remark.

'It's my destiny, my ancestry. My bloodline.' Still perplexed, Tate took a couple of sideways steps to offset Lena's advancement.

'Caravaggio fathered a child during his last days in Rome before fleeing in exile. The woman who bore that child was Maddalena Antognetti. She was my ancestral Grandmother, some twelve generations ago. My family name before adoption was Antognetti. The picture I stole is a portrait of her. Caravaggio painted the Magdalene after receiving news from Maddalena of the conception. The rapturous state of delight he captured in the face of the Magdalene is for the child she is secretly bearing. That child was the first of the bloodline and I am the last.' Lena stepped down once more, moving ever closer to Tate. Again, he moved to maintain some distance. He posed another question, partly to distract Lena, whilst he discreetly glanced for something with which to arm himself.

'Why the Narcissus and why me?'

'In mythology, the Narcissus was a beautiful hunter. Along with the mother of my bloodline, we have hunted those who have for so long avoided punishment. They were so easily allured by her beauty within the picture. I thought you would be the one person to understand. People like this have been committing crimes in front of our eyes, yet they evade detection and prosecution. Millions of pounds of art are stolen each year, most is never recovered and the majority is sold on the black market. Galleries are finding it harder and harder to obtain works of art. They are constantly outbid at auctions by individuals with bottomless pockets, who are ignorant to a pictures true value and pay outlandish prices, to then hang these lost works where they will be seen by so few. They themselves are crucifying the world of art.' Lena caught sight of Tate's scouting and pulled a revolver from the waistband of her trousers. She had the upper hand and wanted to keep it that way. She motioned with the gun for Tate to move to the side of the plinth.

'I knew the messages would eventually grab your attention. I needed you to recognise that these people are constantly falling through the net. I wanted to open your eyes because you have been blind for so long. These people are the murderers not me.' Tate realised that the more she answered the more she started to sound delusional. She seemed to believe in all she had done. She could not see her own misdoings. Where had all this escalated from and more importantly what had happened to the woman he thought he knew so well?

'You are as guilty as they are,' snarled Lena, her voice becoming more aggressive as she let fly with a barrage of accusations. Tate tried desperately to tune out the verbal abuse as these were now the ramblings of someone who no longer had a grip on reality. However, it was difficult when you were the subject of such bitter resentment, whether the accusations were true or not. He could see an anger building behind her eyes but did not anticipate Lena's next move.

Out of nowhere, Lena suddenly sprang in Tate's direction. He was taken off guard and could not react in time. The butt of the revolver struck Tate on the side of his temple. The energy of Lena's forward momentum causing the strike to be delivered with great force. Tate slumped to the ground, dazed and confused. Lena stood astride of Tate's collapsed body. She held the barrel of the gun to the side of his head and looked into Tate's barely conscious eyes. They still showed signs of awareness. She shook her head and sniggered, before lowering the gun.

Caravaggio had painted a pair of flagellations. The Western chimney offered a second pillar and Tate would become her second Christ.

Battersea Power Station

London, England

91

Harriet had only overheard the final part of the exchange between Tate and Lena as she crept ever closer behind the advertising hoarding. She had removed and extended her police baton upon seeing Lena pull the gun. She had been waiting for the best tactical moment, coupled with the element of surprise before striking out. She too had been taken aback when Tate had been knocked to the ground. She had almost engaged into action then but had held off in fear of further injury to Tate. She remained crouched in her concealed position watching and waiting for the best possible chance of catching Lena off guard. She knew by now that DS Richards would have assembled the tactical team and secured all exits. As instructed, he would now be waiting further commands. She checked her radio was still muted and cautiously moved further along to the end of the hoarding. As Harriet stood to position herself behind the corner of the scaffold, Lena turned to one side and knelt to retrieve the whip.

Harriet seized her moment.

She leapt from her concealment and in one complete motion, she struck Lena across the forearm of the hand holding the gun and rolled to one side. The revolver clattered to the floor. Harriet spun and made a lunge for the weapon. As her hand met the stock, Lena kicked out and the gun slid across the roof further from reach. Lena continued her offensive and lashed out with the scourge in her other hand. The leather thongs struck Harriet across the chest of her tactical vest before striking at the hand clasping the baton. She lost her grip and the baton. The thongs struck her arm a second time. Harriet back tracked on all fours. Lena was now upon her like a ferocious animal, lashing out time after time, flaying at any part of Harriet within her grasp. Harriet glanced over her shoulder; she was nearing the edge. She looked back, Tate was still semi-conscious. She needed to act fast. Lena struck once more. This time though Harriet held fast and clasped a firm hold on the flaying end of the whip. Using Lena's weight as a counterbalance she pulled at the whip and regained her feet. Both women held firm on the whip and struck out at each other with their spare hand and kicked out with their feet. Lena used her height advantage and the rage that blazed within her to gain ground and Harriet soon found herself standing on the edge of a very long drop.

She teetered on the edge, her feet fighting for purchase on the tightrope that was the edge of the building. The leather of the whip cut into the flesh of her palms as the thongs slowly slid through her grasp and she fought to maintain a grip. But her desperation was in vain. Her lifeline suddenly going limp as Lena released her hold on the other end of the whip's handle.

Harriet toppled backwards into the void, grasping at the emptiness. Her arms cartwheeling as her hands desperately clawed at the nothingness, much in the way a drowning victim fights to stay above the surface. As she continued to freefall, her face suddenly brushed against something. The same something then struck her torso and then her arm. Her first thoughts had been that the whip was simply tumbling with her. But it was not the whip. Her eyes fixed on a length of chain, of which she was now falling back into. She reached out through the air, her arms swimming upwards for a second lifeline.

Her hands fought to secure a grip on the chain as she continued to plummet towards the ground, whilst her fingers desperately grappled with the thick interconnecting links. She clasped hand over hand as she struggled to find some traction. The chain momentarily stiffened in her hands as she finally secured a hold before it too began to fall away alongside her. For a fleeting moment, Harriet's life flashed before her eyes. Was this the end? Not in her wildest nightmares had she imagined this was how death would take her. She had envisioned getting shot in the line of duty, maybe stabbed by a drug crazed killer or as a victim of an RTA during a high-speed pursuit, but never falling from the roof of a building.

But then she was no longer falling. The chain suddenly tightened and Harriet's grip held firm. Her body jerked to a halt and she hung spinning at the end of the chain like a puppet bouncing hopelessly from its strings. She looked up the line of the chain. It ran through the pulley wheel of an industrial block and tackle which was attached to the scaffolding a couple of metres above her head. Harriet took a second to contain herself and to take stock of the situation. It appeared that a galvanised bucket attached to the other end of the chain had jammed on contact with the pulley wheel and arrested her fall. Her relief was only brief as she quickly realised she was unsure how long she could maintain a grip or even how secure the entrapped bucket was.

Harriet tried to climb hand over hand up the chain with one eye constantly on the wedged bucket. She only managed a short section before having to stop. Her hands bleeding from the cuts sustained from the leather thongs of the whip. But she held strong, determined that this would not be how her life ended. She still had more to give; it was not her time to bow out. She could not take the risk of reaching for her radio as she was unsure whether she would be able to maintain her hold with a single hand. She looked to the roof once again and caught sight of Lena moving away towards the opposite chimney. Harriet called out for Tate, not knowing if he was even conscious. She called his name a second time but heard no response.

Battersea Power Station

London, England

92

His mind was fuzzy and a drumming filled his head. Not the usual rhythmic, melodic drumming of the bands he enjoyed hearing, but the thumping throb of an intense headache. The pain reverberated about his head.

Tate sat himself up, scrunched his eyes and felt for the source of the pain. He winced as his hand found the contusion on his temple. He held his hand to it and then checked his palm for blood. There was very little. He thought he heard someone shout his name but could not be sure. He shook his head and thought nothing more of it. He tried to stand, feeling slightly lightheaded as he straightened his legs and pushed himself upwards. As he did so, recollections of where, what and who, began to materialise in his memory.

He looked around, cautious of another attack. Jeremy was still hanging limp at the chimney. Using one hand to steady his climb, Tate made his way up to the lifeless body. He checked Jeremy for a pulse. It was weak, but he was still alive. However, he needed immediate medical attention if he were to survive. Tate looked at the fastenings securing Jeremy to the chimney. There was no way he could remove them without inflicting further injuries. He would need to get help.

Movement further along the roof drew his attention. Lena. Memories of their altercation minutes earlier flooded his mind, but he was still at odds with how things had escalated to this point. Whatever he thought, Lena had committed crimes and she was now answerable for them. He could not let her get away. He checked his temple again. Apart from the headache, everything else seemed to be in one piece. Tate clambered down from the chimney and headed off in the direction of where he had last seen Lena, only to stop just as immediately as he had started. He heard someone shout his name once more. Recognising the voice, he looked around for the source. He turned through 360 degrees, but saw nobody but Jeremy and Lena, who was now nearing the end of the building. He knew the voice had been Harriet's.

'Tate!' He heard it again. He sensed a state of distress and desperation in the calling.

'Harriet. Where are you?' She replied immediately, an urgency in her voice.

'Oh thank God. Hurry. I'm down here, over the side. Look for the chain. I don't think I can hold on much longer!' Tate saw the chain and hurried across to the scaffolding. He stood at the edge and looked over the side. Harriet hung precariously in a loop of chain. He could see by the anguish in her face that her strength was fading. He hesitantly looked across at Lena and back at Jeremy. But his decision had already been made.

'Hold on,' he hollered, 'I'm going to start pulling the chain through the pulley.' He grasped the chain at the point where the bucket was attached and began to pull it through. Harriet held fast as the chain rose upwards. Being a block and tackle designed to lift heavy objects with minimal effort, Tate made easy work of hauling Harriet back to the roof. He helped her back over the scaffold and she slumped to the floor. She held up her arms, her hands contorted like crab claws, but she managed to manipulate them enough to depress the mute button of her radio with a knuckle.

'Tactical team, roof now. Suspect Lena Johnson last seen heading for the Northwest chimney. Immediate medical assistance required.' Harriet looked up at Tate and smiled. A smile that said it all. 'Alright?' she enquired.

'Yeah, fine. You?'

'Nothing a good manicure won't sort out.' They both laughed and looked mercifully at each other. But Tate's gaze was drawn past Harriet. He looked across in the direction of the other chimney. He could no longer see Lena. An urge gnawed at him from within. His instinct telling him the fight was not over. He still had time to put a stop to this madness. Harriet sensed Tate's hankering.

'Go. I'll be fine. Not much use as back up I'm afraid,' she said, raising her injured hands once more. 'I'll stay on the radio and control things from here.' Without hesitation Tate darted off across the roof. 'Just be careful,' she called over his shoulder. Her past feelings for Tate briefly re-emerging in the adversity of the situation. Harriet watched Tate as he dashed off in pursuit of Lena before DI Stone took control. 'Tactical Team. DCI Tate Randall also in pursuit of suspect. Approach with caution.'

Tate skirted the Northwest chimney as figures dressed in black military apparel began to emerge from all sides of the roof. The tactical team converged towards Tate's position. At this precise moment, he was unsure how to confront Lena. Her current state would need a tactful approach. He would need to treat her as a friend and colleague rather than an adversary. Confronting someone you held in high regard was never easy at the best of times. But on the roof of a building, a dying man crucified to a chimney, a police officer left hanging for her life and four previous cold-blooded murders would mean something very different for Tate. It was far from questioning somebody about a stolen vase in Chingford. Their earlier confrontation had made Tate realise that Lena was far beyond reproach. She was in complete denial of the misjustice she had delivered. She would need to be accountable for her own misdoings. But Tate could not see that happening. He could only see this ending in a way he did not wish to see.

Turning the corner caused Tate to freeze in his tracks. Maybe that ending would be much more than he had ever envisioned. Lena stood at the edge of the building; her arms stretched out like Christ the Redeemer. She stood on the edge of Battersea Power Station reaching out for forgiveness, her arms spread in repentance.

Lena allowed herself a satisfying smile and with that she stepped off the side of the building.

Battersea Power Station

London, England

93

As she went over the edge, her feet found the brick work and the arresting device attached to the harness she had stepped into moments earlier engaged with the rope. She remained with her hands outstretched and ran in a forward abseil down the face of the building. She let the rope run freely until she was only metres from the plaza below. As the bottom of the rope ran out Lena slowed her descent and simply stepped out onto the paved area.

Tate watched as Lena nonchalantly walked across the plaza below. She was calm and callous enough to just walk away. Passers-by having been oblivious and unobservant of her descent of the building. Tactical personnel were now transecting the roof and covering the exits. But no-one was covering the corners of the building. Lena merged into the crowds and casually walked towards the Coaling Jetty Pier.

Tate looked at the rope running down the line of the brick work. It would have been left in situ by a team cleaning the façade of the building. He knew he could not attempt to ascend the length of rope without the appropriate equipment. Lena had meticulously planned her escape. Whilst keeping one eye on following Lena's movements below, Tate looked for the quickest way from the roof of the building to the Thames side path. At first there was no obvious solution. He looked along the frontage of the structure below him. Nothing offered any further possibility. Looking further afield, he noticed two cranes moving materials back at the Northeast corner. Calculating this as his only option, he raced back across the building. Below, Lena began to descend the jetty.

Tate came back into Harriet's view as he ran the entire length of the Northern side of the power stations' roof. He did not stop as he passed.

'She's heading for the river. You might need a boat and an eye in the sky,' he shouted as he sped past. He reached the edge of the roof as the nearest crane swung its load over the corner of the building. He took a moment to assess the feasibility of his plan. Happy it might just work, he took three extra-large steps back, like those of an Olympic long jumper, before sprinting towards the edge of the roof.

He launched himself from the corner of the building, his legs peddling at thin air, whilst his arms grasped for imaginary monkey bars as he fought to maintain his forward momentum. His hands reaching out in a do-or-die attempt as his fingers grasped to latch onto the load swinging beneath the crane's jib.

Battersea Power Station
London, England

94

Clive does not like working Sundays. Sundays are about lunchtime beers with the lads, football on Sky and a roast dinner. The council do not usually allow works on a Sunday, giving local residents a break from the humdrum of the site. However, occasionally due to special circumstances a permit would be issued. This was one of those Sundays.

Materials needed to be moved ready for a new phase of the latest developments due to start first thing Monday morning. He was one of two crane operators contracted that day. Still the sun was shining, it paid double time and the football was broadcasting on Five Live in his cab.

Tower cranes were now commonplace on major construction sites. Their triangulated lattice mast rising over two hundred feet to the drivers cab and the rotating platform. Here, the horizontal jib intersects the mast, allowing the crane to reach out up to a further two hundred feet depending on the weight of its workload.

Clive had been tasked with moving pre-cast concrete slabs from the delivery site, past the front of the original building, to a new construction area on the banks of the river. He was engrossed in the commentary of the football's second half as he eased the jib past the Northeast corner of the power station.

'What the…?' He could not believe what he was seeing. It took a moment for his eyes and mind to make sense of what had just happened. Someone had just jumped from the edge of the roof and was currently clinging to the side of the concrete slab he was moving. Clive continued to watch, unsure quite what to do. His training and the handbook said to cease movement of the jib if there is imminent danger to co-workers or members of the public. He eased the trolley carriage to a stop, unaware that he had done so, as he remained captivated by the escapade on his jib hook. The man swung his legs and hoisted himself up and over onto the top of the concrete slab. Clive had become so absorbed in the reckless exploits of the daredevil that he did not hear Arsenal score and take a 2-1 lead.

The man stood and held the jib line. He started to wave and gesticulate, pointing in the direction of the river. Clive reached beneath his seat and retrieved the pair of binoculars he kept in his cab for as he put it, 'a spot of birdwatching' whenever he ate his lunch. He raised the binoculars to his eyes. The man was definitely waving his hands erratically in the direction of the river. Clive noticed a glow of blue flashing lights converging below as a voice cut in over the two-way radio.

'Clive. Jess. Are you receiving?' Both acknowledged the call.

'I have a DS Richards here in the office,' declared their supervisor, 'he is going to relay messages to you from his superior officer who is on the roof of the old building.' Clive was startled and unsure how to react.

'One of you currently has a man on top of your load.'

'That will be mine,' Clive replied.

'Please move the cranes arm in the direction of the river.' Clive did as commanded, slowly engaging the trolley once more, whilst swinging the jib to the right.

'Can the other crane nearest to the river move their hook to intercept with the first cranes load.' Jess acknowledged from the other crane. The ends of the jib arms began to converge. After a minute or so, both cranes slowed to a stop.

Tate held firm as the concrete load shuddered and swayed beneath his feet. The other crane's empty hook had stopped about six feet short of the load he stood upon. He could just about hear Harriet as she called out to him. Apparently the cranes were both at their limits. If his plan of reaching the river was to succeed, he would need to make the jump. But at over one hundred feet above the ground, six feet looked an awfully long way. He weighed up the situation. At least he had the length of the slabs to give him something of a run up. He looked over the edge. He could no longer see Lena. But she could not have gotten far. The longer he thought about the pros and cons, the more reasons he would find to stay put. He took a large gulp of courage and let go of the wire. Unsteadily Tate edged back to the far side of the load. He stood for a moment waiting to see if the wind changed or if the swaying would subside. When nothing dramatically improved he focused on the other cranes hook. It looked considerably smaller than it probably was. He rubbed his hands together. He wasn't sure whether this was to clean them or make them stickier, but it did the job.

Courage bolstered; Tate began to run at the jib hook. The concrete slab below his feet began to sway with his forward momentum. No going back now as he reached the edge and launched himself for a second time into thin air. He hit the jib hook hard and promptly wrapped his arms around its wire. His feet slipping and sliding to gain purchase within the curve of the hook. He retained his hold for a few seconds before raising a hand to signal he was safe.

The jib began to move, swinging back in the direction from which it had come. As it moved towards the river, Tate caught sight of Lena once again. The realisation of her actions took a moment to sink in. She now straddled a jet ski and was heading West towards the Chelsea bridge. Tate looked down; he was still over solid ground. He repeatedly motioned towards the river and cried out hoping Harriet could still hear him. He hopelessly watched as Lena disappeared beneath the bridge.

Finally the Thames appeared beneath and the jib continued to extend towards the centre of the river. Tate clenched a fist and pointed his thumb downwards. He over exaggerated the movement for the driver to see. The hook began to descend. Tate looked again for Lena. She had cleared the bridge and was accelerating away upriver. The crane was taking too long to lower. He looked down at the distance between him and the water. It was still a considerable drop. He needed to act now or fear losing sight of Lena all together.

Without a second thought he stepped from the jib hook and tombstoned into the water below.

River Thames, Battersea

London, England

95

Tate surfaced from the water. He had landed a hundred yards from the boat moored at the jetty. He knew he could make quick time of that distance. But it was against the tide. He would have to dig deep. However, his early morning swims paid off and he covered the distance with relative ease.

'Who are you, MI6?' said the man in the boat having just witnessed Tate plummeting from the crane jib into the Thames.

'No. Art and Antiquities Department,' replied Tate struggling to retrieve his ID from his pocket as he hauled his torso up and over the gunnel of the RIB. 'I need you to follow that jet ski and pronto,' pointed Tate as the jet ski began to disappear from view. With no further questions the man started the boat and spun it into the flow of the incoming tide. As he fully engaged the throttle, the twin outboard engines rose the boat from the water and within seconds they were planing across the river's surface in quick pursuit.

As the boat accelerated under Chelsea Bridge, Tate pulled his phone from the back pocket of his trousers. The screen was cracked, probably from the impact with the water. He hoped that the manufacturers specifications regarding water submersion were accurate. He searched his recent call history and hit the call button hoping it would connect. It did and Tate gave the answerer no time to talk.

'Harriet. She is on a blue jet ski heading upriver towards Albert Bridge. I am on a yellow RIB craft registered to "Spirit of the Thames Jet Boat Rides", approximately five hundred metres behind at present.' He did not hear Harriet's reply as they hurried after Lena's ski. Tate was unsure what he would do if and when they finally caught up with Lena. He still felt an unease at the thought of confronting her again. Did she still have the gun? If so, would she think twice about using it to gain an advantage. Tate looked about the boat in an attempt to find something with which to arm himself. Nothing jumped out at him. He looked to the bow of the RIB and noticed they had started to gain on Lena when a thought suddenly struck him.

'Do you have a flare gun onboard?'

'Not a gun, but I have flares. It's a regulation to carry them,' the driver shouted, Tate finding it difficult to hear the reply over the drone of the outboard and the rushing of the wind. 'They're in here.' The driver pointed to a hatch below his jockey console.

'I might need them.' Without questioning or losing speed, the driver retrieved an orange tub and handed it across. Tate had seen similar kits and hoped this one had more than just hand-held smoke flares. He unscrewed the lid and found exactly what he had hoped for.

The twin engines of the RIB were now eating up the distance between them and the jet ski. They passed under Albert Bridge and started to turn a significant corner in the river. Tate pointed to the inside line and the driver followed his direction. His plan was to intercept Lena as she continued her current line around the curve. As they powered through the corner, the driver turned the wheel and the RIB cut back across to the outside curve of the bend and directly across Lena's path. Lena abruptly turned the ski and cut behind the RIB's line, the jet ski bouncing as it passed through the boats choppy wake.

They continued to slalom across each other's line, twisting and weaving in a game of cat and mouse. As the chase approached the Battersea Rail bridge they split paths and passed either side of the pillars. Lena looked back over her shoulder as she punched the jet ski's throttle forward, looking to squeeze every scrap of power from its engine. Enraptured by the thrill of the chase, the driver of the RIB, swung the boat sideways, making contact with the gunnel of the ski. Lena veered away as the RIB swerved to make contact for a second time. However the sudden movement made the RIB driver overcompensate and he needed to substantially reduce his speed in order to regain control. Lena sped forward.

A reasonable stretch of water lay ahead before the next bridge. Tate secured his footing on the hull of the boat and levelled one of the hand-held rocket flares in the direction of Lena's ski. He pulled the ignition wire. The flare ignited and launched from the cannister. It blazed a trail across the water, arcing past the bow of the ski. Lena turned sharply and leaned away, having by chance looked back at precisely the right moment to notice the approaching projectile. She headed for the South bank and the bridge ahead, hoping the urban infrastructure would make Tate think twice about firing any further flares. But her optimism was short lived as a second projectile struck the aft of the ski causing her to veer sharply onto the absolute edge of capsizing. She battled as the ski rocked from gunnel to gunnel and needed to over steer in opposing directions to fight the ski back into a straight line. She regained control and once again pushed the ski to its limit and weaved under the Wandsworth bridge, knowing that her planned exit point lay just up ahead. The rib driver cut to the other side of the bridge stanchion and exited just behind the fleeing ski.

Feeling a new sense of vigour in the realisation that her escape plan might just work, Lena rode the ski with confidence, standing above the seat and allowing her legs and knees to act as shock absorbers as the ski bounded across the rivers surface. She constantly glanced over her shoulder to check the proximity of the chasing boat.

Tate on the other hand, slowly saw his chances of intercepting Lena diminish as she suddenly changed course and swung the ski into the mouth of a small inlet on the southern bank. Without easing off on the throttle, she sped into the narrow channel of the river Wandle. The RIB driver at first followed her line, but it quickly became evident that there was insufficient water at this stage of the tide for them to continue. The driver stalled the power and the rib sat down in the water as it slowed to a stop. Lena disappeared upstream as Tate hit the call button on his phone.

'She has turned into the Wandle River creek. The water's too shallow for the draft of our boat. We are no longer in pursuit.'

Lena continued along the river for a few hundred metres before slowing the ski as she approached a low footbridge ahead. As the jet ski passed under the nearside of the bridge, she straightened her legs astride of the seat and reached to grasp at pipework running along its underside. She then released her knee grip and the jet ski continued its forward momentum leaving her hanging from the underside of the bridge. She see-sawed her legs back and forth several times to gain some momentum. Then in one single motion she pulled up on her arms, swung her feet up onto the side of the bridge and pushed up and through into a kneeling position. She checked along the river. As planned she was no longer being followed. With no time to hesitate she turned and sprinted towards a riverside industrial area.

Lena had planned her exit strategy down to the last detail. Her motor bike was only a few hundred yards away in the corner of a car park. Along with the jet ski she had strategically positioned them earlier that day in the event of her needing to escape. So far it had all gone to plan, but there was still one small matter to be taken care of.

Woodford Green
London, England

96

It was late into the night as Harriet and Tate continued to pursue any and every lead in the hope of picking up on Lena's trail and shedding some light on her current whereabouts. They had drawn a blank. Lena appeared to have disappeared with the tide.

But whilst they turned over every stone, unbeknown to them, for one final time Lena was hunting as the Narcissus. She lurked in the shadows patiently waiting for the prey she sought. Lying in wait knowing that at some point her final target would eventually return home. Shortly after Midnight, the Narcissus watched as Rebecca put the key into the lock. She was returning after a long evening reporting on developments of an incident which had unfolded at Battersea earlier that afternoon.

Rebecca had just poured herself a well-deserved glass of Malbec when a knock at the door disturbed her sanctuary. At first she was surprised by the presence of the female detective, her surprise quickly turning to concern as she suddenly had a realisation that something may have happened to Harriet. Her worries quickly subsided as the detective offered a bare all, no holds barred, inside story on the recent celebrity killings. An opportunity that Rebecca would never turn her back on and she welcomed the stranger into her home with open arms.

Lena had her swan song securely in her sights, with the knowledge that Harriet's current predicament would keep her at work through the night and therefore there was little chance of being interrupted. The offer of 'sharing a glass' whilst they talked, presented Lena with the perfect opportunity as Rebecca left the room to collect a second glass. It took Lena a split second to drop the Rohypnol into Rebecca's wine. Lena cleverly kept the conversation casual and chatty until the effect of the drug began to take hold. At first, Rebecca tried to resist, but it was not long before she had succumbed to the drug and her lifeless body slumped paralysed in the chair with the ability to listen and nothing more.

Lena then bared all. Laid it all out in detail. She revealed her true identity as the Narcissus. She wanted to tell her story. This was her confessional. She knew the recording on Rebecca's dictating device would eventually be found. Rebecca would be part of that story and it would only be fitting for her to get her moment of glory too. Although it would be a shame she would never bear witness to her crowning moment. Her story would be told posthumously.

There would be no reason to rush. Lena being quietly confident of not being disturbed. It would most probably be several hours before Harriet would venture home, if at all. Firstly, she would finish her wine and acquaint Rebecca with her plans for her final symbolic work. She wanted Rebecca to be conscious and aware during her final moments, so she could speculate how her body would be found and how her demise would most likely be reported. But that was probably the least of Rebecca's worries, judging by the terror that filled her eyes.

Lena left Rebecca to ponder her fate as she wandered to the bedroom to prepare her canvas. The sight of the full-length mirrored doors caused a warm gratifying feeling to rise through her veins and she gave herself a self-approving nod. It would make the posing of the body far more memorable than she had envisaged. The doors came away from their hinges with relative ease and Lena laid them mirror side up across the bed. She had to do no more. The setting of the scene was simplistic. Rebecca would be the focus.

She lumbered Rebecca's immobilised body into the bedroom and removed her clothing. Rebecca tried to protest, but only murmurings slurred from her torpefied vocal cords. Lena had chosen a simple white blouse from the wardrobe and slipped it over Rebecca's naked torso. It would give Rebecca the look of innocence that Lena wished to portray. She then carefully moved Rebecca to the bed and onto the mirrored doors. With every further movement, trapped frustrations and the imminent dread of what was to come could be seen building in Rebecca's eyes. The narcotics effect inhibiting anything more. Her debilitated limbs unable to offer any defence.

Lena manoeuvred Rebecca along the mirrors to the head end of the bed. She wrestled with the dead weight of the body until Rebecca was crouched in a kneeling position. She took a moment to ponder the original pose she wished to emulate. She pulled the left knee forwards into a prominent position and slid the right knee backwards to balance the body. She then moved both of Rebecca's arms forward, bending them slightly at the elbow, before placing the hands, palms down on the mirrored surface. She then adjusted the arms into a position to support the weight of the torso. Finally, she moved Rebecca's head forward, turning the face down to look at its own reflection. Lena then spent several minutes rejigging the limbs until she was completely satisfied with their final positioning. All the while, Rebecca was trapped within. Tears now welling in the corners of her eyes. Incapacitated and unable to prevent this inescapable torment. Her mind bedevilled as it agonised over her looming fate.

Lena stood back and admired her work. The body positioning gave the impression she was looking for, but the lighting was wrong. The background needed to be darker. Much darker. She closed the blinds and moved a bedside lamp to a dressing table at the side of the room. She manipulated the lamp until the light shone across the bed from a different angle.

Then she turned off the overhead light.

The solitary light source now illuminated Rebecca's reflection and the anterior of her torso and face. The surrounding room was now in semi-darkness. Her finale was complete.

Lena stood before Rebecca holding the syringe. A fear glazed over Rebecca's eyes as the trepidation of her own death erupted into the panic of a silent scream. She did not wish to die, but for one of the few times in her life she had no control. She was at the mercy of another's actions.

'You have been the tempter and you are also the tempted. You show no consideration for others, only a desire to inflate your own self esteem. Your temptation has this time been your undoing.' Lena eased the needle into Rebecca's neck and slowly depressed the plunger.

As the cocktail of drugs began to slow her heart, Rebecca stared into the soulless eyes of her reflection and a single tear dropped towards its mirrored form. She would be forever captured in this moment in time.

Her reflection staring back at her in the pose of Caravaggio's 'Narcissus.'

Printed in Great Britain
by Amazon

28150001R00182